Dear Reader,

This month I'm delighted to include another book by Kay Gregory, whose first *Scarlet* novel, *Marry Me Stranger* was such a hit with you all. You can also enjoy the second book in Liz Fielding's intriguing 'Beaumont Brides' trilogy.' Then we have another romance from talented author Maxine Barry. *Destinies* is a complete novel in itself, but we're sure you'll want to read *Resolutions* next month to find out 'what happens next!' And finally, we're very pleased to bring you another new author – Laura Bradley has produced an exciting and page-turning story.

Do let me know, won't you, what you think of the titles we've chosen for you this month? Do *you* enjoy linked books and books with a touch of mystery or do you like your romance uncluttered by other elements?

By the way, thank you if you've already written to me. I promise I *shall* answer your letter as soon as I can. Your comments will certainly help me plan our list over the coming months.

Till next month,

Sally Cooper

SALLY COOPER,
Editor – *Scarlet*

About the Author

Liz Fielding was born in Berkshire and educated at the local convent school before training as a secretary. At the age of twenty, she took a post with the Zambian Government. Liz met her Coventry-born husband John in Lusaka and after their marriage Liz and John spent some time in the Middle East, Qatar, Bahrain and the UAE before returning to Botswana and Kenya.

After their children were born, Liz remained in the UK and began to write in the long evenings while John was working abroad. The family now lives in a tiny village in West Wales surrounded by romantic crumbling castles and beautiful countryside. Liz's first romance was published in 1992 and *Wild Lady* is her second *Scarlet* novel.

Other **Scarlet** titles available this month:

THE SHERRABY BRIDES by Kay Gregory
WICKED LIAISONS by Laura Bradley
DESTINIES by Maxine Barry

LIZ FIELDING

WILD LADY

(Part 2 of The Beaumont Brides)

Enquiries to:
Robinson Publishing Ltd
7 Kensington Church Court
London W8 4SP

First published in the UK by Scarlet, 1997

A copy of the British Library Cataloguing in
Publication data is available from the British Library

ISBN 1–85487–718–6

Printed and bound in the EC

10 9 8 7 6 5 4 3 2 1

CHAPTER 1

When Claudia Beaumont, late and pushing her new sportscar hard through the narrow Berkshire lanes, finally spotted the entrance to the airfield, she experienced two distinct and warring emotions. Relief and dread. And dread was winning by a country mile.

But she knew that the letter was simply the product of a sick mind. Someone was trying to frighten her, make her look feeble and if she backed out now her anonymous correspondent would have succeeded. For heaven's sake, she *expected* to be frightened. Who wouldn't be? And who was she to deprive millions of television viewers of a vicarious thrill? She slowed and turned into the gate. There had damned well better be millions or she would want to know the reason why.

The security guard checked her car registration against a list he had on a clipboard, then directed her to the far side of the field where the OB unit was set up beside a large aircraft hangar. Even at a distance the scene gave the appearance of organized chaos. Excitable men, earnest young women milling about in an attempt to give an impression of their own enormous importance, heavy cables snaking through the grass, vehicles everywhere, the essential catering truck doing a roaring trade in coffee and bacon sandwiches.

And a small aircraft, a very small aircraft, was parked on the apron in front of the hangar, waiting to take her several thousand feet into the air so that she could jump out of it for the amusement of the vast audience of Saturday night viewers.

'Do the show, darling,' her agent had coaxed. 'It's popular family entertainment, not in the least bit tacky, all the money the viewers pledge goes to a charity of your choice. And we'll get a big plug for the new television series.'

He'd forgotten to mention the fact that one of the guests would be landed with an amusing little forfeit. And with three envelopes to choose from she'd managed to find the parachute jump. It was quite possible, she realized with a belated flash of insight, that they all contained the same forfeit. It was highly probable that she'd kill her agent.

'You'd better put your foot down, miss,' the security guard advised. 'The weather looks as if it might be closing in and if you don't get off the ground soon, you'll have to come back another day. And that won't please Mr MacIntyre.'

It wasn't her eagerness to please Mr MacIntyre, whoever he was, or to get on with the jump that sent the little car leaping forward. If the film crew had a wasted day because she was late, Claudia knew she would be about as popular as an outbreak of rabies in a boarding kennels.

There were a number of cars parked in a neat line facing the hangar. Her car was lipstick-bright against the greyness of the morning and, aware that every head had turned at her approach, she did a slick change down as she drove onto the grass, planning to slide neatly into the space between a gleaming black Landcruiser and the silver Porsche that she recognized as the pride and joy of the show's director.

There was only one problem. When she put her foot on the brake it went straight to the floor without resistance. For a split-second she froze. It couldn't be happening. Her car was brand-new. Two days old. But it *was* happening. And she was heading straight for Barty's Porsche.

She wrenched hard on the steering wheel, somehow expecting that it, too, would fail to respond. It didn't fail. It responded with fingertip precision. And after that everything seemed to happen at once. The jolting tango along the black bulk of the Landcruiser, the bruising jerk as her seat-belt locked and bit into her shoulder, the airbag exploding into life. The final nightmarish sound of rending metal as she collided with the hangar.

Then everything went very quiet for a moment before the door beside her was wrenched open. If she had had the time to anticipate any reaction from the horrified onlookers, she would have expected

3

sympathy, concern, even worry that she wouldn't be able to go ahead with the planned jump.

What she got, apparently, was a bear with a sore head. And he was growling at her. 'What the hell do you think you're playing at?' Definitely a growl. The kind produced by low, controlled anger. It seemed par for the course today, Claudia thought, that the gap between expectation and reality should be so vast.

She turned, unhurt, but somewhat dazed by the rapidity with which events had overtaken her and was confronted by a pair of large boots, combat trousers that seemed to ascend into the stratosphere and the kind of taut, aggressive hips that would normally give her a pleasurable tingle of expectation. The voice however, did not encourage her to expect anything except . . . well, aggravation.

At a disadvantage in the near ground level car, she unfastened the seat-beat, leaned out and looked up. She was right about the stratosphere. Wrong about the bear. But not that wrong. The man went up a very long way before widening out into a pair of shoulders that would have done justice to a barn door. He also had a thick pelt of black hair that would have curled had it not been ruthlessly trimmed into submission and the kind of blue eyes that any girl would gladly die for. From the expression in them, she thought, this girl just might be required to. But she didn't like his immediate assumption that she was to blame for the accident. She would go down fighting.

4

'Playing at?' she enquired, determined to show him that she was not in the least bit intimidated by his size, or his damped down anger. Or by his eyes. 'Why, musical cars of course,' she said, with a careless wave of her hand. Her shoulder complained but she ignored it. 'Care to join me?' she invited.

It was perhaps fortunate that at that moment they were inundated by near hysterical television personnel. 'Claudia! Darling! My precious girl, are you all right?' Barty James, the programme's director waggled his hands dramatically. 'Shall we call an ambulance?' He turned to his harassed assistant. 'Shouldn't there be an ambulance standing by? Isn't there supposed to be a doctor – ' He began issuing a tirade of instructions, sending minions flying in all directions, but mostly for cover.

Claudia, used to theatrical hysteria, took no notice. Instead she swung long, silk-clad legs out of the car and waited for someone to help her to her feet. Barty was still busy berating his hapless assistant for the lack of an ambulance. Blue Eyes had swiftly removed himself from the scene and was more concerned with the damage to the Landcruiser. Abandoning all hope of immediate aid and succour, she climbed from her car unaided and joined him. His concern was well placed. The damage, although superficial, was widespread. She had scraped and dented every panel, leaving streaks of scarlet paint like careless kisses along the entire right-hand side.

5

The hangar didn't look much better. She hadn't hit it hard, but had still managed a pretty spectacular job of buckling and splitting the elderly corrugated metal.

But her lovely new car had far the worst of it. The left-hand side had suffered horribly in the encounter with the Landcruiser and the bonnet now looked as if a very heavy-footed figure skater had been practising triple toe loops on its glossy paintwork. It was not a pretty sight, but as she turned to Blue Eyes she managed a smile, quite prepared to be brave about it although under the circumstances hysterics would have been quite permissible. Blue Eyes was unimpressed.

'I do hope you're properly insured, Miss Beaumont,' he said, curtly, in case she had missed just *how* unimpressed he was.

Claudia, who could usually reduce a man to stuttering incoherence in less time than it took to say it, was seriously shaken to discover that this man was quite immune to her particular brand of magic. Insurance? That was all that bothered him? He wasn't in the least concerned about her health, the fact that she might have broken her neck? Apparently not. As their eyes met across the wreck of her car she received the very strong impression that he was quite prepared to break it himself. Well, the day was still young and if her anonymous correspondent was right, he might yet get his wish. The thought was enough to drive the smile right off her face.

'Why wouldn't I be properly insured?' Her premium was, in her opinion, large enough to insure any ten cars. 'But if you think I'm paying for this, you can forget it,' she said, nettled by his manner into displaying a little irritation on her own account. 'For your information my brakes failed and since this car is only two days old it's going right back to the manufacturer. I suggest you call them and tell them your troubles.'

'The brakes . . .' There was a twittering of excitement from the television men.

Blue Eyes didn't twitter. 'You really expect me to believe that?' It was quite obviously not a question to which he expected an answer. He had made up his own mind and disbelief was written in every tightly controlled line of his face. 'You were showing off and driving too fast for the surface. Damp grass is like ice if you hit the brakes too hard.'

'Is it? And if you hit the brakes and nothing happens?'

'You lost control. If your brakes had simply failed you wouldn't have hit the Landcruiser, you'd have hit the Porsche.'

'I *know* that. It's why I swerved. I didn't want to hit Barty's Porsche . . .' Something in his expression warned her that she wasn't helping matters and her voice died away.

'Are you saying that you hit my car on purpose?' He spat out the words, one by one.

'It seemed like a good idea at the time.' She glared at him. 'It still does.' Then she threw up her hands in despair. It had been a bad day from the moment she got out of bed and found that horrible anonymous

7

letter on her doormat. 'Is there any chance of a cup of coffee around here?' she demanded.

'Claudia, darling, why don't we forget this for today?' Barty intervened, quickly. 'You're over-wrought. It's quite natural,' he added quickly, as she glared at him, too. 'I'll run you down to the local hospital for a check-up. Since you've had an accident we'll be covered by insurance and we don't want to take any risks, do we?'

'Don't we?' Claudia asked. Blue Eyes was giving her the kind of look that suggested she might have man-ufactured the accident simply to get out of the jump and she didn't like it. 'Oh, for heaven's sake, Barty, I'm not made of glass. Let's get all my bruises over with in one day.' She looked around. 'Where's Tony?' Tony Singleton was the one bright spark in this entire fiasco. Her role in *Private Lives* kept her on stage until eleven every night, but it had still been worth dragging herself out of bed first thing for Tony's training sessions, even under the watchful eye of the television crew. They had filmed her swinging gracefully from a tower in a harness under his careful instruction, learning how to fall, even packing the parachute she was to use.

Today they were going to celebrate her maiden jump. Without the cameras.

'Tony's wife telephoned this morning to cancel.' Blue Eyes regarded her steadily. 'Apparently he's feeling a bit under the weather. She didn't think it was a good idea to take any risks with him.'

Wife? He was married? The low-down sneaking rat. Some days it was just not a good idea to get out of bed.

'His wife?' she enquired, coolly. Being an actress had its advantages. The ability to hide feelings was one of them.

'She's expecting a baby next month.' He punctuated the remark with a speaking, one-shouldered shrug. 'Didn't he mention her?'

No. He seems to have overlooked that minor point, she thought. After all, actresses, were notorious for sleeping around so it didn't really matter, did it? *Like hell it didn't.*

'Not that I recall,' she replied.

'Perhaps he didn't think it was important. But don't worry, Miss Beaumont. I'm here to look after you in his place.'

Now why wasn't that a comfort?

'Really?' she said. 'And who the devil are you?'

His face finally cracked into something that might have been a smile, although she could see that his heart wasn't really in it. 'Gabriel MacIntyre. But Mac will do.' He didn't offer his hand; instead his eyes made a rapid transit of the space between her feet and her carefully tousled blonde hair, making an instant judgement on her short, flirty little skirt and loose silk jersey top. She had dressed to spend the day with Tony, not for a parachute jump, and he knew it. 'And you are the glamorous Miss Claudia Beaumont,' he said pointedly. He seemed singularly underwhelmed by the fact.

9

'I know that,' she informed him, crisply. It was odd how very *crisp* she was feeling considering the fact that she'd just run into the side of an aircraft hangar. The man had much the same bracing effect as the blast from a bottle of smelling salts. 'But please don't stand on ceremony,' she added. 'Miss Beaumont will do just fine.'

'Darling, don't be naughty!' Barty, his thin body encased in a close fitting silk shirt, a toning scarf knotted with studied carelessness around his throat, intervened nervously, throwing a jittery look in the direction of Mac.

'Mr MacIntyre will think you don't like him.'

'Then he'd be right. I don't.'

'Claudia!'

'Well, what do you expect? I told him that my brakes failed and without the slightest evidence to back him up he chose to believe I was lying.'

It was clear he believed a lot of other things about her. None of them were true either.

Mac, Blue Eyes, was unrepentant. 'I saw the way you were driving.'

Barty was beginning to unravel. 'Are you quite sure you want to go ahead with this, Claudia, darling?' He pulled her aside, lowering his voice to a whisper. 'We'd all quite understand . . . shock, what have you . . .'

Claudia realized the crew were looking at her expectantly. Things had changed. With the insurance company paying, they'd all have an extra day's work if she decided to throw a wobbly and put the stunt off

10

until a later date. But they didn't have to jump out of an aeroplane for the titillation of all those millions of television viewers, every one of whom was no doubt hoping to see her fall flat on her face. Especially the one who sent her that nasty little note.

'We do it now, Barty, or not at all,' she announced. This was not a day she wished to repeat. She turned to Gabriel MacIntyre. 'Come on, Mac. I can see you can't wait to push me out of an aeroplane. Lead me to my overalls and let's get on with it.' It gave her considerable pleasure to see that she had taken him by surprise. Although he didn't flicker so much as a muscle, Claudia knew that he'd been convinced she was going to bottle out. She would rather die than give him that satisfaction.

Slowly and with obvious reluctance, he jacked up the smile. If he ever made an effort, she thought, he might be dangerous, but there didn't seem much likelihood of her finding out.

The equipment was laid out on a trestle in the hangar along with a pair of bright red overalls with her name printed across the back because it had looked good on the ground shots. And it would make identification easy, she thought with a wry little smile, if she simply ploughed straight down into the nearest field. Then the boots. Her helmet was next, a mini camera and microphone already attached and ready to be hooked up to the power pack she would wear at her waist. Goggles. Finally, the parachute that she had packed herself under Tony's supervision.

The crew were already suited up, running last minute checks on their cameras and microphones with the OB unit.

'Is there somewhere I can change?' she asked.

Mac's eyes flickered over her unsuitable clothes. 'I hope you're wearing warm underwear,' he said. 'It'll be cold up there.'

'I've a nice line in silk thermals. Would you care to check them out?' He handed her the overalls and pointed her in the direction of the office without another word.

Claudia strode off jauntily enough, but once the door was shut behind her she let out a deep breath and sank into a chair. She was beginning to shake and wasn't sure whether it was a reaction to the shunt with the car, or whether she was just plain scared.

She shed her skirt, her top, her tights, then retrieved from her bag the thermal vest and long drawers that Tony had advised, pulling them on as quickly as her shaking fingers would allow. Damn Tony and his boyish charm. He could have got her through the next half an hour without a qualm, unlike Mr MacIntyre. At least she had nothing but a few stolen kisses to reproach herself for. Although why she should reproach herself for anything when *he* was the cheating bastard, she wasn't quite sure. But she did. And so did Mac.

By the time she came to fasten the front of the jumpsuit her fingers were shaking so much with a mixture of nerves and anger that she couldn't keep hold of the zip pull. A sharp rap on the door, making her jump, was the last straw and she gave up trying.

'We haven't got all day, Miss Beaumont.' *Miss Beaumont*. He made it sound like an insult.

Clutching the overalls together at the front she emerged from the office. 'I'm having zip trouble,' she said loftily. 'It seems to be stuck.'

Mac didn't say a word. He simply took hold of the pull and the wretched thing slid smoothly up to her neck. Then he pushed down the velcro flaps. 'You should have asked for help sooner,' he said, when he was satisfied. 'I told you I'd take care of you.'

She cleared her throat, nervously. The crew had moved outside, leaving just the two of them in the hangar. 'So you did,' she said.

'Is there anything else?'

'No.' She reached for her helmet and tugged it on. 'I can manage now.'

'I hope so. We've all been waiting quite long enough. You were very late.'

She tucked in her long blonde hair. It seemed to take forever and he finally lost patience, finishing the job for her without much care for her scalp. Then he fastened the chin straps. 'I couldn't find the airfield,' she said. 'It's not exactly well sign-posted.'

He ignored the implied criticism and picked up her 'chute. She flexed her shoulders and held back her arms for him to lift it on. He didn't.

Now who was wasting time? 'What's the matter?' she asked, looking behind her.

13

'Nothing. I'm just going to change this 'chute.'

'What's wrong with it? I packed it myself and Tony said I'd made a perfect job of it.'

'Then Tony must have had his mind on other things. I'll get you another one from the store. Why don't you wait outside?'

She glared after him. It wasn't such a hardship. He was six foot two inches of unadulterated masculinity. He might raise her hackles, but after the narcissism and hothouse atmosphere of the theatre she had to admit that there was a rough hewn, unfinished freshness about the man. Not that he was her type. She liked sophisticated, well groomed men who knew how to treat a lady. Gabriel MacIntyre appeared to be the kind of old-fashioned chauvinist who preferred his women barefoot and pregnant. He probably had half a dozen baby MacIntyres to prove it.

And she made it a rule never to play house with other girl's husbands. But men didn't make it easy to be noble. Tony, lying and potentially cheating Tony, for instance, had looked as if butter wouldn't melt in his mouth. At least Mac wore a wedding ring.

Ten minutes later, buckled, fastened, wired for sound so that every gasp of fright could be experienced vicariously by the television audience, she was hurtling down the runway in a noisy, comfortless aircraft. She forced herself to smile. The fuselage had been fitted with tiny cameras to catch every fleeting expression and she was supposed to be enjoying herself. This was all good, clean *fun*.

Ideally they should all be chatting and laughing but thankfully it was too noisy. No doubt someone would add on the kind of jokey commentary that would make the studio audience roar with laughter. She smiled harder, hoping that she hadn't chewed all her lipstick off. It was the performance of a lifetime.

Nothing could go wrong.

The cameramen, all experienced freefallers, were relaxed as they circled the airfield, gaining height, double-checking camera equipment with the OB crew on the ground.

Mac was standing behind the pilot, waiting until they reached the right height. He turned for a moment and stared at her, his eyes thoughtful, his forehead creased in a deep frown. It was unsettling, but she met his gaze, challenged it. Then the pilot shouted something to him and he looked away.

Claudia tried to remember everything that Tony had told her, but found her mind was a blank. Then, in the noisy cramped space of the aircraft, with the jump only minutes away, the letter that had been pushed through her door in the early hours of the morning floated back to the surface of her mind and began to fill the vacuum with its insidious poison.

What kind of sick mind did it take to do something like that? To take so much trouble to find all the right letters in a newspaper, cut them neatly out and then arrange them precisely, sticking them down one by one? She tried to blot the whole thing out. It was rubbish, nonsense, some sick person's idea of a joke.

Any successful actress was bound to provoke jealousy. It was inevitable. Especially when her path was perceived to have been eased by famous parents, a mother who had been a legend, a father who had directed the play she was appearing in right now. The letter was nothing. She had torn it up and thrown it in the bin with the rest of the rubbish.

Everything had been checked a dozen times. She was jumping from a static line. The 'chute would open automatically. All she had to do was go through the drill Tony had taught her. It was no big deal. She looked up as Mac tapped her on the shoulder. It was time to go.

Nothing could go wrong.

But her skin was slicked with sweat as she watched the camera crew jump out of the open doorway, moving away from the aircraft, getting into position to film her own exit from the plane. They made it look so easy. It was easy. She adjusted her goggles.

Nothing could go wrong.

Mac hooked her to the static line then guided her into place in the doorway. Below her the ground was like a picture from a storybook. Small, clean, beautiful. The rushing wind tugged at her, eager to suck her into the void, but she held on, waiting for Mac's signal. It seemed forever coming and she glanced at him. He smiled reassuringly. He'd picked a hell of a time to decide to be friendly, she thought, as at last he slapped her on the shoulder with sufficient impact to ensure she didn't change her mind and mess up everyone's day.

Then, as she plunged downward, dropping towards the Berkshire countryside at thirty-three feet per second, she quite suddenly recalled that Gabriel MacIntyre had changed her carefully packed parachute at the last minute. And no one else had seen him do it.

The fields, the hedges, the silver ribbon of river all seemed to merge and resolve into a sheet of cheap lined paper covered with a jumble of newsprint:

I'VE FIXED YOU, DARLING CLAUDIA. OR RATHER I'VE FIXED YOUR PARACHUTE. ENJOY YOUR JUMP. YOU WON'T BE MAKING ANY MORE.

Gabriel MacIntyre stood in the open doorway of the aircraft and watched Claudia Beaumont fall, counting the seconds, releasing the unexpectedly held breath as the parachute streamed out behind her and the canopy billowed and spread as it filled with air.

He had been so angry when he had seen the envelope tucked in the 'chute she'd packed herself, certain it was a message from Tony. It had been something of a shock when, in the privacy of the store room, he'd opened it and seen what was inside.

She was floating gently now, drifting slightly in the light breeze, the jeep with the ground camera crew chasing after her. He hoped that despite her apprehension she had managed to relax sufficiently to enjoy herself, but the irony of the situation was not lost on him. Her celebrity had put her in a situation where she had been forced to do something she would gladly have avoided. And he had been forced to stand by and watch, instead of being out there, skimming the air for those few magical seconds, the closest sensation to flying a man could ever hope achieve.

He pulled a face as she hit the ground heavily, almost feeling the bone-jarring shock of a bad landing. She had been too tense to collapse and roll the way Tony would have shown her. She'd be stiff tomorrow. And if she'd cut her lip maybe it would be her understudy's lucky night. He hoped she hadn't. She had the kind of mouth that dreams were made of even when she was chewing off her lipstick with nerves.

He watched for a moment longer as the ground camera crew homed in on her, determined not to miss anything that would give the viewers a buzz, hoping that the cool Miss Beaumont would be sufficiently shaken to say something that needed a bleep. That was always good for a laugh.

His lips twisted in disgust at his own feelings of superiority. He was taking their money, for God's sake, part of the circus whether he liked it or not. And what a circus it was.

He saw her rise to her feet, apparently unhurt by her heavy fall, then peeled away from the doorway, dropping into the canvas seat that Claudia had so recently vacated, rubbing at a knee that was never slow to remind him that he wasn't quite the man he had been. Be patient, give it six months, the specialist had said and they'd look at it again. He didn't need six months. He knew he'd never jump again; not and walk away.

He pushed the thought away, taking the envelope he had retrieved from Claudia's parachute from his pocket, shaking out the pieces of a photograph and putting them together. He'd seen the picture on the cover of one of the Sunday supplements a week or so earlier; Claudia Beaumont dressed and made up for a role that, according to the headline, her mother had once made her own. Despite the artificial, stylized glamour of the photograph, the girl's almost luminous beauty shone through and he could see why someone as gullible as Tony had been bowled over. He had thought himself utterly immune to anything that obvious, but when she'd put her head out of that ridiculous little car and looked up at him with those huge silver fox eyes he had been uncomfortably aware of his own stampeding testosterone. He'd been so busy defending himself from her siren beauty that he'd bawled at her like a barrack square bully instead of checking to see if she was hurt.

His mouth twitched in an involuntary smile. She hadn't needed anyone to look out for her; Miss Claudia Beaumont might look like an angel but she was quite capable of giving as good as she got. Sometime within the next half an hour he would have to apologize to her and he had the distinct feeling that when he did she would be laughing at him, knowing precisely why he had responded in the way he had.

Was there a man alive who wouldn't?

He looked at the photograph again. It had been cut into six pieces. Arms, legs, head, each neatly severed from the body. The effect was distinctly chilling and obviously calculated to scare Clauda silly. It had to have been Adele. When she was happy, contented, at peace with herself and the world, she was a delightful young woman. Jealous, she was a tiger, quite capable of reacting to any threat to her marriage with that kind of over-the-top gesture and she had been at the airfield yesterday evening, blazing with indignation and fit to kill.

He shrugged, pushed the envelope back in his pocket, wishing he'd never got involved in this pantomime. The money the television company was paying for the use of his field, his team, would help to underwrite the cost of training a bunch of written-off youths into a talented free fall team, but when he had been approached with the idea he hadn't anticipated someone like Claudia Beaumont as part of the package, disrupting their lives.

He shifted uncomfortably. Maybe he was misjudging the woman. Once Tony had set eyes on her it was inevitable that he would start thinking with his hormones and it was quite possible that Claudia hadn't known that he was married. She hadn't erupted like Adele when he had told her, but the anger had been there, just for a split-second before she had covered it with that cool dismissal. He looked up as the pilot caught his attention. 'How'd it go?' he mouthed over the noise of the engine.

'No problems.'

No problems. He may have had doubts about Claudia Beaumont's morals but there was certainly no doubting her courage. Because it took courage to jump when you were frightened out of your wits. And she had been frightened despite all that brittle-edged bravado. He'd seen too many first-time jumpers to miss the signs. Men usually went through with it because they didn't want to look stupid in front of their mates. Claudia Beaumont would have looked stupid in front of millions of television viewers. And from what he'd heard, she hadn't been given much of a choice to start with.

He bit down hard. She didn't deserve his sympathy because he certainly wasn't misjudging the situation that had developed between her and Tony. Damn the man. Why the hell couldn't he grow up and realize just how lucky he was?

The aircraft wheels touched down on the runway with a bump and a screech and moments later they were taxiing onto the apron in front of the hangar, followed by the jeep that had brought Claudia and the rest of the crew in from the far side of the field.

He lowered himself through the door, taking care to put his weight on his right leg first and by the time he had turned Claudia had taken off the helmet and goggles and her hair was flying about her face. Even with a slightly swollen lip and a graze beneath her left eye she looked incredibly beautiful as she held the flirtatious film crew at bay with an easy grace. He really hated having to admit it, but he was seriously impressed by her composure. He'd seen grown men throw up, cry even, with relief that it was over, that they were still alive.

Then she saw him and her smile faded to be replaced with a tiny frown as he stepped forward to help her down. After a moment's hesitation she put her hands on his shoulders and he gripped her waist. It fitted comfortably between his hands and as he lifted her, her hair swung forward, enfolding him in some faint exotic scent that mingled with the everyday scents of clean fresh air and bruised grass that clung to her jumpsuit. She was tall for a woman, no feather-weight as she hung momentarily above him, yet he would rather have held her than let her go. And when he set her down, his hands remained at her waist.

She didn't move but remained perfectly still within the circle of his arms, that tiny frown still puckering the wide space between her eyes. Without thinking, Gabriel MacIntyre bent and kissed her. Her mouth tasted the way he knew it would, honeypot sweet, seductively so and he had a momentary sense that quite suddenly everything was right with the world. Then she stepped back, raised her hand and slapped him. Hard.

For a moment nobody moved. Then one of the cameramen grinned at him. 'Don't worry mate, for a small consideration we'll edit that bit out.'

CHAPTER 2

Gabriel MacIntyre's cornflower blue eyes darkened. It was like a shadow crossing the sun and Claudia, heart pounding from an adrenalin rush that sent her blood zinging through her veins, saw it and was glad. Men kissed her at her invitation and Mr MacIntyre hadn't been asked to the party. After what he had just put her through, he wasn't about to be.

She would never forget the long seconds of nightmare fall, the flashing certainty that she would never see the baby that her sister Fizz was expecting, never have a baby of her own . . .

The sudden jerk of the parachute opening had come as such a shock that she had forgotten everything Tony had taught her and she'd been flailing about like an idiot when she hit the ground. Her ankle had twisted beneath her and instead of falling in the controlled roll she had been practising, she had crumpled up awkwardly, scraping her mouth against the harness, banging her cheek against the rough grass. All because Gabriel bloody MacIntyre had decided, for no good reason, to change her parachute at the last moment.

And to cap it all he thought he'd take up where his precious partner had left off. Well, now he knew better.

There was a pop and a cheer as someone opened a bottle of champagne and she turned away, taking a glass, playing up to the camera as her fellow parachutists gathered round to offer her congratulations, and to these gentlemen she offered her cheek, although if her mouth hadn't been bruised, she wouldn't have hesitated to rub salt into Mac's wounds. She sipped from the glass gingerly, the champagne fizz stinging against her lip when what she really wanted was a cup of strong, nerve-steadying tea.

'Where's Mac?' Barty shouted from the trailer. 'Get him in the picture somebody.'

Claudia swivelled round defensively, her eyes daring him to come one step closer. But he hadn't moved from the jeep. He was standing just where she had left him, very still, very contained, his whole being focused on her. The imprint of her hand had faded from his weathered, outdoor skin more quickly than he deserved, but at least he was making no effort to join in the celebration.

Claudia blinked, uncertain. There was something unnerving about the man. A detachment. Although there had been nothing detached about the way he had kissed her. That had been the real thing and for a moment his look held her before she turned away, handing her glass to one of the breathless young men hanging on her every movement.

'That's enough, Barty,' she called out. 'I have to get back to London.' She glanced at her poor, battered car. 'Can you give me a lift?'

'If you're quick,' he said, a certain stiffness betraying his irritation with her for cutting short the filming. 'I can't wait all day.'

'Neither can I,' Claudia muttered, under her breath. 'The sooner I get out of this place the better.' She turned quickly in the direction of the hangar, a move she regretted as she came down awkwardly on her left ankle. She stumbled and although he had been yards away a moment earlier it was Mac who caught her.

'Your landing looked a bit heavy,' he said, his face expressionless. It was impossible to tell if he was delighted by this, or merely bored. He nodded in the direction of her foot. 'Is your ankle very painful?' Claudia received the distinct impression that he hoped it was.

'My ankle, for your information, hurts like hell but it proves I'm alive and I can assure you that there is no feeling to beat it.'

It was possible that a spark of humour flashed briefly across his face at the intensity with which this was uttered, but she couldn't be sure. Blue Eyes was not a man to give himself away unless thoroughly provoked; she wondered, briefly what had provoked him into kissing her.

'No assurance is necessary, Miss Beaumont. I know exactly how it feels. And any time you'd like to repeat the experience, just give me a call.' With considerable restraint, Claudia resisted the temptation to slap him again.

Instead, she said, 'Any time I feel like repeating the experience, Mr MacIntyre, I shall go and lie down in a darkened room until I have recovered.'

'I'm sorry you didn't enjoy yourself.'

'Are you? It's odd, but I had the impression that if you could have thrown me out without a parachute you would have done it gladly.' She tilted back her head to stare up at him. He didn't bother to deny it, just stared right back and after a moment she lifted her shoulders in the slightest, but most speaking of shrugs.

'You should have relaxed, Miss Beaumont, let yourself go. Parachuting is the nearest you'll ever get to flying – '

'When I want to fly, Mr MacIntyre, I'll audition for Peter Pan.'

'Attached to a harness?' His scorn was undisguised.

'Very firmly attached to a harness.' She hadn't taken her eyes from his face and now she challenged him. 'And if parachuting's such fun why did you stay put in the safety of the plane?' The muscles around his mouth tightened ominously, but Claudia was into her stride and didn't wait for him to answer. 'Tell me, Mac, why did you really change the parachute? Was it simply to frighten me?'

'Frighten you? Why would I do that?' This time she had the distinct impression that he was laughing at her even though his face didn't betray him by so much as a crease around his eyes. 'You were quite scared enough without any help from me.'

She didn't deny it. 'Then why?' she persisted.

Mac, until that moment rock-steady in his regard, suddenly discovered something in need of his total attention just an inch above her head. 'I told you,' he said, dismissively. 'The packing was sloppy.'

'Bullshit.'

He blinked. 'I beg your pardon?'

Claudia did not believe she was being invited to repeat herself. Although maybe she was wrong about that. Maybe this towering hulk of Neanderthal manhood was so stunned by the fact that she had dared to contradict him, he was finding it difficult to believe his own ears. One thing was certain however, contradicting Mr MacIntyre gained her his absolute and undivided attention. She didn't waste it.

'Are you sloppy when you pack your own parachute?' she enquired, with rather more politeness than she considered his due under the circumstances. 'Or do you concentrate very hard?' Her expression encouraged him to give the matter his deepest thought. 'I imagine you have a pretty fair idea of what would happen to you if the canopy didn't open?'

His face tightened. 'Yes, I have a good idea what would happen.'

'Of course you do. Well, believe it or not, I have an equally well developed sense of self-preservation.' Gabriel MacIntyre's arm was about her waist, taking her weight as she leaned into his shoulder. It was probably the most accommodating shoulder, Claudia decided, that she had ever leaned against, broad and comforting despite the very obvious fact that comforting her was the furthest thing on this man's mind. She thought it would be safer to remove herself from his vicinity immediately. But first she was determined to set the record straight. 'I took the very greatest care when I packed that parachute. And Tony didn't take his eyes off me while I was doing it. If you don't believe me, every minute of the operation was filmed . . .'

'I believe it,' he said, quickly.

'So?' she demanded, finally detaching herself from his arm and turning to face him.

This time he resisted the urge to look somewhere else. She wondered why he found it so difficult. It wasn't as if she was particularly hard on the eyes.

'I just wanted to be sure, that's all.'

She stared at him for a moment. 'Shall I tell you something, Mr MacIntyre?' He raised no objection, so she continued. 'I don't believe you. I think you wanted to give me a fright and for your information you succeeded.' With that she pushed passed him and limped across the hangar.

'Claudia, how much longer are you going to be?' Barty complained.

'As long as it takes,' she snapped. 'Wait.' Barty, brought to heel like a badly behaved dog, waited while she collected her belongings, not bothering to change back into her own clothes. Then, in an effort to appease her for his impatience, he clucked around her while she settled herself in his car. 'Oh, don't fuss so, Barty,' she said, slapping his hand away as he fastened her seat-belt and closing her eyes. 'Just get me out of here. Fast.'

Barty didn't need telling twice and he reversed away from her own battered vehicle and drove off with exactly the kind of flourish that Mac had accused her of. Claudia pulled a little face. Men were allowed to show off, women were supposed to drive sedate little hatchbacks designed for the transportation of the average two point four children to schools, cubs, ballet classes and swimming lessons. And if that wasn't enough, there was always the excitment of collecting the weekly shop from the supermarket. Not her style at all. She wasn't domesticated, and she wasn't in the market for a husband or a family. Except for that brief moment when she thought she would die, the idea of having a baby, a child of her own, had never crossed her mind.

She glanced back, but Gabriel MacIntyre had already turned away, obviously more interested in the damage to his own car than whether Barty could be trusted to get her home in one piece.

Mac kicked the tyre of the Landcruiser. Damned woman. He turned to the remains of her showy little sportscar. Scarlet. Well it would be. Screaming for attention, like Claudia Beaumont. Except of course she didn't have to do anything to attract attention. She had that tall, willowy, head-turning presence that drew every eye to her, whether they wanted to look or not.

It was precious little wonder that Tony had fallen for it. There wasn't any doubt that she'd be dynamite in bed. And just as dangerous. Tony was fortunate that he'd managed to convince Adele that he hadn't got around to finding out. As it was she'd keep him on an emotional diet of bread and water until she considered that he had paid thoroughly for even thinking about it. Which was no more than the idiot deserved since it was obvious that Claudia Beaumont had simply been toying with him, using the glamour she exuded to tempt him for her own amusement.

He opened the door of the car. Typical of a woman, he thought, as he reached for the keys she'd left so carelessly in the ignition. Not that her car looked as if it was going anywhere ever again. But looks could be deceptive. He slipped behind the wheel, pushed back the seat and started her up, smiling despite himself at the rich throaty purr from the engine. It was a lovely machine, utterly wasted on the likes of a woman like Claudia Beaumont who only wanted it to draw attention to herself.

He reversed slowly away from the hangar so that he could get a better idea of the damage she had caused. And when he touched the brakes nothing happened.

He wasn't impressed. Undoubtedly the line carrying the brake fluid had fractured on impact. He pumped the handbrake and the car, moving slowly, stopped without a problem. He turned off the engine and got out, inspecting the grass in front of him. Apart from the marks left by the wheels, the grass was clean.

It was with some relief that Claudia was decanted at her own doorstep rather less than an hour later. When she had said fast, Barty had taken her at her word.

'I'll see you tomorrow, Claudia,' he said. 'And wear those overalls, they'll look very dashing on the show.'

'Dashing isn't my style, Barty.'

'Dashing and sexy,' he amended. 'The overalls, complete with grass stains. And if that bruise develops nicely I'll want to see that as well.'

'Barty!'

'You want the viewers to know how hard you worked to part them from their money, don't you?'

For a moment she considered arguing, but then she shrugged. 'Whatever you say.'

'I'll send a car to pick you up at the theatre after the matinée.' He waited for her to get out. She didn't and after a moment he came around and opened the door for her, impatiently offering her a hand as she levered herself awkwardly onto the pavement on an ankle which would have already swollen but for the tightly laced boot. It was difficult not to contrast his grudging manner with Gabriel MacIntyre's instinctive offer of assistance. Barty wouldn't win any awards for his manners. But then Barty wouldn't kiss her, either.

She winced as the thought provoked a smile. She'd better get some ice on her lip. And some professional strapping on her ankle if she wasn't going to limp through her performance tonight.

'Are you crazy, Mac? I know better than to play about with parachutes once they're packed.'

'I had to be sure. You were madder than a wet hen yesterday . . .'

'It was what I needed, a chance to blow off steam. I've been cooped up at home for weeks, just waiting. God, you men have no idea how boring it is just sitting about knitting booties.'

'You can't knit.'

'Exactly! Is it any wonder I've been a pain in the backside to live with? If I'd been Tony and some glamorous female had looked at me twice I'd have been panting like an eager puppy, too.'

Mac had been uneasy about confronting Adele. She was less than a month from delivery and had a temper like a volcano, a combination that was distinctly unsettling. But although Tony was undoubtedly in the doghouse, it was clearly more to impress on him the error of his ways than because she was still seriously angry. Although whether Tony was privilege to that information was open to question.

And he was somewhat disconcerted to discover that she found the whole incident at the airfield highly amusing. 'Claudia Beaumont actually admitted choosing to hit your car rather than upset the television producer?'

'That's what she said.'

She laughed. 'I wish I'd been there to see your face.'

Mac was not proud of the way he had reacted and he was heartily thankful that his performance had not been witnessed by anyone whose opinion he cared about. 'You are on maternity leave,' he said, roughly. 'I don't want you coming down to the airfield until you're ready to start work again.'

'Which, according to you, is when my offspring has finally left school?'

'That's about right.'

'God, but you're old-fashioned, Mac,' Adele said, totally exasperated with his pig-headedness. 'I'm entitled to keep my job, you know. You can't get rid of me just because I've had a baby. There are laws – '

'So, sue me.'

'I will.'

'I look forward to it.'

'Then you're a bigger idiot than I took you for.' Then, 'Oh, look, I'm sorry. I understand the way you feel, Mac, but I'm not Jenny. You have to trust me.'

'I know you wouldn't do anything to hurt your baby, Adele. But I can't have you or – ' he waved vaguely in the direction of her bump – 'it, on my conscience.'

'I know. I do understand.' She held out her arms to him. 'Come and give me a hug.'

Claudia was dabbing at the bruise developing below her eye with a concealer when Melanie put her head round the dressing-room door.

'Still in one piece, then?'

Claudia glanced at her half-sister through the mirror. 'Just. But coupled with the fact that I managed to all but write-off my new car, I have to say that I'd give a big thumbs down to leaping out of an aeroplane as a way to spend the morning.' Leaning forward to examine the result of her camouflage job more closely, she said, 'Will I get away with that, do you think?'

'You've had an accident? Should you be here? What happened?' Anxious questions bubbled out in a rush.

'Nothing much. I put my foot on the brake pedal and, well –' she shrugged – 'as I said, nothing much happened.'

Shaken, Melanie, although she had worked for five years in Australian television, was younger than her twenty years might suggest and still endearingly impressionable. She sank into an old-fashioned basket chair set at an angle beside the dressing table. 'You mean the brakes failed?' she whispered in a shocked voice.

'You could say that.' Claudia mentally reviewed her conversation with the manager of the garage which had supplied the car. 'I believe I said something along

34

those lines when I called the garage and asked them to pick up the wreck.'

'But how did you stop? I mean – '

'Stopping was no problem. An aircraft hangar obligingly got in the way.'

'A what!'

'An aircraft hangar.' Claudia tossed a grin in her sister's direction. 'Eventually. First I bounced along the side of a very large Landcruiser that belonged to an equally large man.' She gave another little dab at the bruise. 'He wasn't very pleased. In fact a short while later he pushed me out of an aeroplane.' She indicated the bruise beneath her eye. 'It's been a fun day all round.'

'It doesn't sound like my idea of fun. Should you be here?' she repeated.

'The bruise is that bad?'

'The bruise doesn't show. Well, not that much. But you must be pretty shaken up.'

'Shaken, my dear, but not stirred. The show must go on.' There was a tap at the door. 'Come in.'

Jim Gardner, who worked the stage door, brought in a hand tied bouquet of roses. 'A gentleman just brought these to the stage door for you, Miss Claudia. There's a note. He's waiting for an answer.'

'Is he, indeed?' Claudia took the pale yellow roses and picked out an envelope tucked between the stems. If it was Tony he'd get all the answer he could handle.

'How lovely. Who are they from?' Melanie asked.

'I've no idea.' Her name, written in bold, black ink, gave her no clues. She flipped it open and slipped out the card. *It's important that I speak to you. I'll come backstage after the performance. Gabriel MacIntyre.*

Claudia laughed. 'Well, well. It appears my very large, very angry man wants to see me.'

'Maybe he wants to apologize for pushing you out of that aeroplane,' Melanie suggested, taking the card and regarding it with interest. 'He's a touch dictatorial, but he has lovely handwriting.'

Apologize? For being rude, or for kissing her, Claudia wondered briefly before turning to the waiting doorman. 'Jim, please tell Mr MacIntyre that I'm sorry but I'm busy after the performance.' She glanced defensively at Mel. 'Good handwriting doesn't make up for rude.'

'I didn't say a word.' Then, 'You're keeping the flowers?'

Claudia lifted the blooms to her face, but florists' roses rarely had much scent and these were no exception. 'It would be too cruel to return them. What would a man do with a bunch of flowers? And all that ribbon, too. They'd be nothing but an embarrassment to him.' She grinned at Mel. 'Perhaps I should send them back. I'd enjoy embarrassing him.'

'Would you? Why?' Claudia didn't enlighten her and she shrugged. 'Sending the roses back won't embarrass him unless he's truly stupid. He'll just dump them in the nearest bin,' Mel informed her. She shrugged. 'I tried it once.'

'You have hidden depths, little sister.' But Claudia knew instinctively that Mac wasn't the kind of man to allow a woman to embarrass him that easily. 'In that case I'll keep them. Thank you, Jim, just pass on my message.'

Jim, who had heard just about everything in a long life spent behind the scenes in the theatre and was surprised by nothing, nodded. 'Yes, Miss Claudia.'

'No, wait. I want to be sure he gets the message. Forget the "sorry". Just tell him that I'm busy. And don't on any account let him in,' she warned, as an afterthought. 'No matter what he says.'

'Right, Miss.'

'You're absolutely heartless, Claudia,' Melanie chided. 'If the poor man just wanted to say he was sorry for losing his temper the least you can do is listen. You did run into his car.'

'Yes, I did. But I wasn't showing off.'

'Oh,' Melanie murmured, 'is that what he said?'

'He did. So, if he wants to tell me how sorry he is, he'll have to try a lot harder. Yellow roses, indeed.'

Melanie took them from Claudia. 'What's wrong with them? You didn't expect red, did you?' Then she gave Claudia a thoughtful look. 'Or did you? In addition to being very large and very irritable, is he also very good looking?'

Claudia laughed. 'I'm sure some women would find him absolutely devastating,' she said, remembering those blue eyes, 'but he's a bit rough hewn for my taste.'

'Then why won't you see him?'

'Because in the language of flowers, my sweet innocent, yellow roses indicate insincerity.'

'You can't expect a man to know that!' her sister protested. 'Especially not the rough hewn variety.'

'Maybe not, but I sense that he chose yellow instinctively.'

'But you've already said that red wasn't an option; what does that leave? Pink? You're not the kind of girl a man would send pink flowers to.'

'No?' Claudia considered the matter. 'No, I think you're right. Pink would be altogether too wishy-washy a colour for Gabriel MacIntyre.'

'Gabriel MacIntyre. It's a wonderful name. I'm tempted to go and have a look at him. Perhaps I could stand in for you, receive his apology by proxy? After all, I'm your sister.'

Claudia laughed. 'Oh, no. You're too young and tender a plant for the likes of Mr MacIntyre, my sweet.'

'It sounds to me as if he's made quite an impression on you, whether you're admitting it or not. What a pity he didn't understand about flowers. Although there doesn't seem to be much choice left. White?' she offered, doubtfully.

'White?' Claudia laid her fingers dramatically across her breast. 'For a scarlet woman who flirted with someone else's husband?'

Mel laughed uncertainly. 'Don't be silly.'

'I'm not being silly,' Claudia informed her. 'It appears that Tony was married, a small detail that he somehow overlooked to mention.'

'Married? What a rat.'

Claudia waved an admonishing finger. 'Unkind to rats, Mel.'

'But if you didn't know, why is Gabriel MacIntyre blaming you? And why does he care?'

Why indeed? 'They work together. Maybe it's some male bonding thing. In any case Mr MacIntyre assumes that I didn't care whether Tony was married or not, so you can see that white roses would have been out of the question.' And there was only ever one actress who had commanded white roses by right.

'Obviously,' Mel continued. 'In fact I'm beginning to wonder why he's bothering.'

Claudia shrugged. 'Oh, come on, Mel, use your imagination,' she encouraged, cynically. 'Gabriel MacIntyre may be disapproving, but he isn't entirely immune.'

Mel blushed. 'You're joking?'

'Maybe.' She caught sight of her reflection in the mirror, the curve of her lower lip accentuated by the slight swelling that an ice pack had reduced, but not entirely eliminated. It had a bee-stung look. The look of a woman recently kissed. She lifted her fingers to her mouth as if to still the slight throbbing, then snatched them away. 'Of course I'm joking,' she said, with a rather forced brightness. 'He probably just wants to know the name of my insurance company. Can you give me a lift home this evening, by the way?'

'Of course.' Mel handed Claudia the roses and got up. 'I'd better go and get ready.' At the door she paused. 'Claud? I'm really sorry about Tony. I know you liked him.'

'I should have realized a man that pretty was too good to be true.'

'Maybe you should try the rough hewn type for a change,' Mel advised with a grin as she departed.

As the door closed behind her Claudia lifted the roses to her face, ruffling the petals against her lips for a moment before she tossed them onto the chair Mel had vacated and turned to the mirror to complete her make-up.

'Have you hurt your ankle, Claudia?' She was laughing at something her leading man had said as the enthusiastic audience finally allowed them to leave the stage, but she turned at the stage manager's obvious concern.

'Just twisted it a little, Phillip, but it's nothing serious,' she said, falling in beside him, slipping her arm through his as they made their way back to the dressing rooms. She extended her ankle a little to show the strapping. 'I hope it wasn't too obvious on stage?'

'Not a soul in the audience will have noticed,' he reassured her. 'I saw you limping when you arrived, that's all. Have you had an accident? I thought I noticed a bruise, too. Not that it shows now,' he added, quickly.

40

'Thanks to the miracle of make-up.' Phillip Redmond had been part of the backstage scene ever since she had been old enough to visit her parents in their dressing rooms under the watchful eye of nanny, and he was one of the first people her father turned to when he was mounting a production, more like one of the family than an employee. 'I made a parachute jump this morning for a television programme,' she told him with a grin. 'I wouldn't recommend it as a pastime; I'm bumps and bruises from head to toe.'

He was horrified. 'You shouldn't be taking risks like that, Claudia. If you'd broken your ankle what would we have done tonight?'

'Put on my understudy and no one would even have noticed,' she said, as they reached her dressing room.

'Claud!' Mel came flying out of her dressing room in her wrapper. 'An old friend of mine from Oz just called and we're going to a party. Do you want to come?'

'I think a party on top of the day I've had would just about finish me, sweetheart. You go off and enjoy yourself, I'll get a taxi home.'

'A taxi?' Phillip asked. 'What's happened to that fancy new car of yours?'

'She wrote it off this morning,' Mel told him. 'What with that and a parachute jump, you'd have thought she'd have taken the night off.'

'The public paid to see Miss Beaumont perform,' Phillip said reprovingly, 'not some girl they've never heard of. But you don't have a theatrical background

41

so I wouldn't expect you to understand that.' As far as Phillip was concerned television didn't count and dismissively he turned back to Claudia. 'Don't call a taxi, I'll be happy to take you home.'

Claudia bit back the retort that Melanie Brett Beaumont was her sister, even if a very recent and unexpected addition to the family. Phillip had made no secret of the fact that he thought she was an interloper with no business adding Beaumont to her name. Given time he would probably get used to the idea, but he couldn't be forced into accepting the girl. And although she would rather have called a taxi, she decided that it might be a good idea to accept his offer and attempt a little quiet diplomacy on Mel's behalf. 'That's kind of you, Phillip. I appreciate it.'

'Not at all. I'm happy to take you home any time. I often performed the same service for your mother.' The slightest emphasis on the last word seemed to have been especially for Mel's benefit, Claudia thought, her spirits sinking slightly. Perhaps it would take rather more than diplomacy to reconcile him to Melanie. 'Can you wait about twenty minutes or so?' Phillip asked.

'It'll take me that long to clean off the war paint,' Claudia told him. 'Come along to the dressing room when you're ready to go.'

Mel glared after him. 'Who does that man think he is?' she demanded.

'I'm sorry, but he goes years back with us, Mel. My mother took him on as assistant stage manager when he was a stagestruck youth. I remember him keeping Fizz and me quiet backstage during a matinée once, during a gap in nannies. He fed us toffee non-stop.' She glanced around. 'It was here, I think, in this theatre. It must have been Antony and Cleopatra.'

'If it was Antony and Cleopatra,' Mel said, with a sharp edge of bitterness, '*my* mother was playing the second handmaiden on the left. I've still got the programme.'

Claudia, cursing herself for her lack of tact, put her arm around Mel's shoulders. 'Come on, darling, *we* know Dad loved her, that's what matters. And we *all* love you. Do you really care if the stage manager's just a bit prudish about it?'

'He doesn't let his prudery show when he's talking to Dad. I've heard him. Yes, Mr Edward. Of course, Mr Edward. Three bloody bags full, Mr Edward.' Melanie had lived most of her life in Australia with her own mother. When she was angry she became very Antipodean. 'He missed his vocation. He should have been a butler. He would be a whizz at putting the lower classes in their place.'

Claudia swallowed a smile. 'Darling, try to understand. Elaine French and Edward Beaumont were portrayed as the perfect couple, on stage and off. It might have been a public relations creation but Phillip thought it was true. Everyone did. That's one of the reasons the theatre's full night after night. I've been dressed up to look exactly like my mother and you're Beau's love-child. The nation's prurient curiosity simply cannot resist the temptation to see what we're like together.' She grinned. 'Dad might be a good actor and no slouch as a director, either, but when it comes to marketing he really does deserve one of those little gold statuettes.'

For a moment Mel remained tense and angry, then with a little shudder she let it go. 'Sorry. I shouldn't let it get to me. It's just that everyone thinks your mother was a saint and that mine was no better than she ought to have been. It's a bit hard to live with.'

Claudia hugged her. '*We* know that's not the truth and you shouldn't care what Phillip thinks.'

Mel rested her head on Claudia's shoulder. 'I know. But I'm not as strong as you.'

'Rubbish. You're a Beaumont, strength comes as standard. Now go and have a good time at your party. Just don't forget we've got a matinée tomorrow.'

Mel groaned. 'I loathe matinées.'

'At least you can put your feet up between performances. I've got to rush off to the television studios to accept a cheque on behalf of the hospice.'

Mel grinned. 'And get loads of publicity for that new television serial you're in. It starts next week, doesn't it?'

'Don't remind me. I've got half a dozen interviews lined up already, mostly at the crack of dawn.'

'My heart bleeds for you.'

Claudia laughed. 'Brat,' she said. 'Fizz would never have dared to speak to me like that.'

'If you believe that you don't know Fizz as well as you think you do,' Mel contradicted her. 'But she's a lot nicer than either of us.'

'Nicer than me,' Claudia countered. 'You're not so bad, considering.'

'Considering what?' Mel demanded, hands on hips.

'Considering that you're an Australian, of course.'

It was a running gag between them and Mel, dropping into the flat vowels of her home city, responded in kind. 'Oh, really? Well let me tell you that for a *Pom* you're not so dusty yourself.'

'Compliments, compliments,' she said, laughing. 'I could listen to them all day, but hadn't you better go and get changed if you're going to a party?'

Melanie gave a little yelp of dismay and dived back into her preparations.

Back in her own dressing room, Claudia picked over the messages left at the stage door by her admirers, along with countless single red roses. She was surprised to discover that she felt a certain discontent that Gabriel MacIntyre had not, after all, persisted in his efforts to see her. She had the feeling that he wasn't a man who would easily give up anything he wanted. Or maybe she imagined more in his kiss than he had intended. Maybe he always kissed like that.

She climbed into a pair of close-fitting designer jeans and a silk shirt that clung to her figure, emphasizing her well-shaped bosom and her narrow waist. Then she flicked a comb through her hair, leaving it loose about her shoulders. She had gathered the red roses together and pushed them into a vase already stuffed with similar offerings that stood on her dressing table. The letters were swept up and dumped into her bag to be read and, if necessary, answered at leisure.

Then as Phillip appeared in the doorway she caught sight of the yellow roses abandoned on the chair and in a moment of weakness went back for them.

Phillip gave the flowers a doubtful glance. 'You're not taking those home with you, are you?' he asked.

Claudia smothered a strong inclination to tell him that it was none of his business. She was trying to be diplomatic and that would hardly be a good start. 'Don't you like them? I think they're very pretty.'

'Your mother hated them,' he said, as if that was the last word on the subject. ' "Never trust a man who sends yellow roses," she said to me more than once.' And her mother was undoubtedly an authority on the subject. 'Of course she would only accept white roses. Even from Mr Edward.'

'I know.' The white roses had been part of the Elaine French image and were banked around her dressing room on a first night like a virgin's boudoir. Claudia pulled a face. 'Actually, Phillip, I've decided I don't trust men full stop,' she said, a little sharply. 'Present company excepted, of course. Roses, however, are something else and the colour of these will go perfectly with my new curtains. Shall we go?'

When he stopped outside her door Phillip offered to see her up to her apartment, check it out for her.

'You can't be too careful,' he said. 'A woman living alone is very vunerable.'

'I know,' she said. No one better. 'And I am careful. I had an alarm installed a few weeks ago.' The strain of the day was beginning to take its toll; she'd had all the enthusiastic reminiscences about her mother that she could handle. That, and the lingering scent of tobacco that filled Phillip's car and clung to his clothes even though he had refrained from actually smoking during the drive.

By the time she had climbed the stairs to her apartment, her ankle was throbbing in time with the graze beneath her eye and all she wanted to do was fall into bed. She slid her key into the lock, opened the door and groped to reset the alarm before it woke the neighbours.

It wasn't switched on.

Claudia frowned. It wouldn't be the first time she'd forgotten to set it, but after her fright this morning, she'd been so careful. At least she thought she had been careful. She hesitated for a moment in the hall, wondering whether to run back downstairs and tell Phillip she had changed her mind. He had insisted that he would stay until he saw a light come on. But if he came up she would have to make him coffee and it would be an hour or more before he left. Instead, she ran through the last moments before she had left for the theatre. The taxi driver had been hooting impatiently. It had been a rush.

The flat was absolutely quiet, the only sound her heart pounding in her ears. She was just letting her imagination run away with her. It was that damned letter. But she didn't turn on the light and she left the front door open before edging along the wall to the kitchen, pushing open the door with a nervous little shove. It was dark inside, only the electric green colon on the microwave clock winking at her to warn her that there had been a power failure in her absence. Could that have knocked out the alarm? She tried to remember what the man who had installed it had said. The sound of the refrigerator starting up made her jump and for a moment she leaned weakly against the door frame while her heart returned to something approaching a normal beat.

'Idiot!' she said, and switching on the light she began to laugh at her own stupidity. 'Stupid, stupid – '

Then the front door banged.

She spun around, heart right back in her mouth, pulse rate racketing like an express train. *Who's there?* The words formed in her head, a silent scream. Because she couldn't speak, couldn't call out for help. Her throat had closed with fear, her tongue become thick and rigid as a plank of wood and her voice, the lyrical, laughing voice with which she enchanted hundreds of people every night, deserted her as a dark clad figure detached itself from the shadows of the hall.

CHAPTER 3

'Frightened, Miss Beaumont?'

The voice was low, gravelly, its very softness making it more, not less threatening. It was also familiar and with the familiarity came unrestrained fury and Claudia boiled over.

'What the hell do you think you're playing at, MacIntyre? You frightened the wits out of me.'

'That was my intention.' He stepped out of the shadows and the dark clothing was nothing more threatening than a suit with the collar turned up to cover the betraying whiteness of his shirt.

'You wanted to scare me?' Claudia's voice had returned with a vengeance and she used it. 'Is that what you usually do when a girl tells you to get lost?'

'Making people think about their safety is what I do best. Whether they're packing a parachute, or being threatened from some unknown source. I normally charge heavily for the experience, but in your case I'll consider it reward enough if the next time you come home and find your burglar alarm has been interfered with you'll remember how you felt just thirty seconds ago.'

'Remember?' Claudia knew without doubt that she would never forget that momentary feeling of numbing helplessness; in fact, her sensory input was taking on a major overload for one day.

'Yes, Miss Beaumont. Remember. And instead of behaving like some stupid female in a television drama going to investigate the noises in the attic, get out as fast as you can and call for help.' Claudia, momentarily speechless, just stared at him. 'You've had a shock. Would you like me to make you a cup of tea?'

The sheer matter-of-factness of his offer snapped her out of her temporary paralysis. 'No,' she declared, 'I wouldn't. What I want is for you to go. Right now.'

He ignored her invitation to leave. Instead, he put his arm around her shoulders, eased her through the kitchen door and encouraged her onto a stool before crossing to the sink to fill the kettle. 'Aren't you just a little bit curious to know why I wanted to talk to you this evening?' He turned, his face quite expressionless as he waited for her answer.

Of course she was curious but this man's impassive face gave her no clues. Well, two could play that game. Anyone who had gone to so much trouble to get his own way wasn't going anywhere until he had unburdened himself. She wasn't about to make it easy for him.

Neither did she want him to see just how much he had frightened her. So she propped her elbows on the breakfast bar, rested her chin on her hands to keep them from shaking and waited for him to enlighten her.

He took his time, making tea despite the fact that she'd asked him not to, finding his way around her kitchen with apparent ease. Claudia refused to be impressed. He could have been in her apartment for hours, made any number of cups of tea while he was waiting for her to fall into his nasty little trap.

Nevertheless, she had to admit that he was a pleasure to watch as he set about the task with efficiency and an economy of movement. Men, she had long ago discovered, had a way of making the simplest domestic tasks appear so difficult that women lost patience with them and took over. Most men. Gabriel MacIntyre did not fall into that category. So she watched him. And when he turned with two steaming mugs of tea he saw that she was watching him.

She didn't blush, she didn't look away, covered in confusion. She was twenty-seven years old. Quite old enough to outstare any man. For a moment he returned her gaze and challenged that assumption. Then, as Claudia felt the unaccustomed heat rising to her cheeks he let her off the hook, leaning forward to place one of the mugs in front of her. 'It's weak,' he said, 'but I couldn't find any sugar.'

She was furious with him, with herself even more. 'I don't have any use for it,' she told him.

'I rather suspected that was the case. It's a pity, you might need it when you've seen this.' He lowered

51

himself onto a stool on the other side of the breakfast bar and took an envelope out of the breast pocket of his jacket. 'You asked me this morning why I switched parachutes . . .' He opened it and tipped the contents onto the counter in front of her. 'I switched them because I found this poking out of the one you packed.' Claudia watched as he fitted the pieces of photograph together, then very slowly pulled them apart again so that she could be left in no doubt as to the intended message. He looked up at her. 'Have you any explanation to offer?'

'Explanation?' The word made no sense, but then she wasn't thinking very clearly. Her eyes flickered across the kitchen to the bin where she had flung that horrible letter after she had shredded it with trembling fingers. Could that letter have been a *genuine* threat? A chill feathered her spine and saliva gathered warningly in her mouth.

'What I'm asking, what I need to know,' Mac persisted, 'is whether this could have been a publicity stunt that misfired?' Claudia swallowed hard, sipped the tea, dragged her attention back to the man sitting opposite her. 'Publicity stunt?' She pushed her hair back, desperate for something to do with her hands. For a moment they had stopped shaking; now the tremor threatened her entire body. 'Of course it wasn't a stunt. What kind of sick idiot would engineer something like that?'

'I'm asking the questions.' He didn't care how she was feeling. All that tea and sympathy had been so much guff, she thought and that stiffened her response. She wasn't about to be put through the third degree in her own home by a man who had broken in and scared her half to death just to prove how easy it was.

'Why?' she demanded. 'If it was a stunt it didn't work so why are you getting so steamed up about it?'

'Because someone messed about with a parachute in my care. I intend to find out why and by whom. I've got my own security to think of.'

His security? Oh, la di da. 'You should have lined us all up against the wall and interrogated us this morning,' she snapped. 'I'm sure you carry thumbscrews on your keyring.'

'Maybe I should have,' he replied, in the same cool manner, ignoring the thumbscrews remark, but not denying it. 'But this morning I thought I knew who had done this. I was mistaken. So, was it a stunt?' The last four words were rattled at her like pellets from a gun.

'No,' she declared, instinctively backing away from him. 'Of course it wasn't.' She felt defensive, ashamed that he should think she could be involved in something so tacky. So nastily tacky.

He saw her reaction and pressed her for an answer. 'You're quite sure?' he insisted. 'Think about it.'

Claudia thought about it. Her considered reaction was the same as her instinctive one. Her agent knew better than to involve her in anything of that kind; he was on a knife-edge with her already over a carelessly drawn contract that had cost her a lot of money. The only other alternative was Barty.

Barty was something of an unknown quantity, but she was pretty sure that if he had been involved, it would have been handled with rather more skill. For a publicity stunt to work a whole lot of people had to know about it and on that basis it would have been a flop. But if it wasn't her agent and it wasn't Barty, who had taken so much trouble to cut up her photograph and put it where she would find it? Claudia wasn't sure it was a question she wanted to ask.

Mac wasn't so reticent. 'Claudia?' he prompted, reminding her that he wasn't going away until he had an answer. And if that was what it took to get rid of him . . .

'If Barty had organized a stunt like this,' she said, very slowly, 'it wouldn't have failed. There would have been a reporter and a press photographer on hand. And he would have ensured that someone reliable would have found . . .' She reached out to touch the photograph, then snatched her hand back and put it over her mouth. It had to be connected with the letter. And that meant only one thing. Whoever had written it had meant every word.

'Reliable?' Mac prompted.

She raised her lashes to meet his questioning eyes. 'Someone in on the stunt. Someone who would have known how to make a fuss. The technician who hooked up the power pack probably. Why didn't you say something?' she demanded. 'If I'd known why you'd changed the wretched thing I wouldn't have been so . . .' She made a little gesture.

'So what?' Mac asked. Scared, she thought. But it was stupid to be scared. It was just a prank. It had to be. The alternative was too dreadful to contemplate. When she didn't answer, he continued. 'I didn't say anything because at the time I thought I knew who had done it. I was certain it was just a rather nasty attempt at scaring you. Getting her own back. I didn't think it would help you to know about it. And I didn't believe she would have tampered with the parachute. In fact I know she didn't, because I checked it after you'd gone. Which is why I wondered about a stunt.'

'She?' The penny dropped. 'You were protecting Tony's wife.'

'She's pregnant, a bit overwrought, which is hardly surprising under the circumstances.'

'What circumstances?'

'He'd told her he was going to a regimental reunion and she asked me if I was going. Not unnaturally I didn't know what she was talking about. Then she found a ticket for tonight's show in one of Tony's pockets.'

'You should have told me,' she insisted.

'Why? Since the object of the exercise was to frighten you, if I'd told you about the photograph I'd have done what I thought was Adele's work for her. And I didn't want you scared.'

But she had already been scared. 'You amaze me. I had the impression that "scared" was the very least of the many fates you were wishing on me this morning.'

'Did you?' He seemed momentarily taken aback. Then after consideration he conceded that she might be right. 'Perhaps I was less than sympathetic after you had ploughed into my car, then attempted to demolish my hangar.'

'I didn't do it deliberately.'

'Pardon me?' he said, with every appearance of disbelief. 'I thought you did.' Claudia had known she had made a mistake the minute she'd said it, but it was too late to do anything about it now. She would just have to sit and take it. 'A question of choosing the lesser of two evils, wasn't it?' Mac continued. 'I do hope Barty James was suitably grateful.'

'Barty James is a pain in the backside. And if you think my driving leaves something to be desired, his has to be experienced to be believed.'

'You did say *fast*,' he pointed out. Then he lifted one shoulder slightly. 'But if I'm entirely honest with you,' he continued, 'I did have another reason for not telling you about the photograph.'

'Oh?' She couldn't wait.

'I thought if you had another shock on top of the accident you'd call off the jump for the day. I really didn't want to go through that performance again.'

'Not even for a double fee?' she enquired, remembering the eagerness of the crew to pack up and go home.

He must have remembered it too, because he managed a wry a smile. 'No, Claudia. Not even for a double fee.'

But it wasn't funny. 'You should have told me, Mac,' she insisted.

'There was no risk – '

'No risk?' she demanded. 'No risk?' She was aware that her voice was rising, but the neatly dissected photograph was lying in front of her and she didn't care. 'Who the hell were you to decide whether there was a risk or not? It was my life!'

He regarded her with a thoughtful expression. 'But I changed the parachute,' he said, as if that was sufficient.

'You changed the parachute,' she repeated, 'and that was the answer to everything, was it? Well, Mr Gabriel MacIntyre, you just listen to this. I woke up this morning to discover an anonymous letter on my mat. My kindly correspondent had gone to an enormous trouble, you know, cutting great big letters out of newspapers, just to let me know that my parachute wasn't going to open. So it was a bit late to protect me from Adele's scare tactics. She had already scored a bulls-eye.' She had finally shocked that careful, interrogative expression off his face, Claudia thought. Mac was a man it would be hard to shock, but she had just managed to seriously disturb him. If she had had the time to think about it, she would have applauded herself for such an achievement. But she was too busy telling him exactly what he had done this morning. 'I had actually managed to convince myself that it was just a sick joke – '

'A joke?'

'Some people have a very weird sense of humour,' she told him. 'And approximately eleven million people saw me on television last week. They all knew I was going to make a parachute jump this morning. When you're in the public eye that kind of thing goes with the territory.'

'You didn't consider cancelling today?'

From somewhere she found a smile. 'Believe me, I wish I had. The entire twenty-four hours. But I figured that since the idea of the letter was to scare me out of making the jump, it had to be from someone with a motive for making me look pathetic. I mean, who would believe it? Really? If you'd read about it in the newspaper you'd have thought I'd done it myself just to get out of it. Wouldn't you?'

'Maybe I would,' he agreed, without apology. 'But it would have been wise to mention it so that I could have double-checked – '

'Mention it?' She regarded him with scorn. 'Just when would I have *mentioned* it? After you started yelling at me? I don't believe I had much time before.'

He ignored this. 'You obviously didn't take it seriously,' he said. 'No one could be that stupid.'

'Oh, right. Give the man a coconut. I didn't take it *seriously*. It made me feel sick to my stomach but I had still managed to convince myself that everything was fine. Who could tamper with my parachute? It was safely in the care of Tony and he wouldn't do anything to hurt me. *Would he?*' she demanded and was glad to see an angry colour darkening his cheekbones. 'Of course not. Then, just as I stepped through the plane doorway I realized that *you* had changed the parachute, Mr MacIntyre. That no one had seen you do it. And quite suddenly it occurred to me that I didn't know you from Adam . . .'

'Claudia?' He stood up. 'You didn't think . . . Oh, my God, you did . . . you thought it wasn't going to open – '

The recollection of that horrible moment was suddenly too much for her and she was off the stool and running for the bathroom as the bile rose to her throat, stinging, foul. She had eaten nothing all day as events had piled one on top of the other, conspiring to rob her of her appetite, but her stomach muscles reacting belatedly to the day's traumas weren't bothered about that. Now all she could taste was the acid of the few sips of champagne she had swallowed after the jump as she slumped on the floor, her back against the bath, her cold clammy forehead on her knee.

'Claudia,' Mac said, gently, his hands on her shoulders. 'Come on. Get up.'

She jerked away from his touch. 'Go away,' she muttered, through the rawness of her throat. 'Just leave me alone.' He took no notice. Instead he lifted her to her feet, propping her on the edge of the bath before ringing out a flannel under the cold tap.

He wiped her face, pressed the cold cloth to her forehead. 'There,' he said, as if that would make everything better. 'Come and lie down.' His concern was obvious, but she didn't want his concern. She just wanted him to go. And so she repeated her request for him to leave, somewhat less politely. But he appeared to have been afflicted with sudden deafness since instead of doing what he had been told, he picked her up and carried her through into the sitting room and put her on the sofa. 'Lie down,' he said, 'and put your feet up.'

Claudia gave in, not gracefully, but she gave in; deep down she knew that she didn't have a choice. It was obvious that Gabriel MacIntyre was a man who gave orders rather than took them and so she stopped protesting and allowed him to remove her shoes, prop her feet on a cushion. 'How's the ankle?' he asked as an afterthought when he noticed the strapping.

'There's nothing wrong with my ankle that a pain-killing injection and some efficient strapping couldn't handle. I thought I told you to go?'

He went, but almost immediately returned with a glass of water. She shook her head and he put it on the table beside her. Then crouching down he took her hands, chafed at them.

'For heaven's sake,' she declared, snatching them back. 'Do I look like some heroine out of a Victorian melodrama?'

'Yes, and from your colour one about to expire from consumption,' he confirmed, but he stood up. 'I did what I thought was best this morning. I know you must have had a horrible few seconds – '

'Seconds?' She let her head fall back against the cushions, closing her eyes in an attempt to blot it out. 'It felt like years. Falling and falling . . . Time to think of all the things I wouldn't see, wouldn't ever do . . .' And for a moment he was holding her, as if trying to absorb the fit of trembling that had overtaken her. His chest had the solidity of a cliff and as she clung to him, for the first time that day she felt safe. It was an illusion, of course. Cliffs were dangerous places, continually undermined by the waves and slipping into the sea. And men had feet of clay. 'Are you in love with her?' she asked.

'In love?' He pulled away to look down at her. 'I don't follow you.'

She thought he did, but she was prepared to humour him. 'With Tony's wife. That is why you tried to protect her, isn't it? You're in love with her yourself.'

'Adele?' The corners of his mouth creased in the wryest of smiles. 'No, Claudia. I'm not in love with her. In fact I'd say she's about the biggest pain in the backside it's ever been my misfortune to meet, but since she's my sister I have to put up with her.'

She regarded him with disbelief. 'Tony's married to your sister and he's prepared to risk fooling around?'

But Mac's mouth lifted at one corner in the wryest of smiles. 'Under normal circumstances Adele is quite capable of handling Tony. She knows that he's weak.'

Claudia sighed. 'But he's very pretty.'

'As to that, I couldn't offer a comment. He's not my type.'

'You don't go for tall blondes?' Claudia asked, and remembering his kiss, wondered what kind of woman he would go for. The dark-eyed, warm-skinned mother-earth type ... She touched the wedding band on his left hand. 'And what about your wife, Mac? How does she feel about you kissing other women? Does she know where you are right now?' His face darkened. She'd touched a raw nerve. She poked it harder. 'Does she care?'

'I kissed you because I thought you'd done really well. It's tough making that first jump.'

He was lying. Which was interesting. She would have sworn that he wouldn't lie. She lay back against the cushions. 'Is it a courtesy you extent to all first-timers, Mac?'

'Of course,' he said, quickly. Too quickly.

'Or just the women?' He stiffened, but she didn't wait for his answer. 'Tell me, do you and Tony normally hunt in pairs?'

'Hunt in pairs?'

'He softens the girls up with his winning smile and sugar-coated charm. You offer the shoulder to cry on when they find out he's a rat. It's a nice act. What do you do for an encore?'

He stood up. 'You've had a bad day,' he said, 'so I'll forget you said that.'

'Too damn right I have. And you and Tony are the cause.'

'Are we?' She raised a hand, the smallest gesture that left him to provide his own answer. Mac shrugged. 'Tony's an idiot. But Adele's been giving him a hard time for the last few months. I can see why a smile from you must have seemed like a raft to a drowning man.'

'Well, that's a very pretty compliment.' She waited. He wasn't going offer any excuses on his own behalf?

'Have you still got the anonymous letter?' he asked.

No excuses. 'It's in the bin under the sink. Watch out for the – ' For the used teabags, she was going to say, but he had already gone. He was gone for a long time and when, finally, she couldn't stand the silence any longer she went to see what he was doing.

He glanced up briefly from the breakfast bar where he was trying to piece the threatening letter together. She'd made a thorough job of tearing it into small pieces. 'You shouldn't have got up,' he said as she slid onto the stool opposite him.

'If you'd said that before I got out of bed this morning, you'd have contributed immeasurably to my well-being. As it is, you're hours too late.'

'Go to bed now and I'll suggest it tomorrow if you like,' he offered.

Her head was thumping and she felt like death lightly warmed over. The temptation to go to bed and stay there for a week was almost overwhelming. 'Tomorrow I have two performances of *Private Lives* with a trip to the television studios in between,' she said, resting her head on her arms.

'At least you don't have to get up at the crack of dawn to leap out of a plane. What time shall I bring you a cup of tea?' he asked.

What was it about married men, she wondered? Were they all utterly insensitive? One inadequate apology, one bunch of yellow roses and he actually thought he was going to stay the night. The roses, she noticed, had been picked up off the floor where she had dropped them in her fright and had been put into a jug of water. 'You've a whole lot of nerve, Gabriel MacIntyre,' she mumbled into her arms.

He finally gave her his full attention. 'It'll take me a while to piece this together, Claudia. I shan't disturb you.'

'No you won't, because you won't be here. I don't recall inviting you in and now I'm asking you to leave.' She lifted her head off her arms to look at him. 'How did you get in anyway?'

'I told you. Security is my business. If I can't crack a system, then it's reasonably safe.' He obviously hadn't taken her request to leave at all seriously. Instead he slotted another piece of the letter into place. 'Yours was a piece of cake.'

'Really?' She was unimpressed. 'Actually I'm pretty sure I forgot to switch the alarm on before I went out,' she said, yawning. 'It's been one of those days.'

'You switched it on. In fact after the kind of day you've had it would be have been strange if you hadn't remembered. But using your birthday as the code number was not very bright.'

She stared at him. 'You're guessing,' she said, finally.

'One seven zero eight. It's not a state secret, Claudia, in fact it was in that article.' He nodded towards the segmented photograph. 'Your locks need changing, too. The average ten-year-old could get in here.'

'They have to get through the front door first. There's a speaker system.'

'I got past it,' he reminded her.

He had a point. 'How?'

He glanced up. 'It wasn't difficult I was helped by a utterly charming lady, somewhat past middle years, who was struggling through the front door with a large bag. She was very grateful for the assistance and she didn't even query my assurance that Miss Claudia Beaumont was expecting me.'

'I don't believe you.' His description of Kay Abercrombie was close enough, but his assumption that she had such a continual stream of 'gentleman callers' that he wouldn't be challenged was galling. It was also incorrect.

'You should believe me. The lady wasn't in the least suspicious. I was well-dressed, polite, helpful. And a burglar wouldn't carry your bag for you. Would he?'

Claudia was disgusted. 'I can't believe you'd take such advantage of that sweet old lady.'

'Can't you? Well, if it hadn't been her it would have been someone else. People are dangerously gullible and your anonymous correspondent got inside somehow. Unless you think someone in the block might have written this?'

'Someone I know?' She was horrified. 'None of my neighbours could have written that.'

'You'd be surprised what envy and spite will do to even the sweetest of old ladies,' he told her. 'But you can go to bed in perfect safety tonight. In fact I suggest you go right now before you fall off that stool.'

She was too tired to argue, but she turned in the doorway. 'Why did you come to the theatre tonight, Mac? Your note said it was important.'

'Did it? Well you obviously didn't believe it was that important. Certainly not important enough to spare me a few minutes of your time. Or did you think I'd be waiting for you at the stage door like some lovelorn pup?'

Maybe, if she was honest with herself, the idea of bringing Gabriel MacIntyre to heel had had a certain appeal, but she wasn't about to admit it. 'You're no pretty pup, MacIntyre. You're pure wolf hound. But I was sure that if you were determined to see me, nothing I did would put you off.'

'That sounds like the voice of experience.'

'It is.' She glared at him and he glared right back. 'So? What was *so important*? I don't believe you were that desperate to check out a non-existent publicity stunt?'

'Don't you? Then it's taken you a while to get around to the most obvious question.'

'It's been a long day.' And she was too tired to rise obligingly to his bait. 'Well?' she demanded. 'Are you going to tell me?'

For a moment he hesitated. 'There are a number of reasons I came up to town this evening. First I came to apologize for shouting at you this morning. You might drive like an idiot, but that was no excuse for me to behave like one as well.'

'If that's the best you can do by way of apology I'd advise you not to take it up for a living,' she warned him. 'You'd starve.'

'I had intended to make my peace with you before you left the airfield this morning, but something must have put it clean out of my head.' His head moved slightly to one side, his expression close to mocking and Claudia felt like slapping him all over again. But she didn't. She told herself she was far too tired. She also had a very strong suspicion that he wouldn't let her get away with it a second time.

'And?' she demanded.

'And?'

'You didn't drive all this way, then break into my flat just to say that. How did you find out where I live, anyway?'

'Tony gave me your address.' He glanced around. 'Has he been here?'

She was going to tell him he could go to hell before she'd tell him that. Something about the way he was looking at her suggested he was expecting as much. 'And?' she pressed.

He smiled slightly. 'And I did have a free ticket for *Private Lives*.' He gave the smallest of shrugs. 'My brother-in-law discovered he no longer had a use for it.'

'So he passed it along?'

'Well, no. Not Tony. Adele. Although come to think of it she didn't exactly give me the ticket. As I recall she threw it at me, along with a less than flattering assessment of my character for having let Tony anywhere near something as dangerous as you.'

What about his own wife? Didn't she care?

'Your apology is noted, Mr MacIntyre. Kindly let yourself out when you've finished playing with the contents of my dustbin. You know how to reset the alarm.' She slid off the stool and headed for the door.

'There was just one other thing.' Something about the way he said it brought her to a halt. She turned and waited. 'You said your brakes failed this morning.'

'They did. As I recollect, you didn't believe me. Or am I overstating the case?'

'Not at all. But when I moved your car after you left, in order to assess the extent of the damage to the hangar, I discovered for myself that you were telling the truth.'

'Then I think that calls for another apology, don't you?'

He ignored that. 'And once Adele had assured me, somewhat astringently, that she didn't plant the photograph in your parachute, I decided to put your car on the ramp and check it out.' He was taking a long time to come the point, but she continued to wait. 'I think you should know that your brakes failed because they'd been tampered with.'

She laughed. It was a small, uncertain little sound. 'You're joking. I mean this time you *are* joking?'

'I told the mechanic who came to pick it up what I'd found. No doubt the garage will give you a full report which you may wish to pass on to the police. That's the *important* reason I'm here, Claudia. The parachute was a distraction,' he said. 'But I don't think there's any doubt about the intent.'

'Intent?' Her brain had stopped functioning, it was merely recycling the last word it heard. Then it sank in. 'Do you mean someone really wants to kill me?'

He paused just a fraction too long before he said, 'I doubt it. With your seat-belt and an airbag it's unlikely you'd have sustained any serious injury. But it could certainly have been a lot worse.'

'Yes,' she said, slowly. 'I could have hit Barty's Porsche.'

'Claudia? Are you all right?'

Was she all right? She was in one piece, so that had to be a good start. But she wasn't sure whether she should laugh or cry. She decided that neither was appropriate. Not until she'd had a few hours' sleep. 'I'm going to bed, Mac. Don't wake the neighbours when you let yourself out.'

Claudia stirred to the sound of a cup being placed by her bed but didn't open her eyes. She ached in every bone and her eyelids were just too heavy to lift.

Then there was a touch on her shoulder, warm fingers against her skin. 'Claudia?'

She recognized the voice. Gabriel. She had her own personal archangel to bring her a cup of tea. That was nice. She smiled, but despite a latent curiosity about angels, she decided it was altogether too much effort to do more.

'Claudia, please wake up. It's eleven o'clock and I have to be somewhere else.'

She blinked into her pillow, opened her eyes and immediately forgot all about angels. Gabriel MacIntyre was no angel. Far from it. 'How the hell did you get in here?' she demanded, lifting her head to turn and look at him then, as she realized that she hadn't made it into a nightdress, clutching her sheet to her before turning to confront him. 'I *know* I locked my bedroom door.'

'Do you?' He might think it funny but she didn't.

'Yes, I damned well do,' she said.

'Then I'm sure you did,' he replied, gently. 'But don't worry about it. I'll be back in a while with something that will keep you just a little more secure.' He paused in the doorway. 'In the meantime, don't answer your door to anyone.'

'Anyone?' she queried. 'You mean anyone I don't know?'

'I mean anyone. I'll be a couple of hours,' he said, turning to leave.

'It won't do you any good, I won't be here,' she called after him.

He came right back, which was not exactly what she had intended. 'Where are you going?' he asked. 'And when?'

She considered telling him to mind his own business, but since he seemed to consider her life was his business it would probably be easier to tell him. It was hardly a state secret. 'I'm going to work. I've a matinée and I have to be at the theatre at two o'clock.'

'How do you plan to get there?'

'You should take this up for a living, you know. If you bought yourself one of those big, bright torches to shine in your victims' eyes they wouldn't stand a – '

'How do you plan to get there?' he insisted.

'My sister will pick me up.' And this time she did tell him it wasn't his business. She might as well have saved her breath.

'Call her and tell her you'll make your own way to the theatre.' He produced a card from his pocket and placed it on the table beside her bed. 'Ring that number when you want a car.'

'Why?'

He sat down on the edge of her bed. 'There are two reasons. *If* someone is trying to hurt you it's almost certainly someone that you know.'

'And you suspect Melanie? Are you mad?' But even as she said it she remembered Melanie's bitterness the night before. Then she gave a little gasp. *How could she even think such a thing?* But even as she asked the question, she knew the answer. It was what suspicion did to you. It poisoned your mind, warped your thinking until you'd believe anything. It was what the letter writer wanted. She pushed the black thought firmly away. 'What was the other reason?'

'If someone is trying to hurt you, you won't want any of your family or friends to become unintentional victims.' She said nothing. 'I'm sorry, Claudia. The letter and the photograph might have been a nasty joke. The brakes weren't. You're going to have to take this seriously.'

'Oh come on . . .' she began, then her voice died away. He meant it. He really and truly meant it. 'How seriously?'

'Very seriously. In fact until we discover who's been sending you nasty notes, chopping up your photograph and interfering with your car, I'm going to have to insist on a few simple precautions. Transport is the most obvious.' She picked up the card, turned it over. It didn't bear a name, simply a telephone number. 'Don't worry if you're not here when I get back, I'll let myself in.'

'Don't you dare break in here again,' she warned him.

'I wouldn't dream of it. I found a spare set of keys in the kitchen drawer.' She was still staring after him as the front door clicked shut.

Claudia clambered from the bed, dragging the sheet with her as she flew down the hall to wrench on a bolt that had been painted over half a dozen times since it had been last used. It didn't budge and she had to push the slider up and down several times to loosen it. Eventually it shifted under her determined onslaught

72

and she slammed it home. 'Get through that, Gabriel MacIntyre,' she challenged him, with satisfaction.

Then, taking him at his word that she should trust no one, she tipped the tea he had so carefully made her down the sink and set a pot of coffee to drip before retreating to the bathroom where, with the door defiantly open, she took a leisurely shower, washed her hair and generally took her time about getting ready, indulging herself in a manner that the previous week's training sessions had not allowed.

She was covering the bruise beneath her eye with cosmetic concealer when the telephone rang. She loved the telephone, enjoyed hearing from her friends. Now she stared at the instrument as if afraid that it might bite her. The very anonymity of the caller seemed suddenly threatening; she had no idea who might be at the other end, what awful things they might say. As she eyed it suspiciously it rang again and she gave a little gasp of irritation at her pathetic response. 'Sticks and stones . . .' she muttered, picking up the receiver.

'Claudia Beaumont,' she answered, the firmness of her voice challenging anyone who thought she was an easy target to think again.

'Heavens,' Mel laughed. 'You do sound fierce. You're not still cross about those roses, are you?'

'Roses?' She was shaken by the depth of her relief that the call was innocent. 'Oh no. I was expecting the garage to ring,' she lied. 'I didn't want them to think I was a push-over. Good party last night?'

'Great,' Mel enthused and Claudia winced. How could anyone be that eager so soon after getting up? Then she smiled ruefully at her own reflection. It wasn't so long ago that she would have partied half the night away and still been button-bright the following morning. These days she didn't even want to. It was a daunting thought. 'The thing is, Claud,' Mel was running on, 'I met a guy who has some kind of radio show and he asked me to do an interview today so I won't be able to pick you up.' Claudia didn't say anything; something had clammed her tongue. 'Claud? Did you hear me?'

She took in a long breath. 'Yes, Mel, I heard. Who's show is it?' she asked, casually.

'Josh somebody. Roads?'

'Oh, right. Josh Rhodes.' For just a moment, for just one awful moment, she'd allowed herself to think that Gabriel MacIntyre was right. That someone was out to get her and that they'd invented some spurious show to get Melanie out of the way. But Josh Rhodes was a popular talk show host. 'Don't worry,' she said. 'I can get a cab.'

As she hung up her glance fell on the card lying next to the telephone. She picked it up, tapped it against her thumb-nail. Then, with a shrug of resignation, she dialled the number. Before it could ring, she slammed the receiver back onto its cradle and stepped back, glaring at the instrument as if it had personally done something to offend her.

This was no way to live. Jumping when the telephone rang, afraid to go out into the street. Whoever had written that note and planted the photograph had had their fun and she refused to be driven onto the defensive.

The garage had offered to loan her a car until hers was repaired or replaced. She'd take it and go home to Broomhill after the show tonight. She needed time to think and she wanted to talk things over with Fizz. Her younger sister was down-to-earth, practical. If anyone would know the best way to handle this, she would. And the decision made, she called the garage and then hauled an overnight bag down from the top of her wardrobe.

Half an hour later, wearing a pair of black leggings with a vivid oversized silk jersey top that draped her figure provocatively in a manner designed to turn heads in the street, or anywhere else for that matter, she grabbed her bag and defiantly set her alarm before letting herself out of the flat. Gabriel MacIntyre could go and frighten someone else because one thing was certain: if the day came when she didn't dare to step out of her own front door and hail a black cab, she'd enter a convent. The thought raised the smile that had been absent all morning and without another thought she walked to the corner, saw a cruising taxi and began to raise her arm.

Then, suddenly uncertain, she snatched her hand back and stood and watched it go by.

'You're an idiot, Claudia Beaumont,' she said to herself, as it slowed to turn the corner. 'I really can't believe you just did that.' And waving frantically she chased after it.

CHAPTER 4

Claudia, already zipped into the overalls that she had been wearing the day before, was lacing up her boots when there was a tap on her dressing-room door.

'The car's here to take you to the studios, Miss Claudia.'

'Thanks, Jim. Tell the driver I'll be with him in a couple of minutes, will you?'

She finished lacing the boots and checked her reflection in the full-length mirror fastened to the wall. The bruise was showing nicely through a minimal layer of foundation, the jumpsuit was suitably crumpled and stained and her limp was sufficient to arouse sympathy without being grotesque. Barty would no doubt be thoroughly pleased with her. She pulled a face at herself. Pleasing Barty James came very low on her list of priorities.

After letting that first taxi go, she'd quickly pulled herself together and had determinedly shaken off the sense of unease that Mac had stirred up. All she had to do was get through the television appearance and the

77

second house and then she was going to spend the rest of the weekend with Fizz and Luke. Nothing could be more guaranteed to put her life back in perspective.

She picked up her handbag and walked out to the stage door. 'Warn the front-of-house manager that it might be a bit tight this evening, will you, Jim? I've asked for my piece to be in the first part of the show, but I'll ring if there's a problem.'

'I'll warn him.'

She opened the door and stepped confidently into the early evening sunshine, her panic attack long since evaporated in the warmth of sweet reason.

It was all so obvious. Adele, despite her denials, had tried to frighten her. Who else had the slightest reason to scare her? No one. Not one single person. It had to be Adele. She could understand that, even sympathize with her.

As for the brakes, well the manager of the garage had been reassuring. He clearly thought talk of the car being tampered with was the imaginings of a man out to impress a glamorous young woman. He'd as good as said as much, promising her a full report as soon as possible. She'd wait for that rather than rely on the opinion of an amateur who seemed to suffer from delusions that he was James Bond.

A sleek black car was waiting at the curb, engine running and as she leaned forward to speak to the driver, her hair swung forward so that she sensed rather than saw the man who grabbed her round the waist, lifting her clean off her feet. And before she could react, cry out, alert Jim on the other side of the stage door, a hand was clamped over her mouth and she was bundled unceremoniously into the rear seat. She struggled, but his arm was a band of steel around her waist and her back was jammed hard against his chest as they pulled rapidly away from the curb.

She was angry, she was incensed at the indignity of it, but she wasn't fooled for a minute. Gabriel MacIntyre couldn't scare her twice in twenty-four hours. She kicked back with her boot and connected in the most satisfactory manner with an unguarded shin. The hand at her mouth loosened and she bit down, hard.

'You cat!' Mac exploded as he released her.

She turned on him, furiously. 'You're lucky to have got off so lightly. What the hell do you think you're playing at?'

'Lightly?' He sucked on the pad of his thumb, glaring at her over his hand.

She pushed back her hair, wriggling to the opposite end of the seat. 'Well, what did you expect? Another kiss for your trouble?'

'I expected you to take the simplest of precautions for your own safety. You chose to ignore me.'

'Of course I ignored you. You're crazy.'

'I'm crazy? I'm not the one on the receiving end of a threatening letter. And I'm not the one with a sudden brake failure.'

'Two quite unrelated incidents. I'm quite certain I know who was responsible for the first – '

His eyes narrowed. 'Who?'

She didn't bother to answer. Why should he believe her when his precious sister had already denied responsibility. 'And the second was just some mechanical foul-up,' she concluded.

'You're a trained mechanic, are you?'

She regarded him with irritation. He clearly thought he was helping, but he wasn't. 'Are you?' she demanded.

'I'd take any bet you care to offer that I know more about the internal workings of a motor car than you do, Claudia – '

'I thought not.'

It was obvious from his expression that he wanted to put her over his knee and spank her. He was clearly having difficulty in restraining himself. Well, just let him try, she thought as he regarded her over his still smarting hand. 'I simply suggested you take the most elementary precautions before you went out. It wasn't much to ask.'

'Why?' She was genuinely curious. 'As far as I can see the only danger I'm in is from you. This could be a genuine kidnapping attempt for all I know.'

'Precisely.' He glared at her.

'So, how much do you think I'm worth?' she asked, flippantly.

'To me? Nothing. You're a spoilt woman with nothing but her looks to commend her. To whoever's trying to frighten you, hurt you, I don't imagine money means anything at all. Perhaps you should give some serious thought as to what his motive might be. Then maybe we can discuss sensible precautions.'

'Motive?'

'Yes, damn it, motive. For heaven's sake, Claudia, can't you use the common sense you were born with? Or haven't you got any?'

She ignored his attempts to scare her. She refused to be scared. 'When I asked why, Mac, I meant why are you going to so much bother to offer your protection when you clearly don't think I'm worth my space on the pavement and I've made it more than plain that I don't want you to? And as to common sense, let me tell you I've got more sense than to be scared witless by you three times in two days.'

'Are you saying that you knew it was me back there? I don't mean after the first panic when you had time to think. I mean at the very moment I grabbed you.'

'Yes.'

He sat back, regarding her with disbelief writ large on every feature. 'How?'

A combination of things. The outdoor scent of the rough army sweater he was wearing, the hardness of his chest at her back, the girder-width of his shoulders as he pushed her into the car. The fact that he had avoided the bruised side of her face when he had covered her mouth. 'I just knew, all right?' Then, 'This is crazy, Mac. Haven't you got anything better to do than make my life difficult?'

'Don't blame the messenger, lady. I'm not the one making your life difficult.'

'You underestimate yourself.'

'No. But I think you're underestimating a very real danger. If that had been a genuine snatch you'd have been out cold on the car floor before the door was closed. No kicking. No biting.'

'No one is going to snatch me. No one wants to hurt me. Adele did the stuff with the photograph, she just doesn't want to admit it and I can't say I blame her.' Claudia didn't think Mac would be slow to make his feelings felt, no matter how pregnant his sister was.

He didn't bother to argue. 'And the brakes?'

'The garage will send me a report. When I've got it, I'll take whatever action seems appropriate.' She pushed her hair back from her face. 'Now, since this clearly isn't the car Barty promised to send for me, but one from your tame taxi company, with a tame taxi driver who is following your orders, will you kindly tell him to take me to the television studios? I'll be happy to drop you at the nearest Underground station.'

Mac grinned. 'It really would be quite easy to like you, Claudia. You're an idiot but you've got plenty of spirit.'

She arched a brow at him. 'If that was supposed to be a compliment, Mac, it was on a par with your apologies. You're going to have to try harder. Much harder.' She leaned forward and tapped on the window. The driver slid the glass back. 'Stop at the nearest convenient spot, please. Mr MacIntyre wishes to get out.'

The driver glanced at Mac for instructions. He shook his head. 'Mr MacIntyre has the same destination as you, ma'am,' he said, with every appearance of regret. Then he closed the glass.

She turned on Mac. 'Is that true? Are you going to the studios?'

'Of course.' He indicated his clothes. Like her, he was dressed as if about to take a parachute jump. 'You don't think this is my normal evening wear, do you?'

'I'm not prepared to hazard a guess at what you might choose to wear at any time of the day,' she replied, stiffly.

'Tony was supposed to come along and tell the viewers what a feisty girl you are and how well you did. But since I'm on the film and he's still confined to barracks . . .' His gesture said it all.

'Tell me, Mac, if your sister thought you were at risk from my vampish behaviour, do you think she'd react in the same obliging way and keep you locked up?'

He regarded her sourly. 'I think my sister has her hands full already, don't you?'

'With one baby on the way and another on leading strings? More than full,' she agreed, then she kinked an eyebrow at him, refusing to let him duck the rest of her question. 'What a pity your wife doesn't keep you on a closer rein.'

'My wife is in no position to do anything of the sort,' he said, his voice expressionless. 'My wife is dead.'

Claudia felt her insides curl up with embarrassment. The man was a grieving widower and she'd just jumped all over his wife's grave. There were days when her mouth seemed to attract her foot. For a moment he continued to stare at her, then he turned away and looked out of the window. 'I'm sorry,' she said.

'We're here,' he said.

He didn't want to talk about it; he couldn't have made it more obvious. She glanced at him as they reported to reception, signed the visitors book. He met her gaze. He knew all about the questions rattling around her brain but his eyes made it quite plain that it was none of her business.

A girl in a pink wraparound overall appeared at her side, diffusing the sudden tension. 'Hello, I'm Jill,' she said, brightly. 'If you'd like to come this way, Miss Beaumont, Mr MacIntyre, I'll take you through to make-up.' She ran a professional eye over Claudia's bruise. 'We should be able to do something about that.'

'No. The bruise stays, Barty's orders. All I need is a comb through my hair.'

'Your lipstick could do with some work,' Mac suggested, helpfully. Claudia glared up at him. 'It's a bit smudged.'

'Just wait until they start to work on you,' Claudia muttered.

Jill smiled up at Mac. 'I don't think Mr MacIntyre needs any make-up. He has a natural tan and with his bone structure . . .' Apparently Mac's bone structure defied description. 'Why don't you go along to the

Green Room,' she suggested, helpfully. 'It's just down there on the right.'

But Claudia wasn't about to let him get away with it that easily. 'I'm afraid Mac will have to stay with me,' she said, turning an innocent expression on him. 'I'm sure you'll want to check everything out.' She laid her hand on his arm. 'Just in case . . .' she whispered, leaving the implication hanging in the air. She didn't believe it, but he was the one making all the fuss. 'Unless of course you're desperate for a drink? Kid-napping is such hard work.'

His smile was grudging, but it was there as he followed her into the make-up suite, leaning against the door as Claudia was seated and swathed in a large pink cape. Jill began to blot off her lipstick, cleaning off the smudges where Mac had covered her mouth with his hand to stop her screaming. When the girl had finished and had decided on a replacement colour, Claudia leaned around the chair to look at him.

'Do you think you ought to test it first?' she asked. 'Just in case it's been tampered with?'

'I think I can restrain myself.'

Jill, apparently used to odd behaviour, took not the slightest notice of this exchange. 'Just tilt your head back, please,' she instructed, then began to paint on the colour. 'There, that's better.' She eyed Claudia's bruise through the mirror. 'You're sure about that? I can cover it up in a tick.'

'I'm sure.'

The girl shrugged. 'Do you want to do your own hair?'

Claudia regarded her reflection. Her sleekly styled hair was tousled from her recent close-arms engagement with Mac. It went with the bruise perfectly. 'My hair's fine the way it is.' She pulled off the cape and thanked the girl before slipping her arm through Mac's. 'Come on, darling. I have a yearning for a glass of something wet and fizzy before the sound man comes looking for us.'

'More champagne?' he asked.

'No, water. I'm less than halfway through my day's work,' she said, propping herself up on a bar stool.

He eased himself onto an adjoining stool. 'I didn't get a chance to tell you what I thought of the play last night.'

She took a sip of water. 'Discretion,' she reminded him, 'is the better part of valour.'

'Well, I wouldn't have bought a ticket,' he confessed, 'but it's very stylish and the jokes still seem to work. The other girl is your sister?'

'Melanie's my half-sister. We've different mothers. It seems impossible to believe now but none of us knew she existed until a couple of months ago, not even Dad.'

'Really?' He wasn't convinced. She didn't blame him.

'It's true. My own mother was Elaine French – '

'I know. Everyone's heard of her.'

Who hadn't? 'Yes, well, she was badly hurt in a car accident at about the same time that Mel's mother

86

discovered she was pregnant. Rather than ask my father to make a choice she just went away and never told a soul who the father was. Not even Melanie. She died last year and Luke – ' She paused. This was getting complicated. She wasn't even sure why she was telling him.

'Luke?' he prompted.

She shrugged. 'Luke Devlin. He's Melanie's uncle, her mother's younger brother. He discovered that Dad was Mel's father and came looking for him with malice aforethought. Fortunately he met Fizz first and fell in love with her. She's my other sister, a whole one this time, not half like Melanie.'

'And she's the pregnant one?'

'That's right. Felicity. The one who isn't an actress.' Claudia gave a little shrug. 'She runs a radio station.'

'You're quite a family,' he said.

There was an edge to his voice that she didn't quite like. 'Theatre is the family business, Mac. Is house-breaking yours?'

'No. That's an entirely new line of business.' He stared into his glass. 'In my family the men are soldiers. They always have been.'

'Always?' She regarded him coolly. 'How long is always?'

'How long have men been fighting? There was a MacIntyre with John Churchill at Blenheim. A couple battled across Spain with Wellington, one actually survived the charge of the Light Brigade – '

87

' ". . . the glorious madness . . ."?'

'– and on a single day two brothers and a cousin died in the mud at Ypres.' He glanced at her. 'Not glorious, Claudia. War is a bloody business.'

She didn't flinch from his criticism. 'I'm sorry, I didn't mean to be flippant. Go on.'

'There are always wars, Claudia. And always men stupid enough to fight them.'

'You?'

'I'm as stupid as the next man, I guess.'

Or maybe a man with little choice. 'That's quite some burden to carry around with you,' she said. 'How do you live up to that?' She saw that she'd surprised him. Did he think she wouldn't know what it was like to follow an illustrious line, to have everything you did analyzed and compared?

'Claudia, Mac,' Barty gushed, as he pounced on them. 'Thanks for coming. I'll just run through what I want and then you can go and get miked up.'

Claudia almost felt the relief emanating from Gabriel MacIntyre. He was perfectly willing to tell the world about his illustrious ancestors, but she sensed a reluctance to talk about himself. Was he a flawed hero? Or not a hero at all? He was too young to have retired.

'Claudia?' Barty was looking at her, obviously expecting an answer. 'Weren't you listening?'

'Sorry, I was distracted. I thought I saw somebody I knew.'

'Well, you can go and talk to him afterwards.' Why did everybody always assume it would be a *him*? 'Now, listen,' he instructed, as if it was her first day at primary school and he was the headmistress. Barty, Claudia thought, would make the perfect headmistress in one of those 'Carry On . . .' films. 'Since you made such a fuss about getting back to the theatre I've changed the running of the show and you're on first. Mike'll explain in the introduction why you've got to rush off.' He gave her a petulant look. 'That will give you a nice little hype for *Private Lives*.'

The play was sold out for weeks, but since gratitude was evidently expected, she smiled like a good little girl. 'Thank you, Barty.'

'And then we'll run the film and when that's over you'll be called on; there'll be loads of applause so I want you to run down to the centre of the studio, arms raised in triumph.'

'Oh, God,' Mac groaned, as Barty demonstrated exactly what he wanted. Claudia coughed loudly to cover him.

Barty waited impatiently for her to finish. 'Then Mike'll tell you how much you raised for your charity and present the cheque.'

'What is your charity?' Mac asked, turning to Claudia.

'A children's hospice in Broomhill. My home town. Fizz began a campaign for it on her radio station last year. Luke has donated a site for it and raised some of the money through the City. But building work is starting next month and – '

'Yes, yes,' Barty said, impatiently. 'It was a lovely choice. You'll be glad to know that we've had an enormous response to the appeal and some lovely letters. A lot of people still remember your mother with great affection and you are so like her.'

'I'm not in the least bit like her, Barty. She was – ' Mac's fingers tightened warningly on her arm and she dragged at a breath, caught back the words. 'She was a real star,' she finished, slowly.

'Yes, dear. She was utterly radiant. Your father must miss her dreadfully.' Then he gave an awkward little laugh as he realized he had said something that perhaps wasn't quite as true as everyone had once thought.

'My father devoted himself to her until the day she died,' Claudia said through barely clenched teeth.

'Yes. Well.' He turned quickly to Mac. 'Once we've given Claudia her cheque, we'll thank you for all the work your team put in to make the jump a success and since you're not taking the payment for your services personally, but for your own good cause, Mike will then tell everyone about it, run the little film we made about it and after that you'll get your own cheque. Okay? Right.' He glanced at his watch. 'You can get miked up now and in ten minutes we'll be ready to go.'

'Is it too late to tiptoe out?' Mac asked, as he watched Barty buttonhole his next victim.

'Just grin and bear it,' Claudia said. 'Think of the people who'll benefit because you were prepared to make a fool of yourself for a few minutes. And

Mac . . .' He tilted a questioning brow in her direction. 'Thanks for stopping me from saying something I'd regret.'

'Anytime.'

'How did you know?'

'You went sort of white around the nose. Adele does that just before she hits the roof. I had a very recent reminder of what that's like.'

'Oh.'

'It's all right, Claudia. I understand.'

'Do you?'

'It can't be much fun living in your mother's shadow.'

'Really?' She stared at him, furious with herself for hoping that a man who lived under the weight of a whole regiment of heroes might actually have been just a little more sensitive. 'I suggest you save your amateur psychology for those it impresses, Mac. You've got me all wrong.' She spotted the sound man and crossed to him, leaving Mac to stay or go. She didn't care either way.

He stayed and when he had been rigged up for sound he came to stand alongside her as the show started, watching the monitor as the film of her training sessions and the jump was shown. He put a hand on her arm as she tensed, but it didn't look as bad as she had feared although her insides contracted uncomfortably as she hit the ground. The next shot was her arrival back at the apron, the waiting champagne, Mac lifting her from the jeep. Mac kissing her. She held her breath and it was Mac's turn to go rigid.

Surely they wouldn't show her slapping him? But the film froze on her just-kissed face, her lips soft, slightly parted, her eyes bright, filling the television screens in eleven million sitting rooms throughout the country.

She didn't have time to think about it; instead the floor manager was waving at them frantically to get onto the set. Mac caught her hand and they ran down onto the set to thunderous applause from the hyped-up studio audience.

Mike Grafton, the show's host, beamed at them before turning back to the audience. 'Let's hear it for a brave young lady.' The audience went wild. 'And the lucky man who gave her all that support.' Another cheer. 'Do you think he deserves another kiss?' he asked them.

'You kiss him,' Claudia muttered, but no one heard. The audience, being worked skillfully by Mike, was loudly roaring its assent.

'How much is it worth?' he asked them.

'One thousand pounds,' they shouted back with one voice.

He put his hand to his ear as if he hadn't heard them. 'How much?'

'One thousand pounds, one thousand pounds, one thousand pounds,' the primed audience chanted glee-fully and Claudia's insides curled up at this further indignity as Mike turned to her and Mac, hands open in an 'over-to-you' gesture.

Claudia felt her insides contract again as Mac turned his blue eyes upon her. 'It's all in a good cause, sweetheart,' he murmured, with the slightest lift of his brows.

'Sure it is.' She'd been set up, the audience primed in advance by the warm-up man and there was no way out, but if Barty James thought he was going to get off that cheaply he had seriously underestimated her. She turned and looked up at the audience, then putting her hand to her ear in an imitation of Mike's gesture she called out, 'How much?'

She made an upward gesture with her other hand and the audience, assuming this was all part of the fun, didn't need any encouragement. 'Two thousands pounds,' they chanted, noisily.

Claudia placed her hands on her hips and stared up at them. 'Only two thousand?' she demanded. 'You can do better than that. Think of all those sick children.'

'Three,' they shouted back, gleefully. 'Three thousand pounds.'

She turned to Mac with a broad gesture of disgust at their cheapness. Mac, taking his cue from her, joined in. 'Come on now,' he encouraged them. 'It isn't coming out of your pockets. Mike's got the money burning a hole in his pocket right now. Just say the word.' The audience obliged.

Mike Grafton, realizing his show was being hijacked, quickly joined in hoisting up the price until Barty James' frantic signals brought him to a halt. 'Well, Claudia,' he said, turning to her. 'The audience want another kiss and we like to keep our audience happy even if it means we have to give seven thousand pounds to your good cause.' Off camera, Barty's expression suggested that it was coming straight out of his own pocket. 'What do you say?'

Claudia smiled sweetly. 'I say you should double it.'

Mike gave a nervous laugh. 'Double it?' On the edge of the set she saw Barty groan, but he knew when he was beaten and he nodded once before disappearing to grab a large whisky that had magically appeared in front of him. Mike, determined to make the most of this turn of events, turned to the audience.

'Double it!' he repeated. 'Shall we ask Gabriel MacIntyre if he thinks she's worth it?'

Claudia was aware that Mac was looking at her, but she was incapable of meeting his eyes. Instead she kept her professional smile turned on the audience as an expectant silence settled over the studio.

'She's worth every penny,' Mac said.

The audience loved it, but Mike held up his hand for silence, then as the studio darkened, he stood back, leaving them in a sudden bright spotlight.

It was nothing, Claudia told herself. A stage kiss meant nothing. But Mac made no move to help her out. Maybe he was remembering what had happened last time and he was leaving it up to her to take the lead. Slowly she turned to him, took his hands in hers for a moment. 'We'd better give them their money's worth, darling,' she said, then reached up to put her arms around his neck.

'Have we got that long?' he murmured softly.

She didn't answer, she simply raised herself on tiptoe and pressing herself against him, she kissed him. Cold, calculated and entirely without feeling, it was undoubtedly the most brazen kiss she had ever given, on stage or off. An unabashed, no-holds-barred plundering of his lips and for a moment she felt him tense against the unexpected onslaught. Just for a moment, then his arm tightened about her waist and he was in control, kissing her back, raiding the softness of her mouth, stealing the very breath from her body. One moment she was firmly in control of the situation, dictating the pace, the manner of a very public kiss. Then, quite suddenly she wasn't. Startled by the sudden switch, she froze. But as his body moulded itself to her, his arms about her waist lifting her from the floor, taking her weight, all the anger at being set up like this seeped away from her and she bunched his sweater beneath her fingers, clinging to him. Somewhere in the back of her mind she could hear the audience clapping, counting out the seconds as the kiss went on and on. But this final humiliation didn't seem to matter. Nothing seemed to matter, except the heat of Gabriel MacIntyre's mouth and the slow, deliberate way in which he was taking possession of her.

Then suddenly it was over and as she leaned back against his arm, her hair falling away from her face, his eyes were shuttered, giving her no clue to the way he was feeling. Furious with him, furious with herself, she barely managed to keep her own emotions from spilling over. But despite the provocation, the temptation to do exactly what she had done the first time he had kissed her, she knew better than to lose her temper in front of an audience of millions. Instead she briefly lowered her lashes. 'Tell the people, Mac,' she murmured huskily, 'was that kiss worth fourteen thousand pounds?'

'It's your good cause, Claudia, you tell me,' he replied, his voice soft as tearing velvet.

'Don't even talk to me,' she said, as Barty followed her to the door. 'I never want to be involved in a show with you again.'

'It was just a bit of fun, Claudia. And you did very well out of it – '

'No thanks to you. And it's still chickenfeed. This is the cheapest kind of television going. You get celebrities to appear for nothing but their expenses because the proceeds are all for charity and you get the public to put their hands in their pockets to support them. And tomorrow I'll be all over the tabloids locked in his arms.' She glared at Mac. 'I suppose you knew all about this? So much for your objection to making a fool of yourself.'

'I didn't as a matter-of-fact.' He shrugged. 'But as you said, it was for a good cause.'

'No, Mac. It was for cheap publicity for his show.'

'Not that cheap,' Barty complained.

'No,' she agreed. At least she had the satisfaction of knowing that she had squeezed him until he squeaked.

She glanced at her watch and headed for the door. 'Just consider yourself lucky that I have to be somewhere else, Barty. You've got off lightly.' Mac beat her to the door, opening it for her, but as he took her arm she shook him off. 'Will you stop manhandling me?' she demanded, eyes flashing as her temper turned on him. He lifted his hands, holding them palm up to show that he had got the message. 'Right. Let's go.'

He held the car door for her, but did not offer her a hand as she climbed into the car. And he didn't try to make conversation as they sped back to the theatre. But he did follow her inside when they arrived.

'Get lost, Mac. I've had all I can take of you for one day.'

'Not quite, I'm afraid. You won't be able to get into your flat. I've changed the locks and the combination on your alarm. I'll take you home after the performance and run through it with you.'

'No, Mac, you won't, because I'm not going back to my flat. I won't be back until Monday afternoon,' she informed him. 'Which will give you plenty of time to put everything back exactly the way it was. And, since you're such good pals, you can leave my spare set of keys with Mrs Abercrombie.'

With that she turned on her heel and went backstage to her dressing room. She was still shaking with rage as she applied her make-up.

'Five minutes, Claudia.'

'Right.' She put the finishing touches to her hair and stood up, taking half a dozen slow breaths. Then she opened her wardrobe door to take out the long white lace *peignoir* that she wore in her first scene.

It was in shreds.

'Darling, you looked absolutely fine,' Melanie reassured her. 'Your wrap is lovely, no one could possibly have known you weren't wearing your costume.'

'Unless they'd seen the show before,' Phillip said. 'Or they had looked at the production stills outside the theatre. Or they checked their programmes.' He was white with rage. 'Have you any idea how this reflects on me? On my staff? I don't know what Mr Edward will say.'

Melanie turned on him. 'Is that all you can think of? Your own selfish concerns? Have you any idea what it must have been like for Claudia to walk on stage, carry on as if nothing had happened minutes after finding something like that? I don't know how she did it.'

Claudia raised a hand. She was not about to referee an argument between the two of them. 'Phillip, will you please see that the garment is replaced by Monday evening and ask wardrobe to ensure that there are spare costumes available in future.'

'For Miss Melanie as well?'

Claudia considered telling him that it wasn't necessary. But that would draw unnecessary attention to her own predicament and the fewer people who knew about that the better. 'Of course. And when I come to the theatre on Monday I will want a full list of everyone who has been through the stage door since the first performance today. Staff and visitors, anybody working here.'

'You'll have it.'

Mel touched her arm. 'Can I give you a lift home, Claudia?'

'No, I'm going to Broomhill for the weekend.' She had a sudden urge to tell Melanie where she would be. 'I'm staying with Fizz and Luke.'

'What about transport?'

'The garage loaned me a car. And before you ask, I'm quite capable of driving myself.'

'Are you sure?' Claudia gave her the kind of look that brooked no argument. 'Right. See you on Monday then,' she said, melting through the dressing-room door.

'Claudia,' Phillip began, but she cut him off.

'Monday, Phillip. And will you close the door on your way out please.'

Alone in her dressing room, Claudia sat very still and considered what had happened. Thought about someone walking into her dressing room, slashing her costume to ribbons and then walking out again. And she thought about the car the garage had loaned her sitting outside the theatre since she had arrived just after two. Out in the open. Unprotected. She thought about it for a long time.

Then she opened her bag, took out a card and dialled the number on it.

A man answered with the number, nothing else, and waited.

'My name is Claudia Beaumont,' she said, and realized that there was a noticeable shake to her voice. 'Gabriel MacIntyre told me to call you if I needed transport.'

CHAPTER 5

Gabriel MacIntyre arrived at the theatre twenty minutes after her call and the doorman directed him backstage.

When he had left her three hours earlier, she had been angry with him. Now he was angry with himself. He had attempted to scare her into listening to him. He had *wanted* to scare her. Whether he wanted to punish her for what she had put Adele through, or perhaps for what she was putting him through was something he refused to contemplate.

But as she opened her dressing-room door to his knock, he knew his own feelings were of no importance. She was pale, her skin drawn tight across her face, her eyes full of apprehension.

'Mac!' For a moment he might almost have been convinced that she was glad to see him, but she quickly disabused him of that. 'You didn't have to come yourself.'

'I was there when you rang in. I thought . . .' Had he thought? Or just reacted? 'Well, I just thought if something else had happened you might be happier with someone you recognized.' He glanced around. The room, a muddle of telegrams, letters, make-up, was almost like a stage set of what an actress's dressing room should be. Even down to the vase of red roses that adorned her dressing table. But there was nothing to account for her pallor. '*Has* something happened?' he asked.

Claudia didn't answer him; instead she crossed to the wardrobe and slid back the door. Then she made a helpless little gesture at the white lace *peignoir* hanging inside. She had worn it on stage the night before. It was cut low enough to display the promise of firm and generous breasts, the bodice fitted tight to her neat waist before flaring out into a full-length skirt. There had been an almost audible sigh from the audience as she had swept across the stage and he remembered how his body had tightened in desire at her seductive beauty. His and every other red-blooded man's in the audience. But he had known what it was like to hold her, breathe her scent, kiss her. And to suffer her indignation for his presumption.

Turning away abruptly he lifted the beautiful lace frippery out of the wardrobe and his stomach turned over as he saw what had happened. No wonder she was white to her gills. He carried it to the dressing table and examined the slashes in the brightness of the mirror lights. It had been done with a razor. An old-fashioned cut-throat razor. His blood ran cold at the thought of what else such a weapon might do.

'It happened while I was at the studios,' she said, her voice not quite steady. 'I found it . . .'

'Have the police been called?' he interrupted briskly, only managing to keep his voice matter-of-fact with considerable difficulty.

She shook her head. 'The curtain was about to go up when I found it, and after the show . . . everyone was exhausted, I couldn't put them through an interrogation. On Monday the stage manager will compile a list of everyone who had a legitimate reason to be backstage this evening, and he'll question them to see if anyone else was seen.'

'Seen but not remarked on at the time?' He wondered if she realized just what she was saying.

She nodded. 'Visitors have to sign in, but people are in and out all the time, particularly between matinées.' She shrugged, as if she knew it was hopeless anyway. 'The backstage crew tend to send out for pizzas.'

'And they just get waved through.'

'It happens. Jim knows them, you see, and if he was busy . . .' She turned her huge silver eyes on him. 'Well, someone who was known, recognized, wouldn't have been challenged once they were inside the theatre.'

Known. Recognized. She knew. She had realized that the person who had done this must be someone who could walk through her tight little world without question. Someone she knew. Maybe even someone she called a friend. It was no wonder she looked like a ghost. It had gone beyond the point at which it could be brushed off as a sick joke. At best someone wanted to frighten her. He didn't want to think about what the worst might be, but he would have to. And so would she.

'You're very vunerable here, Claudia. There are dozens of places someone could hide.' She didn't flinch from the thought and he knew that she had already worked that out for herself. It was why she had telephoned the number he had given her. She could no longer trust anyone. She was being forced into the arms of a stranger, an outsider with no axe to grind, someone outside the world of the theatre with no grudge, real or imagined, to fuel this nightmare. 'Perhaps you should consider taking a break, disappearing for a week or two, until whoever's doing this has been found.'

'I can't do that.'

'Not even a week? Even stars get sick sometimes.'

'No, Mac.' He hadn't noticed the stubborness of her chin before. He'd been too intent on her mouth. But it suddenly demanded attention. 'I won't be driven out of the theatre. And I have interviews arranged all next week. There's a new television serial starting at the weekend.' She managed a wry smile. 'It's about a girl driven to the edge of suicide by a stalker.'

'Are there any parallels with this?'

'I hope not. The girl I play is finally driven to kill the man involved. She can't see any other way to reclaim her life.' She regarded him without resentment. 'If you're thinking that this is another candidate for a publicity campaign – '

'No.' He said it too quickly, but she was right. The thought had bubbled up like poison. He turned away to hang the remains of the gown back in the wardrobe. If it came to the police, they would want to see it, keep it for evidence, although heaven alone knew how many people had touched it since it had been slashed. He sensed a reluctance in Claudia to involve the police and her reasons for not calling them this evening had been flimsy. It was possible that despite her denials she knew who was doing this or at least had her suspicions.

'I wouldn't blame you, Mac,' she said, with the tiniest of sighs, an unconscious gesture that betrayed her own uncertainties. 'To tell you the truth, I rather wish it was something that simple.'

Despite the colourful top she was wearing, she looked fragile and haunted. He wanted to go to her, hold her, reassure her that everything would be all right. That no one would hurt her.

Instead he picked up her overnight bag and opened the door. 'Come on. I think you should get out of here. Right now.' She might be at home in the theatre, but to him it was alien, full of shadows, a place where danger had too many hiding places. As he urged her towards the stage door his skin crawled with tension as he thought of some crazy with a razor on the loose, capable of anything.

The tall, slight figure of man was waiting by the stage door and Mac, hand on Claudia's arm, kept himself between her and the unknown, although it was soon clear that Claudia knew him. 'Phillip, I thought you'd gone home.'

'Not while you were here,' he said, with just a touch of reproach in his voice. 'I thought you might need a lift. I didn't want you to think of going home alone. Not after . . .' Redmond paused, apparently unwilling to mention the attack on her gown in the presence of a stranger. 'You know I'm happy to take you anywhere you want to go.'

Mac, on the receiving end of a long hard look that came close to a challenge, kept his face expressionless even though every nerve ending was on alert and urging him to get her out of there as fast as possible.

Claudia, despite her shock, continued to be gracious. 'How thoughtful of you, Phillip, but as you see I have a lift tonight.' She turned to him. 'Mac, this is Phillip Redmond. The mainstay of our whole operation. Without him everything would grind to a stop. Phillip – '

'I recognize Mr MacIntyre from the television,' he said stiffly, barely acknowledging his presence.

'You watched the programme?' Mac looked around. 'I would have thought television was banned from such an august establishment.'

'Hardly. Mr Beaumont has television interests and the VTR is a very useful aid. Everyone was in the green room to watch Claudia.' Everyone? Not the dress slasher. Had he known that everyone's attention would be distracted? Mac kept his thoughts to himself, but he felt Claudia's arm twitch nervously beneath his fingers. 'Well, if you're quite happy with your transport arrangements?' Redmond murmured doubtfully, as he turned back to Claudia. If the man had been ten years younger, Mac thought irritably, he would have been inviting a black eye.

Claudia, however was gentle. 'Quite sure.' She touched his hand, lightly. 'Thank you, Phillip.'

Outside, the not-quite-dark of the August night was cool enough to raise a shiver. He felt it as she hesitated in the doorway, no doubt remembering the way he had jumped her earlier. Then he had wanted to frighten her. Now she flinched as he put his arm reassuringly about her shoulder to ease her towards his ill-used Landcruiser. 'It's all right, Claudia.'

But she didn't move. 'The car. It shouldn't be left here.'

'What car?'

She pointed to the small saloon parked twenty yards behind his. 'The garage loaned it to me.'

He didn't have to ask why she'd changed her mind about driving it. Someone had breached the security of her dressing room. Her car, standing out in the open since early afternoon, was a much easier target for a man who had shown himself mechanically skilled, and equally adept at creating diversions. 'I'll get it picked up and checked over.'

'Straight away? If some youngsters decided to take it . . . I wouldn't want anyone to get hurt because of me.'

If they got hurt, he thought, it would be because they couldn't keep their hands off someone else's property, but he didn't argue.

'Straight away,' he said. 'It'll take a good hour to get to Broomhill, even at this time of night. Do you want to get in the back, try and sleep?'

'I won't sleep, not straight after a performance,' she said, with an effort at a smile. 'The adrenalin keeps on pumping.'

'I suppose so.' But he didn't think there was too much adrenalin pumping around her system right now. She looked bloodless, a pale shadow of herself; he couldn't begin to estimate the strength of will it must have taken to step out on the stage and carry on as if nothing had happened. And it had taken everything out of her. She'd lost that feisty, do-it-or-die look that had struck him so forcibly when, despite her fear, she had stepped out of the plane and into thin air. Even then she had come up fighting, but right now she looked fit to drop.

Perhaps she didn't want to risk sleep, was afraid of the demons that might come if she allowed those heavy, silk-lashed lids to close. A queasy wave of anxiety for her swept through him as he stood over her. Then, impatient with himself, he switched off the alarm and opened the passenger door. She had made it more than plain that she didn't want him worrying about her. In truth she wasn't the kind of woman he would normally worry about. Glamorous she might be, but her entire life was a performance. Even thanking Phillip Redmond for his concern, he had sensed that was all it had been. A beautifully judged performance. Not genuine at all. And now she was making a drama about climbing up into the Land-cruiser.

Then he remembered her ankle and cursing to himself, lowered his shoulder so that she could put her hand on it before lifting her up into the high seat. 'All right?' he asked.

'Fine,' she said, fastening her seat-belt.

He watched her for a moment before closing the door on her and settling himself in the driving seat. She glanced behind her, still on edge about the sedate little saloon car the garage had loaned her. He was pretty certain that no self-respecting joy-rider would be want to be seen behind the wheel of such a vehicle, but he made the phone call anyway.

'Someone will be here in five minutes,' he promised, replacing the receiver. Then he put the keys in the ignition and started the engine. She'd asked him why he had gone to so much bother to protect her when she had made it clear she didn't want his protection. He glanced across at the slender figure pressed back in the seat, cheeks and eye sockets nothing but dark shadows in her face. He'd been asking himself that all day.

Her full lips shone in the street light and he remembered how her mouth had been warm and alive beneath his. She might be self-absorbed but she had her own kind of courage; she had certainly made Barty James smart for taking advantage of her.

And she was, without doubt, the most vivid woman he had ever met. Pure drama. She rolled her head towards him, looking at him from beneath lowered lashes and his body responded with an urgency that bucked through him like an electric shock.

Christ, but he was in trouble. He'd never wanted a woman like he wanted Claudia Beaumont, wanted to feel her body soft and yielding beneath him. He didn't doubt he could take it. Or that he would be one in a very long line. He wasn't that kind of fool.

'Is something wrong?' she asked, her voice husky with tiredness, twisting his guts.

'I just wondered if you'd like some music, or the radio?' he said, turning away abruptly.

She shook her head. 'Absolute silence will do very nicely.' And she closed her eyes again. Then, 'But you could lower the back of the seat just a little.'

'The lever's on the other side of the seat.' She made no move to adjust it herself and after a moment's hesitation he reached across her. If he tried very hard, he could shut out the image of her as he stretched across her body, taking care not to touch her. He could somehow ignore the way her hair spilled across the black upholstery like spun gold. But her scent cried out to him, haunting, subtle, like an elusive memory that shifted out of the corner of your mind even as you thought you had it pinned down, inviting you to follow. He lowered the back of the seat so that she was stretched out, more lying than sitting, beneath him. 'Is that more comfortable?'

110

'Thank you.' She caught his arm as he straightened. 'And thank you for coming tonight, Mac. I didn't deserve it, not after the things I said. You tried to tell me – '

'Forget it,' he said, his voice shockingly harsh in his own ears as he cut off the words, but she didn't seem to notice, reaching up to him, holding his face between her hands. Then, for just a moment, she pressed her cool, smooth cheek against his. It was wet and as she fell back against the seat he could see the shining marks that tears had left on her face. A lump formed in his throat as he wiped them away with his thumbs. 'Don't cry, Claudia,' he said thickly. 'Go to sleep. I promise, nothing's going to hurt you.'

'I know.' She closed her lids and even before he had pulled out into the main road she had obeyed him, her lashes dark fringes against the translucence of her skin.

He glanced at her from time to time. She trusted him. No one else. It should have made him feel like a giant; instead he felt terribly afraid. He had promised her she was safe with him and no one could ever guarantee that.

'Claudia?' She stirred, sighed, opened her eyes and looked at him. 'We're in Broomhill. Can you give me directions to your sister's house?'

She yawned, stretched, looked at the clock on the dashboard. 'It's very late, perhaps we shouldn't disturb them. We could always go – '

'Are they expecting you?' he interrupted.

111

'Well, yes, I telephoned to say that I was coming, but – '

'Then you must go straight there. From now on you must always do what you say you're going to do, or make sure everyone knows you've changed your plans.'

'Must I?' Sleep had restored her and now her eyes glinted with amusement as she turned to him. 'That could prove to be a real nuisance.'

'Nuisance or not,' he said, tightly, 'they're the rules and you're going to have to live with them for the time being, no matter how much it affects your love life. Now, can I have those directions before we end up in the sea?'

Claudia, slightly ashamed of baiting him no matter how much he deserved it, told him the way to her sister's home and fifteen minutes later they pulled up in front of the low stone manor house nestling in a fold of land above a small bay. Luke opened the door as they came to a halt and she didn't wait for anyone to open the car door, jumping down onto her sound foot and flinging herself into her brother-in-law's arms. He hugged her, held her briefly.

Then he looked over her shoulder at Mac standing beside the Landcruiser. Claudia watched in sly amusement as they sized one another up and then Luke, apparently satisfied with what he saw, moved towards him, hand outstretched. 'Luke Devlin,' he said.

'Gabriel MacIntyre.'

'But you can call him Mac,' Claudia said.

Luke grinned down at her, arm still around her shoulders. 'Can I?' He offered Mac an apologetic smile, the kind of smile that men use when a woman has done something charmingly silly. Mac, she noted, did not respond. But then he had made no secret of the fact that he didn't think she was in the least bit charming and a lot worse than silly. He had made up his mind exactly what she was before he had even set eyes on her. Which made his concern for her all the more puzzling. 'Well, come on in, Mac,' Luke said. 'Make yourself at home.' He turned back to Claudia. 'But do it quietly, Fizz is asleep.'

Mac retrieved Claudia's bag, shut the car door softly and using a remote, set the alarm before looking up at the red box attached to the side of the house, just beneath the eaves. Apparently satisfied, he followed them over the threshold.

Claudia crossed the black and white chequered floor of the hall. 'If nobody minds,' she said, 'I'm going straight to bed. I'm suffering a serious shortfall of sleep.' But at the foot of the broad oak staircase she turned back. 'Well? Are you coming, Mac?' she asked. Despite her tiredness she was unable to resist the opportunity to torment him again, just a little. He might think she was wanton, but he wasn't entirely unaffected by her. Or why would he have raced to the theatre when she had momentarily lost her head and called for help?

'Coming?' She was interested to note the slight flush that darkened his cheekbones.

113

'I thought you'd want to look under my bed, check out the wardrobe.' She paused. 'In fact I was sure you'd insist on sleeping at the foot of my bed like a faithful watchdog. You're not going to disappoint me, are you?'

'I think I'm going to have to.' She saw him relax as he realized that she wasn't serious. It was an interesting reaction; most men she knew would have leapt at the chance, which was why she didn't issue the invitation to every Tom, Dick or Harry. But it was hardly surprising that a man called Gabriel would defy that kind of simple categorization. 'I don't believe I know you that well, Claudia.'

'No? Try convincing the eleven million people watching your performance on television tonight and see how far you get,' she reminded him.

'Neither of us had much choice about that.'

'Not the most gallant response, Mr MacIntyre. You could at least pretend you enjoyed yourself. You certainly convinced me.' She turned away to hide the little flush of annoyance that heated her cheeks. 'Did you see how much we raised for the hospice, Luke?'

'We were glued to the screen and Fizz was deeply touched at the personal sacrifice involved,' Luke replied, with the straightest of faces. 'However, there's no need for either of you to suffer further since we've plenty of room. But Claudia . . .' She waited. 'Fizz doesn't know about what happened at the theatre tonight. I'd rather you didn't tell her. I don't want her upset.'

Claudia forgot about teasing Mac in her concern for her sister, coming back down the stairs a little way. 'There's nothing wrong, is there?'

'Nothing at all and I intend it should stay that way so, as I said, I'd be grateful if you didn't wake her.' He turned to Gabriel MacIntyre, directing him towards the study. 'Mac, can I interest you in a drink?'

Claudia, lingering on the stairs, watched them disappear into the dark panelled interior of Luke's study. Mac was going to tell him what had happened. Everything. They were going to talk about her. Decide what was best for her and then tomorrow they would certainly insist that she take a break from *Private Lives* until the nightmare was over. She felt like going back downstairs and telling them that they might as well save their breath.

But she also felt bone-achingly weary, certainly too weary to go back down the stairs and argue her corner, so she left them to it. Tomorrow would be soon enough. They could demand all they liked, but it wouldn't make any difference. She wasn't about to walk away from the theatre, even for a day. Not because she was enjoying the part particularly. But the run had been extended because of the demand for tickets and an awful lot of people were depending on her for a job.

'Whisky?' Luke Devlin asked.

'Thanks.'

Luke was puzzled. He hadn't known Claudia for much longer than six months and he hadn't seen a great deal of her in that time. But he thought he knew the kind of men she liked to be seen with. The kind of men who paid a fortune to have their hair cut twice a week, wore Italian suits and handmade shoes and who had soft, well-manicured hands. 'Water?' he asked.

'Just as it comes, thanks.' Luke handed him a heavy crystal tumbler and poured one for himself. 'I'm sorry to impose on your hospitality so late at night.'

'It's no problem. Claudia's always welcome. And her friends.' Luke motioned to one of a pair of leather chairs set in front of wide open French windows. He and Fizz had been sitting there earlier, enjoying the night scents from the garden, the sound of the sea washing against the rocks at the bottom of the cliff. 'Have you known her long?'

'No, only a couple of days. And we're not exactly friends.'

'Well, I have to admit that I did notice the slightest suggestion of a clash of temperament, but you can never tell with Claudia. She is very good at hiding her feelings beneath that provoking manner of hers.'

'I hadn't noticed her making much effort to hide her feelings,' Mac said. 'On the contrary, I find her bracingly direct.'

'I'd say that's a good sign. If it matters.'

'Is it?' When Mac looked up from his glass his face was creased in a rueful smile. 'You clearly haven't been on the receiving end.'

He wasn't saying whether it mattered, Luke noticed. Which probably meant that it did, so he changed the subject. 'You'd better tell me what happened at the theatre tonight.'

Mac told him about the dress, then about the letter, the photograph and finally about his suspicions that the car had been tampered with.

'Can I ask why Claudia turned to you for help?'

'She didn't. I rather imposed myself on her. She didn't seem to be taking the danger at all seriously. She's convinced the letter and photograph were just a rather tasteless joke.'

'And the car?' Luke probed.

'The car is more difficult. She doesn't want to believe that, because it clearly takes the whole thing way beyond even the nastiest kind of joke. She's insisting that I've got a James Bond complex.'

'But you haven't?' He didn't want to the offend the man, but it did all seem rather far-fetched and if it weren't for this latest incident with the gown he'd be inclined to agree with Claudia.

'If someone can convince me that I'm wrong I'll be happy to admit my mistake. I've arranged for an independent assessor to look at the car. Ostensibly for insurance purposes.'

'In the meantime you think she'd be safer here?'

'I didn't say that. I brought her here tonight because it was what she wanted and I didn't think she could face any more. But your wife is pregnant, I believe?'

'Well, yes. But it won't be any trouble having Claudia here. We've got a housekeeper – '

'That wasn't what I was getting at. If someone really wants to hurt Claudia he may come after her. I don't think she should stay beyond the weekend.'

'She'll be perfectly safe here.'

'Will she?' Mac gestured towards the open window. 'Did you leave this open when you came to the front door?'

Luke regarded him thoughtfully. 'You mean anyone could have walked in? It would have taken a lot of nerve.'

'He walked into the theatre this evening and slashed her costume to ribbons. He managed to get that photograph into a parachute inside my own security cordon. Don't doubt his nerve.' He took a swallow of whisky. 'Keeping a house of this size secure in high summer would be a real strain. Locked windows, closed doors. Your wife couldn't fail to notice something was amiss.'

'Are you offering to help?'

'Security is my business, Devlin.'

'I see. Then you'd better tell me what you have in mind.'

'Claudia? Are you awake?'

She opened her eyes, blinking sleepily. 'I am now,' she grumbled, then smiled as she saw who it was. 'Hello, Fizz. How are you?' Her sister put the cup she was carrying on the night table and perched on the side of the bed, her hand curled protectively about the noticeable bump where her baby was growing. Claudia didn't need to ask how her sister was. She was glowing. Marriage and the approach of motherhood had put a bloom on her that made Claudia suddenly feel very empty and alone.

'I'm feeling wonderful,' she confirmed. 'How about you?'

'Me? Same as ever. I'm just dandy.'

'Are you?' Fizz asked, her smooth forehead creasing with concern. 'You look a bit . . .' Claudia watched her sister struggle for some tactful way to say that she looked washed out.

'Tired?' she offered.

'Mmmm. A bit. Have you been overdoing it?'

'Burning my candle at both ends? At every conceivable opportunity, darling. It's what life is for. My life, anyway.'

'I don't know, even Luke mentioned that you look a bit . . .' Again the hesitation.

'Tired?' Claudia offered again.

Fizz grinned. 'Exhausted, actually. And Mac seems to be very concerned about you.'

'He's very caring,' Claudia assured her.

'Then perhaps you should take a week off and let him care for you?'

Claudia laughed out loud. 'Trust a pair of men to get a woman to do their dirty work for them.'

'I don't know what you mean,' Fizz declared.

'Your nose will grow, miss,' Claudia warned and her sister gave a little shrug. 'You have you been elected to persuade me to take a week off, admit it.'

119

'Now I've seen you, I really think you should.'

'Don't be silly, Fizz. You know I can't do that.'

'Why not?'

'A fully booked theatre?' Claudia offered.

'I suppose a few people will be disappointed.'

'Well, thank you, darling,' Claudia replied, with the gentlest touch of reproach.

'Maybe a dozen then.'

'Oh, wow. A whole dozen.'

'All right, all right,' she laughed. 'They'll be riots in Shaftesbury Avenue. But you've been working so hard these last few months and you saw what happened to Dad when he drove himself to the limit. If you carry on and collapse from exhaustion you'll be forced to take a break whether you want to or not.'

'Dad was suffering from stress. I'm just suffering from a surfeit of early mornings and late nights. Parachuting isn't all it's cracked up to be. It isn't *all* fun, you know.'

'*Really*? It looked a heck of a lot of fun to me. Tell me about it.'

'You're too young. But I promise you I'm not about to collapse. Besides, that would be different. People would be sympathetic. And they would feel uncomfortable about asking for their money back. If I just swanned off for a holiday with some hunk of a man the public would, quite rightly, lose confidence in me and they wouldn't book in advance.'

'For this particular hunk of a man it might be worth it.'

Mac must have made quite an impression on her sister, Claudia thought. And she wasn't easily impressed. 'He's not my type, Fizz.'

'The way that Julian and David Hart and goodness knows how many other smooth and beautiful young men were your type? For all of ten minutes.'

'There weren't that many,' she protested. 'And David is just a friend. He was never interested in my body.'

Fizz's eyebrows shot up. 'I didn't know that. I thought he worshipped you blindly. I thought you rushed into his bed whenever life was letting you down – '

'His spare bed. Not that it's any of your business. And Julian was in love with you, not me. I refuse to be a consolation prize, no matter how pretty the man.'

'Then if he isn't "your type", why is Mac here with you?'

'Here? With me?' Claudia made an comically elegant performance of looking about her. She peeked under the covers of the bed, leaned over the edge and looked beneath it, lifted a pillow with exaggerated care. 'No. I don't see him. In fact I didn't see him all night. He doesn't know me well enough for anything like that. He said so. Ask Luke.'

'Claudia!'

'We are not an item, Fizz. He gave me a lift last night because I had a little shunt in my new car.'

'How little?'

'A few dents and scratches. Nothing to worry about.'

Fizz stood up and crossed to the window, drawing back the curtains. 'Mac has a few dents and scratches in the side of his car too,' she said, looking down onto the drive. 'Coincidence?' she asked. 'Or do they match? Your car is red, isn't it?' She looked back at Claudia. 'Did you hit him, or did he hit you?'

Claudia laughed. 'You mean he didn't tell you? He's not usually so reticent on the subject.' She flung back the bedclothes and made a show of bouncing out of bed. 'Enough of such nonsense,' she declared brightly. 'I'm going to have a shower, then I'm going to give Mac the grand tour of Broomhill.'

'I'm sure he'd much rather have the grand tour of one of Broomhill's most interesting inhabitants,' Fizz replied with an infuriatingly smug little smile.

The trouble was, Claudia realized as she stood beneath the shower a few moments later, she really wasn't at all sure what Mac wanted. Which on its own made him more interesting than most men she met. Most men only had one thing on their mind and boringly let it show. She raised her face to the warm water, letting it stream through her hair and down her body, wondering just what it would be like to have him there, kissing her, not with half the country watching them, but alone and with no holds barred.

Not boring.

Then, furious with herself, she reached out and snapped off the water. What the hell was she thinking about? The man thought she was easy. A loose living actress without a moral to her name. The way he had kissed her proved it. Well, let him think it. He wouldn't be the only one. If she laid down a penny for every man her name had been linked with they would stretch the length of Broomhill Pier. But linked with and lain with were very different.

Gabriel MacIntyre was very different.

She examined her reflection in the glass. For all her sister's concern, she didn't look so bad and the fading bruise and faint shadows beneath her eyes were quickly dealt with. Mascara lengthened her lashes and a hot lipstick did the rest. But she ignored the baggy shorts and t-shirt she had brought with her, originally planning to spend the day quietly on the beach with an undemanding book. If she was going down into Broomhill with Mac she wanted heads to turn. She wanted him to see heads turn.

The wardrobe contained an assortment of clothes that she and Melanie had left behind on earlier visits and she picked out a little dress, a swirl of bright colours with a skimpy halter neck and a skirt short enough to display her long legs to advantage. It was Melanie's, but she wouldn't mind Claudia borrowing it. And it was a head turner if ever she'd seen one.

She found Mac leaning against the balustrade that overlooked a tiny private beach tucked below the house in a crack in the cliff. He was no longer wearing the macho combat gear he had been pressed into wearing for the television programme. This morning he was altogether less aggressive in a pair of light coloured chinos topped with an expensive jersey polo shirt the colour of bluebells, a shade that perfectly matched his eyes. Only a man who was vain about his appearance would have been so careful with the colour. She had met enough of them in her business to recognize the type and Gabriel MacIntyre was definitely not the type.

So it had to be a present from a woman, a woman who wanted to display her man, show him off. His dead wife, then, or was there someone else in his life? If there was, she had to be a pretty relaxed sort of girl, Claudia decided. A great deal more relaxed than she would be in similar circumstances.

Whoever had chosen the shirt knew her business. In the olive drab sweater Mac had just looked big. But the silky material of the shirt accentuated his shoulders, putting her in mind of the iron girders that framed multi-storey office blocks, draping a torso equally lean and hard. And the forearms on which he was resting as he stared out to sea had the kind of mass that only hard manual work could develop. Broomhill had better brace itself.

Heads would turn for sure, but not just to look at her.

'Do you always carry an overnight bag with you?' she asked, turning her back on the sun-spangled sea, propping herself on her elbows as she leaned back against the parapet, her arm not quite touching his.

He glanced down at her, his eyes lingering momentarily on a hint of breast where the bodice divided to fasten about her neck. 'Doesn't everyone?'

124

'Not without the expectation of a night in a strange bed.' She lifted her face to the sun so that her hair hung down behind her and she closed her eyes. 'Whose bed were you planning on sleeping in, Mac?'

'I carry a sleeping bag, too. One can never be sure of a bed.'

'Single or a double?' she continued, deliberately provoking him.

'This is a very pretty spot,' he said, refusing to take the bait. 'Devlin was lucky to find a place like this on the market.'

'Luke's the kind of man who makes his own luck. He's worked for everything he owns. And so has my sister.' She realized that she sounded defensive. There was something about him that put her on the defensive and she wasn't used to it. She was used to being in control. All the time.

'Fizz was telling me about the radio station. She suggested you show me around.'

'Did she? There's not much to see. A radio station is a rather boring place unless you're actually broadcasting. But it's usually fun walking along the pier on Sunday. There's a lot of live entertainment.'

'Unfortunately fun isn't on the agenda.' He produced an envelope from his pocket. 'This was on the mat when I got up this morning.' She took the envelope, opened the letter it contained. YOU CAN RUN, the evil letters screamed at her, BUT YOU CAN'T HIDE FROM ME. I KNOW EVERY

MOVE YOU MAKE. 'It's all right,' he said quickly as she dropped the letter, her hands covering her mouth. He pulled her into the safety of his arms and for a moment held her there while the tremor swept through her body. For a moment she allowed him to. 'It's all right, Claudia.'

'All right,' she moaned. 'How can it be all right?' She took a grip of herself and pushed away from him. 'It's not all right. I shouldn't have come here. If Fizz had found that filthy thing . . .'

He retrieved the letter from the gravel, put it in his pocket. 'She didn't. I'm an early riser.'

'But whoever sent that is earlier.'

'Not sent, Claudia. It's Sunday. It was pushed through the letterbox. But your sister doesn't know about it. We thought it best.'

'You were right. She mustn't ever know about this. I'm afraid you'll have to forgo your tour of the local beauty spots, Mac. The sooner we leave here the better.'

'I wasn't sure you'd see it that way.' She sensed his relief and it infuriated her.

'What kind of a person do you think I am, Mac? Do you think I'd risk my sister's peace of mind, her safety, for one second longer than necessary?'

He looked awkward. 'Luke didn't think you should be left to deal with this by yourself. He wanted you to stay.'

'Then you should have told him that you'd appointed yourself my personal bodyguard.'

126

'I did.' He saw her face and made a move to calm her down. 'He took a lot of persuading but I told him that I'd take care of things. Until we know what kind of person we're dealing with – '

'You don't have to spell it out, Mac. Why the devil didn't you call me earlier?' She glared at him, furious that he could have delayed, even for a minute.

'Luke thought it best to act as if nothing had happened and he took the view that calling you before twelve unless there was a national emergency might just alert Fizz to the fact that there was something wrong. We had a good look around but whoever left the note didn't hang about.' They exchanged a glance. 'What excuse shall we give Fizz for leaving so soon?' he asked.

'You have to ask? Like all new converts my sister believes she has a mission to urge others to take the path to wedded bliss. She'll do everything she can to foster romance.'

'Maybe.' He didn't quite grit his teeth, but it was a near thing. 'But I did get the impression that she's expecting you to stay until tomorrow. Something about you making a recording for one of her programmes?'

'Oh, God, *Holiday Bay*,' Claudia said, with a groan. 'It's a soap she broadcasts from the radio station. A sort of Archers by the seaside. The whole family has been co-opted into taking part, whether they want to or not. But it's not a problem. I'll take the scripts with me and record my bits in London. The rest of the cast can record around me. Mel and I do it all the time when we can't get home. And you can leave Fizz to me. If I tell her that we're moving down to my flat for a little more privacy she won't be surprised.'

'Your flat? You have a flat, here in Broomhill?'

'Just a small self-contained apartment at home. In my father's house,' she explained, when he looked blank. 'I'm not here often enough to make anything bigger worthwhile.'

He looked doubtful. 'Why on earth would Fizz think we've gone there? If your father – '

'He isn't. Dad's away drumming up finance for a television series he's going to make later in the year. We'd have the whole house to ourselves.'

His mouth tightened. 'I see.'

'Do you, Mac?' Of course he did. 'Well, call me clairvoyant,' she said, 'but somehow I never doubted that for a moment.' She hadn't expected anything else, but it still hurt that he would jump to the boringly obvious conclusion that it was a common occurrence. 'I'll go and tell Fizz we're leaving. It'll only take me a minute to pack.'

'There's just one thing before you do.' She waited. 'I told you that Devlin took a lot of persuading.'

'Yes?'

'I had to promise him that I'd take care of you.'

He didn't have to make it sound quite such a chore. She hadn't asked him to involved himself in her troubles. 'It's all right, Mac. Once we leave here I won't hold you to it.'

'I'm afraid you don't have a choice in the matter. I gave the man my word that I'd look after you and I intend to keep it. If you don't agree to do exactly as I say, Claudia, you'll have to stay here.'

Claudia's hard front came close to crumbling. In her experience men only wanted one thing from her. Borrowed glamour and bed. She lent her glamour when it suited her, her bed had been given to few. Her heart she had managed to keep entirely to herself.

But no one had ever insisted on taking care of her with quite that ring of sincerity. She was almost fooled by it.

CHAPTER 6

Take care of yourself, Claud,' Fizz instructed earnestly, hugging her sister as Mac started the Landcruiser. 'No more late nights.'

'I'll do my best to see she's tucked up in bed before midnight,' Mac said softly as Claudia climbed in beside him. And he made a great performance of fastening her seat-belt. If they had been lovers it wouldn't have bothered her in the least, she would have been too busy enjoying the attention. But they weren't and it embarrassed her and she discovered to her chagrin that she was blushing. She could have sworn she had forgotten how.

'And I'd leave the driving to Mac for the time being,' Luke advised. 'He knows what he's doing.' His words were invested with extra meaning for those who knew what he meant.

'You're a chauvinist, Luke Devlin,' she called back to him as Mac let out the clutch and rolled away down the drive. She stuck her head out of the window. 'I don't know why Fizz puts up with you.'

But as they stood in the driveway, Luke's arm protectively about Fizz, she knew. She sat back in her seat. She knew and she thought her sister was probably the luckiest woman in the world.

At the gate Mac eased out into the lane and then turned to Claudia. 'It might be a good idea to check out your place down here before I take you back to London.'

It was almost a relief to be confronted with reality. No matter how brutal. 'You think my correspondent will have visited there, too?'

'It's possible. He might have hedged his bets.'

But the house was quiet, peaceful, undisturbed. There were no unpleasant surprises. 'Whoever is giving you a hard time seems to know you pretty well,' Mac said, as they locked up and returned to the car. 'Did you tell anyone at the theatre you would be staying with your sister rather than coming here?'

She shook her head. 'Only Melanie.' He looked thoughtful. 'For goodness' sake, it's not Melanie,' she declared hotly.

His expression didn't change, but he didn't press it. 'It's possible you were overheard talking to her. Or maybe someone was listening in when you telephoned Fizz to tell her you were coming. Or maybe someone checked your phone to see who you had called. It wouldn't take much working out – '

'For goodness' sake, Mac, leave it, will you? Just take me home. I need to think about this, decide what to do.'

131

'I'll take you home, but only to pack. You can do your thinking somewhere safer. Somewhere no one will find you.'

He wasn't listening, so she said, very carefully and quite slowly as if talking to someone whose wits had gone walkabout, 'No. Thank you. I've done with sticking my head in the sand and last night I did my one and only impression of a headless chicken. I can't ignore this, but I'm damned if I'll run and I'm damned if I'll hide.'

'There's nothing wrong with your spirit. Unhappily your reasoning isn't in such good shape.'

She was determined not to lose her temper. He'd come running to her rescue when she'd screamed for help, but now it was time for the professionals. 'My reasoning is just fine and dandy. I'm not ignoring the problem, I'm going to call the police the minute I get home and put the whole thing in their hands. And you assured me that with your new locks I'll be perfectly safe.' She wanted him to be perfectly clear that he was off the hook. That she didn't take his promise to Luke seriously. 'You won't forget to send me your bill?'

He sent her a scathing look. 'Perfect safety is unobtainable, you should know that. Even with security cameras and round the clock monitoring, the determined intruder will always find a way inside. And you've still got to get to the theatre and back again late at night.' He didn't mention the possibility of attack coming out of the dark shadows of the theatre itself. Perhaps he was being kind. But she didn't think

132

so. He simply left it to her own imagination. And her imagination obliged him.

'I refuse to live in a cage,' she said, a touch desperately. 'I won't be driven behind locked doors by some nasty little cockroach who gets his rocks off –'

'All right,' he said, quickly. 'I understand how you feel. But you'll still have to take precautions. I can organize proper protection for you.'

'Can you?' It didn't take too much imagination to guess the role he had picked for himself. The night watch. 'What would that involve?'

'A driver trained to deal with any emergency, someone who can stay with you at all times, monitor your mail, filter incoming calls and watch your back at the theatre.'

'A bodyguard,' she said, dully.

'Not a bodyguard. This is real life, not the movies. Just someone who will allow you carry on with your life, as near normally as possible, until whoever is threatening you is found and dealt with.'

'No.' It sounded appalling. 'Thanks, but no thanks. I know you're only trying to help, but your idea of normal doesn't coincide with mine.'

'*Normal* just isn't going to be possible for a while, Claudia. You must see that.'

'No.'

'Think about it.'

'No.'

'For goodness' sake, be reasonable – ' he began impatiently.

133

'The police will deal with it,' she said, cutting him off.

'The police will do what they can. But they can't be there every minute of the day.'

'Good. I don't want some stranger at my back every minute of the day.' Her huge eyes challenged him to defy her. As they pulled up at a long line of traffic held up by roadworks, he turned and challenged her right back.

'Whoever is writing you unpleasant little notes is at your back every minute of the day,' he reminded her. 'Whoever is chopping up photographs of you is at your back every minute of the day. Whoever is – '

She wanted to put her hands over her ears to shut out the words. She wanted him to take her in his arms and promise that no one would ever hurt her. She suddenly wanted all kinds of impossible things. Her hands tightened in her lap, but her voice betrayed nothing. 'I couldn't possibly afford that kind of protection,' she said.

'How much is your life worth? Less than one of your couture frocks? Far less than one of those fabulous jewels you inherited from your mother.' He turned briefly to look at her. 'I hope you weren't relying on those pathetic locks to keep them safe?'

That made her laugh but when he turned to look at her, she didn't bother to explain why. 'This is not a matter of life and death, Mac,' she declared. 'It's nasty. And I'm not denying that last night came as a bit of a shock. But anyone who knows me could have

134

guessed I'd go down to Broomhill and with Dad away, that I'd go to Fizz and Luke. No one would want to be in that great big empty house by themselves. Not after a fright. And that is the purpose behind all this nonsense. To shake me, make me run.' Her hands were tight little fists. 'But I can ignore it if I try hard enough.'

'Can you?' He gave his full attention to the road as the traffic began to move. 'Should you?' His eyes met hers briefly. 'You may be right, but if you insist upon carrying on as if nothing has happened it's possible that he'll try harder to get a reaction.'

'He?'

'He,' Mac affirmed. 'Or are you still trying to convince me that Adele had something to do with this?'

'You know her better than I do, Mac. But do you really think that a man would have slashed my costume? That was such a bitchy thing to do.' Her eyes dared him to deny it.

He didn't; instead he rubbed absently at a small scar just above his right eyebrow. 'Maybe that was the intention. To make you think it was a woman.'

'That's a bit convoluted, isn't it?'

'Maybe. The trouble is, I can't see a woman meddling with your brakes.'

Brakes, brakes, brakes. Why couldn't he forget about the brakes? It was a fault, nothing more sinister. It was just a coincidence.

'You're a chauvinist,' she snapped.

'I'm a realist.'

Claudia, despite her reservations, conceded the point. 'You're probably right. I certainly wouldn't know where to begin. But it doesn't rule out the possibility of Adele recruiting a man to do her dirty work for her. She *was* the first person you thought of,' she reminded him.

'She might have done the parachute thing on the spur of the moment. But not the brakes. She was angry but I think with herself as much as Tony or you. She knows she's been hell to live with for the past few weeks. And she was home watching us make fools of ourselves on television when your dress was slashed.' He glanced across at her. 'I checked with Tony.' She arched a finely honed brow at him and he shrugged. 'I had to know. If it had been Adele, she would need some professional help.'

'Somebody needs professional help,' she agreed, with feeling.

'You really don't have any idea who could be behind this, Claudia?'

'You think I'd keep quiet about it?'

'Maybe.' He shrugged. 'You didn't seem to take the first letter very seriously. And you've been slow to put the matter in the hands of the police. Are you sure you can't think of someone you've upset recently?'

'Are you suggesting that this is the work of a disgruntled lover?'

'Did I say that?'

'No, but I believe you were implying it.'

'Maybe I was,' he conceded. 'Or maybe you just have a good idea who's behind it. You're in a funny business. The people in it are . . . volatile.'

'Is that a fact?'

'Don't think you can handle this by yourself, Claudia.'

'I can't think of a single person I know who would do this to me. I don't go out of my way to make enemies. And I'm a great deal choosier about lovers than the popular press would have you believe.' She grinned humourlessly. 'Read tomorrow's tabloids and you'll see what I mean.' She looked around as he signalled and slowed to turn off the main road. 'Where are we going? This isn't the way to London.'

He glanced in the rearview mirror. 'I thought we'd take the scenic route.' As Claudia stared at him the down rose goosily on her skin and she gave a little shiver of apprehension. 'We can stop at a pub I know. For lunch,' he added quickly.

'You're checking to see if we're being followed.' He didn't deny it and she looked back nervously but the road behind them was busy with holiday traffic. 'How can you tell?'

His mouth creased slightly in a suggestion of a smile. 'I don't think you have much to fear from harassed parents with roof racks full of luggage and cars filled with restless children.'

'I don't suppose I have anything to fear at all. Nothing real. Only fear itself. That's what this is all about, isn't it?' She glanced uncertainly at him. 'Making my life miserable.'

137

'Probably.'

Not particularly reassuring. But she refused to be cowed. 'Well, I refuse to be miserable. And right now I'm at greater risk of dying from hunger than anything my nasty little friend can dream up,' she declared. 'Is this pub far?'

'You should have got up for breakfast,' he told her, with a distinct lack of sympathy.

'You may have forgotten, but I was working until way past eleven o'clock last night.'

He checked the mirror again. 'So was I.'

So he was. And he had been up long before her, too. Another minute and she'd be feeling guilty. 'You didn't have to. I didn't ask you to don your breast-plate and come galloping to my rescue like some latter-day Galahad.'

'Didn't you, Claudia? I rather thought you did.'

She felt her cheeks heating up beneath his gentle challenge. She may not have asked for him specifically, but her relief when he had turned up last night must have been plain enough. 'I can assure you that any driver would have done,' she declared, crisply. 'And as you know, Fizz would be startled to see me downstairs before lunchtime on Sunday.'

'So she said.' He signalled and slowed, turning off the main road to head across country. 'You're not a bit like her, are you?'

'You mean she's kind and gentle and charming, while I have a tongue like a bandsaw as well as being as flighty a piece of work as you're likely to meet this side of Christmas?' Claudia's response was as light and as brittle as spun toffee.

'You said it.' Mac continually checked the mirror as they drove between high hedges, then as a gap approached, he pulled off the road, turned to face the road and drew up under the shelter of a thick canopy of trees. He turned off the engine and for a while the only sound was the ticking of the engine as it cooled and the gradual return of birdsong as the inhabitants of the copse became used to their presence.

'Well?' Claudia whispered, after long tense moments when she held her breath, half expecting to see some vehicle come speeding by in search of them. 'Are we being followed?' He didn't immediately answer her and she glanced across at him. In direct contrast to her own tense and expectant state, Gabriel MacIntyre was utterly relaxed, leaning back in his seat, eyes closed. Clearly not. 'Why have we stopped?' she demanded, suspiciously.

'I wanted to think.'

'Think? You can't think and drive at the same time?'

'That depends on the thought.' He opened his eyes and turned his head towards her. 'I had an idea that required my undivided attention. And it seemed a good idea to be stationary when I put it to you.'

'That suggests I'm not going to like it.'

'I very much doubt it,' he agreed.

'Then I advise you to trust your judgement and keep it to yourself. Forget lunch, just get me home without delay.'

'That's what I've been thinking about. Taking you home.'

'Don't waste time thinking about it,' she encouraged him. 'Do it.'

'All in good time. 'When we've settled the question of protection.'

'I don't want protection.'

'You don't have any choice in the matter. I have a personal score to settle with your "cockroach". And I gave Luke my word that I'd take care of you,' he added, as if that settled it once and for all.

'Luke had no right – '

'But it occurred to me that if a stranger suddenly appeared at your side, it would alert the enemy.' He finally opened his eyes and turned their blue depths upon her. 'And then it occurred to me that your performance on the television last night was very convincing.'

'My performance? Don't underrate yourself, Mac. You gave as good as you got.'

'Thank you. I'm glad you appreciated the effort.' She glared at him. 'You said it would make the tabloids. Did you mean it?'

'I shouldn't think there's any doubt about it. Barty probably had someone lined up to run the story even before the show went on air. He'll want a return on his investment, especially since it was a great deal heavier than he had anticipated.' That thought, at least, gave her immense satisfaction.

'So it shouldn't be too difficult to start a few rumours of lust at first sight?'

She waved a hand in weary resignation. 'Stopping them will be the problem.'

'I don't think we should even try.' He took her hand, held it for a moment. 'You see, don't you, what I'm getting at?'

'I'm having a slow brain day. Enlighten me.'

'As your latest and most ardent lover I don't suppose anyone would be surprised to see me at your heels twenty-four hours a day. Would they?' And with that he lifted her hand to his lips in a courtly gesture. But his eyes when he lifted them to meet hers were anything but. 'What do you say, sweetheart?'

Claudia didn't say anything for the simple reason that she was speechless. If he thought he would convince anyone who knew her that he was her lover . . . it was laughable. He just wasn't her type. No way.

He was still looking at her in that intense, self-mocking way that gave her goosebumps. He was waiting for her to answer, waiting for her to leap into his arms in gratitude. Well he could wait.

'Actually, Mac, I'd say you were quite mad, but since I don't think very well on an empty stomach I'm prepared to give you the benefit of the doubt,' she said, with exquisite politeness. 'For now.' And since she was a talented actress she had no trouble at all in finding a smile with which to humour him. Then she realized that he was still holding her hand and she snatched it back, rather spoiling the effect. 'Were you serious about lunch, or were you simply tormenting me with the promise of food?' she snapped. 'It's a long time since the sandwich after yesterday's matinée.'

'You haven't eaten since yesterday afternoon? And you think *I'm* crazy?' He leaned forward to start the engine. 'It sounds to me as if you need a nanny as well as a bodyguard.'

Claudia recalled the competent way he had moved around her kitchen and it occurred to her that being looked after by Mac might have its advantages. 'It's a long time since I had a nanny. Can you cook?' she asked.

'I wasn't volunteering to double up.'

'Weren't you?' She shrugged. 'That's a shame. But I suppose living on take-aways goes with your line of work. I'm afraid I've never quite managed to get the hang of domesticity.'

'I don't suppose there's much cause for you to develop your domestic talents. Not when you have so much else to offer.'

It was truly incredible the way Mac managed to invest even the most innocent of statements with insult, Claudia decided, and she hit right back.

'No doubt your wife was a wonderful cook. In fact I imagine she was perfection personified.'

'You know nothing about her.'

There was a satisfactory tightness in his voice. Well, it would do the man good to realize that verbal fencing was a two-way sport. 'Maybe not. But I know about you. And it's clear that nothing short of perfection would ever have satisfied you.'

142

'Your mouth will get you into serious trouble one day. If it hasn't already.'

'Personally I distrust perfection. My mother was reknowned for it. Perfect wife, perfect mother, perfect actress.'

'You don't take after her.'

'No, thank God.' She suddenly lost interest in baiting him. 'Will you stop the car here please. I'd be happier in a taxi whose driver wouldn't feel he had a right to continually criticize me.'

'I'll do you a favour and pretend I didn't hear that.' He tossed her a warning glance. 'It's a couple of miles to the pub and there's not much in between. You'll never make it in those sandals.' She opened her mouth to tell him what he could do with his two miles, his pub, his protection, but he lifted his left hand from the steering wheel and laid his fingers lightly on her lips. His touch went through her like a lightning bolt, fizzing, explosive, dangerous. 'Enough, Claudia.' She jerked her head away from him and his hand dropped back to the steering wheel. But the point of contact just went on burning.

They drove on in silence, but Mac's mind was seething. Why wouldn't she accept the reality of what was happening to her? Last night she had been terrified and he had thought it would be the simplest matter to persuade her to take all the necessary precautions for her safety. This morning she had anticipated the danger to her sister without him having to spell it out. If he was prepared to reorganize his life to make sure she was safe, why wouldn't she just accept his offer gracefully?

He wanted to stop the car, but not to let her out. He wanted to take hold of her by the shoulders and physically shake her. Worse, he wanted to kiss her, to touch her, to carry her deep into the woods and make love to her, anything that would put a stop to the infuriating, reckless way she let her mouth run away with her. He wanted her soft and warm in his arms, her voice silky with longing. He gave a little gasp from somewhere deep in his throat.

She turned to him. 'Did you say something?'

'No.' Then, 'But I'm sorry.'

'I beg your pardon?' She touched her fingers to her ear and leaned towards him. 'I don't believe I quite caught that.' Her voice was rich with sarcasm. Well, she had a voice that had been developed to show any emotion, any feeling she chose. 'Was that an apology, Mr MacIntyre?'

Of course it was an apology. She knew that. Did she have to make a meal of it? Gloat? Why couldn't she just accept it? But it was too late to retract. 'I'm sorry. I've no right to make comments about you or how you live.'

'Too damn right you haven't. You know nothing about me.'

Her sharpness sparked an instant echo in him.

'On the contrary, I know too much about you and I don't much like it. But you know nothing whatever about me. Or my wife. And that's the way I'd like to keep it. As far as I'm concerned this is purely business,' he said, responding in kind. Another minute and they'd be shouting at one another.

He gave a little exclamation of disgust. Whatever had happened to his self-control? He glanced at Claudia. *She'd* happened to it. He'd been on a knife-edge since she crossed his path, crashing her way into his life. He loathed everything she was even while he burned with an insane desire to hold her, to protect her, to feel the heat of those long legs wrapped about him. For a moment it hung in the balance. He could see the battle raging within her. She wanted to tell him to go to hell. But he couldn't let that happen. Someone wanted to hurt her and she didn't know where to turn for safety. He couldn't allow her push him away. 'Why don't we discuss terms over lunch?'

'That suits me just fine,' she declared. Then suddenly she said, 'And I'm sorry too. About your wife.' She made a tiny, rather helpless little gesture that might have meant anything but told him more than any number of words that her edginess had far more to do with being scared than being angry. She hadn't mentioned the second letter, but it had shaken her far more than she would ever admit. Claudia Beaumont, he realized with something of a shock, was a great deal tougher than she looked. But she was still one very frightened lady.

Tempting as it was to offer bland reassurance he was glad she didn't underestimate the danger because something about the whole series of incidents worried

145

him more than he had admitted, even to Luke. The lack of pattern was puzzling. The only links so far were the letters and maybe the photograph in the parachute. Unpleasant in themselves, but not life threatening. The incident with the dress seemed much more personal, so much closer, and that made it especially frightening, but all of those things had the same feel to them. The car was something else entirely. That had been potentially lethal. He had played it down, but in a car built for speed, driven by a woman with an inclination to show off, sudden brake failure could have been catastrophic. And without that first letter or the photograph, who would have looked for evidence of foul play?

'What's the matter?'

He kept his eyes on the road. 'Matter?'

'You frowned. I hope you're not lost.'

He had the distinct feeling that he was being teased. Claudia Beaumont was a creature whose moods changed as quickly as the weather and he discovered that it was very easy to respond to them. 'No, ma'am. In fact you can tell your frantic stomach that we've arrived.' And as he took a long right-handed bend a small village opened up before them. It had everything. A cluster of cottages, an ancient church, a green complete with a pond and a family of ducks. And the perfect picture postcard thatched village inn. Mac pulled into the small, but packed car park, squeezing the Landcruiser into the last space. 'What do you think?'

'I think it's lovely. I just hope we can get a table.'

'Leave me to worry about that. I'm a particular friend of the landlady.' He opened the door and swung her down onto the tarmac, but although her scented hair brushed his cheek he stepped back quickly, turning away to usher her through the door into a low, oak-beamed bar. There was an instant shout of joyous recognition.

'Mac! You should have let me know you were coming.'

Claudia watched him lean across the bar and take the hand of an elegant silver-blonde, probably in her early forties, but whose perfect bone structure and flawless skin gave her the kind of ageless good looks that would never fade. He kissed the woman's cheek and seeing the very real warmth in Mac's eyes, Claudia felt a stir of something possessive grip her. When they were with her, men weren't supposed to notice other women.

But he hadn't lied when he said he was a particular friend of the landlady. 'Diana, it's good to see you,' he said, still holding her hand. 'How're you both keeping?' Both? Claudia looked around for the woman's husband. There was no sign of him.

'We're fine, Mac,' Diana replied. 'But run off our feet as you can see. Heather, look who's here.'

'Hello, Mac.' The girl was longing to fling her arms about him, Claudia could see. Instead she stood awkwardly, waiting for him to notice her. It was impossible to miss her in her Doc Marten's, a pair of thick black tights she was wearing in defiance of the August sunshine, a miniscule tartan skirt and a baggy black t-shirt. Topping the lot was a thick cropped head of henna'd hair.

Mac managed not to flinch. But he wasn't tactful either. 'Hello, carrots,' he said, flicking the top of her cropped hair-do. 'What happened to the pigtails?' The deep flush of red that coloured the girl's cheeks, clashing horribly with her hair, must have alerted him to his mistake because he quickly turned to introduce Claudia. 'Claudia, Diana Archer and her daughter Heather.' No husband, then. 'Diana, this is – '

'Introductions aren't necessary.' Diana smiled warmly and detached herself from Mac's hand to offer her own. 'Miss Beaumont, you're very welcome.'

'Claudia, please,' she found herself saying. Diana was impossible to dislike. Natural warmth exuded from every pore and it was little wonder her pub was so popular.

'We saw you both on the television last night,' Diana said.

'Did you?' Mac asked, with a grimace. 'I was hoping there might have been a nationwide power cut.'

Heather's eyes flickered defiantly in Claudia's direction. 'I'm not surprised, it was dreadfully tacky.'

'Heather!' Diana protested, but Mac laughed.

'The child's right. Tacky scarcely covers it,' he assured her. 'But Claudia raised a lot of money for the hospice. And the donation to the club will come in useful.'

148

'When are you going to let me join?' Heather asked, placing her hand proprietorially upon his arm.

'I'm not.'

'Mac!' she protested.

'You lack all the necessary qualifications, sweetheart. You aren't an underprivileged youth from some inner city slum with at least one conviction for anti-social behaviour to your name.'

'And you're not a boy,' Diana added quickly.

'You don't just take boys, do you, Mac? You teach girls to jump.'

'It has been known. Why don't you to ask Claudia what she thought of the experience? I don't think she'd willingly do it again.'

'Not for an Academy Award,' Claudia responded, obligingly.

'Well, she's just a bimbo, what do you expect?' Heather retorted, then blushed so hotly that no one had the heart to upbraid her for her rudeness, although Claudia thought that might have made things even worse.

But Diana wasn't prepared to allow her daughter any further leeway. 'Heather, the table by the window needs clearing. Will you see to it? Now.' The girl glared at her mother as she walked away, furious at being dismissed to undertake such a menial task. Claudia felt a twinge of compassion for the girl, even though she probably deserved worse. She was clearly besotted with Mac and her mother knew it. But then Diana was a good looking woman and it was entirely possible that she had plans of her own in his direction.

'Are you staying for lunch, Mac?' Diana asked.

'If you can find us a table. I didn't expect you to be this busy.'

'Thank goodness for the tourists,' Diana said, with feeling. 'They see us through the winter. We can fit you in in about ten minutes. Or you can come through to the back if you'd prefer to be private?' She glanced enquiringly at Claudia.

'There's no need to go to any bother for me, Diana. I'm perfectly happy in the bar. Why don't we have a drink while we're waiting, Mac? I'd like a spritzer.'

He turned back to Diana. 'Just a mineral water for me.'

'You're driving again?' she asked, as she put two glasses on the bar and proceeded to fill them. 'How's the leg?'

'Nothing to grumble about. It's propping up the left-hand side of me fairly adequately.'

'Will you be able to jump again?'

'It's too soon to say,' he hedged. 'Tony's taking care of the club for the time being.' He picked up their glasses. 'We'll take our drinks outside. Will you give us a shout when there's a table?'

'It won't be long,' Diana promised. 'Take a menu with you.'

They settled themselves on an old rustic bench under one of the windows that overlooked the village green and for a moment neither of them said anything. Claudia finally broke the silence.

'What happened to your leg?'

For a moment she thought he wasn't going to answer. Then he shrugged. 'It collided with a bullet on my last visit to Bosnia.' She winced. 'I'm not complaining,' Mac said. 'It was aimed at my head.'

'But it brought your army career to an untimely conclusion?'

'I was luckier than Mark. Diana's husband,' he explained when she asked. 'He was killed in the Gulf War.' He leaned back, his arm along the top of the bench behind her. 'They'd just bought the pub. Mark had done his twenty years in the army and he was due to retire . . . but he had some very special skills . . .' Mac stared into his glass. 'He said he didn't want to miss the fun.'

'And was it fun?'

He intercepted Claudia's thoughtful glance at his leg. 'There's not much amusement to be gained from a posthumous medal. Diana's got a pension, of course, and she puts a brave face on things, but it must be hard work running this place on her own.' He indicated the postcard-perfect village with a broad sweep of his hand, taking in the distant shimmer of the sea on the horizon. 'Even with the perfect setting dreams don't always come true. What do you want to eat?'

He had changed the subject before she got too inquisitive about his own special skills, she noticed. He didn't want to talk about the army. Or his leg. Or his life. But she didn't pick up the menu.

'At least she has Heather.'

'Yes, she has Heather. She didn't lose everything.' The vivid blue sparkle died from Mac's eyes and Claudia realized that she had touched some nerve, something buried very deep. *He'd* lost everything. *Had there been a child?* 'But Heather's getting to the age where she'll want more out of life than a quiet country pub can offer, no matter how picturesque,' he continued, somewhat brusquely. There had been a split-second when anything might have been possible, but now it was gone and Claudia knew better than to pursue it.

'Yes, I suppose she is.' She wondered if he realized the girl had a crush on him. 'I'm sure she could be persuaded to stick around if you're a regular customer,' she said, sucking in her cheeks.

He looked up, startled out of darker thoughts. 'Me?' He suddenly realized what she meant. 'For heaven's sake, Claudia, she's just a child.'

'Old enough to think of leaving home. I would have said she was seventeen or eighteen.' And right now bitterly regretting what she had done to her hair.

'Eighteen, I think. I'm certainly old enough to be her father.'

As if that made any difference. 'Then it's a pity you haven't had the decency to go bald, or lose your teeth, or run to fat,' she told him. 'As it is I'm afraid that to a suspectible girl you're probably the most dangerous kind of man there is.'

'Dangerous?' he growled, turning on her. 'What the hell do you mean by that?'

'For heaven's sake, Mac, calm down. I didn't mean anything sordid. It's just that she's a romantic teenager. Your age, your experience will be half the attraction for a girl of her age. And you have the kind of lived-in face that some girls seem to find irresistible.'

She didn't say they were crazy, she didn't have to, her voice did it for her. Mac didn't seem to notice any insult, he was too intent on dismissing her theory as madness. His lack of vanity was rather endearing, Claudia thought, but she didn't make the mistake of telling him so.

'Beauty and the beast is an enduring fantasy,' she assured him. 'Kiss the frog and find the prince . . . you know the sort of thing.'

'I'm beginning to get the picture. Which am I, the beast or the frog?'

'Take your pick. Then, of course, you're a widower. Hurt, suffering, a man in need of the most tender, loving care. What spotty youth could possibly compete with all that?'

'You're serious, aren't you?'

'Trust me, I'm a woman. I know these things.'

'I've got a gammy knee,' he offered.

'It doesn't show.'

'You've caught me on a good week.'

'And it stops you parachuting for the pure pleasure of flying through the sky?' Claudia recalled the his intensity as he had described the sensation to her.

Mac apparently did not wish to discuss his injury. 'I've still got a stick in the car if you think it would help – '

'Good grief, no,' she exclaimed. 'That would just make you seem even more glamorous to an impressionable teenager.'

'Glamorous? For goodness' sake, Claudia, you're being ridiculous – ' he began, but she cut him off.

'Glamour is all in the eye of the beholder. Believe me, Mac, I was eighteen myself once and I had a crush on an actor who was even older than you.'

'Did he have a limp?' he asked sourly.

'No, he didn't limp, but he wore a patch over one eye. Just for the part he was playing at the time. A black patch. It made him utterly irresistible.' A fact he knew and exploited to the full. Why else would he have worn the thing when he wasn't on stage, she suddenly thought.

'Did it?' Mac wasn't impressed. 'Well, don't suppose you tried very hard.'

He had an almost uncanny ability to find the weak spots in her armour, Claudia realized, which was odd, because she didn't think she had any. But she refused to give him the satisfaction of seeing that he had hurt her with his careless remark.

Instead she tutted, gently. 'I thought you were trying to keep personal remarks out of this relationship, Mac. That wasn't very businesslike.'

He dragged his hand through his hair. 'No. I'm sorry.'

An apology? He could take her by surprise too. But Claudia had a use for his unexpected vulnerability.

'You're right of course. I didn't resist at all, in fact I'm afraid I rather threw myself at him. I suppose I must have been a tremendous nuisance, but he relieved me of my virginity with the stylish elegance and skill that any eighteen-year-old would be grateful for.' She raised her lashes and looked him straight in the eyes. 'I'm sure you would earn Heather's undying gratitude if you – '

'Don't you dare say it!' he warned her.

'You're not the tiniest bit tempted?'

His brows shot up. 'You're not serious?'

'Actually in your case, no. You'd feel so guilty that you'd feel you had to marry the child and that would be a disaster.' Claudia eyed him over the rim of her glass. She felt sorry for Heather, but that kind of agony was part of growing up, something to be got through. She had implied that her actor had done her a favour, but a true gallant would have laughed at her precociousness, been cruel to be kind. Mac would probably react by staying away from his friends, which wouldn't be good for any of them.

She reached out and touched his face with the tips of her fingers. It was hard bone and she could feel the stubble that already shadowed his jaw. He turned to the gentle pressure of her fingers then, as their eyes met, became very still, as if the slightest movement would be a risk.

'What about me, Mac? Are you tempted by me?' He didn't answer. 'Would you kiss me if I asked you to?'

'Why would you do that?' She didn't answer. 'The last couple of times you didn't seem terribly keen.' His voice was gravelly, just a little ragged.

'Three's a charm,' she murmured and sliding her fingers into the crisp, close-cut hair, she leaned into him so that the swell of her breasts brushed against his arm. 'Try it and see.' And she closed her eyes.

CHAPTER 7

For a moment nothing happened. It seemed she had hung herself out on the washing line and he was leaving her there to dry. Then his lips touched hers, his mouth extraordinarily gentle as it moved over her own, asking questions to which she had no answers. Quite without warning, what had been nothing more than a skilled performance, a scene acted out for the benefit of the girl watching them from the window, became more. Much more.

Claudia found herself the victim of her own trap as her body was invaded by a delicious weakness, a barely remembered yearning that had too much in common with Heather's adolescent fantasies for comfort. As Mac raised his hand to cradle the back of her head, to hold her, claim her, she recognized a very real hunger to be loved.

She had thought she was totally in control of the situation, she was always in control, but as Mac deepened a kiss that was beginning to spiral out of control, she was seized by an almost forgotten blissful feeling of vulnerability . . .

A sudden crash behind them put an abrupt halt to the moment as he released her and swung round, startled.

'What the hell was that?'

Claudia opened her eyes with the tiniest of sighs. 'I'm rather afraid it was the sound of Heather's heart breaking.'

He swivelled back to face her. 'She was watching us?'

'She was clearing the table in the window,' she admitted.

He stared at her for a moment then looked back towards the pub but the girl had disappeared. 'That was a pretty cruel trick – '

'Possibly, but it was kinder than leaving her yearning hopelessly for something she can't have, don't you think?' She was distinctly irritable on her own account. She wasn't much given to hopeless yearnings and it was disconcerting to be caught out by one. 'Or were you getting to like the idea?' she added, unkindly.

'Don't be ridiculous. She's a child.'

'No. She's not a child.' Heather was feeling the kind of pain that every woman went through and right at that moment Claudia had more sympathy with the girl than she would have believed possible. 'Don't worry, Mac. She'll go and have a good cry, she might even tattoo my name on an old Barbie doll and stick pins in it. Then she'll realize that you're having fun while she's being miserable so she'll decide to make you jealous by flirting with some local boy. With any luck he'll flirt back. And that's the way the world goes round.' She felt him relax slightly. 'But I warn you, if she tips soup in my lap you'll get the cleaning bill.'

He grinned. 'It might be a good idea to avoid the soup.'

She grinned back. 'Cheapskate.'

'Actually, I was thinking of you. Heather doesn't do things by half. It would be scalding.' He looked up as Diana put her head around the door. 'Are you ready for us, Di?'

'Any time you like, Mac.'

He stood up and offered Claudia his hand. 'What do you say? Are you prepared to risk it?'

'I'll have to, or faint from lack of nourishment.'

Diana led them to the table that Heather had been working on. 'Have you decided what you want?'

'Oh, no. I'm sorry.' Claudia looked up from the noticeable damp patch on the carpet. 'I'm afraid I've been too busy admiring the view. It reminds me of something . . .' She glanced out of the window to the village green.

'It is lovely, isn't it?' Diana smiled at her. A genuine smile full of warmth. And she felt slightly ashamed of her earlier suspicion that the mother, like the daughter, harboured fantasies about Mac.

'Have I seen it on the television? It's like something that might have been used for one of those dreamy pre-war family – ' Claudia stopped. She suddenly knew what it reminded her of. She'd been reading the script of the television film her father was planning to produce in the autumn. This village would make the perfect location. 'Has it ever been used for filming?' she asked.

'Not that I've ever heard of. Now that would be good for business.' Then she sighed. 'Not that everyone appreciates living in rural tranquillity. Heather can't wait to get away to university in October.'

'What's she going to read?' Claudia asked.

'English and drama. I think she's probably kicking herself for being so rude to you. I'm sure she'd love to talk to you about working on the stage.'

'If she can come up to town one day tell her to give me a ring and I'll be happy to show her around the theatre. In fact why don't you come with her and you can both stay and see the play . . . although I don't suppose it's likely to be Heather's cup of tea.'

'Maybe not, but it's certainly mine,' Diana said. 'Mark and I used to go to the theatre all the time.'

'Don't leave it too long.'

'I won't.' Diana gave a little sniff. 'I'll send one of the girls over in a minute to take your order. Excuse me.'

'Oh, Lord,' Claudia remarked, as Diana hurried away, 'I'm afraid she's going to cry. I haven't done much for Diana or Heather, have I?'

'I can't speak for Heather, but Diana likes to talk about Mark. Remembering him, remembering the good times we all had together keeps him alive for her.'

His forehead creased slightly and Claudia wondered if it worked two ways. Diana was someone who knew

160

his wife, someone he could talk to about 'the good times', while she knew nothing, not even her name.

' "It's good to talk?" ' Claudia murmured, just a touch wryly.

'Doesn't your father talk about your mother?' Mac asked.

Claudia retreated, her insides contracting as they always did when she thought of her mother. 'He prefers not to,' she said and shifted her attention to the menu.

'It's a mistake to bottle up feelings. They can choke you.'

That rather depended on the feelings, Claudia thought. Some things were better left unsaid. 'I think I'll have the avocado salad and then chicken in a leek sauce with baby vegetables,' she said, pointedly changing the subject on her own account.

He ordered for both of them. Then he sat back and looked at her across the table. 'Tell me about your mother.'

Everyone wanted to talk about her mother. 'Why? You might be old enough to be Heather's father but you're a bit on the young side to have been one of Elaine French's besotted admirers.'

'Perhaps, but I did see her perform once.' She didn't encourage him. 'On a school trip to see Antony and Cleopatra.'

'My father played Antony, he's a pretty good actor too. Why don't we talk about him?'

'Another time. I'm particularly interested in your mother because although you've gone out of your way to trade on your likeness to her, even to the extent of recreating one of her most famous roles, you seem to resent her so much.'

Claudia's hands tightened momentarily in her lap. Then she forced herself to relax, smile. Normally it was easy. Easy to bury the more searching questions beneath all the well known foibles of a star. Like the fact that she would only accept perfect white roses from husband and admirers alike. That her scent was made for her by an adoring perfumer who burned his blending notes on the day she died and scattered the ashes on her grave. That her contracts always included a clause that her costumes were her own personal property and would leave the theatre with her, never to be used by another actress. Somehow facing Gabriel MacIntyre's searching blue eyes she wanted to say much more. 'You said it, Mac. She's a hard act to follow.'

'Then why bother? You don't need a second-hand identity.'

'It was rather thrust on me. Sometimes I think that it's all I'll ever have. Years from now some stone-mason will chisel it on my headstone. Here lies Elaine French's daughter.' She shrugged. 'She had me trained from my cradle to be exactly like her.'

'Just you? Not Fizz?'

At least he hadn't told her she was being stupid. Paranoid. 'Fizz was never really like our mother. Oh, don't get me wrong. She went through the motions, in fact she was tremendously talented, a naturally gifted actress, but somehow she was never quite as dazzled by it all as I was.' Claudia gave a little shrug. 'Just as well; if she had, I wouldn't just be Elaine French's daughter, I'd be Felicity Beaumont's sister as well.'

'I'm sure you underrate yourself.'

'No, it's true. She had that something extra. She didn't rely on technique.'

'So why is she running a radio station?'

'She had a bad experience right at the start of her career and I guess she saw it all for what it was. So she stepped back, let it go. For a long time I thought she had made a mistake. Now I'm not so sure.' She gave an awkward little shrug. 'I'm not deliberately trading on the likeness to my mother, Mac. I did *Private Lives* for Fizz.'

'Oh?' He sounded just a touch sceptical, as if he doubted her capable of an unselfish act. She stabbed at her salad with a fork and he caught her wrist. 'I'm sorry, Claudia. Tell me about it. Please.'

Claudia flickered a glance at him, uncertain of his motives. But he seemed sincere enough. 'Fizz and Luke had the most enormous row after Dad collapsed from exhaustion back in March. The doctors said it was stress-related and she blamed Luke for it.'

'Why?'

'Oh, it was all to do with Melanie. Anyway, she wouldn't see him, speak to him, even tell him that she was expecting his baby.'

'Wouldn't he have noticed, sooner or later?'

'Well, no. That was the problem. When Fizz sent him about his business he went off to Australia to lick his wounds out in the outback somewhere. And she wouldn't let anyone else tell him. She was hurting so much that we didn't dare take the risk of defying her.'

'So, how did *Private Lives* help?' Mac prompted, when she seemed reluctant to continue.

She straightened. 'Luke had already put up the money for the show because he wanted something light to launch Melanie in the West End. Did I tell you that she's his niece?' Mac nodded. 'She'd done plenty of television, soaps and suchlike in Australia, but she wanted to get into real theatre. He insisted I play the lead opposite her.' His brows rose insistently and Claudia pulled a face. 'You suggested a while back that my tongue might get me into trouble. I'd been a bit rude about Mel's acting ability in the past. Luke thought sharing a stage with her would teach me to be a little more polite.'

'In other words you did it under duress?'

'No. I thought it was the most likely way of getting Luke and Fizz back together. I knew that nothing would stop him from coming home for Melanie's first night and I hoped, I believed, that once Fizz had had time to calm down, getting them together would be enough.'

'It obviously worked.'

'Oh, I'm sure it would have done. But Fizz didn't wait. She realized all by herself that she couldn't live without the man and flew out to the back of beyond only to find him packing up to come home. He'd

164

decided that no matter what she had said, he was going to lay siege until she agreed to marry him.'

'Make him a willow cabin at her gate?'

Shakespeare? A poet soldier? Perhaps he wasn't so rough hewn after all. 'Fortunately it wasn't necessary. He'd have almost certainly developed pneumonia.'

'It was a very damp spring,' Mac agreed, solemnly.

'And in the meantime I was stuck with *Private Lives*. Not that I'm complaining and Mel is a dream to share a stage with. But Dad, bless him, realized the publicity potential of me stepping into my mother's shoes. Literally. The dress I was wearing in the photograph was one of hers.'

'Really?'

'They're all still wrapped in tissue in Dad's attic. All her costumes, all her gowns, lingerie, shoes in their original boxes, furs. They'd make a wonderful bonfire.'

In the silence that followed, the waitress brought them the next course. Claudia picked up her fork, speared a mange-tout and ate it slowly. Then she said, 'Now it's your turn.'

'You want to know about my mother?' he enquired.

She had known that he would put up a brick wall. He expected her to ask him about his wife. About his leg. About the army. 'Only if you want to. I'd rather you told me about your business. Security? What is it that you do exactly?'

'If I told you exactly, I wouldn't be in the security business,' he pointed out.

'If you want me to employ your company, I think I'm entitled to some details.'

'I've changed my mind. This is personal. I'm still not happy about the way that photograph got into your parachute pack.'

'Can you afford to get personal?'

'Even the boss is entitled to a few days off. I'll take a busman's holiday.'

She was beginning to lose patience. Wasn't he listening to anything she said? 'This is my life, Mac. I thought I'd made my feelings plain.'

'Ad nauseum.'

'But I might as well have saved my breath?' She tilted her head slightly, inviting contradiction.

'I'm not holding mine. But I'm not wasting any more arguing with you, either. And since I still have your keys and you can't get into your flat without me, you might as well stop being difficult and enjoy your lunch. I intend to.'

'I enjoy being difficult,' she informed him. 'Being difficult is what I do best. It's part of my charm.'

'I agree about your talent, I don't quite see the charm in it.'

'You, I take it, majored in rudeness?'

His smile was slow and deliberate. 'If it seems that way I can only put it down to your influence, Claudia. You just seem to bring out the worst in me.'

'I had noticed.' Then she gave a little shrug. 'Since you won't talk about your business can I ask one simple question?'

He looked at her warily. 'You can ask. I'm not promising an answer.'

'Trust is a two-way thing, Mac. You're going to have to trust me a little, too.'

After the longest pause he finally nodded. 'Go ahead. I'll do one question.'

'Will you tell me your wife's name?'

For a moment he stared at the plate in front of him and she thought he wasn't going to answer. 'Jenny,' he said, finally, his voice catching on the word. Then he looked up, looked her straight in the face. 'Her name was Jenny Callendar,' he added, as if that should mean something to her.

For a moment her brain wouldn't co-operate. Then she remembered. 'The climber?' she asked.

'You said one question. That's it.'

It wasn't it. Not by a long chalk. The questions were tumbling around in her brain like the weekly wash in the dryer. Jenny Callendar had been killed a couple of years ago . . . How? Where? She realized that Mac was watching her. Knew she was trying to remember, but he didn't help her out. Claudia let it go. It would come to her in time.

Instead she gave her full attention to the careful dissection of her lunch which provided the perfect cover to consider the enigma of the man sitting opposite her.

He had kissed her more than once and once was usually enough to make a man her willing slave. By now he should be eating out of her hand, promising

167

her the earth. The fact that she didn't want it was unimportant. She had learned to control men at her mother's knee but she wasn't controlling Gabriel MacIntyre. He was far too complex a character for that. He was keeping a careful distance, refusing to be twisted around her little finger. That he desired her, she knew by instinct, but for some reason he was determined to resist her. Then she remembered his kiss and a small dimple appeared beside her mouth as she recalled just how difficult he was finding it.

She looked up to find him watching her and her heart gave an odd little flip. She wondered what it would take to seduce him. She was sorely tempted by the challenge; the trouble was he wouldn't like her, or himself much afterwards. He was a man who needed to care for a woman he made love to.

Which brought her back to his wife. Jenny Callendar. But she kept her curiosity to herself. She had made a start and if he was planning to stick around there would be time enough to discover all Mr MacIntyre's darkest secrets.

There was another letter waiting at her flat.

Mac produced a serious-looking set of keys for the new locks and when he opened the door, it was there on the mat. A cheap white envelope with her name printed on it in large, plain letters using a black ballpoint pen.

For a moment Claudia simply stared at it, numbed, paralyzed by the awfulness of the realization that

168

someone actually wanted to make her feel just this way. Sick, frightened and very, very alone. Her hand flew to her lips as the bile began to rise, then she choked out a little sound, something approaching a hysterical laugh as she realized her mistake.

It wasn't the same at all. The others envelopes had been addressed in letters cut from newsprint. This time her name had been neatly printed in ballpoint. Relieved, she bent to pick it up.

'Don't touch it,' Mac warned sharply, as he turned from the burglar alarm. 'The police might be able to lift fingerprints.' And he pushed her back out into the hall.

'No, Mac. It's all right. It isn't the same,' she protested, but he still held her back. 'It isn't,' she said stubbornly, meeting his eyes. She didn't want it to be the same.

'The envelope's exactly the same,' he pointed out, gently. 'I warned the rest of the tenants about letting in unidentified strangers. It may be that your correspondent was forced to leave this in the letterbox downstairs. Would someone have brought it up and pushed it through your door?'

'Kay Abercrombie usually takes the newspapers and post around to everybody.' She looked away, hope dying as she realized what must have happened. 'She wouldn't have touched something addressed with letters cut out from a newspaper,' she said, slowly. 'He would have realized that, wouldn't he?'

'This guy might be crazy, but he's certainly not stupid. He wants you to think he's been up here. Right up to your door. Touching it.' He was being deliberately unkind. He wanted her to understand the kind of person they were dealing with.

'But if he couldn't get into the building – '

'We mustn't assume anything, Claudia. He may just have wanted you to believe that.'

'Oh, God. I think I'm going to be sick.'

'Don't you dare,' he said, sharply. 'You're going to stay right here while I look around.' Too weak to argue, she leaned back and slid down the wall, wrapping her arms around her head.

Mac came back. 'No one's been inside,' he said. He meant to be reassuring, but Claudia still felt as if her living space had been in some way defiled. He touched her shoulder and she looked up. 'Come on,' he said more gently, and she allowed him to help her to her feet before she shook him off and, stepping over the letter, closed the door on the outside world and rammed home the bolt with shaking fingers.

All that casual bravado undone by the sight of something as innocent as an envelope lying on the mat. And suddenly she had to know what it said. Before Mac could stop her she had bent and picked it up, ripping it open savagely. For a moment she stared at it, uncomprehending, her hands shaking. Then she laughed. She put the back of her hand to her mouth to stifle the sound, but it gurgled from her,

170

unstoppable as the tears that began to stream down her cheeks.

He took the paper from her unresisting hand. There wasn't much. But then none of them had said much. It was what they said. And this one was no different in its sly nastiness.

HELLO CLAUDIA, HOW DOES IT FEEL TO BE HOME? SAFE?

He released a small, explosive sound and folding his arms about her, pulled her hard into the protection of his body, holding her tight, crooning softly to her until the hiccuping sobs began to subside and she laid her head into the curve of his neck, quietly resting against him until her own racketing pulse matched the slow, steady thump of his.

And even then she didn't want to move. But she had to. 'I'm sorry, Mac,' she said, pulling away a little. 'I know I've been nothing but a nuisance since the first moment you set eyes on me. I'd quite understand if you don't want anything to do with me. You can go any time. Really. I'll be fine.'

He looked down at her, but her eyes were closed and she was unaware of the softening of his mouth, his eyes. She looked bruised. Nothing to do with the slightly darker patch under one eye, or the slight swelling of her lip, but emotionally beaten. He could think of any number of ways to soothe her, bring the colour back to her cheeks. It took every ounce of will-power to reject every one of them.

Instead he said, 'Do you remember what you said to me at the airfield on Friday morning? When you thought I was stringing you a line about changing the parachute?' He saw from her blush that she did. 'Then consider it returned with interest. Now why don't you go and make yourself useful while I make some calls?'

She withdrew reluctantly from the comfort of his arms. 'What do you want me to do?'

'What every red-blooded English woman does in a crisis. Make a pot of tea.'

'You're joking.' The moment of tenderness was over and he didn't even bother to answer her. But even as she opened her mouth to tell him in no uncertain terms that he could make his own damned tea Claudia realized that he was just giving her something to do, keeping her busy. She gave a little shiver, rubbed her arms, decided to find a sweater. She stopped in the doorway. 'If you're staying what will you do for clothes?'

'You can leave me to worry about that.' It hadn't taken him long to return to his usual stonewalling. Why wouldn't he talk to her?

'I suppose at the snap of your fingers one of your personal army will jump to attention and pack a bag for you.' He took no notice of her, but lifting the telephone receiver he began to punch in a number. Claudia wasn't used to being ignored. 'I suppose they're all ex-soldiers?' she persisted.

He cut the connection and turned to her. She expected him to be angry, but he wasn't. 'They're not *my* army, Claudia. They're not *my* anything. We're just a group of friends who do what we're good at and help one another out from time to time. That's all,' he said, clearly trying to be patient, as if he was talking to a slightly tiresome child.

She didn't think it was quite that simple but on the whole thought she preferred him mad. 'Like your discreet chauffeur service for instance?' she asked, provoking him further. She could be wrong but that had seemed just a bit too well rehearsed to be some casual arrangement.

'It's a perfectly normal car hire business, Claudia. In fact they specialize in weddings using vintage cars. But when I need a car and driver for something special I know I can count on them.'

'I'm not sure that I believe you.'

The patience was wearing thin. 'I'm not sure I care very much what you believe. It's really none of your business.'

'It is if you're planning to take over my life.'

He was taking over *her* life? Did she think he had nothing better to do than play nursemaid to a frightened actress? He felt the quick surge of anger drain away from him. Frightened. That was the key word. She was frightened out of her wits and trying very hard not to let it show. Perhaps he was being a little hard on her.

'We're not some gung-ho outfit, Claudia,' he said, more gently. 'The whole thing is very low key. A group of communications specialists, transport experts, couriers – '

173

'And security. They all fit together very nicely.'

'When necessary. Mostly we do our own thing, but we complement one another and we work well together. Occasionally I put a team together for a special job but that's the exception.'

She still looked doubtful. 'I hope I don't come under that category.'

'That rather depends how sensible you're going to be. If you insist on carrying on with nightly appearances in *Private Lives* I'm afraid you probably will.'

'I don't have a choice, Mac. People are relying on me. You should understand that.'

'But you don't have to stay here.'

Her mouth took on a stubborn line. 'I won't be driven out of my own home.' Even when it felt comfortless and chilling. She shivered again. 'But I'd be a lot happier if you'd stay with me.'

Mac noticed the shiver. Every instinct screamed at him to go to her; he ignored them all. It was tough, but he didn't want to make it easy for her to stay put.

'I suppose we could install CCTV on all the entrances,' he offered, unenthusiastically. 'And we'll need a porter downstairs to monitor the post, check visitors in and out. You know your neighbours. How do you think they'll react?'

'By asking their insurance companies for a reduction on their premiums if they've any sense.'

He'd hoped this vision of disruption to other people's lives would have given her pause. But she was probably right, the rest of the tenants would no doubt welcome the extra security, especially if they didn't have to pay for it. 'What about the landlord?'

'You'll have no trouble from the landlord,' she assured him.

'I see.'

'No, you don't, Mac. *I'm* the landlord but I'd rather you kept that little gem to yourself since none of the other tenants know.' She gave a little shrug at his raised eyebrows. 'Mother left Fizz and me some money. Fizz sank all hers into her radio station, I bought this block. But I prefer the managing agents to deal with complaints about dripping taps.'

'You don't have to excuse yourself to me.'

'Don't I? Then why do I feel you're constantly judging me?'

He didn't know. He had no idea why he felt the constant need to test her. Or maybe he knew only too well – he just wasn't ready to admit it to himself. 'You're determined to stay put?' he countered.

'I need to be in London, Mac. And I refuse to hide.'

She looked the way she had before she'd jumped out of the aircraft. Scared but determined. She was going to stay in her own apartment and nothing he did was going to persuade her otherwise. 'In that case I'd better get on with organizing it.'

'You do that. I'll go and make your tea.' She turned towards the kitchen, but instead of getting back to the telephone, Mac followed her. 'You know this isn't over, don't you? This guy isn't going to give up and go away.'

'Maybe if I don't react he'll get bored.'

'He might. Or he might just be driven to do something more dramatic, simply to get your attention.'

'More dramatic?' The wobble in her voice gave him hope and he went to her, took her shoulders, forced her to look up at him.

'For the last forty-eight hours you've been on the run from this, Claudia. He's been in control, jerking your strings, watching you jump. For heaven's sake, walk away. Give yourself a bit a space.'

'And where will I go?'

'There must be somewhere, someone who could offer you a . . .'

'A bed?' Some man, he meant. 'Melanie?' she offered. 'Would that be wise? He anticipated I'd go to Fizz.'

'He knows you. He knew you'd go there first. And I didn't mean family.'

'I know what you meant, Mac. But for your information I don't keep a handy cache of lovers just on the off-chance that I might need a bed for the night, although even if I had it would be none of your damn business. And perhaps now is as good a time as any to tell you that if you stay here, you'll be sleeping in the spare room.'

He stared at her for a moment. 'Then I guess we understand one another,' he said, at last.

'I understand you, Mac. Whether you understand me is a moot point. Meanwhile, whoever this person is, he'll almost certainly catch up with me sooner or later no matter where I go. At least here you can install your toys, watch my back. If you still want to, that is.' She rubbed at the gooseflesh that stippled her arms.

'We'll stay here if you insist. But on my terms. I'll be laying down a whole heap of rules and you'll have to do exactly as I say.'

We. He was staying. She hadn't realized how much she was relying on that. 'You expect me to do exactly what you say?' she repeated.

'Without question.'

'I've never done exactly what I've been told in my entire life,' she warned him.

'Then the next few days should prove interesting. Shall we have a trial run?'

She held up her hands. 'I know, I know, you're still waiting for your tea. I'm afraid I'm not very good at the domestic stuff.'

'I'm sure we'll manage. But forget the tea for the moment. Right now I want you to go and find something warmer to wear. You look like a plucked chicken.'

'Well, thanks. Compliments are always welcome. But it's nerves, not cold,' she told him, changing her mind about the sweater. 'I'm just the same before I go on stage.'

'How interesting. Shall we try that one again?' he suggested, very softly, the words dropping against her breastbone with an almost tangible insistence. 'Go and change into something warmer.'

He was *ordering* her to change her clothes. *Without question?* 'You don't like my dress, is that it?'

'Your dress?' Mac tried not to think about the way the scrap of bodice clung to her breasts, the way the shortest of skirts swirled around her long slender legs. He had been trying very hard not to think about it all day, without notable success. 'Your dress is fine,' he said, woodenly, 'as far as it goes. But it doesn't go very far does it?'

'It suits me.'

She was challenging him. Now that she had got her way about staying in the flat, she was making a push to establish herself as the one in control. He knew that if he shrugged and told her to do what she wanted, she would immediately do what he had told her do and find something warmer to wear. Adele had been just the same as a kid. Maybe it was a female thing, but Claudia wasn't kidding when she said she didn't like taking orders.

'It suits you just fine, Claudia. In fact you look quite stunning in it.' The gooseflesh, he noticed, disappeared as she relaxed a little, warming to his compliment. He took two sets of door keys from his pocket and placed them on the kitchen counter. 'Now, here are your keys. Two sets. I'd advise you not to let them out of your sight.'

'I won't, I promise.' She'd promise him anything, but she was only delivering when it suited her.

'I don't think it would be a good idea to give a set to one of your neighbours, or your cleaning lady, or even

178

your managing agents for the time being.' He turned back into the hall and tapping the alarm box as he went, but not stopping, he said, 'I've changed the code on your alarm system to nine two five seven – can you remember that?'

'Nine two five seven. Consider it done,' she said as he unbolted the front door and finally turned to face her. 'Where are you going?'

'And I would advise you to be extremely wary of unexpected packages. Even packages that you are expecting.'

She looked confused, and he noted with interest that the gooseflesh was back. 'Mac?'

She looked like a child, he thought. Lost and alone. He wanted to race back to her, sweep her up into his arms and hold her. Keeping his expression detached, his voice brisk, was as hard a thing as he had ever done. 'Goodbye, Claudia,' he said, and without waiting for her reaction, he closed the door behind him. He was halfway down the stairs when she wrenched it open again.

'I'm sorry,' she called after him. He didn't stop, didn't look back and after a second he heard her footsteps behind him. 'Mac, please. I understand what you're doing and I'm sorry.'

He stopped then and turned. 'Sorry? Why are you sorry?'

She gave a helpless little shrug, looked up at him with those big silver eyes. 'I warned you that I wasn't very good at taking orders.'

She was acting. It was a pretty performance, but that's all it was. 'Don't worry about it. It doesn't matter. I'll look out for your television programme.' He turned and headed for the front door.

'Mac!' She was angry now. With him, but with herself too. 'Come back here!' He opened the front door. 'Please!' He hesitated as the fear crept back into her voice, overlaying the disbelief that he could do this to her. 'Please don't leave me on my own. I'll be good. I promise.'

It was the hardest thing Mac had ever done, but he kept his ground. He couldn't let her off the hook that easily. 'You don't know how to be good, Claudia. You've been spoilt all your life. You want me to look after you but you'll argue with everything I say. When I say "duck" you'll still be arguing when the bullet hits you.'

'No, really I won't. Please, Mac. Come back to the flat and I'll go and change. Straight away.' And she would. This time. But the next time he asked her to do something it might mean the difference between life and death and Claudia Beaumont still had the look of a woman who thought she could twist him around her little finger. All big moist eyes and soft tempting mouth and he knew from personal experience just how hard that mouth was to resist. 'If you'll stay, I'll do everything you say.'

'Will you?'

Drawing a cross over her heart, Claudia offered him an uncertain, wavery little smile. 'I promise I'll duck the minute you say the word.'

She did it so beautifully, he thought, that it would be a pleasure to surrender. But this wasn't a game, it was for real. 'Without question?' he asked.

'Without question.'

'Prove it to me.'

'Prove it?'

'Give me your dress.'

'My dress?' She looked slightly startled, but agreed readily enough. 'Oh, my dress. Of course,' she said, retreating back up the stairs.

'No, Claudia,' he said, standing his ground at the entrance to the flats. 'Right here and now.'

He saw the beginning of laughter form on her lips, then falter as she began to realize that he meant it. 'Here? But the door's open,' she protested. 'Anyone might see.' He took a step towards the open door and he saw from her face that she was finally getting the picture. 'But I'm not wearing anything . . .' She waved her hand vaguely in the direction of her bosom. 'Mac!'

He wasn't going to back down, Claudia realized with horror. She had pushed him and this was his way of letting her know that he wouldn't be pushed. How dare he! She felt a cold shiver feather her spine as the answer filled her head. *Easily. No problem.*

He'd told her his terms for staying at the flat and she had immediately put them to the test. She'd always been the same, at home, at school, even on stage she'd always pushed against authority, testing the opposition to see just how far she could go, taking the boundaries to the limit. But what kind of idiot would try to push a man like Gabriel MacIntyre? She didn't have to look far for the answer.

'You want my dress? Here and now?' He didn't answer, but then she hadn't expected him to. She did as he said or she was on her own. Yesterday she would have told him to go to the devil. Yesterday she had been convinced this was all some sick joke. Now, slowly, never taking her eyes off his face, she unfastened the buttons at the neck of the sundress and let the straps fall, still holding the tiny bodice against her breasts.

She paused there, certain that obedience demonstrated he would call a halt. He didn't. Nor did he look away. Not quite Galahad, then. She found that oddly reassuring. A man without any kind of weakness would be unbearable.

She lowered the halter neck to the waist. There was no visible reaction, except for the tiny betraying beads of sweat that appeared above his lip. But it was enough, and satisfied, she unfastened the buttons at the waist and let the dress puddle at her feet. When she stepped out of it she was wearing nothing but the briefest white pants and a pair of strappy high-heeled sandals.

'There,' she enquired, softly, when he didn't speak. 'Are you quite satisfied?'

Satisfied? By a pair of the shapeliest legs he had

ever encountered at close quarters, legs that reached to the stratosphere? Satisfied by full generous hips that tilted provocatively towards him and breasts that were the stuff of dreams? Gooseflesh, Mac decided, was catching.

But although his mouth had gone suddenly very dry and his treacherous body had tightened with barely containable desire, Mac knew that if he allowed her to see the effect she was having on him he would have lost. And for her sake it was important that he didn't lose.

So, offering up a silent prayer that it wouldn't shake, he raised his hand, holding it out in a wordless demand that she bring her dress to him. Surrender completely.

For one long moment she made him wait, made him endure the torture that he had inflicted upon himself, before bending gracefully to pick up her discarded dress, carrying it towards him in two outstretched hands like a precious votive offering from some heathen priestess. But if her stance was that of a supplicant, her eyes were not downcast, they were bright and knowing and her lips were set in a provocative curve. For a moment his resolve wavered as he realized that she had not surrendered. She would never surrender. The game had simply moved onto another level.

Then he grasped the dress, tightening his fist about it and holding it out in front of him for just long enough to prove that he had complete mastery of his reactions before letting it fall to his side. It was, he thought, a pretty damn close thing.

'Now,' he invited, through a throat that felt as if it had been stuffed with hot gravel, 'why don't you go and put on something warmer.'

CHAPTER 8

Claudia was very conscious of eyes following them as she led the way backstage the following afternoon. She had warned Mac that rumours of a romance would be flying about, but even she had been surprised by the number of photographers camped out on the theatre doorstep to await her arrival.

'I'm sorry, Mac,' she murmured as he brought the four wheel drive to a halt. 'They're not normally this eager.'

'Maybe they'd heard you wouldn't be alone,' he replied, coolly. Maybe they had. He caught her expression and shrugged. 'If he knows you're not alone your nasty little letter writer might think twice about trying anything.'

'So you rang around and invited the press to see just how cosy we've become?'

He couldn't miss the chipped ice in her voice. She didn't mean him to. But he ignored it. 'That's right. And this way no one is going to be surprised if I tag along everywhere you go.'

'Everywhere?' she enquired tartly.

'Like superglue,' he promised.

'Can we have a photograph, Claudia?' one of the men called, as they paused at the stage door.

'Haven't you got enough, Jimmy?'

The motorwinds of the cameras had been working since Mac had driven up to the theatre, but if she was going to be plastered over the dailies she'd prefer it not to be an inelegant picture of her climbing down from the four wheel drive. 'Are you sure about this, Mac?' she asked, as he took her arm. 'It won't be much fun.'

'It's no fun at all,' he assured her. 'I'm glad you realize the sacrifice I'm making.'

'You ain't seen nothin' yet,' she warned, as she slipped her arm through his and leaning against him, looked up at him with an idiotically besotted smile.

He returned her smile for the benefit of the cameras, but only she could see the look in his eyes. 'You're enjoying this, aren't you?' he demanded.

'Only because I know you're not,' she replied, sweetly. 'And this was your idea, remember?'

'Then we'd better be convincing.' She anticipated his next move, but trapped between the stage door and his equally hard body, she could do nothing to avoid it, but was forced to wait while he slowly lowered his head to hers, while he brushed her lips with tormenting sweetness for the benefit of the photographers.

'Are you sure you haven't done this before?' she asked, a little breathlessly. 'You really are very good at it.'

'High praise indeed from an acknowledged expert.'

Claudia resisted the temptation to say something extremely rude; instead she turned a blazing smile on the photographers and blew them a kiss before punching the code into the stage-door security pad.

It was the most they had said to one another since the incident with the dress. She had been genuinely cold by the time she had walked up the two flights of stairs to her flat. She had wanted to run, certain that any second a door would open and one of the other tenants would see her. But she didn't run. She had walked as sedate and straight-backed up the stairs as if she had been dressed for a debutantes' ball, refusing to let Mac see how upset she was.

Once inside her apartment he had rapidly lost interest in what she was wearing, shutting himself away in the living room with the telephone. That suited her fine and she had locked herself in the bathroom for a long hot soak and then, wrapped in silk pyjamas and a warm dressing gown had finally made a pot of tea.

Mac had barely looked up when she placed a cup beside him and she hadn't encouraged conversation, taking her own cup to her bedroom. She had locked that door too, although more as a gesture than in any hope of keeping him out should he decide he needed to open it.

He hadn't. Apparently he was too busy to give her a wake-up call and when she finally emerged, tousle headed and heavy eyed, it was to discover that her apartment was overrun with total strangers doing complicated things to her telephone, her windows and her doors. The smell of cooking drew her to the kitchen. 'What's going on?' she asked a man busy at the grill pan.

'Nothing to worry about, miss. Just fixing up a few odds and ends. Fancy a bacon sandwich?'

Claudia knew, in theory, that breakfast was a good thing. In practice she rarely indulged in anything more challenging than a slice of toast before lunch. About to refuse politely and withdraw, Claudia caught Mac's expression as he worked at the laptop computer propped on the kitchen counter. It was quite evident that the idea of her eating one of the doorsteps being dished up was causing him some amusement and she just had to wipe that look off his face.

'Thank you,' she said, pushing back her hair and tightening the belt of her robe. 'I'd love one.' With the sandwich came with a mug of thick, dark coffee. She eyed her breakfast with misgiving before picking up the plate and mug and backing towards the door, planning to retreat to the privacy of her bedroom where she could decide what to do with the contents.

'Don't let us drive you out, Claudia,' Mac said, without looking up.

'I don't want to get in the way.'

'You won't. There's plenty of room.' He patted the empty stool beside him. 'And I want to check your plans for the rest of the week.' He looked up and smiled then. 'You can tell me about them while you have your breakfast.' And under his watchful eyes she had been forced to eat every mouthful of that damn sandwich, drink every drop of coffee so strong that it would keep her awake for a week.

And now he had kissed her again, this time for the newsmen and that wrankled. He kissed her a damn sight too easily. They might be playing at lovers, but they didn't have to do it in the street, did they?

The buzzer sounded to indicate the door was open and she pushed through it but Jim, having been given a severe talking to about lax security by Phillip Redmond, immediately stopped them. 'Will you sign your visitor in, Miss Claudia,' he asked a little nervously. He'd known Claudia a long time and recognized the expression clouding her eyes.

'Visitor?' She looked around, ignoring Mac. 'I haven't got a visitor,' she said, and began to walk away. Let Mr MacIntyre chew on that, she thought crossly. But Mac grabbed a handful of her expensive silk shirt and ignoring her yelp of outrage, hauled her back to his side. There was a spattering of applause from a group of backstage workmen who were making a meal over moving some boxes that had just been delivered.

'I thought you were going to behave,' Mac reminded her.

'It's a two-way deal, mister,' she hissed back. 'Now get your hands off me.' There was a snigger from somewhere behind her and she swung around. 'If you people haven't got anything useful to do, I suggest you find something. Quickly.'

The men suddenly found the boxes were a great deal easier to move than they had supposed, but as they disappeared into the shadowy recesses of the theatre Claudia heard one of them say, 'I'll give it a week at the most.'

'Amen to that,' Claudia murmured softly, but with deeply expressed feeling.

'You want to bet?' Mac asked her, and raising his voice and investing it with rich irony he called after the retreating figures, 'If anyone's running a book I'll have a piece of that action.'

Laughter greeted this and, the tension broken, Mac turned to Jim and offered his hand. 'Gabriel MacIntyre.'

'I saw you on the television, Mr MacIntyre. Nice to meet you. Will you sign the book for me?'

Mac glanced pointedly at Claudia and she quickly intervened. 'That won't be necessary, Jim.' She handed over a small photograph that Mac had given her. 'Mr MacIntyre will be a regular visitor so it will be simpler if you make him a security pass.'

Jim grinned at Mac. 'I guess that means you'll be around for a while?'

'Well, for a week anyway.'

Claudia, irritated by all this male bonding, interrupted. 'Jim, will you find Phillip and ask him to come along to my dressing room as soon as he's free.' Then she extended her hand to Mac. 'Come along, sweetheart,' she said, with a distinct lack of warmth. 'I'll show you around.'

'I'm all yours,' he said, reaching out to take her hand, folding it into his own much larger one.

It was odd. He infuriated her, he made her feel scratchy and cross, yet she had to admit that she enjoyed the feel of his hand about hers. It was a slightly battered hand, and although the nails were clean and neatly trimmed there was nothing manicured or pampered about it. It was rather like Mac, she thought, as nature had intended, but tough as they came and very strong. Wrapped around her fingers like this, it had the effect of making her feel cherished and protected. Not that she would was going to admit it. Ever.

Claudia's silver fox eyes gleamed softly as she looked up at him. 'All mine?'

Mac, his fingers wrapped around the small, delicately boned hand of this unreadable woman, felt as if he had been kicked by a mule. She had that effect on him. One moment he was as irritated as hell because she was behaving like a wayward brat, the next she looked at him with those extraordinary eyes and he was gasping for air. Yet even as he acknowledged that she was the most bewitching, the most desirable creature he had ever met, his skin crawled with the thought that flirting was something she did as naturally as breathing. That it didn't mean anything. *And if it did*? The question was there at the back of his mind and wouldn't go away.

But damn her, he refused to make a fool of himself over her. He'd do his best to clear up the mess she was in and then he'd forget her. And quickly.

'Just as long as you behave yourself,' he told her, brusquely.

'I'm trying to be good.' Her husky voice teased him, just as her eyes had and the mule kicked again.

'No, sweetheart, you're just trying.'

She looked up at him, startled, but something in his expression must have reassured her because she laughed, her lips parting softly, the sound as sweet and warm as cinnamon toast.

It was all pretence of course, but her hand felt good in his and the elusive flowery scent she was wearing seemed to fill his head as she leaned against his shoulder, turning to smile up at him as they walked to her dressing room, making certain that everyone they passed knew she was in love. He swallowed, hard, and smiled back. After all, this had been his idea.

'Oh, dear Lord,' she exclaimed as she saw the pile of newspaper clippings placed in a neat pile on her dressing table. She reclaimed her hand, crossing swiftly to look at them.

Mac, missing the small hand tucked trustingly into his, somehow managed to stop himself from going after her, concentrating instead on the room itself. Concentrating on the job. Without a window the room was invunerable from outside. He opened the door to her private bathroom, glanced around, but it had an electric ventilator. Whoever had slashed her costume had come through the door from the corridor, passing goodness knew how many people on the way. But no one had noticed. Which strongly suggested that it was

192

someone who had every right to be there. An inside job.

And if whoever it was had left any clues they had all been cleaned away since Saturday night. The surfaces had been thoroughly polished, the floor vacuumed; the pots of make-up had all been wiped and were laid out along with brushes in all shapes and sizes in neat rows, waiting for her to transform herself into her character.

The roses in the tall vase had been beautifully arranged, the fading blooms removed. There was nothing hurried or slapdash about it. It hadn't been a quick flick over with a duster. Someone had done this for her, did it for her every day with care and devotion and for the first time he was forced to confront the fact that she wasn't just some tiresome actress who was in a bit of bother, but that she was the centre of this small universe, that her talent, her name brought in the crowds whose money paid the wages. That she was, in fact, a star.

'Claudia – '

'I'm afraid this is worse than I expected,' she said, turning to him with a sheaf of clippings in her hand, interrupting him before he could make an utter fool of himself. He had to make a serious effort to concentrate on what she was saying.

'Worse?' he demanded. 'What could be worse?'

'This,' she said, with a giggle as she held up a sheet of newsprint to show him the headline. STAR FALLS FOR PARACHUTE HERO, he read and

193

groaned. 'Are you a hero, my darling?' Her voice was teasing. 'I think I ought to know.'

'I would have thought you'd know better than to believe what you read in the newspapers,' he reminded her.

'Oh, *I do*,' she replied, lightly. 'But I find it odd the way everyone says that when *they* are in the news, yet still seem to be taken in by stories about other people.'

Mac mentally flinched, aware that he had just been quietly reprimanded, gently but firmly rapped over the knuckles with the equivalent of a velvet covered cane. Guilty as charged.

'I suppose,' he said, slowly, 'that if a thing is repeated often enough it achieves a certain mythical status.'

'Hang onto that thought, Mac,' she told him, her laughter deepening the tiny lines around her eyes, lifting her whole face, giving it character, depth, offering him a glimpse of the woman beneath the public image, a real woman, warm and full of life. He realized, quite suddenly, that he had been wrong about her. He had judged her on newspaper gossip and his own prejudiced attitudes. He'd made no secret of his feelings and because of that he had only been allowed to skim the surface shell of Claudia Beaumont, to know the part of her capable of taking on the sharpest television host around and steal away his show, the woman who flirted her way across the gossip pages, the part of her the public thought it knew and owned. But there was more, much more and he wanted to break through the shell and discover the whole woman, find out what had made her so very protective of her inner self that he suspected she almost forgot it was there herself. 'I think you're about to become a myth in your own right,' she added, then glancing obliquely at him, said, 'I do hope you're up to it.'

'Why? What does it say?' He was floundering, trying to regain a foothold as the ground shifted treacherously beneath him.

'I did warn you. I'm afraid that since rumours of our romance were too late to catch the Sunday papers, the dailies have rather gone to town.'

'I imagine I'll survive,' he reassured her, but as she looked at the photograph accompanying the headline, Claudia caught her lower lip between her teeth. It gave her a curiously vulnerable look and he moved closer, resting his hand on her shoulder as he looked over her head to see for himself.

What he saw made him frown. It was an almost indecent close-up of that television kiss, although why, frozen like this in a grainy black and white photograph, it should seem so much worse than live and in full colour before an audience of millions, he didn't know. But live, it had been over in moments, it had been a performance and no one had been looking that closely. But the photograph captured something that the viewer would never see; something that wasn't quite make-believe.

'You did say that Barty James would probably have a journalist on standby,' he reminded her.

'*Journalist* rather overstates the case,' she said, touching the photograph with just the tip of her forefinger. 'But you're right, as the whole thing had been set up in advance it seemed logical that he would want to take full advantage of the situation.'

'We might not have . . . co-operated.'

'Then he would simply have used the kiss on the film.'

'But that wasn't . . . you didn't . . . Oh, I see.'

'I knew you would.' Eventually. He'd kissed her and that had given Barty James the idea to use it for the show. And now it was Claudia's name that was being bandied about. Oh, he was there, but no one was really interested in him except as an accessory for their story. And that was how reputations were forged in the heat of the press room. Except of course there was no hot lead these days. It was all done clinically, by computer. She hadn't said he was slow on the uptake, but then she hadn't needed to.

He swallowed and turned back to the clipping for another lesson in reading between the lines. In fact there wasn't much more than a caption, leaving the journalist little room to speculate on their relationship. But then he hadn't needed words; the photograph said it all.

Other newspapers hadn't been so restrained. Without the picture of the kiss they had simply printed a stock photograph of Claudia and made up for the

196

omission by telling their readers what they had managed to dig up in the meantime. All of them reported that the two of them had met during a charity parachute jump, all of them repeated the 'hero' motive although mercifully without any details, which suggested it was just a useful word to go with parachute. Thankfully none of them had taken the trouble to look up his record. Or anything else. Several had made a big point about the instant attraction between them.

'There was an attraction all right,' Mac said. 'Your nearside wing was instantly attracted to the offside of my Landcruiser. I'll bet none of them mentioned that.'

Claudia looked back up over her shoulder at him, laughing at his obvious indignation. 'Oh, yes they did,' she said, rifling through the cuttings. 'Listen to this.' She put on a pompous voice. ' "Claudia Beaumont suffered a minor accident on arrival at the airfield, skidding on the wet grass in her new sportscar. Gabriel MacIntyre immediately rushed to her assistance" – rushing to wring my neck more like – ' she countered – ' "and his deep concern was obvious to everyone present." ' She turned to face him without dislodging his hand from her shoulder. 'Nicely done. You were concerned, weren't you, Mac? About your shiny black car. And your aircraft hangar.'

'I did apologize.'

'Mmmm. I don't think you've quite got the hang of apologies, Mac. You should consider taking lessons.'

'I thought you'd forgiven me.'

'Well I have,' she said, 'for that. But you will keep doing and saying things that mean you have to say you're sorry all over again. You're beginning to slip seriously behind. That comment you made outside the theatre for instance,' she said, ticking it off on her fingers. 'Then grabbing my shirt and telling me to behave in front of the crew wasn't exactly gentlemanly – '

And apologizing for his thoughts would take a month. Fortunately Claudia couldn't read his mind. Interestingly she hadn't mentioned the incident with the dress . . . Maybe that was her way of admitting she had been in the wrong. Maybe he should . . . No. She just wanted to forget about that. He certainly wished he could. Right now she was simply teasing him a little so he kept it light.

'Lady, you could do with a few lessons yourself. Your own manners leave something to be desired. Just because you're a star – '

'A star?' She laughed. 'I'm sure you don't think I'm a star.'

'A wild star, a slightly wicked star, a star that twinkles when it thinks it will rather than according to any rules of physics, but I don't think there's any doubt about it, Miss Beaumont. You're a star by any definition of the word.'

She laughed again, but this time a little uncertainly. 'I do believe that was a compliment.' She lifted her hand to his cheek, touching it lightly with just the tips of her fingers. 'Rather a nice one. Perhaps there's hope for you yet.' On an impulse she raised her lips to his and kissed him, equally lightly. 'Thank you, Gabriel.'

Gabriel. His name had been something of an embarrassment to him as a boy and he had ditched it the moment he had left school. And Jenny had hated it. But on Claudia's lips it suddenly sounded wonderful.

'Any time,' he said, his voice thick, his body tight with a sudden and very urgent need for her and without allowing himself to think about what he was doing he caught her about the waist, drawing him into his body and as he lowered his mouth to hers, she closed her eyes.

They were alone, no audience, the only reason to kiss her was because he wanted to. And he wanted to. If he was honest with himself he'd wanted to since he'd wrenched open her car door and first set eyes on her. Oh, he'd been infuriated by her careless driving, but that had been nothing compared to the wave of anger that had overwhelmed him as he realized that none of the barriers that he had erected to protect himself from his emotions, from feeling anything for a very long time, were one damned bit of use when confronted by Claudia Beaumont. All it had taken had been one look from those incredible eyes, one throwaway line in that low, husky voice and his defences had begun to crumble. And no amount of reinforcement had helped.

His lips brushed over hers and he felt her tremble slightly, unexpectedly, against him. After the confidence of her embrace in front of the cameras he had expected her to respond with a rather more immediate fire. Passion or fury. Instead she seemed to be holding her breath, waiting for him to take the lead. Her hesitancy took him by surprise, emboldening him and he took her lower lip between his to taste its warm sweetness, dipping his tongue against her teeth in the gentlest exploration. She gave a little sigh, moved slightly to fit herself more closely against him, raising her lashes over a pair of startled eyes as she became aware of his all too obvious arousal. 'Is this the way you take care of all your clients?' she asked, her voice more breath than substance.

Clients? Did she really think of herself as his client? If that was the case, he'd be giving serious thought to the way he collected his account. 'It's the most effective technique I know,' he assured her, softly. 'If anyone wants to get to you, they have to get past me first.'

She thought about it for a moment, then said, 'That makes sense.' And apparently quite happy with that closed her eyes again. He looked down at her. Her lids were heavy, lightly dusted with the same silver grey as the colour of her eyes, her lashes were unbelievably long and thick, like the glossy furs worn by his grandmother when he was a boy. He touched them very lightly with his lips and was rewarded with a tiny sound that came from somewhere deep inside her, tightening his skin, making him very aware of his own desire. But he refused to be rushed by a racketing libido. It had been a long time since he had made love to a woman and he was determined they should both enjoy the experience.

With that firmly in mind, he began, very slowly, very thoroughly to trace the finely moulded bones of her face until he reached the small crease just above corner of her mouth. Her lips, he had noticed, tilted up slightly, so that she looked as if she was smiling even when her eyes were saying something else, but the crease only appeared when she was genuinely happy and it seemed that she was happy now. Rather happy himself, he touched the tiny indentation with the tip of his tongue.

Claudia turned slightly as if seeking his mouth with her own, but then she hesitated and looked up at him, her eyes full of question. 'This is just for us, Mac?' she asked, with touching uncertainty.

'Just for us.'

And she gave a little sigh. He took his time, aware that for both of them this was something new. Not the kissing; he had kissed her before, first without quite knowing why, and then he had kissed her because . . . well, there were all kinds of reasons, none of them to do with the way he was feeling right now.

Now he tasted her lips, the smooth minty freshness of her teeth, met and slowly acquainted himself with the heady pleasure of her tongue, drifting away on a tide of this new sensual pleasure. *New*. The word mocked him. He was thirty-five years old. There was not much left for him to discover, pleasure or pain, that was entirely new and as the kiss deepened a warning bell reminded him that he'd been here before.

Yet not quite here. Not feeling quite like this. This was like being fifteen, knowing nothing and kissing a girl for the first time, all mixed up with those years of experience. The combination was so heady that he didn't even hear the door opening behind him. It took a low cough to warn him that they were no longer alone, to drag him back from the dangerous territory into which he had strayed.

It took a moment longer before he focused on the figure standing in the doorway. Mac had seen him before and he didn't much like him. His brain began, slowly, to click into gear. Redmond. Phillip Redmond, the theatre manager.

'You sent for me, Claudia?' Redmond said, with the barest touch of something insolent in his manner. 'I did knock.' But he hadn't waited for her to answer and he had interrupted them when anyone with an ounce of good taste would have simply closed the door and gone away, Mac thought. No, he didn't like him. And he fully expected Claudia to tell the man to get lost in her own inimitable style.

Instead she took a little shuddery breath. Mac felt it beneath his hands before she gathered herself and not quite managing to meet his eyes, turned away from him, putting a yard of distance between them. It felt like a mile, a great yawning empty space.

'Yes, Phillip, I did.' Mac took comfort from the fact that her voice shook just a little and that she sat rather

202

suddenly on her dressing stool. 'I want to know the progress you've made so far in your enquiries about what happened on Saturday.' She avoided looking in the mirror, Mac noticed, avoided looking at him, while Redmond fussed around picking up the cuttings that had slipped from her hands. 'Leave those,' she said, impatiently. 'I'll pick them up later.'

She wasn't quite in control, Mac thought, but she was getting there. Phillip Redmond, however, was too intent on the photograph in the newspaper to notice Claudia's lack of poise. 'Your mother would never have done that,' he said, holding it out to her.

She didn't take it. 'It was just a kiss, Phillip,' she said, blushing a little. Mac was surprised that she felt the need to explain herself to the theatre manager. He was even more surprised by the blush. 'It was just a bit a fun to raise money for Fizz's charity.'

'Your mother raised a great deal of money for charity without the need to make an exhibition of herself,' Redmond replied. 'But then, she was a lady.'

Claudia finally took the paper, looked at it for a moment and then at Redmond. The sudden flush of colour had been leached from her skin and she was perfectly still. 'Just what does that mean, Phillip?' she enquired, softly. 'That my mother was more competent at raising money for charity than me?' Her pause was epic. 'Or that I am not a lady?'

CHAPTER 9

There was a horribly long moment when the tension was so thick that it could have been cut into wedges and served with whipped cream. Mac finally broke the silence.

'Miss Beaumont asked you a question, Redmond.' His voice was scarcely above a whisper, but it was the kind of whisper that would have hit the back wall of a hushed theatre, Claudia thought, and no one would have been left in any doubt about his feelings. 'It would be ill-mannered to keep *a lady* waiting for an answer.'

A lady? Used by Mac to describe her, the word caught her by surprise. She fought back the urge to look at him and read his face, see if he really meant it. It was too important. She cared too much. So she kept her eyes fastened on Phillip Redmond.

But Phillip was defensive, rather than apologetic. 'I didn't say that, Claudia. You know I didn't mean to imply – '

'Didn't you?' With his mean-spirited attempt to justify himself something snapped. Claudia knew the way Phillip felt about her mother. He'd placed the image of Elaine French on a pedestal a mile high and worshipped at her feet.

It had been obvious from the first that he bitterly resented Melanie's presence. She had told Mel that Phillip would get used to her, but it was quite obvious that he had been getting more, rather than less difficult during the run and, Claudia realized with a sinking heart, she was partly to blame.

With the benefit of hindsight she believed her father had been unwise to bring Phillip in to work on *Private Lives*, a play so much associated with the Elaine French legend, although heaven knew that he would have been terribly hurt if he'd been left out of the team. But he had been getting increasingly difficult during the run because she and her father had preferred to overlook his behaviour, excusing it as a slightly irritating eccentricity instead of confronting it. It had been a mistake, a mistake she had to address right now.

Phillip wanted her to behave like her mother, or at least the woman he thought she had been. No problem.

Lifting her head, she tilted it slightly to one side in the pose that was the very essence of Elaine French and then very still, very poised, she became her mother.

It wasn't difficult. She had been brought up to it, had performed the trick as a child, for her mother's friends, for eager photographers when they came to take 'family' shots, even at school.

'I think,' she said, in that cool dismissive voice her mother had used when she was particularly displeased, 'I think that you came very close to it, Phillip.'

Redmond blinked, his shoulders dropped and he took a step back, almost for a moment as if he'd seen a ghost. Then he raised his hand to his forehead. 'I'm sorry, madam. I'm sorry. You know I wouldn't do anything to hurt you.' He made a helpless little gesture.

Madam. He had always called her mother that and Claudia froze, momentarily horrified by what she had done, how convincing she had been.

'Perhaps you'd better try harder,' Mac suggested, stepping forward, a supportive hand beneath her elbow. 'Miss Beaumont was put in an impossible situation on Saturday. Do you think she enjoyed performing like that?'

'Miss Beaumont? Claudia.' Phillip stared at her for a moment and then with a long shudder turned to Mac. 'I'm sorry. It's just that Claudia looks so much like her mother. I can't . . .' He made a helpless little gesture, as if incapable of putting his feelings into words.

Claudia made a small sound, deep in her throat. It might have been the beginnings of a laugh. But then again, it might not, she couldn't be sure. If Phillip had ever seen the ladylike Elaine French screaming abuse at her hapless husband because she was no longer beautiful, because she couldn't bear to look at herself in the mirror and he was the only available target for her venom . . .

206

But no one knew about that. Oh, Fizz had told Luke, and Melanie had been told just a little about why Edward Beaumont hadn't left his deeply damaged wife to be with the girl he loved. But no one who hadn't been there could possibly *know*. Who could you tell? Who would ever believe it? They had never discussed what they should do. They had each simply chosen to lock away the terrible memories and so the legend had remained intact.

She realized that Mac was looking at her, his eyes suggesting that Phillip was expecting something from her, the gentle pressure of his hand on her arm assuring her that she was not alone. Slowly, with conscious effort she came back to the dressing room and reality.

'The standards of behaviour that my mother set were so –' she struggled for the right word – 'so *taxing*, that few of us can ever hope to achieve their like, Phillip,' she said. It was as near to an acceptance of his apology as she could manage.

He didn't appear to notice the reservation. 'She was unique,' he agreed, solemnly, as if that answered everything.

'I believe she was.' She sincerely hoped so. And she made a silent promise to herself that, no matter what the provocation, she would never, ever, impersonate her mother again. And once this run of *Private Lives* was over, she would never recreate one of her roles, or even allow herself to be made up to look like her.

A shiver ran through her, as if someone had walked over her grave.

Mac felt it and moved closer. 'Claudia?'

She put her hand over his for just a moment while she gathered herself and he saw the brief internal struggle as she reclaimed herself, put on the public smile. 'Darling,' she said, with forced brightness, 'why don't you sit down over there. This won't take long and then I'll show you around.'

For the moment Mac accepted that he had temporarily lost the woman he had discovered a few minutes ago. Warm, a little uncertain, a very different woman from the one who wore her couldn't-care-less front so convincingly. But he was concerned about her, too. Just now something had happened inside Claudia's head that he didn't quite understand. She had done something to herself, something that had sent a shiver down his spine.

As she hesitated, she gave him a playful push and taking his cue from her, he reluctantly resumed his self-inflicted role as infatuated lover and retreated to the velvet covered chaise. The temptation to flatten Phillip Redmond was still making his knuckles tingle but it would serve no purpose, Mac decided, other than to make himself feel better and that wasn't why he was there. So he picked up a programme to flick through idly as though the business of the theatre bored him rigid.

Nothing could be further from the truth. Phillip Redmond interested him a very great deal. He was clearly obsessed with Elaine French and obsessive characters were dangerous. Especially when the object of that obsession, apparently reincarnated in the shape of her daughter, refused to conform to the proper standards of behaviour.

Mac wasn't a psychologist but to his layman's mind it had all the hallmarks of a disaster waiting to happen. Or maybe it had already happened. The destruction of the dress would have presented no difficulty for Redmond and he undoubtedly knew where both Claudia and Fizz lived. He could have followed them easily in the heavy traffic of London and once he had seen they were headed for Broomhill he wouldn't have needed to stay on their tail.

The photograph in the parachute was more difficult.

'That's it?' Claudia looked up as Phillip finally came to the end of a long list of names. 'Wasn't there anyone who was unaccounted for?'

'Well, there might have been someone. We're not quite sure. Jim says he caught sight of someone hurrying out through the door at about half past six.'

Even from the other side of the room Mac felt her tense up. 'A man or woman?' she asked, carefully.

'A woman. Quite tall with long blonde hair. He just saw the back of her and assumed it was one of the staff dashing out for something before the second performance. But he doesn't remember her coming back.' He gave a small shrug. 'That, of course, means nothing, Jim is about as reliable as a weather forecast, but there are quite a number of girls who could fit that description.'

'Perhaps you could check with them, see if anyone went out about that time?' Mac suggested impatiently, tossing the programme to one side and giving a fair impression of a man tired of waiting for the woman in his life. 'Or just call the police and leave it to them. It's their job after all.' Mac expected Phillip to protest that calling the police would be bad for publicity. He didn't.

'I wanted to call the police, but Claudia won't hear of it. I imagine she thinks this attack is by someone she knows, someone who needs help rather than punishment. All very noble I'm sure, but that costume cost a fortune.' He seemed to take the loss personally.

'It could just have been a dissatisfied customer,' Mac offered flippantly.

Phillip Redmond clearly didn't think that remark worthy of an answer. 'I'll ask everyone to account for their movements,' he told Claudia, just a little testily, making it clear that while Mac might be Claudia's personal champion, *this* wasn't any of his business. He had quite recovered his aplomb, Mac noticed. Beneath that lugubrious, faintly subservient manner, the man had an ego as big as the Eiffel Tower and that made him uneasy. He'd read somewhere that the one thing murderers had in common was an over-developed sense of their own importance. 'But a lot of the staff won't be in until later.'

'They're the front of house people,' Claudia, intervened, in an effort to smooth things over. 'Box office, usherettes, programme sellers, bar staff. And on matinée days, like Saturday, there are cleaners as well.'

'Why on matinée days?' Mac asked.

'Think about it, darling. You wouldn't want to pay a fortune for a seat that was knee deep in someone else's ice cream cartons and chocolate wrappers, would you?' She turned on a mischievous little smile. 'And we don't like to provide dissatisfied customers with the ammunition with which to demonstrate their feelings, eh, Philip?' The man attempted a smile but it really didn't suit him and Claudia stood up, indicating the meeting was at an end. 'I'll leave it with you, Phillip,' she said. 'Has the replacement costume arrived?'

'It's in the office, with Angela and Pam. I didn't want to leave it unattended. The spares will be here by the end of the week. There's quite a bit of post, too; maybe you could look at it.' He glanced back at Mac. 'If you can spare the time.'

'No problem, I came in early for that very reason. Mac? Are you ready for that tour I promised you?'

'Sure,' he said, noting the switch back to *Mac*. He'd have to remind her that they had moved on, but in his own good time. 'There's no hurry if you have things to do. Why don't you look in at the office first in case there's anything urgent? Maybe Redmond could give you a hand.'

The idea of spending any more time in Mac's company clearly didn't fill the man with enthusiasm. 'Actually I'm needed up in the lighting gallery. There's some kind of problem with the new electronic board.'

'Then we won't keep you. Claudia?'

'Well, I would like to check my costume.' She slipped her arm through his. It was nice but Mac had the impression it was more for Redmond's benefit than for his. He caught her hand and raised it to his lips. That was for Redmond's benefit too. He wanted to check the man's reaction. There was none. Maybe that was because Redmond had learned his lesson. Or maybe he'd got a tighter rein on his feelings. Or maybe, Mac thought, he wanted the villain to be Redmond so much that he was simply letting his imagination run away with him. Claudia retrieved her fingers and kept them lightly tucked under his arm until Redmond was out of sight. Then she pulled away. 'I'm hoping to hear from Beau, too,' she went on, with a determined brightness that didn't fool him. She was still upset about what Phillip had said.

And she wasn't quite sure about what happened before Phillip interrupted them. He liked that. He wasn't exactly certain what was going on, himself. 'Your father?' he enquired. If she wanted to be businesslike he was happy to oblige.

'He's due back from the States any day and I promised to pick him up at the airport.'

'If you tell me where and when I'll organize a car for you.'

'Will you? I didn't think ferrying him about would come under the job description.'

He glanced down at her, outwardly so in control, but beneath the surface he could plainly see the welter of uncertainty clouding her eyes. It hadn't been there before. Or maybe it had. Maybe because of his new insight into her character he was just seeing her more clearly. 'Oh, I'll have to charge extra,' he informed her, his face as straight as a stick.

'Oh, well, in for a penny,' she said, carelessly. 'Just put it on the bill. Or perhaps you'd prefer to have your pick of my mother's "fabulous" jewellery?' she added, in a clear reference to his observation that her safety would be ample compensation for parting with a piece. She gave him an oblique look. 'I'm afraid none of my "couture frocks" will fit you.' Then, as an after-thought, she added, 'But don't take the diamond drops.'

'Why? Are they a particular favourite?'

'No. They're fake.'

He laughed. Her sex appeal had never been in doubt, but she had a sly sense of humour, too. In fact he was in grave danger of seriously enjoying Claudia Beaumont's company. 'Definitely not the diamond drops, then.' She had known he was kidding and she was kidding him right back. It was like being hugged. 'I'll remember.'

The office was the domain of two middle-aged ladies, Pam and Angela, who kept the accounts and the correspondence of the production company running like oiled silk. Mac was introduced, offered coffee and cake and generally fussed over.

He accepted the coffee, refused the cake and watched while the replacement costume was taken from its box and shaken out. 'It is so beautiful,' Pam exclaimed. 'The lace is just unbelievable.'

'You wouldn't believe the price, either,' Angela said, dryly. 'You'd better try it on, Claudia. Just in case it needs adjustment. Five minutes before curtain up will be too late. Would you like me to give you hand with the buttons?'

'Would you? Do you mind, Mac? It won't take a minute.'

'Ask him nicely and I'm sure he'll give you hand with the buttons himself, dear,' Pam suggested with a giggle.

Mac backed away in apparent horror, knocking over the telephone as he did so. The next time he gave Claudia a hand with her clothing he wasn't planning to have an audience. He bent down, picked up the telephone, made a point of checking that it was still working and grinning at his own clumsiness he replaced it on the desk. Then, his listening device planted and his main purpose in encouraging Claudia to go to the office achieved, he made his excuses. He was quite happy to have Claudia safely occupied for a while. He didn't want her to know about the bugs, but if he went around knocking over telephones it wouldn't take her long to guess what he was up to.

'Take all the time you need, sweetheart,' he said. 'I'll go and get that security badge from Jim.'

'I thought you were planning to stick to me like a tube of instant glue,' she protested mildly.

'You'll be safe enough here for a while. But don't go wandering off without me,' he said, his voice teasingly light for the benefit of the ladies. His eyes issued a much sterner warning for her alone. 'Not for *any* reason,' he warned, as she accompanied him to the door.

'What shall I do if I need the loo?' she enquired, making her eyes large and innocent.

'Cross your legs.' Then, because the office closely resembled the tropical house at Kew Gardens he added, 'Of course, if you get really desperate you could use the nearest plant pot.' He didn't wait for her answer, which he was fairly certain would be unprintable.

Jim, Mac discovered when he called at the stage-door office, was not averse to a little gossip. 'Phillip said you might have seen the woman who slashed Claudia's dress,' he prompted, as he made an apparently ham-fisted business of fastening the badge to his shirt. He'd noticed that few people were surprised that a big man should be clumsy.

'I saw *someone*.' Jim's shrug suggested there was more if he was interested enough to ask. But Mac didn't probe. Gossips just had to talk. Silence offended them. 'Of course it could have been one of the cleaners,' he added, after the pause went on too long. 'They come and go at such a rate you can't keep up with them.'

'You don't issue their IDs then?'

'I've got quite enough to do without that.' Jim didn't appear busy, but Mac was too polite to say so. 'The cleaning contractors issue IDs to their own staff.'

'Oh, right.' Mac glanced up as a light began to flash over the stage door and Jim lifted himself heavily out of his chair. 'What's that?'

'Someone's at the door. It wouldn't do to have people ringing a great loud bell whenever they felt like it, would it?' He sniffed at the ignorance of outsiders and left the office. Mac, who had been expecting the interruption, knew that the courier at the door would keep Jim thoroughly occupied for at least two minutes. Nevertheless he wasted no time in attaching a listening device to the telephone on the man's desk and when the door keeper returned bearing a package he was innocently contemplating an old framed poster of Elaine French and Edward Beaumont, who had apparently appeared together at the theatre twenty years earlier.

'It's a package for you, Mr MacIntyre. You know most of those couriers can barely wait long enough for you to sign once,' Jim grumbled, 'but this one wanted me to sign more forms than the tax man.' He waited, clearly expecting to be given chapter and verse of the contents, but Mac accepted the large padded envelope without comment. 'You'd think he was handing over the blooming crown jewels,' he prompted.

'Not quite the crown jewels, I'm afraid. Just something for Claudia.'

'Ah, well.' Jim's face softened. 'She deserves a treat after what happened on Saturday night.'

'I quite agree. But don't say anything, it's to be a surprise.' Surprise was right. The package contained the small recorders he needed to pick up transmitter signals from his bugs. He very much doubted that she would approve of what he was doing which was why he wasn't telling her. He certainly didn't want her warning anyone, her half-sister for instance, not to make calls they wouldn't want overheard.

'*Say* anything?' Jim responded with scorn. 'With women? When do you get the chance?'

'That was a nasty business with the dress,' Mac dropped in casually, giving him a chance to vent his feelings. 'I don't understand why Redmond didn't call in the police.'

'The police?' Jim laughed, although not with much humour. 'What would we want to bother them for? I'm sure Miss Claudia knows perfectly well who did it.'

'You think so?' Mac didn't need to act surprised. He might have his own suspicions that Claudia knew more than she was saying but Jim's casual comment, added to Redmond's earlier suggestion that she suspected who the culprit might be, was unexpected.

'With these actresses it's all up one minute and down the next. The *jealousy*. You'd have to see it to believe it.' He shook his head. 'I've seen girls trying to scratch one another's eyes out over a walk-on part. And the men are worse if anything. No,' he said, with the wisdom of someone who has seen pretty well everything in a long lifetime behind the scenes in the theatre. 'It's best to keep these things quiet. There's nothing to be gained from a lot of tacky publicity and it'll all blow over.'

'Will it?'

'Sure to.' Mac hoped the man was right, but he had a feeling that with the kind of media interest Claudia was generating at the moment, keeping it quiet would be easier said than done. He weighed the package in his hand, thoughtfully. If anyone in the *Private Lives* company decided to enrich themselves and enliven the nation's breakfast table with the story, they'd better not use any of the telephones in the theatre or they'd have to answer to him. 'Are you going out, Mr MacIntyre?' he asked as Mac made a move towards the door.

'Just to the car.'

'Then you'll need the code for the keypad to open the door.' Mac gave an inward sigh. He considered asking how often the number was changed, but he didn't. It wouldn't make any difference. A day after it had been changed it would be in the possession of an unquantifiable numbers of spouses, partners, friends and quite possibly chalked up somewhere in half the local fast food delivery services in the area. He hated door codes.

He collected a briefcase from the Landcruiser and then back inside asked Jim for directions to Phillip Redmond's office.

'Just down the corridor on the right,' he said. Then as an afterthought called after him, 'But Phillip's up in the lighting gallery at the moment.'

Five minutes later he was back in Claudia's dressing room, having placed his tiny transmitters on all the backstage telephones. He wasn't sure what he would pick up; probably nothing more exciting than orders called into the nearest pizza parlour on the coin operated telephone in the green room; Angela and Pam's calls would prove to be a mixture of business and homely personal calls; Melanie was an unknown quantity, he hadn't met the girl and as for Redmond . . . personal dislike was probably accounting for his hopes in that direction.

But in truth he was unlikely to discover anything of world shattering excitement. Claudia's cockroach hadn't yet stooped to using the telephone; he or she was probably only too aware of how vunerable the system was to eavesdroppers. But it was wise to cover all options. And covering all options was what he planned to do. But he still felt decidedly seedy as he attached one to Claudia's dressing-room telephone. Telling himself that it was for her own safety didn't make him feel any better about it.

The package that had been delivered contained a number of small voice-activated recorders each no bigger than a personal stereo and having tuned them

219

in he placed them back in the envelope and out of sight on top of the wardrobe. Judging by the amount of dust up there, it seemed there was little likelihood of them being disturbed.

Then he opened the briefcase he had brought in from the Landcruiser. It was packed with state of the art listening equipment to pick up the mobile phones. The recordings might overlap, but they could be unravelled by an expert. And he was an expert.

'What are you doing?'

He had heard the door open and closing the briefcase without obvious haste he turned to face her, holding out a small device for her inspection. Claudia was in the doorway holding her costume over her arm and staring at him, her face rather pale.

'I fetched this from the car for you. It's a panic alarm.'

She came closer to look at the small tube. 'Like a mace spray?'

'Carrying mace is illegal, Claudia.' And so is bugging telephones, his conscience reminded him. He ignored it. 'This just makes a dreadful noise when you push it. *Don't*!' he said, quickly, as she took it from him. 'Don't press it unless you mean it. But keep it handy.' Then, 'I thought I told you to stay put.'

'For how long? And anyway there was a message from Dad on the fax asking me to ring him. I didn't want to use the office telephone.'

He crossed to her, took her by the shoulders and gave her a very small shake. 'You know, Claudia, it might not have been me in here.'

'I know.' She looked down suddenly. 'Actually, you did give me a bit of a start.'

'Good,' he said. 'You deserved it. Now I'll leave you to talk to your father in private if you promise to stay here until I get back.'

'Where are you going?'

'Not far. Promise me, Claudia.'

She looked up at him with those huge eyes. 'Or you'll make me take my clothes off again?'

'You've got to take this seriously.'

'I do. I am.' She shook her head. 'Then it all just seems so silly that I can't believe there's any real danger.'

'I know it's hard. You don't want to believe it and I can understand that.' He released her, took the costume from her and held it up. 'But when you feel tempted to think all the precautions are rather silly, consider what happened to your costume, Claudia. Consider the possibility of that happening to you.'

'You can't really believe that.' But her dismissive laugh was uncertain. 'It's so . . . so melodramatic; like something out of *Maria Marten and Red Barn Mystery*.'

'Maria Marten was a real girl, Claudia. And she was murdered.' He waited for a moment until he was sure the unspoken threat had sunk in. 'Now promise me you'll do as I say or I'll make sure this theatre doesn't open tonight, or for the foreseeable future.'

'You wouldn't,' she declared. Then, less certainly, 'You couldn't.'

221

'You could put me to the test,' he invited. 'I almost wish you would, then I could take you to a quiet place in the country where keeping you safe would be a whole lot easier.'

'You mean that, don't you?'

'Yes.' In fact, the more he thought about it, the more certain he was that she was in very real danger. The trouble was, he thought, personal feelings were beginning to intrude, confusing concern with anxiety. But he wasn't prepared to take the chance. 'I've never been more serious in my life.'

Her shoulders slumped. 'I'm sorry, Mac. I'll do everything you say, I promise.' She looked so down that he put his arms around her and pulled her against his chest.

'Gabriel,' he murmured.

'What?'

'It's my name.'

She looked up at him, her fears momentarily forgotten. 'I know, but everyone calls you Mac. You said so.'

'Maybe they do. But you are not everyone.' He paused long enough for her to digest this information. 'And you promised you'd do everything I say?' He touched her lips, very lightly, with the tip of his finger. 'Gabriel,' he insisted.

'Gabriel,' she repeated, her voice barely above a whisper.

'Good, I'm glad we've settled that. Now I'll leave you to call your father,' he said, straightening. For a moment she looked confused. She had thought he was going to kiss her again. She was waiting for him to kiss her and something dead inside him reignited with the power charge from that knowledge.

He would kiss her. He would most certainly kiss her. But not yet. Certainly not here. Not, if he had any sense, until this nightmare was over.

He opened the door and looked back. She was standing where he had left her in the centre of the room, looking a little bemused, as if not quite certain where she was and what had happened to her, a million miles from the assured and confident star who'd invited him to play musical cars just a couple of days ago. Or perhaps not. 'Tell me, Claudia,' he enquired, from the doorway, 'are you familiar with *The Taming of the Shrew*?'

He didn't wait for her answer, but as he closed the door behind him, something hit it with great force before clattering to the floor. His laughter was drowned out by a sound so terrible that the entire backstage crew came at the run.

He beat them to it. Twisting the tube sharply to switch off the sound.

Claudia removed her hands from her ears and shrugged. 'I was just testing it,' she said.

CHAPTER 10

Something woke Gabriel MacIntyre and for the smallest fraction of time he froze, sorting out the messages bombarding his brain. Strange bed. Strange room. *Claudia*! Then he was out of bed, on his feet, his body on automatic as he tackled the intruder, his mind racing away to the other room where Claudia was sleeping . . .

But it was Claudia he cannoned into. Soft, warm, smelling like a dream in something silky that slipped beneath his fingers. Enticing, flimsy . . .

'Mac!' His name was expelled from her on a sharp breath as he pushed her back against the wall with the rush of his attack. 'Mac, let me go!'

She was backed against the wall, her arms pinned at her sides, her body yielding against his. The last thing on earth he wanted to do was let her go. He wanted to pull her back down with him into the warm cocoon of bedclothes, unwrap the silk and make love to her. The idea took a lot of resisting.

He managed it, just about, but he didn't immediately let her go. 'Gabriel,' he insisted.

'Come on, Mac,' she said, struggling ineffectually against him, 'this is ridiculous.' Ridiculous he might argue with, but it certainly wasn't wise. She was not doing her cause any good at all. 'For heaven's sake – ' she exclaimed, then realizing she had no choice but to obey him, she conceded. 'Gabriel,' she snapped, crossly.

'Try harder, Claudia.' The scent of her skin was undermining his good intentions and the bed was still very tempting.

She glared up at him. He smiled lazily back and he saw, in the semi-darkness, the very moment when she realized exactly what was going on, felt the stirring of his arousal against the smooth curve of her hip.

Her eyes widened slightly, the tips of her breasts tightened to hard peaks and her lips parted slightly as she cooled them with the tip of her tongue.

For a long moment the room was filled with a quiet so intense that the sound of his own heartbeat began to sound like a drum in his ears.

'Please, Gabriel,' she said, her voice mostly breath.

Very slowly he took his arms from about her and straightening, let her go. Equally slowly, it seemed to him, she eased away from him, backing along the wall so that they were no longer touching. Then she took a long, slightly unsteady breath and looked up at him with eyes that should carry a health hazard warning. 'Tell me, Gabriel, did you forget to pack your pyjamas?' she asked, her voice shaking noticeably. 'Or do you always sleep in your skin.'

'Did you want something, Claudia?' he demanded brusquely, his voice thick with gravel. 'Or are you just sightseeing?'

'Sightseeing?' She blinked, swallowed, fixed her gaze firmly on his face. 'I thought I'd better give you a call,' she said, quickly. 'I'm due at the television studios at six thirty. For an interview.'

'What!' he demanded, grabbing a sheet from the bed and wrapping it about him.

'I forgot to tell you last night.'

He couldn't believe it. 'And when did you remember?'

'When I was in bed.' She had been going to tell him. She'd made it as far as his bedroom door, but had lost her nerve. She hadn't wanted him to think . . . well, what he would have had every right to think. 'There didn't seem any point in disturbing you.'

'Lady, you could disturb a three-toed sloth with a look.'

'Could I?' He was no slouch in that department himself and making a slightly nervous gesture in the direction of the night table, Claudia began to back out of the room. 'I . . . um . . . brought you a cup of tea.'

'Well, thank you, Miss Beaumont,' he said, following her, the sheet looped negligently around his waist. 'I surely do appreciate that.'

'We haven't got a lot of time . . .' She gestured vaguely behind her. 'I won't be long in the shower.'

He put his hand on the wall, blocking her exit. 'We could save time by sharing it.'

'Could we?' Her voice was so low that it was almost non-existent and there was a dewy ache between her thighs. Then she caught the glint of something close to amusement in those dangerous blue eyes and she stiffened. 'I don't think so.' And she ducked beneath his arm and beat a hasty retreat.

That would teach her that coming uninvited to a man's bedroom, smelling like heaven and looking like sin when his defences were down, was not the brightest move, Mac thought, a touch wryly. He'd learned quite a bit himself.

She kept coming so close, he thought, dwelling on the lingering image of enticing lips parted over small white teeth, her eyes uncertain as they had searched his face. So meltingly close that all it would take would be one touch to set her off. Dynamite.

Then she backed off like a nervous kitten. In fact, for a lady with something of a reputation for wildness, Claudia Beaumont seemed oddly reticent about embarking on a bed and breakfast flirtation. Or maybe it was just him she objected to. Which was probably as well, he thought, pushing himself away from the wall and closing the door with rather more regret than he would have anticipated. Because he'd lied about the shower. It wouldn't save time. But it would have been a damn sight more fun than an early morning call to a television studios.

The thought brought him to a halt. *Fun*. He couldn't remember the last time he had even thought

227

the word, let alone seriously considered indulging in the experience.

He'd have to go, Claudia decided, as she caught sight of Gabriel MacIntyre's razor laid on the bathroom worktop. She towelled herself dry with a quite unnecessary briskness. There was just too much of the man. He overflowed all over the place, all over her apartment, all over the theatre, all over her life. She could hear him now, moving about in the kitchen, making himself quite at home.

And he would keep scooping her up. And kissing her at the slightest excuse. Her lips burned with the memory of the way he had kissed her in her dressing room. *Like a lover.* She glanced at herself in the mirror, all dewy eyed and idiotic, for heaven's sake! She wasn't fooled by *that,* was she?

She wasn't averse to having men fall in love with her, in fact she rather liked it. She had almost come to think of it as her right. But she didn't encourage expectations of a more physical kind.

What about Tony, her subconscious probed, unkindly. Claudia sighed. She had been so naïve about Tony. She thought he had genuinely liked her when he must simply have been taking sex for granted. Why else would a married man have bothered?

Why else was Mac bothering?

It wasn't as if she'd given him encouragement of any kind. Quite the reverse. Most men who'd been very publicly slapped would have backed off and you wouldn't have seen their heels for dust. But then Mac – no, *Gabriel*, she corrected herself carefully – wasn't like most men. He had a careless arrogance that set him apart. They shared that same cavalier disregard for the opinion of others, Claudia realized, if nothing else.

Except, of course, she *did* care. She just wasn't prepared to let it show. When people saw that you cared, they could hurt you.

She let herself out the bathroom. 'It's all yours,' she called, as she crossed the hall to her bedroom.

He appeared in the kitchen door with the sheet still looped casually about his waist. It was breaking all the laws of physics and defying gravity. But only just. 'What is?' he asked, with look that was clearly calculated to provoke her.

You see, she told herself, closing the bedroom door with a crisp little click. Give him an inch and he'd help himself to the entire tape measure. And if she wasn't very careful she would be the one left measuring out her foolishness in heartache.

The sooner this mess was cleared up and he was on his way, the better. If only she could think of someone who might want to make her life a misery.

It wasn't as if she'd snatched any plum roles from beneath the nose of some other actress. She pulled a face. At least not lately. If anything, it had been the other way around. She'd lost a part in a film because the leading man had wanted his latest girlfriend to have it. But that had been partly her fault too. As her agent, and her father, had both pointed out in an unnecessarily sanctimonious fashion, if she'd signed the contract on the dotted line instead of pushing for a better deal, they wouldn't have been able to switch her at the last minute.

Then a series of chocolate commercials had been cancelled.

She had suggested to Mac that Luke had twisted her arm to appear in *Private Lives*. The truth was that at the time she was glad to do it. And then the television series had fallen into her lap at the last moment. She paused, one leg in a pair of exquisite wide-legged russet trousers; she'd replaced Joanna Gray at the last moment because Jo had broken her arm skiing just before filming was due to start. She might be feeling resentful . . .

Claudia stopped, horrified at the direction her thoughts were taking. Joanna was an old friend from RADA; they'd worked together, partied together, flirted with the same men. And she was a professional. Joanna knew that film companies couldn't wait while broken arms healed. She certainly wouldn't be petty enough to blame her own misfortune on her replacement, or spiteful enough to write poisonous letters. They'd had lunch together just before the weekend and Jo had gone out of her way to reassure her about the wretched parachute jump when Claudia had made her promise she'd step into her role in *Private Lives* if she broke her leg, or worse.

Claudia fastened the trousers, slipped on the long, straight collarless jacket and lifted the collar of her pale peach silk shirt so that it stood up a little. Then she caught her hair back at the nape of her neck with a comb. Elegant, but casual, she thought, pleased with the result. After-dark glamour for breakfast television was so tacky.

Leaning towards the mirror to double-check her light make-up, she realized it hadn't covered the shadow of the bruise on her cheek. She shrugged. She was certain to be asked about the parachute jump and it would provide a talking point. She just hoped no one asked her about Mac . . . *Gabriel*. She'd better not get that wrong again. Why was she finding it so hard?

What on earth had made her call him that in the first place? The way he had held her, the way he had kissed her. *Like a lover.* She recoiled from the word. Was she going quite mad? A tap on the door saved her from the embarrassment of answering herself.

'Good grief,' Gabriel exclaimed as she opened the door.

'That bad, huh?'

'You look fabulous. In less than fifteen minutes. How on earth do you do it?'

She wasn't sure whether to be pleased with the compliment, or cross at his assumption that it would take hours to make herself look presentable. She settled for neutral. 'I've had years of practice, Gabriel.' See, it wasn't so very hard was it? 'The ability to transform yourself into someone else is part of the job. You don't have hours when the performance is live.'

He frowned. 'I hadn't thought of that.'

'So?' Her eyes flickered quickly over the close-fitting denims, the soft linen shirt he was wearing. He looked pretty good himself. Whatever had made her think of him as roughhewn? 'Are you ready?' she asked.

'You should have some breakfast before you go.'

Nobody had been that concerned about her since she had waved goodbye to her last nanny. It was unexpected, a little unnerving. The man had a way of getting to her, but she couldn't afford to be soft.

'Should I?' she asked. 'One of your bacon door-steps?'

'Don't mock, breakfast is the most important meal of the day.'

'That depends who you're having it with.' She threw the words away carelessly enough, but as she deliberately put the distance between them, her throat closed tight. Don't make a fuss of me, she begged silently. Don't pretend to care.

His jaw tightened noticeably. 'I made some toast.'

'How domesticated of you. I never could get the hang of that toaster,' she said dismissively. 'But they'll give us a proper breakfast at the studio. Provided we're not late.'

He glanced at his watch. 'We've got plenty of time. I'd like to call at the theatre on the way. I left my briefcase there last night and if I'm going to be sitting around half the morning waiting for you, I might just be able to get on with some work.'

'Not half the morning.' She managed a smile. 'And I can promise you, darling, you won't be doing much sitting around today.'

'Oh? Is there something else you've forgotten to tell me about?'

'I don't think so. I did mention that I have a late night chat show – after the performance tonight?'

'Yes, you did.' She spread her hands out, as if that was sufficient explanation. 'So?' he demanded, apparently unable to make the connection.

'*So* I need a new dress. *So* this morning I'm going shopping.'

He exploded. 'No. Absolutely not. I forbid it.'

'*Forbid it*?' she repeated, her voice dangerously low.

He must have realized that it was a mistake to challenge her because he immediately changed his tactics. 'Be reasonable, Claudia.' He was learning fast, she thought. 'I can't possibly guarantee your safety while you trawl the shops . . .'

But not fast enough. *Trawl the shops, indeed*! 'I need a new dress, Gabriel, not a parcel of herring.'

'For heaven's sake, you must have something suitable.' He didn't wait to be told, but strode across to the wardrobe and flung open the door while the protest was still forming in her head. 'There,' he said, as if he had proved his point. 'It's full of dresses.'

An exaggeration. It was full of *clothes* and there were quite a few evening dresses, but nothing right. 'I need a new one.'

He wasn't so easily persuaded, but pulled out the first one he laid his hand on. Then he looked at it and swore, very softly. It was that kind of dress, a bright red sheath of clinging material that shimmered from her breasts to her ankles. It was, in fact, the dress she had planned to wear, but she had decided, when she had looked at it last night, that she didn't feel quite comfortable in it any more. He must have felt the same way about it, because he quickly pushed it back, grabbing for the safety of a little black number.

'I don't think so,' Claudia said, regarding the once treasured dress dispassionately. 'It's a style that's become rather *passé*.'

He considered it. 'It does have one thing in its favour.' She raised an enquiring brow. 'If the slasher had a go at it you could just add a few more safety pins and no one would ever . . .' She could actually see the moment he realized he had put his foot in his mouth. Right up to the ankle. 'You're right,' he said. 'You are in desperate need of a new dress.'

'I knew you'd understand. But you don't have to come with me. I was going to ask Melanie to keep me company.'

'Considering the size of my mouth I consider that a most generous offer, Claudia. But I'm afraid I do have to come with you. I promised – '

'Luke,' she completed for him. 'I knew I should never have left you two alone to gang up on me.'

'It wouldn't have made any difference if you'd been there.'

'You really believe that?'

'You're just so used to getting your own way, Claudia, that you think you can ride roughshod over other people. It doesn't always work. I promised Luke I would look after you and that's what I intend to do. Whether you like it or not.' He paused, offering her the chance to argue, but she didn't take it. She knew when she was on a hiding to nothing. And apparently satisfied that he had made his point, he replaced the black dress in the wardrobe and closed the door.

She might have been put very firmly in her place, Claudia decided, but honours were just about even, since she had won over the shopping trip and because of that she was prepared to be generous. 'There'll be no crowds, I promise. Just a few little boutiques. And just to prove how much I appreciate it, I'll take you out to lunch.'

He muttered something under his breath, but he made no further objection to her plans. Claudia tactfully kept her smile of satisfaction to herself, but mentally she chalked it up as a definite win on points.

While Claudia did her stuff for the television cameras, expertly fielding questions about rumours of romance, telling the viewers what it was like to step into her mother's shoes and take over a role she had made her own, Gabriel MacIntyre listened to the tapes he had collected from the theatre.

As he anticipated, there was nothing of earth-shattering interest. Certainly nothing that appeared to threaten Claudia, although that didn't mean anything very much. Only that if someone inside the theatre wished her harm, they were too bright to tell anyone else, at least on the telephone. Disappointingly, Phillip Redmond's calls were strictly business.

He left the tape from Claudia's telephone until last. He found the idea of eavesdropping on her private calls particularly distasteful, but if she did suspect who was involved and was protecting the culprit out of some misguided sense of loyalty, he had to know.

He didn't discover anything about the attacker, but he did discover something else. Something that made him smile. Claudia had suggested to her father that he should go and see Diana, because her pub and the village green were ideal as the location for a new television programme he was planning. And she had suggested Heather might be used in some minor role, a kindness the girl scarcely deserved.

Shopping was a nightmare. In the linen-fold panelled study at Winterbourne Manor it had seemed easy to rationalize his promise to Luke Devlin to look after his sister-in-law. He had his own reasons for wanting to know who had managed to get to her parachute; after all, a security company that couldn't keep its own premises secure wouldn't be in business for long.

236

And Claudia's security wouldn't be a problem. He'd assign someone reliable, install CCTV cameras, intercept her calls and mail and within a week it would all be over.

Then he'd heard himself telling her that the best way to handle close security was for him to move in with her, play the lover for a media panting for the story and throw the anonymous letter writer off the scent.

It had sounded right. He had apparently convinced her. He must have convinced himself because until half an hour ago, Gabriel realized, he had believed it. But the minute he had walked into a Knightsbridge boutique he had recognized the sham for what it was. He would never, *never* have come into a dress shop with another client. He'd have summoned up female reinforcements and retired to a safe distance; there were plenty of well-trained women who would have jumped at the chance to show him what they could do when it came to close protection.

But he discovered that he wasn't prepared to trust Claudia's safety to anyone else, even when it meant he had to sit on a small, spindly-legged chair while Claudia explained exactly what she had in mind to the frighteningly elegant woman who owned the boutique.

'It's not your usual style, Claudia.'

'I know, Lucy. But I think I'm getting a little bit tired of shocking people just for the sake of it. The trouble is whenever I attempt elegance I'm always compared with my mother. Unfavourably.'

'No one can compete with perfection. I know everyone was raving over that photograph of you, but I'm not at all sure it was wise of you to pose for it, even if it meant you were on the cover. You're not a bit like Elaine French.'

'Not perfect?'

'There's something so unnerving about perfection, don't you think? You should be concentrating on your own image, Claudia.'

'It's my image that's bothering me.'

'I'm inclined to agree that you're getting a little bit old to be playing the *enfante terrible*.'

Claudia didn't take offence at this remark. She'd once heard Lucy tell a twenty-year-old she was too old to be wearing white *broderie anglaise* frills. 'It's why I've come to you, Lucy. I need to reinvent myself and I trust your judgement.'

'Reinventing yourself takes time. Unless you do it gradually people are inclined to notice and snigger. Of course you could get married and produce an infant.' Lucy glanced at Gabriel sitting on the far side of the boutique, looking decidedly ill at ease. 'The tabloid press are such suckers for motherhood.'

'Don't even think it.'

'No? Pity. In that case you'd better come through to the fitting room.' She nodded in Mac's direction and raised her voice slightly. 'Will he let you out of his sight for a few minutes? Or shall we have him in to help with the hooks and eyes?'

238

Claudia couldn't quite meet Gabriel's eyes. 'I think between us we can manage.'

'Good, this could take some time and your man appears to be something of a draw.' Lucy looked around at the unusually large number of women who were apparently browsing through the day wear and then smiled at Claudia. 'I don't suppose you'd rent him out by the hour?'

'Mr MacIntyre is a free agent. Why don't you make him an offer?' Hopefully one he couldn't refuse.

For their shopping trip Mac had used the discreet taxi service he favoured, unwilling to risk parking problems and when Claudia emerged from the fitting room without any evidence of having found anything to suit her, he sighed and called it up on his mobile.

'Don't look so desperate. I've found exactly what I wanted, but it needs a tuck. Lucy will send the dress over when it's done. Now,' she said, as they stepped out onto the sunny pavement, 'it's time for lunch.'

'We should get back to the flat. I'll make you an omelette,' he offered, in an attempt to persuade her to behave.

'How tempting.' Her smile was positively wicked. 'But I've booked a table at my favourite restaurant and no one's going to do anything stupid in such a public place.'

He recognized a certain look that he was getting to know rather well. It suggested, quite forcibly, that an argument would be futile. And she was probably right.

Tactics so far suggested the kind of man who crept around in the dark to do his dirty work. A fashionable restaurant, and he was certain that the restaurant would be fashionable, was the last place he would attack.

The light airy atmosphere of the place reassured him and the tables were far enough apart for him to see anyone coming. 'Don't look so tense, darling,' Claudia murmured as they were shown to a table in the window. He wasn't so happy about sitting in the window.

'Anyone could see us here,' he complained. He'd expected to be somewhere in the centre of the room, lost in the crowds.

'That's the point. We're an attraction, that's why we've been honoured.'

'It's an honour to be gawked at while we're eating our lunch?' He wasn't convinced. 'Anyone would think you were trying to draw attention to yourself. What have you got arranged for this afternoon? A quiet bungee jump at Tower Bridge? A nude swim in the Serpentine? A sponsored – '

She laid a hand over his. 'A quiet lie-down in a darkened room with you guarding my door, darling. We can discuss which side of it over lunch if you like.' Then she stood up.

Still open-mouthed at her ability to take him by surprise, he rose quickly to his feet. 'Where are you going now?'

'To powder my nose. Would you like to come and watch?'

'This is ridiculous, Claudia. You're not making any effort to co-operate with me. I absolutely insist – '

'Shush, darling. People are looking.'

'Isn't that what you want?'

'The more people who are looking, the less likelihood that my personal fiend will attack, don't you think? He seems more like a hole-in-the-corner operative to me.' And, having apparently read his mind, she swept from the table, stopping at a number of tables on her way through the dining room to pass the time of day with people she knew.

Mac subsided into his seat. She was right of course. He'd already admitted as much to himself. But she seemed to take enormous pleasure in winding him up. He sat back, shaking his head at his own foolishness. She kept winding him up, because he kept giving her the key.

He glanced out of the window. It was like sitting in a badly equipped goldfish bowl, he decided; there wasn't even a strand of waterweed to hide behind. And there were several photographers outside; he recognized two of the men who had been outside the theatre yesterday afternoon. It seemed Miss Claudia Beaumont was actively courting publicity. Was it her way of poking her tongue out at whoever was tormenting her, saying, 'You can't scare me. See?'

Brave. Idiotic, like poking at a nest of wasps with a stick, but brave. He looked across the room. She had emerged from the ladies' and was talking to a girl, her back to the entrance of the restaurant. He watched her for a moment, enjoying her easy grace, the fluid movement of her hand as she made a point, the way she tilted her head so that her hair, loose now from the comb, swung about her shoulders. He smiled. She might be the most infuriating woman he had ever met, but she was by far the loveliest.

As he watched her, something, some slight movement behind her caught his eye. It was a man, tall, slightly built with floppy fair hair. For just a moment he thought it was Tony and something inside his gut seized with jealousy. But it wasn't Tony. As he realized his mistake he began to relax, watching the man as he approached Claudia. Then his mouth went dry.

Something about the way the man was moving, a certain stealthiness, caution, rather like a cat stalking a mouse, sent warning rockets up his spine and he didn't stop to consider the consequences, but shouting a warning, Mac launched himself across the dining room, grabbing the man by the throat just as he reached out with both hands for Claudia, and slamming him back against the wall. Then before he could speak he yanked him around and twisted his arm hard up behind his back. The man's squeal of pain was the last sound heard in a restaurant where even breathing suddenly seemed too loud.

'Explain yourself, mister.' The words were rapped out into the astonished silence and the patrons, forks laden with food poised halfway to their mouths, held their collective breath. But although the man's mouth opened, nothing came out of it. Mac shook him a little, just to show he meant business, but all it produced was an anguished squeak.

'Come on, Claudia,' Mac demanded. 'Help me out here. Do you know your little cockroach?' She didn't answer and he turned to her. She was staring at him, dumbstruck with shock and horror. She did know him, Mac realized, with a visceral feeling of hopelessness. The whole thing had been nothing but some stupid lover's quarrel. He should have known. All along he had been telling himself that she was trouble. Why on earth he should be so surprised when he was proved right, heaven alone knew.

Claudia shook her head. She couldn't believe what was happening. She tried to say something, but her vocal chords seemed to be glued together and for a moment all she could do was wave her hands, trying to get Mac to let poor David go.

'No,' she finally managed. Then, because he didn't seem to understand what she meant, she managed to croak out, 'Stop it, for goodness' sake.' She pulled at his arm, hanging onto his shirt-sleeve in an attempt to get him to loosen his grip. 'You're hurting him.' Mac was staring at her. 'Let him go.'

'Let him go?'

'*Please*, Mac,' she begged. 'Before you do him some permanent damage.'

'You do know him, then?'

'Yes, of course I know him. We've been friends for years.' And as Mac released him, she put her arms around David and led him to a chair, motioning to a waiter. 'A brandy, quickly,' she rapped out before turning back to David. 'Darling, are you all right?'

He winced as he sat back in the chair. 'I'll live. And I'm sure the feeling will come back to my arm in time.' He flexed his fingers as he looked up at Claudia, his expression decidedly rueful. 'But that's the last time I creep up behind you to give you a surprise.' He jerked his head in the direction of Mac. 'He's a big chap. Protective.'

'He's nothing but a big brute.' She glared up at him. 'What the devil did you think you were doing, Mac?' The entire restaurant appeared to waiting for his answer as were the photographers who had managed to ease themselves in through the door with the help of hurriedly produced bank notes. Claudia scowled at them too. 'What do you vultures want?' she demanded.

One of them, realizing that it was all over bar the shouting, grinned at her. 'We were rather hoping that Mr MacIntyre was going to hit Mr Hart.'

'I'll hit *you* if you don't clear off,' Mac said, through gritted teeth.

'That would do,' one of the other photographers encouraged, hopefully.

'Would it?' He took a step in their direction and as one they backed away.

'Haven't you done enough damage, Mac?' Claudia hissed. 'Please, go away. Just go away.' She was close to tears, but since she refused to cry for the entertainment of the public unless she was playing someone other than herself, she turned to the hovering *Maitre*. 'Can someone get me a cab, please, Lawrence. David, will you let me give you a lift home?'

'No, really. I'm fine. Why don't you stay and have lunch with me?' he invited.

'Because she's having lunch with me,' Mac intervened. 'And since she's got some explaining to do, I suggest we get on with it. So you can forget the cab,' he said, addressing the *Maitre*.

Claudia stood up. 'Lunch?' she repeated, as if it were a foreign word that she hadn't used herself thirty seconds earlier. 'Do you really think I'd have lunch with a man who would cause a scene in a restaurant?'

'Since it will ensure you get your name in the papers, I don't see how you could possibly resist,' he said angrily, taking her arm to lead her back to the table.

But she stood her ground, shaking him off. 'I can resist, Gabriel MacIntyre. It's dead easy. Just watch me.'

She stormed out of the restaurant, hailed her own cab and had the door open before Mac had disentangled himself from the crush at the door and managed to catch her. 'In,' he said, pushing her in front of him. Then having given her address to the driver, he joined her. 'Now tell me what's going on. And who the devil is David Hart?' he began without preamble.

'You really are a blithering idiot, Mac,' she declared. Tears were stinging at her lids, but she was damned if she would let him see. She clenched her jaw and stared out of the opposite window.

'Without a doubt. If I had half a brain I'd have seen that coming. You set me up, didn't you?'

'Set you up?' She turned and stared at him.

'Christ. I can't believe I could have been so naïve. Right from the start I was convinced this whole thing was just a stunt, but I let you kid me on, draw me in . . . when is it going to hit the headlines, Claudia?'

Stunt? Headlines? What on earth was he talking about? And then she knew. For a moment the words hung on her lips, furious words, desperate to spill out and tell him what it was like to have someone you loved think you were a liar.

Loved? A sob quivered on her lips. *Loved*? Oh, no. *Oh, no, not that.* She couldn't have that. Love wasn't something she could handle. And he'd given her a way out. A simple way out.

She buried the sob. Blinked back the tears. Shrugged eloquently. 'You're right of course. It is all an elaborate stunt. David will be explaining everything to the newsmen right now.' She glanced away out of the window. 'How you are simply my minder and you attacked him because you thought I was in danger. A simple misunderstanding of course, but by tomorrow my agent will be besieged and by Friday I might be persuaded to meet the press and tell them how I've been hounded by a stalker . . . just like the girl in my new series.' The little choked sound that came from her throat might have been for dramatic effect. Or maybe it wasn't. But it did the trick.

Mac was staring at her, the blue of his eyes shaded to leaden fury. 'Good God, Claudia, I ought to put you over my knee and spank you.'

She lowered her lashes in a perfectly judged characterization of the vamp. Her voice was more difficult, her throat was tightening with misery and it took every ounce of technique to give it that warm, husky sound. 'Shall we wait until we get home, Gabriel?'

And that apparently, was enough. He leaned forward and rapped at the glass partition. 'Stop here.' The driver pulled over and Mac stuffed a note in his hand as he climbed out. 'That should cover it.' He turned and stared at her for a moment, a slightly puzzled look creasing his forehead. 'You never answered my question.'

Question? She couldn't remember any question. Only answers. And every one of them wrong. 'Which question was that, darling?' she murmured.

'Who the devil is David Hart?'

CHAPTER 11

Claudia stared at Mac. She couldn't believe the nerve of the man. After everything he'd said, how did he dare to stand there and insist she tell him anything? He'd demanded *her* trust and she'd given it, wholeheartedly. But when the chips were down he hadn't trusted her a centimetre further than he could throw her. Not even that far.

How *dare* he accuse her of ensnaring him for her own manipulative purposes? *He* was the one who had insisted she was in danger. Yet after all that had happened to prove him right, one stupid misunderstanding had driven him to the conclusion that she had been lying to him all along, using him to generate publicity for her new television series. He hadn't even given her a chance to explain, he'd just leapt in with both feet. Size elevens if she wasn't mistaken. Not that he'd had so far to leap.

It had to be a publicity stunt, didn't it? She was an *actress* for goodness' sake, and it had been his first thought when he had found the photograph in the

248

parachute. He hadn't seriously believed she was in any danger, he hadn't considered advising her that this might not be the best day to leap out of an aeroplane, he hadn't even contemplated the possibility that it might just be a *joke*, even if it was one in very poor taste.

Well, his first thought would have to be his last thought too, because she'd had enough of his tyrannical behaviour. She didn't *need* him to manage her life. She'd been doing pretty well since she was eighteen years old; she didn't need a man to hold her hand.

Publicity of all things! She still could hardly believe it.

Good grief, hadn't he seen for himself that she didn't need any tricks? Publicity followed her like the hem of her skirt because of who she was, who her mother had been. She'd been surrounded by it since she was a babe in arms. She lived with it because it went with the territory but she hated it. Hated the fact that no matter what she said or did, the newspapers printed the interpretation that suited them best. Hated that they never gave her any credit for what she had achieved . . . only harked back to her mother, compared her to her mother, continually suggested that she owed everything to her mother . . . She hadn't realized just how much she had hated it until now.

But Gabriel MacIntyre hadn't seen. Like everyone else he was fooled by the myth, assuming she must revel in it, that publicity was her life-blood.

Yet even while he was insulting her, accusing her of using him, he still demanded to know who David was. As if, because he had kissed her, he had some right to know.

She had thought he was stronger than that, that he had seen beneath the scaffolding she had erected to keep the world at bay. How could she have been so stupid? Why should he be different?

He was still glowering at her from the pavement, waiting for his answer. Well he could wait. Because as far as Gabriel MacIntyre was concerned, she'd was clean out of answers.

'Drive on,' she rapped out, and the cabbie didn't need telling twice, whipping the taxi out into the traffic. Claudia sat back and sighed as she wondered what had happened in the restaurant after they left. She would have to telephone and apologize. And she would have to ring David too. Poor David. What terrible luck to walk into Gabriel MacIntyre when his macho aggression was firing on all cylinders. She'd heard the way he had hit the wall, the rattle of expensive dentistry. It would serve Mac right if David sued. That would give him all the answers he wanted.

She closed her eyes, hoping to blot out the entire incident. It had been so *idiotic*. David was a dear, kind man, but he had that silly habit of creeping up behind his friends, putting his hands over their eyes and saying, 'Guess who?'

The moment she had heard Mac's warning shout and swung round to see David behind her she had realized what was happening, but it had all taken place at such speed that she had been quite powerless to stop it. Gabriel, fired up on anonymous letters, slashed dresses, car tampering and already unhappy about her insistence on going shopping, had thought her life was in danger. She caught her lower lip as she recalled the effect on the other diners as, Rambo-like, he had hurtled across the restaurant to save her. Because he'd thought her life was in danger.

She gave a little sniff. 'Damn!' she said, searching in her bag for a handkerchief as a tear trickled down the side of her nose. One minute he was prepared to risk life and limb to save her life, the next he had been accusing her . . .

Well? What had she expected? She knew better than to believe in happy endings. 'How stupid!' she declared.

'Did you say something, miss?' the cabbie, asked, half turning.

'No.' She shook her head. 'Nothing. Nothing at all.'

Good grief, she was *talking* to herself, completely losing her grip on reality. Was that what falling love did to you?

Love? The word seemed to leap out of thin air and hit her, taking her breath away. *Love*?

Claudia shook her head as if the physical denial would make it go away. It didn't and she balled the handkerchief in her fist, holding it to her mouth as if that would help stop the word. Love. How could she ever doubt it? Gabriel MacIntyre had filled her every waking moment since she had set eyes on him. Why else, for heaven's sake, would she have slapped him if she hadn't been so disturbed by his kiss?

But there had been so many other things to disturb her that it had been easy to explain away all the oddities in her behaviour during the last few days, her agitation, her jumpiness, a heightened sense of her surroundings and emotions. The fact that when he had taken her into his arms and kissed her like a lover, she still hadn't seen the danger. The trouble was, she had made such life career of avoiding love that she hadn't recognized it when it had slipped beneath her guard and tapped her on the shoulder.

Twenty-seven years old and never fallen in love. She sniffed again. No, that wasn't quite right. She had seen what love could become and so she had never *allowed* herself to fall in love. She had hung on to her heart, resisting every temptation to take her foot off the bottom and swim out of her depth.

Relationships she could handle. She was an absolute whizz at them. Light fun, with no strings attached, certainly not a razor permanently parked in her bathroom. The trouble was, men just didn't see it that way. Suddenly they all wanted to settle down and play happy families.

Well, she had been there, done that. 'Miss Beaumont, the actress's daughter', had seen enough of that game to last her for a lifetime. Not that there had been any shortage of eager young actors knocking at her dressing-room door over the years. But they didn't want her, only the publicity that she could give them. Perhaps that had been Tony's appeal; she knew he didn't just see her as an easy way to get his photograph in the newspapers. Rather the opposite as it turned out. She must be getting careless.

Terribly careless, because when Gabriel MacIntyre had kissed her she hadn't seen the danger. And now, at last, she understood why she had found it so easy to resist the siren lure of love and marriage when all around her had succumbed. She had just never met the right man before. The trouble was, Mr Right was now convinced that she was hopelessly, hopelessly wrong.

Damn. Damn. Damn.

'We're here, miss.' How long had they been standing at the kerb? She blinked back the tears welling in her eyes, put on the blazing smile that came so automatically and the driver leaned back and opened the door for her. Claudia, though, was reluctant to abandon the safety of the cab for the unknown and she stared up at the façade of the building with a sudden clutch of nervousness.

But there was no help for it. There she was. On her own. It was what she had kept saying she wanted and since she liked nothing better than getting her own way, Claudia knew that she should be feeling pleased with herself. But she wasn't. She was assailed by a crushing, bone-deep misery.

And she was scared. Maybe that was all it was, this hollow feeling? Just fear? She clutched at this straw for hope. For the last few days she had been put through the emotional wringer, it was hardly surprising that she didn't know whether she was coming or going, was it? *Love?* What on earth was she *thinking* about?

She had simply overdosed on Gabriel MacIntyre. It was hardly surprising. He had insisted on sticking to her like glue, even when she told him to get lost. Now, suddenly, she was alone, having to face her apartment without him and she was scared.

Even when he was driving her crazy with his over-protective attitudes, he had been there and she had felt safe, his presence a bulwark against the threatening world.

'The gentleman paid, miss,' the driver said, encouragingly. 'More than enough.'

'Oh, yes. Good. Thank you.' The meaningless words tumbled out as she stepped down and then turned to watch the big black cab drive away. She watched it until it disappeared around a bend in road and her very last link with Gabriel MacIntyre had gone. No. It wasn't just fear. She couldn't fool herself that easily.

'Claudia?' Kay Abercrombie was standing on the front steps. 'Are you all right, dear? Only you've been standing there for rather a long time.'

'Have I?' She knew she was smiling because the corners of her mouth were beginning to hurt with the effort. But at least she was smiling. So long as she kept doing that no one would know she was suffering from a strange new malady that she didn't know how to deal with. 'Just daydreaming, I'm afraid. It's a terrible habit.'

'Do you think so? Oh dear, I'm afraid I do it all the time. Now, before I forget, I was looking out for you because I've got a package for you.' Something wobbled inside Claudia. A package. A letter. It wouldn't matter. She would never be able to open one again without a sick feeling, a feeling that someone who meant her harm could reach out and touch her with his grubby little mind simply by putting an envelope through her door. 'It came by courier,' she said, stepping back to let Claudia into her flat. 'It's marked urgent.' Claudia saw the label and realized that it was a television script her agent had promised to send her. Relief made her feel a little giddy but Kay didn't appear to notice. 'Mr MacIntyre didn't come back with you?' she enquired, apparently disappointed not to see him. 'He's *such* a gentleman. He helped me with my suitcase, you know.'

Claudia thought it was a pity that Kay hadn't been home when the first anonymous letter had been delivered. Nothing got past her. 'He was rather concerned that you had let him into the building without knowing who he was,' she said.

'He did warn me to be more careful, but he was so charming.' *Oh, really?* Then Kay Abercrombie gave a little sigh. 'Still, I suppose even burglars are kind to their mothers.'

Claudia, her nerves in shreds, her emotions strung out like a line of wet washing, was suddenly overcome with such a frightful urge to giggle that she had to turn it into a cough.

'My goodness, Claudia, that's sounds terrible. You should look after yourself better. I've got a very good linctus if you'd like some? Or I find lemon and honey very soothing? I brought some wonderful honey back from Wales last week, let me fetch you a jar – '

'No, no. Thank you, Kay, but I have everything I need. Really.' Well, not quite everything. But you couldn't *have* everything. Life wasn't like that. It was a balance of small compromises. To have one thing you sometimes had to give up something else. Gabriel had told her that. She hadn't believed him at the time, but she suddenly saw what he meant. Independence meant making sacrifices. Love meant sacrifice too. If you were lucky you were given the choice. She lifted the package. 'Thanks for taking this in. Now, if you'll excuse me?'

'Oh, yes dear. Don't let me keep you. But if you want that honey you will say?'

'I promise.'

Claudia ran up the stairs to her flat and without waiting to worry about what might be on the other side unlocked the door and stepped inside. It was quiet. Absolutely quiet. She keyed in the new code on the burglar alarm and then, with grim determination, shut the front door. She was alone. And that was how she wanted it. It was how she had always wanted it.

Except of course that everywhere she went there was some evidence of Gabriel's presence. A pile of cold toast in the kitchen. His razor mocking her from the bathroom shelf. The spare bedroom showed no trace of his presence, however; the was bed neatly made, his clothes put away. She opened a cupboard, touched the neatly folded shirts, wondered briefly who had ironed them so thoroughly. Claudia realized just how little she knew about Gabriel MacIntyre. And it was all she would ever know. A small anguished cry escaped her lips and she turned and fled from the room, throwing herself down on her bed, dragging the quilt up and over her head.

Something brought her crashing from a dream in which unseen monsters snapped at her heels. It was the telephone. A new monster, unexpectedly threatening. For a moment she listened, petrified, then furious with herself, she flung herself at it on shaking legs. Before she reached it the intercept clicked in and the tape machine began to record. It was nothing more threatening than the television company wanting to know if she needed a car to pick her up from the theatre and to take her home after *Late Date*.

What had she expected? Whispered threats? Heavy breathing? The whole thing had got out of proportion. Whoever had been tormenting her had obviously been scared off by Gabriel MacIntyre. She didn't need his protection any more, she told herself, she didn't *want* it. He would have to come back to collect his clothes; well he could collect everything else as well. But not while she was there. She wouldn't be able to look him in the face and pretend.

She had the number of his mobile phone, but she didn't want to speak to him either. She could ring Tony . . . No. She couldn't ring Tony. He was in enough trouble already and she didn't want Adele upset again on her account, even if Gabriel was wrong and she had been the one to cut up her photograph and stuff it into the parachute pack.

Then she spotted the card that Mac had given her by the telephone, the one bearing the number of his 'secure' taxi service. They seemed to pass messages along fast enough, Claudia remembered. She could call them. Now. Without stopping to consider the wisdom of her actions, she grabbed the telephone, dialled the number and began to speak the moment the call was answered.

'This is Claudia Beaumont,' she said, quickly. 'Will you please tell Mr MacIntyre that he can collect his belongings while I am at the theatre tonight. I'd like him to disconnect his electronic equipment at the same time. Oh, and he can leave my spare keys in the kitchen. He knows where. I'll expect an itemized account for his services in due course.'

Silence greeted this shaky outburst. Then, very softly, 'I'll see to it, Claudia.'

Gabriel? His voice shivered through her, there could be no mistake. Had he been expecting her to ring? Waiting for her to ring? She opened her mouth but couldn't think of anything to say. And then it was too late, because all she was listening to was the low burring of the dialling tone.

Gabriel MacIntyre cut off the call with his finger while he was still able to, then slowly replaced the receiver.

'Was that her?'

'Yes. It was her.' He turned away, unable to face his sister's inquisitive eyes and stared out of the window. 'You know you really shouldn't be here, Adele,' he said, not wanting to talk about Claudia. 'You should be resting.'

'If I was any more rested I'd be unconscious.' She was lying back on an old sofa, cushions at her back, a notepad propped on her pregnant stomach, the telephone within easy reach. 'You can have no idea how boring resting can be. And I've got my feet up, see?'

He turned obligingly and stared at her. 'Where on earth did you find that dreadful piece of furniture? No other employer would put up with it.'

'There isn't another personal assistant in the country that would put up with you. Besides, you're not just any employer, you're my brother. And I'm on maternity leave.'

'So you keep telling me, with monotonous regularity. So why are you here?'

'Your temp seems to think you work a three day week so I suggested she find somewhere more suited to her social engagements.'

259

'It won't work, Adele. I've told you I won't have you back once the baby's arrived and I mean it.'

'You don't have any choice, Mac. Having a baby isn't an adequate reason for you to sack me. I'm entitled to keep my job.'

Refusing to get into an argument with her, he changed the subject 'Where's Tony?'

'He's flown to Amsterdam. Due back in time for supper. Which, by the way, he'll be making.'

'You've still got the poor dab on a regime of repentance, then?'

'I might have known you would sympathize with him.'

'I know better than to take sides but I know you and I know Tony. Don't be too hard on him, little sister, that baby you're carrying needs two parents.'

'Oh, I'm not that hard on him.' Her smile was catlike. 'He gets to rub my back after he's washed up and done the ironing and I'm sure you think he should be doing those anyway. After all, they're a lot harder work than answering your telephone. What did the glamorous Miss Claudia Beaumont want?'

Glamorous. What a catch-all adjective to describe someone like Claudia, Mac thought. It was a tabloid word, a meaningless label. Claudia Beaumont was a whole lot more than glamorous. 'She wants me to move my things from the flat while she's at the theatre tonight.'

'You mean she hasn't got the nerve to face you? To apologize for what she's done?'

'Oh, she's got nerve, Adele. Buckets of it.' He glanced at her. 'You'd like her. You've got a lot in common.'

'You mean apart from my husband?'

'She doesn't have Tony. She never did. She just needed someone to play a part . . .' He didn't want to think about that, about how far she would have been prepared to go to keep him hooked. Whether it would have mattered whether it had been him or Tony. 'I simply meant that she agrees with you. Like all modern women she thinks that the right place for a baby is in some efficiently run crèche so that the mother can get back to the really important thing in her life; her career.' His jaw worked convulsively. 'She even went so far as to suggest I find one for you.'

'Mac, I'm not Jenny. You can't punish me because of what she did . . .' But he refused to respond to Adele's gentle reproach and heard the small sigh as she let it go. 'Well, maybe you're right, maybe she'd be an ally. I have to admit, she's got the male side of the family all sewn up. I certainly never thought I'd ever see my big brother kissing an actress on television.' Her wide blue eyes were pure innocence. 'You really looked as if you meant it, too.'

'Did I?' He turned back to the window. 'Well, fourteen thousand pounds takes a lot of earning.'

'You're telling me it was hard work?' she teased.

'I'm not telling you anything.' But his sister was right. He had meant it. His hands gripped the sill. He

261

hadn't realized until it was too late just how comprehensively he'd meant it. But there was one thing he needed to say. 'Claudia didn't know Tony was married,' he said.

Adele knew better than to point out that this was the third time he had changed the subject in as many minutes. 'Would it have mattered?' she asked, doodling idly on the pad.

'Oh, yes. It would have mattered.' He knew that. He'd seen her face when he'd told her. It would most certainly have mattered. She had a moral code of sorts. Unfortunately it didn't extend to the use of idiotic men who went out of their way to make things easy for her.

'You're very quick to leap to her defence considering the way she's treated you.'

'She's got her faults, but that's not one of them.'

Adele heaved herself to her feet and joined him at the window. 'It seems she's found herself a champion, Mac. I hope she's worth it.' She glanced at his hands, noted the whiteness of his knuckles. 'Tell me about her, she must be something rather special.'

Something rather special. He'd certainly thought so. Before he discovered that he was being dangled like bait by her publicity machine, that when she kissed him she was simply ensuring his undivided attention for as long as she wanted it. And it had worked. She had it. He watched absently as a twin-engined plane touched lightly down on the runway. 'It looks as if Tony couldn't wait for supper.'

Adele knew her brother too well to push him. But she knew he was hurting. It was enough to make her wish she *had* chopped Claudia Beaumont's photograph into little pieces, but she said nothing, simply looped an arm through his, hugging it as they watched the taxiing aircraft. 'I do like a man to be eager. I asked him to bring me some tulips. Do you think he remembered?'

Mac glanced down at her, a small frown puckering his forehead. 'Isn't it the wrong time of year for tulips?'

'Oh, yes, but it's a test of his ingenuity and creativeness.' Her smiled became enigmatic, mysterious. 'If he's clever, it could be his lucky night.'

'Then, for his sake, I hope he lives up to your expectations.'

'So do I, Mac. So do I. Shall I switch the phones over to the night service before I go?'

'Yes, if you would.' He turned and looked at his desk. 'Was there anything in the mail that needed my attention?'

'No, it was pretty much routine stuff, nothing I couldn't handle. Security sent over a list of people who were checked onto the airfield last week. They said you had asked for it?'

'I did,' he said, refusing to gratify her curiosity. But it no longer mattered. The mystery was solved. Cleared up. Tidied away. He'd done everything that was expected of him when he had publicly assaulted David Hart, right on cue. His only regret was that he

263

hadn't actually hit the man, laid him out on the carpet. He caught himself rubbing his fist into his palm. It was the second time in as many days he'd wanted to hit someone because of Claudia. 'But it's not urgent.'

'Isn't it? They seemed to think it was. Well, it's on your desk. Oh, and there's an envelope marked "personal", but it's from your garage so they're probably trying to tempt you into buying a new four wheel drive. Now that you've battered the Land-cruiser.'

'Then they're out of luck. I've booked it in for repair.'

Adele was standing in the doorway watching him. 'Are you all right, Mac?'

'Fine, sweetheart. I'm fine.' He made himself smile. 'Don't keep Tony waiting.'

Adele lingered in the doorway anxiously so he turned to his desk, picking up the envelope with its enticing 'personal' sticker and ripping it open. 'You're right,' he lied, 'it's an invitation to test-drive their latest model.'

'They never miss a trick. I'll see you tomorrow, then.'

'No, you won't. I'm going to tell security not to let you back on the airfield. Of course you could try climbing the fence . . .'

She would have risen to this challenge before her pregnancy. Now, scarcely able to climb the stairs, she stared at him in absolute fury for a moment before flouncing off as he had known she would. With any luck she'd go and cry on Tony's shoulder. It would do them both good. He raised his head from the report he was holding to watch her slow progress across the hangar. Perhaps flounced was not quite the right word. She was waddling. In the manner of an outraged duck.

As he watched her, he remembered the confident way that Claudia had handled Heather. How would she handle this problem, he wondered? He rather wished that he could ask her advice. Then he called himself every kind of fool, because even if he could, Claudia wouldn't help him. Her sympathy would be with Adele.

He looked down at the paper in his hand. It was the report he'd commissioned on Claudia's car and he opened it up. Not that it mattered any more. It was just that he was interested to know what kind of risk she was prepared to take in the pursuit of publicity. Probably not that much.

He'd thought she was crazy to go ahead with the jump after receiving an anonymous death threat. That alone should have sent the warning signals to his brain. Except that from the first moment she looked up at him with those big silver eyes his brain appeared to have taken a holiday, leaving the thinking in the doubtful care of his libido. And his libido had been having a field day.

He scanned the report from the garage. It was inconclusive. Well, after the scene at lunchtime, he had expected nothing else. It was certain that brake fluid had been escaping before the accident. There appeared to have been a badly fitted connection, there were scratches that suggested it had been adjusted since the car had left the factory and it had most probably jarred free when she drove across the speed bumps at the entrance to the airfield. In the inspector's view, Miss Beaumont's car should be replaced without cost to her or her insurance company, and a claim should be made directly against the garage for damage to Mr MacIntyre's property. Miss Beaumont would no doubt take legal advice about claiming for distress and injury caused by negligence.

Mac thought about the car Claudia had been driving. It wasn't some mass produced vehicle, but had been hand-built by craftsmen and there was a waiting list of years to get hold of a new one. A badly fitted connection seemed extremely unlikely. The manufacturers would certainly say so and once their engineers had looked at the brake line they would, he imagined, tell Miss Claudia Beaumont and her claim for negligence to go and take a running jump.

But he doubted that the manufacturers would ever see the car. Or that any claim would be made. He hoped the television company's publicity budget was a healthy one because it seemed to him, in the light of his newly-acquired hindsight, far more credible that some bright mechanic had been waiting a mile or two up the road from the airfield to loosen the joint. He'd seen the fresh tool marks for himself, marks that had sent him racing to warn her of the danger she was in.

He tore the report in two and dropped it in the bin. He'd leave his insurance company to fight out who paid for what; he didn't want to get involved.

He'd momentarily lost his head, behaved out of character; he hadn't even questioned Devlin's sincerity when he had asked him to look after Claudia. He'd swallowed the deception like a hungry fish because he'd wanted to. He'd wanted to keep her safe, to protect her, to cherish her; all those things and more, much more. Which was quite remarkable considering that when he had stood over Jenny's grave he had promised himself he would never involve himself again with a woman driven to achieve, so driven that she couldn't think of anything or anyone else, not even her unborn child.

His body was racked with a convulsive shiver and for a moment Mac closed his eyes as the pain skewered through him. He knew that Claudia must be driven by some desperate demon. It must take a special kind of selfishness to use people the way she had used him, he thought. A special kind of vanity. And knowing that should make it easy to walk away.

But it wasn't. He still longed to hold her, to hear his name on her lips.

Furious with himself, he slammed his hands flat on the desk and stood up, sending the chair crashing back. He'd had his marching orders and it was time he got on with them. He'd collect his gear from the flat and then wait until Claudia left the theatre so that he could retrieve his listening devices and the recorders from her dressing room. Under the circumstances it would be just as well if no one ever knew they had been there.

'Claudia? Are you feeling quite well?'

Melanie's obvious concern drew Claudia from her bleak contemplation of her reflection. Did she feel quite well? No, she didn't feel quite well. She didn't feel even the teeniest bit well. She actually felt as awful as it was possible to feel and still be walking. And on stage tonight it had showed; she had been about as animated as a sleepwalker. The rest of the cast had worked twice as hard to cover for her but nothing could have disguised her lacklustre performance.

'I'm sorry, Melanie. I was dreadful tonight.' Melanie began to protest, but she brushed her half-sister's objections aside. 'Don't pretend. I know when I'm bad and tonight I was bad on a global scale.'

'You're being terribly hard on yourself.'

'Am I?'

She saw Melanie struggle briefly with the need to reassure her and the truth. The truth won. 'We're all entitled to an off night.'

'An "off night" in the theatre isn't quite the same as a bad day at the office, Mel. A typist could have another go at getting things right, but the people who paid good money for their seats this evening won't come back another day to see if I'm on better form.'

Mel sank into the basket chair beside the dressing table. 'What are you going to do?'

'I've already done it. I called Joanna Gray during the interval. She knows the role, we're much the same size and she can take over tomorrow for a week. There'll be a rehearsal in the afternoon at two.' She smiled reassuringly at Melanie. 'You'll like her, Mel, she's great fun.'

'I'll hate her. And she couldn't possibly be as good as you. But I do think you're doing the right thing; you've been on edge for days.' She lifted her shoulders in a barely perceptible shrug. 'Even before that business with the costume. Dad came home today, didn't he? Will you go and stay with him? Or with Fizz?'

'No. I'm not going to Broomhill. I haven't actually decided where I'm going, but it'll be a very long way from here,' she said, with feeling. 'Somewhere without theatres, or newspapers, or men.'

'Oh, you mean a *convent*,' Melanie said.

Claudia stared at her for a moment then burst out laughing. 'I think that might be overdoing it a bit,' she declared, 'but it's a thought.'

'Overdoing it? You think of somewhere else – ' Claudia held up her hands in mock surrender and Mel let her off the hook. 'Will you be able to get out of doing publicity for the new series? You're doing something tonight, aren't you?'

Claudia groaned and glanced at her watch. 'I'll have to do it too, it's too late to cancel. But as for the rest, well, I'm sure conjecture about my sudden withdrawal from society will excite the public every bit as much as my appearance on any chat show you care to name.'

'Oh, *Claudia*!'

'You don't believe me? Watch this space, kid. You'll see speculation on a scale that will make your teeth curl.' She stood up. 'Now I really must shower and get ready for my appearance on *Late Date*. Are you busy, or do you want to come along for the ride?'

'Me? Where's the gorgeous Gabriel MacIntyre tonight?'

'Not here. Tonight or any night. I told you, darling, he just wanted the name of my insurance company.'

'Sure. And I'm a wallaby's aunt. What happened?'

'Nothing that you won't read about in tomorrow's newspapers.'

'Oh, *Claudia*!'

'Have a care, sweetheart, you're beginning to sound a touch repetitive. Now, are you coming with me? Or have you got something more exciting to do?'

'What could be more exciting?' Claudia gave her an old-fashioned look, but didn't argue; she was too grateful for the company. 'And I can't wait to see you in your new dress.' She glanced at the pale blue silk crêpe halter-necked gown hanging over the wardrobe door, sexy but incredibly elegant.

'Then you're going to be disappointed. It was a terrible mistake, not my style at all. And you know the programme, it absolutely screams for something . . . well, you know.'

'Yes, I do. I guess it's the red dress, then?'

'Give the lady a coconut, she's won first prize.'

It was over.

He had removed every sign of his presence from her flat, disconnected the electronic surveillance equipment that guarded the doors and telephone and then moved on to the theatre to reclaim his bugs and recorders.

It had been the work of moments, but he'd been glad to get out of the place. The centuries old timbers had creaked and strained as they settled in the quiet and although he wasn't superstitious, it didn't surprise him that most theatres claimed a ghost. He'd been startled enough himself when he'd heard a crash and a muttered curse that echoed eerily through the wings until he had realized that it had come from the lighting platform and that, on calmer reflection, he knew the voice. Phillip Redmond had said they had a problem up there and he was obviously taking the opportunity to work on it while the theatre was empty. He offered the man his silent apology for all the bad thoughts he'd harboured about him.

It was over.

Mac dumped his bag on the sofa that Adele had been occupying a few hours earlier and then noticed the light blinking on the answering machine and touched the play button.

Adele's voice broke the silence. 'I'll bring a pair of wire cutters,' she declared, without preamble, then hung up. He smiled wryly at her defiance. He might have known his sister wouldn't let him have the last word.

He unpacked the bag he had carried in from the car, removing the tapes from the recorders, putting the surveillance videos to one side before returning the hardware to the secure store at the rear of his office.

Then he considered the tapes. He ought to look at the videos, listen to recordings from the theatre. He didn't want to, he was certain there wasn't any point. But he couldn't just wipe them. It wouldn't be professional. Finish the job properly, he promised himself, and then it really would be over.

There was a television with a VTR in the corner of the office and he crossed to it and turned it on before bending down to slot in the video.

As he straightened he came face to face with Claudia, her lips softly parted as she laughed at something the show's host had said to her, her hair tossed about her face in an artfully dishevelled style that made her look as if she had just tumbled out of bed, her shoulders pushed forward in an expressive shrug that offered the tantalizing valley between her breasts to the camera's greedy gaze.

And the bright red dress that this morning hadn't been good enough for the show, was now clinging seductively to her body as he had known it would the minute he had set eyes on the wretched thing.

Over? While he could still remember how she felt in his arms. While he could still remember the taste of her mouth, the aching clamour of his body. Who was he kidding?

Mac stretched out his hand to switch channels, but then something else caught his eye. The long diamond drops swinging from her ears as she tilted her head to laugh at something the man sitting next to her was saying. Were they really fake diamonds? For a fake temptress? What else?

He snapped the button, unable to bear it as she flirted with the men around her and the screen fizzed temporarily before the recording began to roll.

It was not the usual kind of security video used by stores: flat, black and white and so fuzzy that it had little real use except as a deterrent. His equipment was concealed, it recorded in good quality colour and anyone who came close enough to be picked up would be identified.

Most of the comings and goings were the tenants of the block. He and Claudia were the first to make a move, just before six. After that it was quiet for a while, Claudia lived in a fairly quiet side street and there was just the occasional passing pedestrian. A few cars and delivery vans.

Nothing.

He ran the second tape. A messenger came with a package for Claudia. Kay Abercrombie signed for it. Then a taxi drew up and Claudia got out. She stared after it for a long time until Kay called her. And when she turned, she looked . . . unhappy. Something inside him twisted painfully. He didn't want her to be unhappy.

Then as she disappeared inside the building he called himself every kind of a fool.

Nothing else happened. Then he stopped the film. There was a van parked on the other side of the road, the driver, wearing a deeply peaked baseball cap that hid his face, was just sitting behind the wheel. How long had he been there?

He rewound the tape.

CHAPTER 12

'Darling, you were sensational!'

Claudia barely stopped herself from flinching as Charley Long, the host of *Late Date*, flung himself at her to kiss her effusively on both cheeks. He might think she had been sensational, she knew that she had been outrageous.

She had flirted with the show's host, she had flirted with the other guests, she had exposed more bosom than she cared to think about and had lived up to her image, or down to it, with a fervour that, now the show was over, made her feel positively sick. And to make matters worse Melanie was looking at her as if she was a stranger, someone she didn't know any more.

It was hardly surprising. Claudia scarcely recognized herself. But since being herself didn't seem to impress anyone half so much as being the person they all seemed to think she was, did it matter?

'We're going on to a party, darling,' Charley was saying. 'You are going to come, aren't you?'

'A party?' The last thing on earth she felt like doing was going to a party. But she didn't want to go home either because when she got home everything of Gabriel would be gone. Her apartment would feel empty in a way that it never had in all the time she had lived there alone. 'Fantastic!' She turned a blinding smile on Melanie. 'What about you, Mel, do you want to come along?'

'It's awfully late, Claud,' Mel said doubtfully. 'Don't you think you ought to go home?'

Her sister's pretty face was creased in concern but Claudia didn't want anyone to be concerned about her. 'No one is forcing you to come, darling,' she said, just a touch sharply.

Darling. Could that false tone be catching, she wondered, from some cold miserable spot deep inside her, along with the shallow posturing, the pretence? Did it even matter since it was simply a game and no one was fooled by it, no one hurt by it? Only the real thing could hurt. She was just beginning to understand how much.

Charley slid his arm around Claudia's waist and pulled her against him. She hated the feel of his soft hand squeezing her waist, hated the overpowering muskiness of his aftershave. Hated everything about him that was so different from the hard-edged physique and the outdoors scent of Gabriel. But Gabriel didn't want her. Gabriel thought she was capable of lying and cheating and anything was better than facing that, facing up to the fact that she would never see him

276

again, never be held as if she was something special, never know what it would be like to love someone who loved you in return.

So she let Charley in on her smile. 'I'm sure this dear man will look after me. Won't you, darling?' she prompted.

'It will be my pleasure,' he murmured reassuringly.

Melanie was anything but reassured. 'Do you really want to go? I just thought – ' she began, but Claudia didn't want to hear what she thought.

'Don't think, Mel.' Claudia leaned forward to lightly touch her sister's creased forehead with the pad of her forefinger, using the opportunity to ease herself out of Charley's clutches. 'Thinking will give you wrinkles.' And looping her free arm through Melanie's she squeezed it. 'Just for an hour, hum?'

'Just an hour, then,' Melanie agreed, giving in with a barely perceptible shrug. 'Someone had better come along an look after you.'

It was nearly three hours later when they pulled up outside Melanie's flat. 'Why don't you stay with me tonight, Claud?' Mel glanced meaningfully at the young man driving the car, but Claudia was apparently oblivious to the hint that it might be advisable to shake off her amorous companion while she could.

'I'll be fine. This sweet boy will see me to my door and he shall kiss my hand for his gallantry. Off you go, now. I want to see you inside before we drive away.'

Mel gave up and Claudia breathed a sigh of relief as the door closed behind her. 'Now, James. Home, I think.'

'My name isn't James, it's Nigel.' There was a touch of petulance in his voice and Claudia turned and stared at him. She loathed men who took themselves too seriously. Especially when they were young and rather silly men who had done nothing to justify their seriousness. Under her disparaging scrutiny he suddenly discovered a need to clear his throat. 'Of course, if you prefer calling me James . . .' he conceded, with something that in a girl would have been described as a giggle.

She didn't even bother to answer. He'd given her a lift home because he'd wanted to be seen leaving the party with Claudia Beaumont. Well, he'd been seen and he'd been photographed and if he was lucky he might get his photograph in the newspapers. If that wasn't enough, he'd discover that sometimes charity had to be its own reward.

'Just down here on the left,' she said, and sensing that he was about to pounce, she had her hand on the door even as they pulled up. But the door was wrenched from her hand and she almost fell out as it was opened without ceremony from the other side. 'What the –?' she began, but never finished her furious demand as two strong hands caught her and hauled her out of the car, dumping her onto the pavement. Then she was looking up into the blazing eyes of one seriously angry man.

'Where the hell have you been, Claudia?' Mac demanded, giving her a sharp little shake. She didn't care about that. All she cared about was that he'd realized his mistake and he'd come back. That he was waiting for her.

Her heart was racketing with excitement, with something so close to joy that she couldn't bear to trust it, refused to trust it.

'Gabriel, how unexpected,' she murmured, her attempt at indifference somewhat marred by the tremulous shake in her voice. 'I thought you'd already said everything this afternoon.'

'Did you? Then you were wrong. I've been waiting here for hours.'

'On the pavement? Don't tell me you were defeated by your own locks? Or did Kay take your warning to heart and refuse to let you in this time?'

'For God's sake, Claudia, I've been worried sick about you. Where have you been?'

Worried? The joy swelled. He'd been worried sick about her! 'I've been to a party. After the show. The chat show, that is. You'd have enjoyed it.'

'I doubt it.' He looked so fierce, deep lines chiselled into his cheeks, his brows drawn down in a dark line. Did it mean that he was jealous? If it had been anyone else she would have enjoyed his discomfort, but she didn't want Gabriel to be jealous, she wanted him to know that she loved him, she just didn't know the right words because she'd never told anyone that before.

'James very kindly brought me home.' She indicated the agitated young man who was practically hopping from foot to foot behind her, not knowing quite what to do, but certain he should be doing something and this gave him his opportunity.

'Look here,' he began. Then, squaring up to Gabriel, he said, 'You can't just – '

But Gabriel was not impressed. 'I can and I will. It was good of you to see Claudia safely home, James, but we won't keep you,' he said without ceremony and taking Claudia's elbow he urged her towards the front door.

'My name is *not* James.' He trailed, somewhat petulantly, after them. 'It's Nigel, Nigel Thomas.'

Mac glared at him, clearly thinking the man was quite mad. 'Well goodnight, Nigel Thomas,' he said, without breaking his stride. And when they reached the door, he turned the searchlight of his attention on Claudia. 'So,' he began, 'tell me about David Hart.'

'David?' He *was* jealous. Claudia, hands shaking, knees giving a fair imitation of warm jelly as she retrieved her keys from her bag, glanced up at him.

Gabriel took the keys from her and opened the front door. 'Yes, David. Is he your press agent? Or just an obliging friend?'

She just hated the way he said 'friend'. It gave her a very bad feeling. The day had been long and stressful and despite that initial leap of pleasure at seeing him, she had a terrible feeling that it was about a get a lot worse. 'I thought you'd already made your mind up about that.'

But he wasn't interested in what she thought. 'Tell me, Claudia. Am I just being made a fool of here, or should I be worrying about you?' Suddenly his anger seemed far more important than the fact that he was standing on her doorstep at three in morning, desperate to see her because he was worried about her. And it occurred to her that he wasn't angry because she'd arrived home late with another man. He was angry with *her* full stop.

The bad feeling was more than justified, she decided. The rush of warmth that had swept through her at seeing him, at hearing him say how worried he had been as he waited for her to come home, ebbed away, leaving her chilled right to the bone. 'You don't have to worry about me, Gabriel. I'm quite capable of looking after myself.' After all, what was the odd nasty letter compared to someone telling you face to face that they thought you were a liar, a fraud? Someone you loved. 'And as it's been a very long day,' she observed, 'you'll understand that I have no wish to stand here on the doorstep playing your silly games – '

'My games? You're the one playing games, Claudia, and since you weren't too tired to go partying until all hours, despite getting up at dawn for the television show and despite your shopping trip afterwards, you can spare me two minutes to tell me exactly what is going on.' His gaze swept over the seductive red gown and his lip curled back in disapproval. 'You can start by telling me what happened to the new dress that you simply had to have this morning? Was there a dress? Or was that all just part of the performance, part of the wind-up to get me good and edgy for the *coupe de grâce* at the restaurant?' He stepped back, releasing her so suddenly that she staggered slightly in her high heels, holding his hands up as if touching her might in some way contaminate him. 'My God. I've fallen for it again, haven't I?' He continued to stare at her. 'I watched that surveillance video and suddenly I was so certain . . . God, what an idiot I am. He was put there to keep me interested, wasn't he? The guy in the van watching the flat? You keep trailing these enticing lures and like a hungry pike, I keep on getting caught. Why?' He was staring at her now with an expression so dark that it sent a shiver up her spine.

'I don't think I can answer that question for you, Gabriel.'

He brushed aside her answer with an angry gesture. 'You know what I mean. Why are you doing this to me? Haven't I done enough for your personal publicity crusade?' Claudia turned away, heartsick at his undisguised contempt, unable to listen any more, but he blocked the way with his arm.

Claudia, her hopes so cruelly raised for the briefest of moments, felt her heart break as surely as if it was made of glass. She didn't know what he was talking about, but it was clear as day that she had got it wrong again. He hadn't come racing back to her to say that he was sorry, to ask her to forgive him for even thinking she could be so false.

282

He'd been lying in wait for her because he wanted more answers. More bloody answers. Well, she didn't have any answers for him and she didn't know anything about a man in a van, but she knew how to get rid of Gabriel MacIntyre. It was easy.

'Why? Because you're a gift, Gabriel.' Claudia was hurting so much that she needed to strike back, so she invested her voice with a deep husky warmth, using his given name because she knew in some deep pocket of her soul that he'd hate that most of all. 'You respond so beautifully to the slightest suggestion of danger . . .' She didn't know exactly what had sent him rushing back to her, so she kept it vague. 'Offer you a clue and you're like a bloodhound after the scent. I knew it would bring you running back – ' she stretched out her hand and clicked her fingers – 'just like that. Am I a clever girl, or what?' She looked about her. 'It's just a pity there's no one about to see your performance.'

Mac lowered the arm that blocked her way and taking her hand in his, dropped the keys he was holding into her palm before stepping back, leaving her alone on her doorstep. Then he stared at her for one long moment before he turned on his heel and strode across the road to the four wheel drive parked opposite her flat.

He smashed his fist against the bonnet. He'd been so stupid. Again. What was it about the woman? She had addled his wits, driven him crazy. He'd been right all

283

along, from the very beginning, he just hadn't wanted to believe it. Couldn't bear to believe it.

Yet something about the man watching the flat had been so disturbing. He'd been there all day. Not in the same place. He'd moved up and down the street, first one side and then the other, avoiding the traffic wardens, not wanting to become too obvious. But he was always watching the flat.

But Claudia had admitted that it was all a publicity scam. So he'd left his office and gone back to the empty soulless flat that had no memories, determined to forget all about Miss Claudia Beaumont. Put her out of his mind. But his mind refused to co-operate. It just kept running a scenario where she went home late at night and when she walked in, the man in the baseball cap would be there, waiting for her in the darkness.

Mac knew it was stupid. He'd changed the locks. He'd changed the code of her alarm. He'd at least made her safe from casual intrusion.

But suppose the kindly old lady downstairs had been persuaded to let someone in? If he was polite, convincing, she wouldn't think twice. How would he do it? Tell her that Miss Beaumont had called the managing agent's office to complain of a leak. In workman's clothes, with the right bag, she wouldn't even ask for ID. And if she did, he would have had something convincing to show her.

He opened the car door and slumped into the seat, glancing up at the window where she was probably right now laughing her socks off. She had made a fool of him and he had let her do it. Then he shook his head. No. *No.* That wasn't right. She'd simply gone along with what he had said, just the way she had this morning.

He was so damned confused. She'd admitted it was all a stunt . . . but she had been angry with him. And suddenly he wasn't sure what she had been angry about. If it had been because he had misjudged her, because he had leapt to the wrong conclusion . . .? He had seen how sensitive she was when her moral integrity was challenged. And she was volatile, she would have reacted without thinking of the consequences; she was quite capable of leaving him to think what he liked and let the devil take the consequences. And if that was the case, she'd *still* be in danger.

But she wasn't. He was the one reacting with his emotions instead of his head. In fact, he was in desperate need of a cold shower. His hand was shaking slightly as he reached forward to put the key in the ignition and he let it fall. Several cold showers. He opened the window to let in some fresh air, sat back, glanced again up at her flat. Her light hadn't come on. He watched for a moment, but her windows remained dark and his gut contracted. It was the same feeling he had whenever he thought of her in danger. The feeling that had sent him rocketing up the M4 without a thought for the speed limit. The feeling that had kept him cooling his heels outside her flat until the small hours of the morning.

285

He reached forward and started the engine. Her light still hadn't come on but it probably meant nothing, except that she was standing behind her curtains in the dark quietly enjoying his vacillations, maybe hoping to tempt him to come up and check that she was safe. Yet he still couldn't bring himself to drive away and leave her alone in the dark even when he knew that to ring the bell because he needed to reassure himself, was to invite ridicule.

What was the matter with him? Why on earth was he still sitting there? Her new locks would take too long to pick for even the most skilled locksmith to take the risk of discovery. Her alarm would have sounded if she hadn't switched it off by now. She had the personal attack alarm he had given her.

Then, quite suddenly, he began to laugh because he knew what had happened. She had forgotten the new code for the burglar alarm. She was standing outside her flat door trying to remember it, knowing that if she got it wrong it would wake the street, bring out the police . . . It would serve her right if he left her there.

But he wouldn't.

He eased himself out of the car and crossed the street to the front door and rang the bell.

There was no response. After a moment he frowned. That was odd. Even if she had got inside, she must know it was him. Surely she wouldn't miss the opportunity to gloat . . .? Some inner instinct for danger raised the tiny hairs on the nape of his neck.

The same instinct that had sent him diving for cover when a sniper had lined up on his head . . .

He jammed his finger onto the bell, holding it down for the count of five. When there was no answer he knew that his instincts were right.

'Claudia!' he called. 'Claudia!' And then he was pounding on the door with his fist, punching at the bell with his thumb, still shouting. Lights began to come on in windows up and down the street and he stepped back to look up at her window, but there was still no sign of life. 'Claudia!' His voice sounded desperate even to his own ears now and he swung again at the door with his fist. But this time it opened to the pressure, swinging back. And Claudia was clinging onto it as if for dear life.

Her mouth was working, but there was no sound. Great silent wrenching gulps of breath were being gasped in but she couldn't catch at them. And in the streetlight, her hair and face were wet, soaked with something that was the same colour as her dress.

'You can come in now, Mr MacIntyre. Miss Beaumont is asking for you.'

The sense of relief that she was well enough to speak was like being given a new life. He'd been driven from the emergency room by a sharp-tongued nurse who'd told him to wait in the day room, but the hour that he'd been waiting had seen more like ten. He'd called Luke who had promised to find Edward Beaumont and tell him what had happened but after that he had nothing to do but berate himself for ever doubting her, blame himself for what had happened.

'How is she?'

'Sleepy. She's been given a sedative, so if you're planning on talking you'd better be quick. Down the hall. Third door.'

Claudia was lying in bed, one side of her face and neck covered in angry red blotches. And great chunks had been hacked from her glorious hair. She was so still that he thought for a moment that she was asleep. Then she turned her head and looked at him.

'Gabriel,' she murmured drowsily. 'I wasn't sure you'd stay.' She thought he'd go away and leave her alone after what had happened. Well, why not? Hadn't he left her when she needed him most? 'I wanted to thank you.'

'Thank me? For what?'

'Being there,' she whispered.

'But I wasn't there.' If he'd been there this would never have happened.

She reached out and took his hand. 'Yes, you were. If you hadn't rung the bell just when you did I would have had a face full of paint, it would have been in my eyes, my nose, my mouth. It could have been a hundred times worse.'

If that was true she'd been lucky. They'd both been lucky. 'Did you see anyone?'

'No.' She yawned. 'I sat on the bottom of the stairs for ages trying to recall the new code for the burglar alarm. I was so tired I just couldn't remember whether you had said five seven or seven five and I knew if I got it wrong I'd wake the whole street . . .' She raised her hand in a gesture of helplessness. 'I finally decided it was seven five – '

'It was five seven.'

'Oh, well. I always was hopeless with numbers. It was why I chose my birthday in the first place.'

'Most people do.'

'Well, whatever. I'd just got to the top of the stairs when you rang the bell. I knew it was you and I was so relieved . . . you can't begin to imagine. Then as I turned to come back down, I heard someone behind me – ' Her eyes darkened as she remembered. 'I . . . I thought for a moment it was acid . . .'

'It was paint,' he said, quickly. Red paint. Thick and sticky and for one terrible moment he'd thought it was blood. He leaned over her, brushed the hair back from her forehead. 'In a day or two you'll be like new.'

'Except for my hair.' Her eyes were getting heavier. 'I've never had short hair. My mother said I should never have it cut . . .'

'It'll grow again,' he reassured her, his voice thick with emotion. 'Why did you do it, Claudia? Why did you pretend it was all a hoax?'

But she had drifted away on the sedative induced sleep. He stared down at her, guilt eating away at him because he knew that he had failed her, that it had all been his fault.

'She's asleep, then?' the nurse said, looking around the door a few minutes later.

'She just drifted off.'

'Good. You look as if you could do with a nap yourself. There's no need to stay you know, she won't stir for a while.'

'I'll stay.' Nothing on earth would move him from her side again unless he could be certain she was quite safe.

'Then you'd better sit down before you fall down.' There was a chair beside the bed. He moved it until it was between Claudia and the door and he lowered himself into it. 'You think whoever did this will try again?' the nurse, who had watched his manoevring with interest, asked curiously.

Not and live to tell the tale. He turned to her. 'It's possible. In case that point was missed by the emergency staff, will you mention that I have put a cross in the box marked "no publicity".'

'Right. I'll be sure to pass on the message.' She backed out of the door. 'Will you be wanting a constant supply of coffee to keep you awake?'

'No, thank you. Staying awake isn't a problem.' The nurse gave him an old-fashioned look and he shook his head. 'I don't need drugs either.'

'Lucky man.'

He was glad she thought so. Doing without sleep was something that he had had to learn the hard way behind the lines in the Gulf and Bosnia. It wasn't a method he would recommend.

Claudia slept peacefully for several hours. The nurse looked in once in a while and he stretched and walked about the room whenever sleep threatened to overwhelm him. Just before seven she stirred and he crossed to the bed.

The inflammation on her cheek and neck where the paint had been removed contrasted starkly with the greyish pallor and dark hollows of the rest of her face. As he reached forward to take her hand, he heard someone behind him and he swung around, but there was no threat. It was Edward Beaumont.

'Luke left a message on my answering machine. I'd taken a pill so I only heard it an hour ago. I came as quickly as I could. How is she?'

'Asleep.' Mac stood to one side so that he could see for himself. For a moment Edward looked down at his daughter, his face grim. Then he turned to Mac. 'You're Gabriel MacIntyre?' Mac nodded. 'Luke told me about you.'

'Then he will have told you that I promised him I'd look after Claudia. I'm afraid I didn't do a very good job.'

'I don't suppose she made it easy for you. She's never made anything easy, for herself or anyone else. I'm Edward Beaumont.' He offered his hand. Mac took it and for a moment the two men sized up one another. Edward Beaumont was tall with an aristocratic bearing. He was elegantly dressed despite the early hour and would never be caught with a hair out of place, or his chin unshaven in public. Mac was twenty years younger, three inches taller and carried a great deal more muscle. He was wearing denims, a well-worn t-shirt and he hadn't had a shave in twenty-four hours. The contrast was striking, but the respect was apparently mutual. 'Luke was impressed with you, Mr MacIntyre. I can see why.'

'I'm not feeling very impressed with myself. Claudia could have been seriously injured and it would have been entirely my fault.'

'Entirely?'

'I offended her and so she sent me packing in the one way she knew would work.'

'Oh?'

'She told me the threats were all part of a publicity stunt.'

'Did she? And you believed her?' He was surprised, but clearly didn't expect Mac to answer because he continued without a pause. 'Actually that wasn't what I meant. I was wondering what you had done to offend her.'

Mac stiffened. 'I asked her to trust me. Unfortunately I didn't return the compliment.'

Edward Beaumont lifted a hand in a supremely helpless gesture and his whole body sagged a little. 'Don't blame yourself, Mr MacIntyre.'

'Beau?' Her voice was unusually small.

'Oh, darling, we've disturbed you,' Edward Beaumont said, turning to bend over his daughter and kiss her forehead. 'How are you feeling?'

'I don't know. Sore. Scared.' Mac heard the rising panic in her voice and caught her hand as she reached up to touch her face.

292

'Leave it.'

'Gabriel.' For a moment she clung to his hand. Then, as she regained her composure, she let go and her voice was neutral, giving nothing away as she turned to her father. 'Will you take me home now, Beau?'

'I think we'd better see what the doctor says. You've had a nasty shock.' He patted her arm gently. 'Whoever could have done such a terrible thing?'

'You have no ideas?' Mac asked him.

'Me?' Edward Beaumont was clearly surprised by the question. 'I haven't a clue why anyone could do anything so wicked.'

'Mac thinks people will do anything for publicity,' Claudia murmured and Mac flinched.

'Don't be ridiculous, Claudia,' Edward said, firmly. 'One thing is certain though, you can't go back to your flat. I'm all over the place for the next two weeks or I'd take you home with me, so I think the best thing is to call Fizz, she'll be able to look after you properly – '

'No. Fizz mustn't know about this.' Claudia's voice was stronger now and she was quite emphatic. 'She'll only worry. And whoever did this knows where she lives. I couldn't risk anything happening to her.' She looked to Mac for support.

'I agree, but your father's right, the flat is out of the question. I don't think you should stay with any of your family. You need to stay right out of sight until . . . well, until the police have made their investigations.'

293

'You called them?' It was an accusation.

'Enough is enough, Claudia. They'll want a statement as soon as you feel up to it.' For a moment he thought she was going to tell him to take his statement and take a running jump. He wouldn't blame her. But then she nodded and let her head fall back against the pillow. Mac hesitated. He'd let Claudia down once and now she was getting over the shock of what had happened she hadn't been slow to let him know it. He wasn't sure how she'd take his next suggestion. 'Look, I've got a cottage . . . it's a bit basic, but it's out of the way and at least no one will look for you there. You're welcome to stay. If you want to.'

'That's very kind of you,' Edward began, but Claudia broke in.

'Are you quite sure about that, Gabriel? You know how much trouble I can be.'

He knew. No one better. But he was pretty sure that grovelling wouldn't win him any Brownie points with Claudia. 'You're the proverbial pain in the backside, Claudia – ' as a spark of animation brought her eyes back to life, he knew he was right – 'and if you misbehave again its quite possible that I'll throw you in the lake but if you'll promise – '

'Lake?' She heaved herself up on one elbow. 'Your cottage has its own lake and you consider it *basic*?'

'Well, I guess your view of basic depends on your priorities. Why don't you come and have look at it? You don't have to stay if you don't like it.'

'I'll come. But no more promises.'

For a moment their eyes locked, then Gabriel nodded. 'No promises.'

Several hours later, standing in the stone kitchen of a cottage which seemed to be suffering from terminal decay, Claudia wasn't so sure she'd made the right decision. Seeing her expression Gabriel lifted his shoulders expressively. 'I told you it was a bit basic.'

'You weren't exaggerating.'

'It has a lot of potential.'

'For what?'

'There are a couple of acres of land with it and the lake. I'm renovating it when I have the time.'

She looked around. The sink was stone with a pump handle attached to the side and an old-fashioned geyser above it that suggested the place had had a brush with twentieth-century plumbing sometime in the fifties and was still trying to get over the shock. The cooker appeared to date from the same period and like the geyser relied on bottled gas to fuel it. A glance at the ceiling confirmed that the suspiciously large number of candles meant precisely what she had feared; electricity had yet to find its way down the long rutted lane that led to the cottage.

She ran a finger experimentally along a shelf and examined the thick wad of dust that piled up beneath it with distaste. 'You must have been somewhat short of time recently,' she said, regarding Gabriel over her finger. 'You don't expect me to stay here, surely?'

'No one will look for you here.'

She couldn't fault him on logic. 'That's true,' she said, brushing the dust of her fingers. 'And even if they did, they'd take one look and go away again.'

'Isn't that the point?'

Claudia knew she was being unreasonable, but she felt dreadful and knew she looked worse. She bit down on her lip. A week from now and her face would be back to normal and a visit to her hairdresser would fix her hair. It could have been a million times worse. But knowing that and believing it when confronted by the result of the attack in the hospital mirror were two different things.

'I'm sorry that the place is so dusty. I haven't been here for a while, but it's nothing a little soap and hot water won't fix.'

'A *lot* of soap and a *lot* of hot water,' Claudia amended, glancing doubtfully at the geyser. It didn't look up to the task. Then she indicated the carton of groceries on the square scrubbed table in the middle of the room. 'Someone must have been expecting us.'

'Not you. Just me. I asked Adele to organize a few essentials but she doesn't know you're here.'

'Why? Just in case it was her all the time?'

'She's the size of a house, Claudia. She couldn't get up your stairs with a can of paint, let alone throw it at you and beat a hasty retreat down the fire exit, but I thought the fewer people who knew you were here, the safer you would feel.'

'So it's just you and me?'

'Yes, Claudia. Just you and me.' He glanced into the box. 'I'll go and stock up the larder tomorrow.'

'And leave me alone?' The panic was already beginning to rise in her throat at the thought. '*Here*?'

'What's the matter, doesn't the lake live up to your expectations?'

'The lake is fine. The cottage is . . .'

'Basic.' Their glances collided and she received the distinct impression that a fit of tantrums and a demand to be taken to the nearest five star hotel would be met with resistance.

Since they had left the hospital, communications had been fairly limited between them, but she had been left in no doubt that for the foreseeable future Gabriel MacIntyre was determined that she would do exactly what she was told. It would have been comforting if she had thought for one moment he was doing it for any other reason than guilt.

And since walking out wasn't an option – they hadn't passed any habitation within fives miles of the place – she decided not to waste her breath.

She turned angrily away and pushed open the door to the living room. It was larger than she had anticipated, with a big stone fireplace at one end and a dusty blue and white jug on the mantle in which some flowers had withered and died a long time ago. Beside the hearth was a basket containing a few logs and yellowing newspapers. In front of it a couple of comfortable armchairs and a thick rug suggested someone had once made an attempt to provide some comfort.

Claudia gave a little shiver. The room wasn't exactly cold, but the August sun hadn't penetrated the thick walls and although the walls had been painted in the not-too-distant past, it had a musty air of abandonment about it, as if the occupants had simply walked out and locked the door behind them and never come back.

Gabriel had followed her into the room and was now watching her, his whole body tense, the skin drawn tight over the hard planes of his face and quite unexpectedly something twisted in her gut. He wasn't finding it easy being in this place yet he had brought her here so that she should be safe. And she was behaving like a spoilt cat. But then, when had she ever behaved like anything else?

'Why don't you light a fire?' she suggested.

His head jerked up, as if for the moment he had forgotten she was there. 'Are you cold?'

'No, but it might cheer the place up a bit.'

'I'll take your bag upstairs first.' The stairs were hidden behind a door and rose, steep and narrow, to the upper floor. He led the way and opened a door to the right, ducking slightly as he entered the room. Claudia too, had to lower her head as she followed him through the door.

The bedroom, like the living room, had been decorated within living memory. The walls had been painted in a pale buttermilk yellow, there were fresh

298

curtains at the window and the pine chest of drawers was genuinely antique. It could have been charming and it would be again as soon as she had cleaned off the dust that had settled over every available surface.

'The bed's more comfortable than it looks,' he assured her.

'Is it?' Claudia regarded the ancient brass bedstead without enthusiasm. It had to be more comfortable than it looked. Less would be impossible.

'You'll find sheets and things in the chest of drawers. It's a good idea to make the bed while it's still light,' he advised. 'Otherwise the candles blow out when you spread the sheets.' He spoke with the voice of experience.

'Candles, she repeated. 'This may come as a shock to you, but the oil lamp has been invented.'

'So I've heard, but I thought I'd skip that phase and move straight on to electricity. I just haven't got around to connecting it yet.' She wondered just what he had got around to connecting. She was beginning to feel distinctingly uneasy about the plumbing. 'These things take time,' he added, as if finding it necessary to justify the omission. 'I'll have to dig a trench from the road – '

'Personally? With a pick and shovel?' she enquired, hopefully. It had to be at least half a mile to the main road.

'This may come as a shock to you but it's possible to hire a mechanical digger.' He waited, but she didn't respond. 'In the meantime we have plenty of candles.'

'Well, candlelight has a certain charm.' An earth privy was another matter. 'Is there a bathroom?' She wasn't hopeful.

'That depends what you mean by bathroom. There's a lavatory downstairs with a washbasin connected to the geyser; baths need a certain amount of organization.' The thought appeared to offer him a certain wry satisfaction. 'But with a little notice they can be managed quite comfortably.'

Claudia, about to ask how, spotted a disturbing glint in those blue eyes of his and changed her mind. Besides, plumbing was not the only thing on her mind. It occurred to her that the bed she was standing beside was double. 'Is that your room?' she asked, making a move in the direction of the second door.

'No.' He didn't exactly block her way, more discourage her with his presence. 'That's empty. I'll stick with my sleeping bag. Downstairs.' In front of the fire, Claudia realized. It sounded a lot more appealing than a sagging mattress on an old brass bedstead. She considered asking him to swop but managed to restrain herself; it seemed safer that way. 'I'll go and clean up the kitchen a bit,' he said. 'Then we can have some supper.'

'I'll come with you. I'm sure you must have a broom and a duster somewhere. I can't sleep with all this dust.' He stared at her for a moment, not moving, blocking the stairs. 'Gabriel?' she prompted.

300

'I'm sorry, I should have asked Adele to organize a clean-up.'

'Wouldn't that have alerted her to the fact that you are not alone? I don't imagine Adele would have taken very kindly to the suggestion that she clean up for me,' she pointed out.

'She wouldn't have done it herself. She'd have sent Tony.' He almost smiled at the thought. 'Stay here. I'll go and see what I can find for you.'

'I'm not an invalid – ' she began, but he was already halfway down the narrow stairs and she wasn't going to argue about it. Instead she crossed to the small casement window beneath the eaves. The room faced south-west and it had taken the full glare of the afternoon sun. It was airless and the windowsill was littered with the dead bodies of insects which had battered themselves against the panes in their desperation to get out. She lifted the catch and pushed on the frame. It was stuck fast where the sun had baked the paint. It needed a couple of hefty thumps with the flat of her hand before it finally surrendered and she was breathing in the cool rush of early evening air, sweet with the heady scent of honeysuckle and roses scrambling over the wall below the window. But it would take a lot of honeysuckle to rid her of the suffocating smell of paint.

The pale yellow striped curtains lifted slightly in the soft breeze. Fresh and pretty, they were the perfect choice for a cottage bedroom. All the room needed to complete the picture was a pot filled with yellow roses.

301

It made her wonder about the jug of shrivelled flowers downstairs and the woman who had put them there. It had to have been Gabriel's wife. It had to have been Jenny Callendar. And once more something tugged at her memory. A tragedy. There had been a tragedy. Something more than her death.

CHAPTER 13

'Making yourself at home?' Claudia jumped guiltily at the sound of his voice so close behind her. She had been making herself at home with his thoughts, his feelings. Letting her mind explore the possibilities of what tragedy had befallen him.

'Do I have to ask your permission to open the window? You should have said.' He clearly didn't believe her question merited an answer, or maybe he, too, was affected by the scene from the window.

The sun was setting, leaving a delicate residue of pink and pearl grey in the sky. The colours were reflected in the stretch of water lapping at the dark silhouette of reeds that fringed the shore of the small lake a hundred feet or so from the cottage. He must have leaned against this sill many times, sharing such a scene with the woman he loved. It was so easy to imagine them standing in this spot, arms looped about each other in the gentle aftermath of love, discussing their plans for the cottage, for their life.

Stealing a sideways glance at his face, Claudia was struck by the lack of any visible emotion. Well, what had she expected? He wasn't the kind of man to break down and sob on her shoulder.

'Nice lake,' she said, as matter-of-factly as a prospective purchaser not wanting to show too much enthusiasm in the presence of the estate agent.

'I like it,' he agreed, in a similarly undramatic tone of voice. 'It's not natural of course, it's an old gravel pit. The area is full of them. Most of them are used by watersports clubs and hotels. Fortunately this one never got big enough to interest anyone very much.'

'Is that a hotel? Over there?' On a rise, beyond a small wood, she could see the roof and gables of a large building.

'No. That's Pinkneys Abbey.'

'Abbey?'

'It hasn't been used as that since the sixteenth century and there isn't that much of the original building left. Everything around here belongs to the estate, even the airfield. You can't see it from here, it's on the other side of the house.'

'Who lives there?'

'No one now. The owner had a problem with inheritance tax. It's let to a company who run management courses.'

'And he sold you the cottage and the lake that was too small for anyone else to bother with?' He didn't make any response and she turned and looked up at him. 'What do you do with it?'

'Do with it? What do you think I do with it? I live in it.' She raised her brows in a deliberately provoking manner. 'I will live in it. It won't always be like this.'

She had been wrong about the emotion. It was there, but it was buried deep. 'Actually, I meant the lake, Gabriel.'

'Did you?' He was angry but not with her. He just didn't like talking about it. 'I swim when it's warm enough and I have been known to fish occasionally. Mostly I just leave it to the birds.' Even as he spoke a pair of swans, necks outstretched, skimmed the water, landing with barely a ripple. 'They're a lot more attractive than beefy skiers in wet suits,' he remarked. 'And a lot quieter. Here, I found you these.' Mac thrust a pump spray of cleaner into her hand with a duster. 'Do you know how to use them?'

The tension that had been almost palpable eased as the subject shifted to more practical matters. 'I think I can work it out,' she assured him. 'What about the broom? I'd better sweep the floor first or the dust will cover everything again.'

'Will it? Fancy you knowing something like that, when domesticity is such a mystery to you.'

'Well, I have to admit that it's not a *complete* mystery,' Claudia confessed. 'I once played a house-maid in a Gothic horror.' She glanced around. 'I have a feeling the experience is going to come in useful.'

She had hoped to make him laugh. Instead he raked his fingers through his scalp. 'I'm sorry, truly, Claudia. I didn't realize how bad it was.'

'Don't worry about it, Gabriel. It doesn't matter.' Without thinking she put her hand on his arm. His skin was warm and dry beneath her fingers, healthy outdoor skin and the fine line of dark hair that emphasized the strength of his forearm was silky beneath her fingers. 'I don't suppose a workout with a duster will kill me.' She could hardly believe she'd said that. And what's more she'd sounded convincing. Given a little encouragement, she might even believe it herself.

'Probably not,' he agreed. 'I'll go and make a start downstairs.' He detached her hand and turned away. 'You'll find the broom on the landing.' It took an act of will to resist the very real urge to follow him and beat him with it.

Instead she searched her bag and found a scarf that Mel had thoughtfully packed for her, no doubt anticipating that she would want to cover her hair, hide it. If she'd been told that Claudia would be wearing it like an old-fashioned Mrs Mop, she would never have believed it. Half an hour ago Claudia would have been hard pressed to believe it herself.

There was a mirror on the chest of drawers and she rubbed at it with the duster, steeling herself to look in it. She had always been told she was beautiful, even as a child. Her hair had been brushed each morning until it shone and because she had so much wanted to be just like her mother she had never complained, even when there were tangles and it hurt. After the brushing it had been rubbed with a piece of silk to add extra gloss

306

before she was taken in to see her mother, who never rose before noon. Sometimes she was allowed to sit on the bed and her mother would take the brush herself, choosing the ribbon she was to wear and telling Claudia that she must never have her hair cut because it was so beautiful.

As she'd got older, her childhood fairness had darkened but she had never had it cut short. But the doctor hadn't been concerned about cosmetic appearances. Her skin, always sensitive, had reacted badly to the paint and he had ordered the nurse to cut away the paint soaked strands to minimize the damage. The poor girl had been so upset that Claudia had had to reassure her that it didn't matter. Did it? After a moment's hesitation she reached up to touch her shorn locks.

Rough where the worst of the paint had been cut out, it felt strange beneath her hand and although the other side was untouched it felt suddenly heavy and uncomfortable. If she'd had a pair of scissors she would have cut that off too. Instead she bound the scarf around it, leaving only her blotchy face to commend her.

All her life her whole being had been concentrated on the way she looked. No one had ever seen anything else in her, looked for anything else, except perhaps, sometimes, her family. She stared at herself for a moment, wondering what she would feel if she had to live with that for the rest of her life the way her mother had had to live with her scars. Would she turn into a monster, too?

Why were there always more questions than answers, she wondered as she turned back to the room and looked around her. For instance, how long was she going to stand there wasting time worrying about nothing when there was so much work to be done? Not a second longer.

She swept and dusted and polished, coughing and sneezing and transferring a large quantity of it to herself until she got the hang of damping everything down with the spray first. Then she turned her attention to the bed. The chest of drawers yielded white bed linen and a yellow and white striped coverlet that matched the curtains, although by the time she had finished it was barely light enough to see anything, let alone the pale stripes.

Downstairs it was much darker. Gabriel had already lit half a dozen or so candles and the soft luminous glow combined with the flames flickering around the logs to banish any lingering cobwebs to the darkness, leaving a small inviting area in front of the freshly cleaned hearth. A window overlooking the darkening surface of the lake had been thrown open wide to let in fresh air. She could hear the disgruntled chuntering of water fowl settling down for the night and a blackbird was making sure everyone knew that he was king of the neglected garden. It should have been idyllic. Instead it was just a little sad.

But, aided by the homely scents of cooking, the long closed-up fustiness of the cottage was in retreat and, suddenly hungry, Claudia was drawn to the kitchen.

Gabriel hadn't wasted his time. The surfaces glistened damply where they had been washed down and now he had turned his attention to the dishes. The scene provoked an image of homeliness, of comfortable togetherness which she found disturbing. They weren't at home, or together, but had been thrust into one another's company by fear and guilt.

She hadn't made a sound, yet apparently sensing her presence, he swung round and the cosy image evaporated in an instant along with the "new" man. Gabriel's features were thrown into sharp relief in the shadowy light, his expression dangerous, his body taut and menacing. She knew she should have been reassured by his alertness, but she found it distinctly unnerving. Seeing her in the doorway he visibly relaxed and she released a long, slow breath, making a mental note to whistle 'Dixie' in future, just to make sure he heard her coming. 'You've been busy,' she said.

'So have you.' Mac scanned her appearance with a thoughtful look. 'The bedroom must be a lot cleaner,' he remarked. 'Most of the dirt seems to be on you.'

'Isn't that supposed to happen?' she enquired, with every indication of surprise. 'Of course when I played the housemaid they didn't have real dirt,' she explained.

'You can have make-believe dirt?'

'You buy it in spray cans. Cobwebs, too,' she told him. He looked slightly perplexed, not entirely sure whether she was kidding him or not and rather enjoying having the upper hand for once, she didn't enlighten him. 'Where shall I put these?' she asked, indicating her cleaning materials.

'There's a cupboard over there.' The door set into the wall concealed the space beneath the stairs. She had been expecting a 'black hole', full of junk and spiders. Instead it was lined with shelves containing the standard array of household cleaning equipment. There were also a number of paint tins, mostly unused and a sad array of paintbrushes stuck into a pot of white spirit that had long since dried up. She quickly shut the door.

'I think I'd better wash my hands before supper.' There was only one other door. She opened it and was disconcerted to discover that several steps led down into the dark interior of a pantry.

'Go out of the back door,' Mac instructed. 'It's the next door along.'

'Outside?'

'I'm afraid so. I can't put in a door from the kitchen because of building regulations. I was planning to extend – ' He stopped rather suddenly, turned away to stare down at the sink.

'That sounds like a good idea,' Claudia said, brightly, when it became obvious he wasn't going to say any more and clearly wished he hadn't started. 'This could be made into a lovely cottage.' It didn't help. In fact, she realized that under the circumstances it was probably rather tactless. It suggested she didn't much like it the way it was. But then tact, like housework, was a skill she had somehow managed to sidestep. 'Gabriel – ' she began, but he didn't want to hear what she had to say.

'You'll need this,' he said, cutting her off as he unhooked a heavyweight torch from behind the door.

She hesitated for a moment, wanting to tell him that she was here for him, a willing ear if he wanted to talk. But his face was blank and discouraging so she looked down at the torch. 'Isn't this rather . . . modern?' she enquired.

He visibly relaxed at her teasing note. 'You can take a candle if you prefer. I always find they blow out at the most inconvenient moments.'

Despite her reservations she discovered the facilities were modern, the water was hot and there were no spiders – at least none that she could see – and Gabriel had put out a clean towel. The torch threw a bright light, but since she couldn't hold it and wash at the same time, the beam was either pointing at the ceiling, or the wall, leaving her reflection little more than a ghostly shadow in the mirror. But she peeled off her t-shirt and did the best she could. Her face stung, but at least she was clean.

'There, it wasn't so bad, was it?' he enquired, as she hung the torch back in its place and took down a tea towel to start on the drying up.

'Ask me again when it's raining. Are those jacket potatoes I can smell cooking?'

'And sausages.' He glanced at her slender figure. 'Maybe you don't eat sausages?'

311

'Not often, but it's long a time since I indulged in comfort food and now seems like a good time.'

Gabriel put down a plate just as she reached for one and their hands collided. It was like a shock going through her, spreading out, heating her, until she was glad of the candlelight to cover her blushes. He moved his hand away from hers as carefully as if he were easing himself away from a close encounter with a landmine. She knew how he felt.

'Comfort food?' he asked, carefully.

She concentrated very hard on drying a plate. 'You know, the kind of food that the best nannies give you to make you feel better. When it's the last day of the holidays and you're dreading going back to school, or when you've got a cold and steamed fish and vegetables, no matter how many times you've been told they're nourishing and good for you, just won't go down. Or when you just need cheering up because . . .' Because your mother is having a bad day. Or someone has thrown a tin of paint over you.

'Oh, *comfort food*. You mean dripping toast and fried egg sandwiches and – '

'Do I?' she interrupted before he got too carried away. 'I don't *think* so. Not fried egg sandwiches, anyway.'

His teeth flashed white as he grinned. 'You don't know what you're missing. Did you have a lot of nannies?'

'I was a bit of handful.'

'You still are,' he assured her, but his look became pensive. 'But it's no way for a child to grow up. Your father suggested as much.'

Most people assumed that she had had an idyllic childhood. His perception was oddly disconcerting. 'Did he?' She lifted a shoulder. 'Well the alternative was boarding school; you pays your money and you takes your pick.' Her mother had wanted to send her away the moment she was eight. Beau had protested, but she would have got her way. She always did. Then there was the accident and boarding school had been temporarily shelved. An eight-year-old couldn't be trusted to keep secrets. Maybe, on reflection, it would have been wiser of her father to have got them both out of the house before their mother came home from the hospital, but he hadn't. He was going through his own personal nightmare at the time, so she and Fizz became extras in the continuing drama of Elaine French's glamorous life. The show must go on. Claudia's hands suddenly began to shake and a saucer slipped. Mac turned quickly to field it and their hands, their arms, their shoulders tangled. 'Are we going to wash the entire contents of this kitchen?' she demanded, jerking away from him, leaving him in possession of the saucer.

'Not tonight. But I thought you would object to eating off dusty plates and it seemed a shame to waste the water.' He took the cloth from her, dried up the remainder of the dishes before emptying the sink and wiping it down. 'Supper won't be long. Could you handle a drink? There might be a bottle of wine somewhere.' He didn't wait for her answer but unhooked the torch from its place behind the door and stepped down into the pantry. He returned a moment or two later with two bottles that clouded with condensation in the warmth of the kitchen.

Curious, she reached out and touched one of them. It was cold. 'All the pleasures of civilization despite the lack of electricity?'

'Civilization was heavily into pleasure long before the National Grid. Or the invention of the refrigerator. They had ice cream in sixteenth-century Italy. I can't manage that tonight, but since the back of the pantry is below ground cold wine isn't a problem. Red or white?'

'White please.'

He uncorked the bottle, poured two glasses and handed one to her. 'What shall we drink to?'

Claudia stared into her glass. 'Why are you doing this, Gabriel?' She lifted heavy lids and looked at him. 'Why are you going to all this trouble when we both know that you don't think I'm worth two minutes of your time?'

'Did I say that?'

'You never say anything, but you think very loudly.' For a moment the air was charged with enough electricity to make the candles redundant. Then Claudia shrugged. 'Whilst I have a reputation for never thinking at all and saying far too much.'

314

'Do you? Well perhaps that's the way you like it because you don't go out of your way to correct the impression people have of you. No matter how mistaken they are.' He gestured towards the door. 'Supper won't cook any more quickly if we stand and watch it. Shall we make ourselves comfortable?'

In reply she settled herself in one the armchairs, kicked off her shoes and tucked her feet beneath her. A piece of wood dropped in the grate, sending up a flurry of sparks, but the flames had died down around the logs and there was more cheer from the glow than heat which was just as well. Her tussle with the dust has warmed her through and Gabriel's words, the intensity of his look, had gone a long way to completing the job of heating her blood.

She waited while he settled in the chair opposite and stretched out long legs that filled the space between them, crossing his ankles so that she was confronted by the largest pair of feet she'd ever seen on a man. When he was upright, they were in proportion and they weren't so noticeable but now she had difficulty in taking her eyes of them. Gabriel, staring into the pulsing embers of the fire, didn't appear to notice.

'Well?' she prompted, gently, when she had waited long enough, reminding him that she was still waiting for an answer to her question.

At least he didn't pretend not to know what she was talking about. 'I told you, it's personal.'

'You're going to all this trouble simply because someone stuffed that photograph of me in one of your parachutes?' Surely he didn't expect her to believe that? 'You know it has to have been one of the television crew. Why didn't you tackle Barty James about it when you saw him on Saturday? He'll have a note of everyone who was there.'

'It could have been Mr James himself,' Mac suggested. 'Have you considered that?' She scoffed at the very idea and he replied with a grin. 'Perhaps you're right. He couldn't have been responsible for the dress, anyway. But I don't need to ask him for a list of his crew, I have my own. Everyone who came onto the airfield was checked in. Maybe you'd like to look at it in case one of the names means something.'

'Maybe.'

For a moment she thought he was going to press her further but he must have thought better of it because he put down his glass and unfolded himself from the armchair. 'Shall we eat here, in front of the fire?'

The gentle warmth had made her drowsy. 'I'd like that,' she murmured and he fetched a low table from the other side of the room. She made a move to rise and offer assistance, but he stopped her.

'Leave it to me, I know where everything is.'

It was only when he'd disappeared into the kitchen that she realized he still hadn't answered her question. And rather to her surprise she found herself laughing.

'What's so funny?' he called out.

'You wouldn't understand.'

'Try me.' He reappeared with a tray and he looked directly at her as he bent to place it on the table. It was slightly intimidating. He was a lot better at interrogation than she was.

'It was nothing,' she said, turning to look into the fire. Then she realized she was doing it too. Side-stepping. Not confronting the problem. Maybe it was catching. Or perhaps a lifetime of avoiding her own black beast had left her with unsuspected skills in the technique. He was very good at it, but she wondered how he would respond to direct assault. There was only one way to find out. Claudia lifted her head, tilted her chin a little to give herself courage and turned to look him straight in the eye. 'I just noticed that whenever I ask you a personal question you always manage to steer the subject away from dangerous secrets.'

'And you found that funny?' Her glance wavered momentarily. In the firelight the vivid blue of his eyes had darkened to slate. But she refused to be intimidated. Or distracted.

'Not especially. But I wondered if you had special training for that in the army?' she asked. 'In case of capture. Or is it a gift you were born with, seeping through in the genes from all those generations of military men? Like acting seems to with the Beaumonts.' The silence that followed this was not promising and quite suddenly she lost her nerve. Ducking her head, she turned with a generous gesture towards the tray and said, 'That looks . . . good.' She had been about to say neat. Ten out of ten. She supposed all soldiers quickly learned the habit. The tray would

317

certainly have passed the toughest of inspections. Even the sausages were lined up with military precision.

Claudia wondered what it would be like to ruffle the man, muss hair kept trimmed to a millimetre, clothes that seemed to leap to attention the moment he put them on. Gabriel was so controlled, so untouchable, so competent in everything he did. He could kiss a woman or cook a sausage with one hand tied behind his back. And they would both sizzle.

She was seized by an almost overwhelming urge to reach up and tousle his hair as he leaned over to pass her a plate. She restrained herself, Gabriel MacIntrye was no teddy bear. The only bear he resembled was a grizzly. And a girl ruffled a grizzly at her peril.

'Would you like some butter for your potato?' he asked, with blade-edged politeness.

'Thank you.' He passed it to her, waited for her to split her potato and place a small nob of butter inside it and then put it back on the tray. 'Salt? Pepper.'

'You don't have to wait on me.'

'You're my guest.'

'An unwanted one. An inconvenient nuisance.'

'That's not true.'

But she shook her head, unconvinced. 'I'm sorry, Gabriel, I'll try to be good. I know you're doing this to help me, that you'd rather not be here.'

'I thought that I would rather not be here, but you needn't feel guilty. It's not as bad as I had expected.'

Claudia felt a queer little flutter in the region of her waist. What on earth was he going to say? He said nothing, turning instead to help himself to butter and pepper. She longed to prompt him, urge him to begin, but for once an unusually acute sense of what was prudent kept her silent as he returned to his seat. She dipped her fork into her potato, swallowed a little. Mac seemed to have forgotten the food on his lap.

'You must have realized,' he said, breaking the silence, 'it must be glaringly obvious, that I haven't been here since Jenny died.' She didn't fall into the seductive trap he offered, managed to withstand the temptation to ask him one of the questions crowding her brain, fighting to get out, questions that would offer him a welcome diversion from his painful thoughts. She held her tongue, waited, and was finally rewarded for her patience. 'I kept putting it off. I told myself that I'd come next weekend, then the next . . .' He paused, waiting, perhaps hoping that she would speak. But Claudia, uncharacteristically, held her tongue. 'When I could no longer fool myself that way, I told myself that it was only sensible to wait until the weather was warmer, the evenings longer and I'd have more time. There was so much to do.' He raised one hand in resignation. 'Then it was winter again.'

And now it was summer. Two years. After a long time Claudia slowly cleared her throat. 'You didn't have to come back at all. You could have sold up. People do. And weekend cottages with the potential of this one, with a lake . . .' But even as she was saying it

319

she knew that he would have found that impossible. And admission of defeat. 'You must have loved her very much.'

'Must I?' There was the briefest pause, before he said, 'Your supper's getting cold, Claudia.' And in case she hadn't got the point, he devoted his entire attention to his own food.

Afterwards he politely refused her offer to help with the washing up and because she had the feeling that he would prefer to be on his own, she didn't push it. But he paused in the kitchen doorway. 'You're going to have to start thinking about who is responsible for this, Claudia. Now might be a good time.' His face was in the shadows and she couldn't tell his mood from his voice. He was back in control and she doubted that he would let the mask slip again. 'And while you're assessing the possibilities I'd like you to consider this. Around eighty per cent of women who find themselves the victim of continual harassment and violence have been in some kind of a relationship with the person who is giving them a hard time.'

So she took his advice and thought very hard about what had been happening. Someone wanted to frighten her. No. The stakes had been upped when that paint was thrown into her face. Someone wanted to *terrify* her. Worse. And Gabriel was right, it had to be someone she knew; no stranger would take so much trouble, or so many risks. She found her handbag and in the back of her diary she began to make a list. Family first, then close friends, then acquaintances. It was a long list and it was nowhere near complete. She looked up when he returned a while later with a couple of mugs of what looked suspiciously like cocoa. He had to be kidding.

He wasn't. He saw her face and smiled slightly. 'I thought since we were into comfort, we might as well go the whole hog, although whether nanny would approve of the Scotch I've laced it with is a moot point. But since there was half a bottle with the groceries . . .'

Only half? Because Adele had thought he might need a drink to get him through his first visit to the cottage since his wife had been killed, but wasn't prepared to take the risk of leaving a whole bottle? 'I think I've let myself go quite sufficiently for one day,' she said, standing the mug on the hearth. 'But don't let me stop you.'

But he didn't seem in any hurry to indulge himself. 'What are you doing?'

'I'm making a list of everyone I know.' She handed it over.

'You know a lot of people.'

'Oh, there are more. A lot more.' She watched as he looked over the names. 'Do you suppose,' she asked after a while, 'that the most likely culprit is a close friend, or a mere acquaintance? Or just somebody I was a bit offhand with one day in a television studio, or backstage, somebody whose name I'll probably never know?' She paused as another thought seized her. 'Or even an outraged theatre-goer who didn't like my performance? Some man who didn't think I was as good as my mother?'

'On that basis it could be half the country.'

'Thank you.'

'I didn't mean – '

'Didn't you?' Their eyes met briefly then he indicated the list.

'Who are all these people? Matthew for instance?'

'He's my hairdresser.' The poor man was going to have his work cut out to make something out of the remains of her hair. 'You can cross him off, by the way, he'd never have done this.' She indicated her turbanned head.

'Peter Jameson?'

'Cross him off too. He's my agent and when I don't work he doesn't get paid.'

'Joanna Gray. Who is she?'

'A friend. We were at RADA together. She's a very good actress, in fact she should have been in *Stalker* but she broke her arm. She's taking my place tonight.'

'I hadn't thought about that. When was that organized?'

'I telephoned her yesterday evening.' She shrugged. 'My performance was beginning to suffer . . .'

'Tell me about Phillip Redmond.'

'Phillip?'

'He seemed somewhat obsessed by your mother.'

'I don't know about obsessed. She gave him his first job in the theatre and you've seen for yourself that he

322

believed she could do no wrong. But he isn't alone in that.' She gave a little shiver.

'You're cold?' He didn't sound particularly surprised, despite the warmth of the August evening and the fire.

'Just a little.' She rubbed at the gooseflesh raised on her arms.

'It's probably reaction. You can't simply block out what's happening.'

'I can try.' Her eyes were dry and painful and she closed them, fighting back the threatening tears. She wouldn't cry. She wouldn't.

'Hey. Hey, come on.' She felt his breath on her cheek as he leaned over her, lifting her from the chair, pulling her into his arms to hold her, warm her. His lips brushed against her temple, but there was no threat, only comfort in the gesture. 'You've had a tough few days. No one's going to ridicule you for letting it show.'

'Oh, no? Let me tell you there are a whole raft of people out there who would love to see the golden girl crumple up, fall apart.'

'Golden girl?'

She buried her face in his shoulder. 'It's what some newspaperman called me once. He said I had it all.'

'No one has it all.' He touched her undamaged cheek, turned her face so that she was looking up at him. 'Sometimes it looks that way to outsiders, but you can't enlighten them because they'd rather believe the illusion.'

Claudia looked up at him. All her life she'd been living with an illusion. 'I'm tired of playing make-believe, Gabriel, but there are some things we can't escape.'

'We can try.' His voice was gravelly and as he held her she sensed that for all the comfort he was offering her as he enfolded her against his strength, he was receiving an equal measure in return. 'We should try.' And without thinking she reached up, touched his cheek as he was touching hers and then followed the gesture with a kiss, the merest touch of her lips on his. It wasn't seductive, or bold, or like any kiss she could remember giving before. It was simply the only way she could think of to thank him.

To thank him for being there, for giving her shelter in the cottage he had shared with his wife, even when it was painful for him. To thank him for just holding her, keeping her safe. The feeling disturbed and confused her. She had never looked to anyone else for strength before and she was beginning to rely on Gabriel MacIntyre far too much. She was beginning to *want* Gabriel MacIntyre far too much.

And because she didn't want to embarrass him, or herself, she drew back, putting a little distance between them, sinking first back onto the chair and then slipping down onto the rug, curling her legs beneath her and reaching out her fingers to the last of the warmth, as if it could replace the warmth that he generated. But it wasn't the same as being held in those strong arms.

Gabriel hunkered down beside her, saying nothing as he stirred the embers of the fire with a long poker before carefully placing a couple of logs in the warmest part of the fire. Then he picked up her discarded mug and placed it into her hands, wrapping her fingers about it and holding them there briefly before disappearing into the darkness to close the window.

Without him at her side the room was suddenly far less friendly and her eyes sought him in the darkness. Her teeth were beginning to chatter and she sipped at the cocoa, the whisky immediately warming the back of her throat and spreading its heat to warm her stomach. But it wasn't the same as having him beside her.

'Do you think all this could be to do with *Stalker*, Gabriel?' she asked, when he lingered by the window. 'The networks started running publicity footage a week ago and it might just have given someone the idea.'

'It could be I suppose,' he said, returning to the fireside but keeping his distance from her. He sounded doubtful. 'But the thing about stalkers is that they are driven to punish their love object for not returning their love. They want their victim to know why they are suffering.'

'And I don't.' For a moment their eyes locked and held then he reached out, touching the unmarked side of her face with just the tips of his fingers.

'Maybe you do, Claudia. Maybe you just don't want to admit it.' She flinched away from him. For a moment his hand remained poised in the air, then he let it fall. 'The subconscious is very good at burying the unpleasant things we'd rather not face.'

'I am not burying anything,' she protested.

He turned and stared into the fire. 'Not deliberately, perhaps. But none of us is immune. Before you go to sleep you should run through any disagreements you've had lately, – ' he paused – 'professional or personal. The mind is very good at finding answers – '

'What answers?' She gathered herself and stood up, looking down into his upturned face. He had this view of her as a thoroughly spoilt woman who had got herself into something she couldn't handle but wasn't prepared to own up. Because of Tony he had got it into his mind that this nonsense was the result of a sexual entanglement that had gone awry, some scorned lover getting his revenge.

Well he was wrong, but he was so fixated on her public image that he wasn't prepared to look beyond it and she certainly wasn't about to explain herself, leaving herself open to an additional charge of lying. Because he wouldn't believe her. In fact, the only reason he was taking such a very personal interest in her problems was because, in trying to get to her, to frighten her, someone had had the temerity to contaminate one of his precious parachutes. He accused her of hiding from the truth, but he was hiding too. 'Maybe you should be asking yourself a few questions, Gabriel.'

'What questions?' His eyes were very still, very intent as he looked up at her. She had his undivided attention and she wasn't about to waste it.

'You're the only person I've fallen out with recently, Gabriel MacIntyre. You knew where I was when I ran to Fizz – '

'Claudia – ' he warned, rising to his feet.

She wasn't listening, she was too busy putting two and two together. 'And you could easily have pushed that nasty little welcome home note through my door when we got home. It might even have been there from the night before. What did it say exactly?' She frowned. 'How does it feel to be home? Something like that. It would have done the job any time, wouldn't it?' She stared at him. *Trust me. Put yourself in my hands.* She had trusted him, accepted his protection and now she was in this isolated cottage, no telephone, no way of escape . . .

As his hands reached out for her she let out a little shriek of fear and stumbled back against the chair. He caught her, his fingers biting into her arms as he stopped her from falling, steadied her.

'Why, Claudia?' he said, very gently. 'Why do you think I'd do that?' She shook her head, unable to answer, but he was insistent. 'That's the second time you've suggested I'm capable of hurting you.' His brow was furrowed in a deep frown that brought his thick dark brows down into a straight line. 'I don't understand why.'

Neither did she. She didn't believe it. He'd tried to

327

protect her from the photograph, the only reason he'd shown it to her was because he was so concerned about her. 'I . . . I'm sorry. I'm so sorry, Gabriel – I don't mean, I know you wouldn't hurt me.'

'You're sure? I brought you here so that you would feel safe. If you're in the least bit uncertain I'll take you anywhere you want to go . . .'

And finally that did it. The tears welled up and spilled over. She shook her head, unable for the moment to speak. Without another word he put his arms about her, drawing her into the warmth of his body, holding her close against his chest as he would a frightened child, so that she could take comfort from the steady beat of his heart.

'It's all right, sweetheart, let it out. You're just scared. Anyone would be.'

'Yes, I'm scared,' she admitted, closing her eyes, as if that would make the fear go away. 'I just feel so . . . alone.'

'You're not alone, Claudia,' he murmured into her hair. 'You won't ever be alone again.'

CHAPTER 14

You'll never be alone. The words had just come out.
But he meant them. Claudia Beaumont had taken his
cold, bitter heart and warmed it with her bright eyes,
her teasing mouth, a heart that he had learned was as
big as a house, despite every effort to keep that fact
hidden.

He had fought it every step of the way, but with that
unpremeditated declaration he knew that he had lost
the battle, that he was hers, for better or worse. That
he would be there for her, for as long as she needed
him.

He knew it might not be for long. She needed him,
but need wasn't love and he wasn't about to load her
with guilt by selfishly declaring his own feelings.

She stirred in his arms and looked up at him, her
eyes wet with tears, her lashes clumped together. He
wanted to kiss them. And because he thought it would
make her feel better, he bent and touched her lids,
tasting the salt of her tears on his lips.

'Gabriel?' The way she murmured his name was like

an intimate caress, her liltingly soft voice stroking him, stirring a response, an ache of longing.

'Why don't you go to bed, Claudia,' he said, thickly. 'You've had a rough day. I'll be here if you need me.' And he eased himself away from her before his reaction to the warmth of her body and the scent of her skin became too obvious.

As he stepped back she turned away from him, but not before a fleeting expression of sadness darkened her eyes and for one treacherous moment every part of him screamed that he had made a mistake, that she wanted him to hold her, wanted him to make love with her every bit as much he was hungering for her. But then she lifted her head and smiled. 'You're right. It's been a bloody awful day and it's time it was over.'

'You'll feel better after a decent night's sleep.'

'Of course.' And there was a bustle while she brushed her teeth, found her handbag and finally departed for bed. Once she had gone Mac stabbed at the dead ashes of the fire, taking his frustration out on the inanimate embers.

Why? She kept asking him why he was bothering with her. Now he was asking himself why he had fallen in love with her. He couldn't come up with an answer to either question that made any sense. Why would he put himself out for a woman he had actively disliked before he had ever set eyes on her? It wasn't as if she had made any effort to change his opinion. On the contrary she had gone out of her way to reinforce it, flirtatious one minute, downright rude the next, eagerly courting the media even while she purported to despise it. Yet all the time, underlying so much worldly cynicism, there was a little-girl-lost fragility that made him want to wrap her in cotton wool. He was sure it wasn't part of the act. The Claudia Beaumont performance.

For a while she had fooled him and it had made him angry with himself for wanting her so much. Angry with her for being so desirable. She was a man-eater. But she was a beautiful man-eater and honesty forced him to admit that he was a willing victim. When she had kissed him for the cameras he had thought he would explode. Yet when she had kissed him this evening if had been different. She had been different.

He poked at the fire again as he relived that moment when she had fallen apart. She hadn't cried. Not then. Wouldn't an actress have cried? Just a little, nothing too messy. But she'd fought tears and when later she had finally succumbed there had been nothing controlled or pretty about them. They had been real enough.

So, was the glamorous image something she put on for public consumption, little more than a disguise to hide behind?

Love was clouding his judgement and he shied away from answering himself, knowing that he wanted it to be the truth, knowing how easy it would be to fool himself into believing that she returned his feelings. He dragged his fingers through his hair, shutting his eyes tightly for a moment to blot out the moment when he had held her, when she had raised her lips and kissed him with an almost childlike innocence. He needed to concentrate, although how he was supposed to do that when he could hear the springs squeak as she climbed into bed just a few feet above his head . . . There was only so much a man could take. It was definitely time for some fresh air.

He dropped the poker, straightened, flexing his aching knee and then quietly let himself out of the back of the cottage, standing for a moment on the step.

The night was clear and the nearly full moon was bathing the scene in sufficient light to make the use of the torch unnecessary. The lake, pink in the dying light of the sun, was now a smooth sheet of steel grey. Everything was perfectly still. He wandered down towards the small dock he had helped his father build years before and out along its length over the lake to stand finally a few feet above the water. He knew he should be doing what he had encouraged Claudia to do, think. Try and work out what was happening. The plain truth was that he was finding it difficult to think about anything but her.

He rubbed his hand over his face. The fire had dried him out, leaving him feeling tight-skinned and hot. He needed a shower, preferably a cold one; what he had was the lake. It wouldn't be the first time he had taken a night dip and now, when his body was tormented with the kind of thoughts that seemed to burn continuously in his brain, seemed as good a time as any.

He turned to look up at Claudia's window, half hoping to see her there, but there was no flicker of candlelight from behind the dark window and he imagined her lying in the big old-fashioned bed and wondered if she was restless too. For a moment he thought he saw a movement, but it was just the curtain shifting in the light breeze, his imagination conspiring with his overcharged libido to show him what he wanted to see.

He wasn't sure whether he was relieved or sorry, but he refused to dwell on it. Instead he reached up and catching hold of the collar of his shirt, he pulled it over his head.

It was too quiet. Used to London, Claudia missed the constant, day-and-night drone of traffic to lull her to sleep. Or maybe it was her thoughts that were keeping her awake, disturbing thoughts of Mac lying in this bed, locked in his wife's arms, the little bedroom filled with the soft murmurs of their lovemaking.

As her imagination began to work overtime it provoked feelings of such self-disgust in her that she threw back the cover and flew to the window, hanging on the sill as, eyes closed, she drew deep breaths of fresh air down into her lungs. His wife. Jenny. It was terribly wrong to be envious of a dead woman, but she wanted Gabriel so much. For just a moment, when he had held her, kissed away her tears, she had been certain that he felt the same way.

The click of a thumb latch being raised startled her

out of the bewildering thoughts that raced through her head, thoughts she couldn't handle but which refused to be blocked out. She turned, hoping that she had been wrong, that Gabriel would be standing the doorway. But the door remained closed. Everything was so quiet here that each sound seemed magnified and after a moment when her confused brain sent her heartrate rocketing with a heady mixture of excitment and desire, she realized that the sound had come not from behind her, but from below.

Peering down into the overgrown garden she saw Gabriel stepping from beneath the shelter of the eaves, his tall frame bleached by the moonlight, his dark hair touched with silver as he covered the ground noiselessly, heading for the lake and out onto the landing stage.

Claudia watched him, an awful longing welling deep inside her to be down on the dock beside him, to go to him, put her arms about him and attempt to offer him some comfort for the pain buried deep within him. To offer him her love.

But she couldn't. There was a barrier between them now. His lack of trust would always be there and it wasn't as if he had come racing back to her side because he realized that he was wrong, that he had misjudged her. He had come back because something had made him uneasy. Because his conscience had pricked him.

She pulled herself together and half turned, determined to return to bed, not to spy on him as he wrestled with memories that had kept him away from the cottage for so long. Then he turned to look up at her window and Claudia froze. Had he seen her watching him in the darkness? For a moment she remained like a statue and hoped she was hidden by the curtains. Her hope was apparently realized because after what seemed an age he turned back to the lake. Before she could make good her resolve to beat a retreat to the bed, he had raised his hand and in one fluid movement pulled his shirt over his head, dropping it at his feet. She remained frozen as he kicked off the soft desert boots he wore, peeled off his socks.

Claudia's forehead wrinkled in a frown, then her hand flew to her mouth to stifle the small hungering sound that bubbled up from her throat. Her earlier shivers had had more to do with the thick walls of the cottage that kept out the August heat, more to do with fear than the ambient temperature. The breeze that brushed against her cheek, moulding the fine lawn nightdress to her figure, was warm. Gabriel MacIntyre was going to swim naked in his lake.

As if to confirm her thoughts he began to unfasten the buckle at his waist. She could hear the sharp slap of the leather as he tugged the end of his belt free and she listened intently for the telltale sound of the zip. Before it reached her, he had pushed his denims over his hips, discarding them and his underwear in one smooth, economical movement. Then, as he stepped clear, she caught her breath.

It was as if he was being revealed to her by layers.

Even on that first encounter, when she had mentally dismissed him as too rough hewn for her taste, Claudia had still been toe-tinglingly aware of the promise beneath the heavy olive drab sweater and combat trousers that he had been wearing.

When, on Sunday morning, he had been dressed in well cut casual clothes she had realized that he was more elegantly put together than first impressions had suggested. He might have shoulders like a girder, but he was tall, well proportioned and the toughness had seemed less obvious. And afterwards, in her dimly lit spare bedroom, when she had been offered a more telling glimpse of the hard torso, a stomach flat enough to iron on and the kind of taut buttocks that a girl's fantasies were made of, a great deal more than her toes had tingled.

More than her toes were tingling now as he stood quite naked on the dock, hers to admire and enjoy at leisure, with every tantalizing promise more than fulfilled. He was awesome. A statue by Michaelangelo, but deliciously, gloriously alive and far more beautiful than any of the pretty actors who had escorted her to premieres and parties.

She sank to her knees in front of the window, propping her chin on her arms to marvel at the way the light muscling of his back was sculpted and accentuated by moonshadow and the deep indentation of his spine terminated in neat, firm buttocks. Then, as he turned to drop his wristwatch on his clothes, she had the briefest glimpse of the spattering of hair that arrowed down his flat belly to his loins, fluffing darkly . . .

She felt herself blushing at her shamelessness, but she still didn't look away and when he turned back to the lake she let her glance trickle down the straight, well-shaped legs. Leg. He favoured one of them. Without his clothes it was easier to see why. Even the soft moonlight could not disguise the scar that jagged viciously behind his left knee and calf where the bullet had sliced through his flesh. Before she could register the extent of the damage he had executed a simple, elegant dive, scarcely raising a ripple on the surface of the water and disappeared from sight.

Her private peepshow was over and Claudia knew she should move before he returned and saw her staring down at him.

But he stayed beneath the water for so long that she began to panic, rising to her feet in her agitation. Suppose he had knocked his head on some rubbish that had been dumped since he was last here? Or had become entangled in weeds? Then, when she thought her lungs would burst from holding her breath and much further out than she had expected, Claudia saw the pale arc of his arm as he lifted it clear of the water, swimming in a slow, deliberate crawl that ate up the distance.

For a while he was out of her sight, hidden by a reed-fringed spit of land, then without any warning he was suddenly back at the dock, hauling himself up on powerful arms, the water streaming from his moon-whitened skin.

She backed slowly away from the window, wanting to stay, but knowing instinctively that if she remained there a second longer he would sense her watching him and look up. And then she knew she wanted him to look up, to come to her.

It was as if her thoughtwaves were plugged directly into his brain because quite suddenly he stopped rubbing himself dry with his t-shirt and lifted his head as if he'd heard something and instinctively he looked to the window and saw her. For a moment he remained perfectly still, then he began to run towards the cottage.

She was still at the window, looking down into the garden, when he burst through the bedroom door. 'What it is? What's wrong?' he demanded.

'Nothing's wrong, Gabriel. Not now you're here,' she said, quietly. The moon was shining through her nightgown, her body a dark silhouette as she turned to him and crossed the room on bare, silent feet. 'But you told me you wouldn't leave me.' She reached out her hand and took his. 'You're cold. Come to bed, my love, and I'll warm you.'

He had been cold, but she'd just turned on the central heating.

'Claudia?' He breathed her name, wanting her to be certain, hoping that she was certain.

'I'll understand if you don't want to make love with me. I know what I look like. But I need you to hold me. I need to hold you.'

She needed reassurance, she needed to be loved. He understood that. He hadn't been mistaken when he had stepped away from her and sent her to bed. It wasn't him she wanted, but comfort. And God help him, she thought it would be difficult for him. At least he could disabuse her of that. He dropped the t-shirt he had been holding in front of him and she gave a gasp as she realized that he was fully aroused.

'Why are you surprised?' he asked. 'Isn't that the effect you usually have on a man?'

He saw her swallow, struggle to find the words. 'It's been a while.'

'For me too.' He lifted the hand linked in his to his mouth and kissed the palm before raising it to his cheek while his other hand found her hip and drew her closer. 'But they do say it's like riding a bicycle . . .'

'Who says?' she murmured. 'What bicycle?' Her fingertips found his mouth, the pad of her thumb stroking the inside of his lip and her mouth, her tongue following in a long, erotic kiss.

And as she kissed him, he eased up her nightdress inch by inch, savouring the torturously slow discovery of her body as it came into direct contact with his. A smooth, satiny thigh and the soft fluff of down that marked her sex moving slowly against the inside of his leg. Her abdomen soft and yielding against an arousal that was almost painful in its intensity. The excitingly hard tips of her breasts against his chest as his hands, on their own journey of exploration, cupped her firm, round bottom, then swooped into her waist before his fingers spread out over her back to hold her even more tightly against him. She moaned softly into his mouth, a small begging sound that left him feeling like a god, her need was so tangible. Then she let her head fall back so that he could pull the gown over her head.

As he dropped it, he bent to taste her skin, breathing a trail of small kisses from her neck to the shadowy valley between her breasts. As his tongue began to circle the dark areola of her nipple and he drew it into his mouth, he felt her begin to tremble and her legs parted eagerly as his fingers touched the dewy warmth there.

'Gabriel, please,' she begged hoarsely and he didn't need a second invitation, scooping her up onto the bed. 'Now, Gabriel, now,' she urged, her thighs parting to him, leaving him in no doubt as to her meaning and near to exploding with his own urgent need, he was inside her with one long thrust.

She had been ready for him, but she was tight. An exclamation of surprise was startled from his lips as he paused above her to wonder.

Claudia opened her eyes and looked up at him. 'I thought you said you hadn't forgotten how to do this,' she murmured, tightening her muscles around him, just in case he needed a reminder.

He caught his breath, for a moment fighting the need to simply let go and take the quick release she offered. But this wasn't about him, or his needs. This was for *her*. For a moment it was touch and go while he struggled to blank out the singing in his ears, the vision of erotic beauty Claudia made lying back on the pillow, her lips parted, her lashes thick fringes against her cheeks. He had to concentrate on something incredibly dull; the formula for working out the speed of a falling object, the battles of the Hundred Years War, the temperature at which . . . then, quite suddenly, he found the strength to rise above his body's clamour and the bucking need for satisfaction was restrained to a steady throbbing heat.

'What's the matter, sweetheart?' he asked, lowering his head to her breast and resuming the torment of one tight nipple with his tongue. She gasped and again the muscles tightened about him, this time involuntarily, but he was ready for it. 'Are you in a hurry?'

'No,' Claudia gasped, her eyes wide with astonishment. 'Take all the time you like.' And as he began to move at a slow, measured pace within her, she reached up, placing both hands on his chest and began to slowly circle her palms over his firm flesh.

His nipples tightened under her hands, grazing her palms and sending small tremors of excitment through her body as Gabriel began to slowly stoke up a deeper heat within her, murmuring soft love words as he nuzzled at her throat, her shoulder, her breasts. She took her pace from him, matching the even rhythm of his hips as he increased the pace and as the heat became an inferno, she began to sizzle. She clutched at his shoulders, digging in her nails as it became impossible to contain the earth-shattering momentum towards a searing, sensually devastating release

341

that seemed to lift her, propelling her into a dizzy world of absolute pleasure that was compounded by Gabriel's shout of triumph and the warmth of his own release deep within her.

She was a long time coming down from the explosive climax of their lovemaking and for a while there was no sound beyond a ragged gasping for air, but Gabriel cradled Claudia to him and pulled the cover over them. She felt glorious, as if she had been found after a long time lost, yet a little frightened at the intensity of her feelings. Afraid, too, of the silence that seemed to be growing between them. Afraid that he was already regretting what he had done. She didn't want him to feel trapped by guilt into some relationship which he wouldn't handle, she wanted him to know that he was free to walk away. So she tilted her head back to look up at him. His head was thrown back against the pillow, the arm not cradling her thrown across his face so that she could not see his expression, had no way of knowing what he was feeling.

'Gabriel?' she murmured, to capture his attention.

'Mmmm?' He didn't move.

'I'm looking forward to seeing you on a bike,' she said.

He turned to look at her, his eyes blank and for just a moment she thought she had made a dreadful mistake. Then he leaned forward and kissed her lightly on the lips. 'If you're good I'll let you have a ride on my cross-bar.'

'I can't wait,' she said, wrapping her arms about his waist, burying her head against his chest so that she could blink back the hot tears that burned at her lids.

'Tomorrow. Go to sleep.'

But Claudia couldn't sleep. And neither, apparently, could Gabriel. For a while they both lay very still, then she sat up.

Gabriel fumbled in the darkness for the matches and lit the candle. 'What is it?' he asked, turning to her. Claudia shook her head, unable to look at him. 'Are you concerned? Because I didn't use anything?' When she didn't answer, he said, 'I haven't been with anyone since Jenny. You've no need to worry.'

Worry? She hadn't worried, hadn't spared a thought for the consequences when she had invited him into her bed. And he had obviously thought she would be on the pill. Well, she wouldn't disabuse him. But she could put his mind at rest. 'I'm not into casual sex either, Gabriel.'

He propped up a pile of pillows and sat back against them, before stretching out his arm and offering her his shoulder. 'I'm beginning to get the idea that your reputation as a wild lady is something dreamed up by a newspaperman on a slow day.'

She settled against him. 'Even newspapermen have to have something to work on, Gabriel; I had a lot of fun to catch up on when I left home. The trouble is that when you've got a famous name it doesn't need much. The smallest indiscretion . . .' She shrugged, tellingly.

'You must have been the gossip columnists' delight.'

'Well, if a girl wants fame and fortune in the theatre she has to get noticed. And at eighteen I was still young enough to take some pleasure in hurting my father.' She sighed, sorry for that.

'Claudia – '

'The best part, though, the one thing that was remarked upon in the disapproving and yet slightly salacious style adopted by all the commentators, was that although I looked like my mother, I wasn't in the least bit like her in any other way.' She felt Gabriel stiffen, knew she had shocked him and she tried to pull away from him. But he held her fast.

'You encouraged them, didn't you? You played up the similarity in your looks and the difference in your behaviour?'

'Congratulations, Gabriel. You've just won first prize.'

'Why do you hate her so much?' She resisted him, but he wouldn't let her go. 'There must be a reason, Claudia.' He sat up, turned her to face him. 'You can tell me. I know what it's like to hate someone.'

'Do you?' She turned her head to look up at him, searching his face for some clue, but finding none. 'You wouldn't believe it. No one would.'

For a long moment he seemed to wrestle with something buried so deep inside him that he couldn't find to way to tell her. Then he said, 'Jenny, my loving wife Jenny, was so desperate to be the world's most famous climber that she was prepared to die in the attempt. It was her life to risk and since I was risking mine on a daily basis, I could hardly stop her. Unfortunately, her ambition was so great that she killed our baby too.'

'She was expecting a baby, I knew there was something . . .' Claudia gasped. Jenny Callendar had been at over twenty thousand feet, climbing without oxygen, when she began to miscarry and she had died before her companions could get her to medical help. 'Oh, Gabriel, I'm so sorry. To lose everything in one – '

'I lost a son or daughter. I don't believe I ever had Jenny. If I had, she could never have done that.'

'You mean she *knew*? They said . . . the papers said . . . that she hadn't realized she was pregnant.'

'When I flew back from Bosnia for the funeral there was a letter from the antenatal clinic about her first appointment.'

'Here?' she asked, very quietly.

'No, Claudia. Not here.' He pulled her back against him, drawing the cover over them both in a gesture that was both protective and reassuring. 'She wouldn't live here. She considered it beneath her. And having the Abbey in sight of the window just added insult to – '

'The Abbey? Then, 'Oh! I see. You're the man with the troublesome inheritance tax.'

'I'm getting there. But I had eighteen years of living in a draughty old house that was impossible to heat. I couldn't wait to escape and I'm certainly not going back. The management consultants are welcome to it . . . at a price. Now, what was that you were saying? Something about me not believing your story? Why don't you try me?'

So she did. As the candle guttered in the balmy breeze that stirred the curtains, she told him exactly why she hated to be compared with her mother.

'My mother had this reputation as a some kind of paragon. Not only was she a great star, but she was the perfect wife and mother. These days it would be impossible to maintain the fiction; even then it must have taken a conspiracy of silence among people who knew her, a willingness to suspend belief . . .'

'Some legends are too big to be challenged.'

'There must be a lot of people who could make a fortune out of telling it the way it really was. Why don't they?'

'Would you like them to?' She didn't answer for a while.

'No. It would hurt Dad too much to drag it all up. He suffered enough when she was alive.'

'Then maybe the conspiracy of silence is to protect him, rather than your mother,' Gabriel suggested. 'After all, there hasn't been anything to stop you telling it "the way it really was". Has there?'

She shook her head. Except that she wouldn't, couldn't put all that nightmare down on paper for everyone to read. 'It never occurred to me that people were simply being kind.'

'What was it, Claudia? Drink? Drugs?'

'No, she didn't drink much, she was too careful of her looks and her figure for that and she despised people who took drugs. It was just plain old sex with her. She was having an affair with a married man. A politician. He drove off the road one night with her. She was terribly injured, her face was scarred . . .' She touched her own cheek in an unconsciously protective gesture.

'You won't be marked,' Gabriel said, quickly, taking her hand away, kissing her blotched cheek.

'I know, Gabriel. But tonight, when I looked at myself in the mirror, I asked myself how I would react if I had to live with these marks for the rest of my life. Supposing I was *really* like her? Deep down?'

'And did you come up with an answer?' he prompted.

'When you've had perfection, I suppose second best is never enough.' She half turned to lay her head against his chest, her arm across his waist. 'At least I was never perfect.'

'That's true.' Then he yelped in protest as she pinched him. 'I was only agreeing with you.

'It isn't compulsory.'

'I'll bear that in mind. What happened to the man? Do you know who it was?'

She shook her head. 'Only that he walked away without a scratch, and that he was powerful enough to ensure that the incident was hushed up.'

'But surely your father didn't let him get away with that?'

'Dad kept the truth to himself to protect her, not her lover. The story was that she had fallen asleep at the wheel, she'd had a minor accident and decided to retire to spend more time with her family after realizing how close she had come to losing everything.' Gabriel made a small disgusted sound. 'No one ever doubted it. Why would they? It was all part of the image.'

'Some image.'

'There was a time, in my early teens, when I used to watch my father's face when the news was on, hoping I might catch some reaction, discover the man's identity.'

'You knew all this when you were still a child?' He was horrified.

'My mother told me. I was to be the new Elaine French, you see. Take her place, keep her name alive. And she didn't want me to make the same mistakes.' Gabriel said something short and damning. 'But she never told me who he was. She always protected him.'

'What a pity she didn't have the same concern for her daughter.'

'I don't think she ever saw me in quite that way.'

'What the devil was your father doing while all this was happening?'

'Suffering, mostly, although I didn't know that until quite recently. He'd fallen in love with Melanie's mother, you see. He'd been planning to leave my mother and take us with him to start a new life with her. After the accident Juliet simply disappeared, went away, because she knew it couldn't happen. Dad didn't even know about Melanie until earlier this year.'

'And *still* no one challenges the myth of the perfect marriage?'

'People believe what they want to believe. And they want to believe in fairy-tales. I thought him so weak for protecting my mother when she made his life a living hell. I suppose I needed to punish him for that.'

'He didn't protect you.'

'And I didn't protect Fizz. But we never told him we knew.' She grinned suddenly. 'Fizz and I used to act out luridly melodramatic scenes in which the tortured soul of our mother's lover drove him to publicly confess all before throwing himself at her feet to implore her forgiveness.'

'Men like him don't have souls, Claudia.'

'No. But each and every day he has to look over his shoulder and wonder if this day will be the one his luck runs out and my father decides to spill the beans.'

'It's a rather subtle form of revenge.'

'I don't think Dad ever thought of revenge. He had his own problems.' Living with the ruins of Elaine French had not been easy. 'Money was difficult, too. He sold the London house and all my mother's precious baubles to pay for the expensive private nursing. The ones we have now are copies.'

'The fake diamond drops?'

'The fake everything.'

Her father had been kinder than her mother had ever deserved, Claudia thought to herself in the quiet of the little bedroom. And perhaps her father had understood, more than she had ever given him credit for, just what living with a mother teetering on the edge of madness had done to her. Because considering the way she had treated him, Claudia realized in the quiet little bedroom, her father had been a lot kinder to her than she deserved, too.

Gabriel shifted slightly, lifting his head to look down at her. 'It's getting light. It's going to be a pretty sunrise. And since sleep seems to be eluding us, we might as well enjoy it.'

'That suits me.' Claudia slid her fingers over the warm skin of his stomach, investigating the dark whorls of hair that stippled Gabriel's chest. 'What did you have in mind?'

He caught her hand and stopped her. 'How do you feel about a sunrise swim?'

'Is that what you meant when you said that baths could be arranged?'

'Not quite. I'll leave that treat until tonight. Bathing by candlelight is one of life's great pleasures.'

'Mmmm,' she murmured, not convinced. 'The lake will be cold.'

'Freezing. But don't worry, love. I'll be there to keep you warm.' And by way of demonstration he began to kiss her.

Later, a long time after a sunrise that had taken place without them even noticing it, they ran back to the cottage wrapped in nothing but towels, laughing and shivering. 'Here let me rub you dry,' Gabriel offered.

'No, I'll do it. For goodness' sake put on the kettle and make us something warm to drink before I shiver to death.'

'I'll warm you,' he offered, wrapping his arms about her and kissing her. For a moment she succumbed, but then pushed him away, laughing.

'Oh, no. Tea first, mister, then we'll discuss heating techniques.' And before he could recapture her she had run away up the stairs, drying herself as she went.

A few minutes later, when she reappeared wrapped up in a fleecy sweatshirt and a pair of jeans, she had something else on her mind.

'Gabriel, we have to talk about my hair.' She lifted the thick hank that hung on one side of her head. 'I've simply got to get up to town and have it cut. I feel ludicrously lopsided.'

'Whatever you say.'

Gabriel was standing in front of the fireplace, leaning on the mantle. He was dressed rather as she was, but in his hand was a portable telephone.

Claudia stopped looking at her hair and looked at him. And as she looked a cold clammy hand grabbed her insides and gave them a vicious twist. Something was wrong. Something was terribly wrong. 'What is it?' she demanded. 'What's happened?'

'I called your father. He asked me to let him know how you were.' He raised his eyes to hers.

'What's happened,' she repeated, her hand at her throat. 'Is he sick again? Is it his heart? Oh, my God. It's Fizz . . . the baby – '

'No!' He reached for her, took hold of her. 'No. Claudia. They're fine. *Fine*,' he repeated insistently, pulling her against him as the shock hit her. 'It's Joanna. Joanna Gray. She's in hospital, Claudia. She's had an accident.'

CHAPTER 15

'Joanna has had an accident?' Claudia repeated dully, unable to take it in. She looked up at Gabriel. '*Joanna?*' Then, 'Oh, my God, you mean she's the victim of something meant for me. That's it, isn't it? How is she? Will she make it? Tell me, Gabriel?' She pulled free from his arms. 'Tell me!'

'She's under sedation.' Claudia gasped. 'It's more shock than anything,' he added, hurriedly.

'I've got to go to her.' She cast around for her bag. '*Now*, Gabriel. This is all my fault and I have to be with her.'

He caught her arm. 'That's not a good idea.'

She shook him off. 'Don't be silly. Of course I must be with her.'

'She won't want to see you. Not for a while.' Something about the way he said that brought her to a halt. 'Sit down. Please, Claudia. I have to tell you something.'

'There's something else.' She subsided into one of the armchairs, not out of instant obedience, but because her legs were suddenly rubber. 'Something

353

worse.' And when Gabriel knelt down in front of her and took her hands in his, she knew that the attack of nerves was justified. 'What happened last night? Was it a disaster? What went wrong?'

'Nothing went wrong, love. Joanna was great last night. Your father was there with Diana and Heather. He said she was really good.'

'Gabriel, please . . .'

'Afterwards Edward took them backstage to meet her, to congratulate her . . . They found her sobbing her heart out in her dressing room.'

'It gets you like that sometimes,' Claudia said, shakily. 'And it's an awful strain standing in for someone else at short notice. I remember – ' She was beginning to babble.

'Listen to me,' he said, sharply and she stopped. Waited. Knowing that it was going to be awful. 'Darling, it's Joanna who's been sending you those horrible letters. She slashed your dress, too.'

'Joanna?' She stared at him. 'I don't believe it.'

'It all ties in. She knows where you live . . .' Claudia didn't answer. 'She told your father that she did it because she was so angry with you for taking her place in some television programme.'

And then she knew it was true. 'Not *some* television programme, Gabriel. *The* television programme. *Stalker*.' She stared at him. 'But that's silly. She broke her arm. Someone would have had to do it.'

'But you had so much already. She said you didn't appreciate how lucky you were. Edward tried to calm her down, but she broke away from him and ran out of the theatre. She was hit by a car.' She groaned and let her head sink to her arms. 'Darling, she's going to be all right. Bumps and bruises, nothing broken. Shock mostly.'

She straightened, slowly. 'Take me to her, Gabriel. I've got to see her. She's got to know that I'm still her friend.'

He hesitated. 'You mean that? After what she did?'

'Of course I mean it. Can't you see how she must have been suffering? It'll be so much worse now. She'll think everyone will find out. I've got to reassure her, tell her that I understand.'

'Do you?'

'Of course I understand. This is a tough business; luck is an important as talent, who you know, family connections. She's right. I've never appreciated how lucky I am. Take me to her, please, Gabriel. I must see her as soon as possible.'

'Yes, of course you must. I just wasn't sure you would be able to. I'm sorry, I should have known.'

'Why?' Her eyes flashed angrily. 'You don't know me, Gabriel. No one knows me.'

Gabriel knew there was no point in trying to convince her that she was wrong. She was upset and with good reason. To discover that someone you trusted could do such a terrible thing was the worst of betrayals. So he stood up and stepped aside. 'We'll go as soon as you're ready.'

'Now. I'm ready now.'

He didn't argue, bit back the suggestion that she should at least have something to eat. He simply picked up his keys and headed for the door.

They travelled most of the way in silence, Claudia lost in her own deep thoughts. He glanced at her from time to time. She must have known, but she made no effort to respond and he didn't push her to talk. She needed time to come to terms with what had happened. It was even possible that she was regretting the impulse to rush to Joanna Gray's side. Then, as they approached London, Gabriel was forced to concentrate on steering the Landcruiser through the early morning traffic piling into the capital.

As they neared Knightsbridge, Claudia stirred. 'Will you take me to my flat first, please.'

Her flat. With the thick gouts of red paint plastered up the walls and over the carpet. Edward was going to have it cleaned up, decorated, before she returned, but he wouldn't have had time. 'I don't think – '

'No, I don't suppose you do. But I can't let Joanna see me like this. I need to put on some make-up, cover my hair.'

He bit down on the angry feelings that boiled up in him. She was probably right, but she was a damn sight kinder than Joanna Gray deserved.

He warned her what to expect, but when she reached the top of the stairs and saw the mess for herself, she came to an abrupt halt, clapping her hand over her mouth, swaying just a little as the reality hit her. She didn't object when he put his arm around her and she didn't argue when he took the key from her and opened the flat door, bundling her inside. For a moment she let him hold her. Just for a moment. Then she pulled away. 'I won't be long, Gabriel,' she said, absently. 'Make some tea if you want some. There's a carton of long-life milk somewhere.'

'Can I get something for you?'

'No.' So he didn't bother. He heard the shower running briefly, then her bedroom door closing. Twenty minutes later she reappeared looking as poised and as stunningly beautiful as ever. Make-up, rather heavier than usual perhaps, covered the worst of the blotches on her face and neck. Her eyes and lips had been made up brightly to draw attention away from what could still be seen. And her hair had been covered by an elegant arrangement with a scarf that didn't look out of place with the wide cotton trousers and silk tunic. She looked, every inch of her, a star. But somehow he didn't think she would appreciate compliments.

'Ready?' he asked.

'Yes. Let's go.'

Joanna was in a side ward and Claudia insisted on seeing her alone. Gabriel watched from a distance through the glass walls as she bent over her friend, kissed her cheek and held her hand. Then she sat on the edge of the bed and began to talk. She was there a long time.

Edward arrived after a while and sat with him. 'This is a very sad business, Mac.' He nodded towards his daughter. 'How did she take it?'

Mac considered the question. 'I think she feels guilty. That somehow it's all her fault for having so much.'

'She doesn't need to feel guilty,' Edward Beaumont said angrily. 'Everything she has came at a terrible price.' Mac shook his head, aware of Edward's scrutiny. 'She's told you.' It wasn't a question but a statement, and it didn't need an answer. 'She's an extraordinary girl, Mac. Infuriating at times, I'll admit. And there have been times I've been terribly afraid for her. If she trusts you sufficiently to tell you about her mother, I don't need to explain.'

'No.' He turned away from Edward's shrewd eyes, standing up as Claudia reappeared. 'How is she?'

'Just bruised and sore. She'll be allowed out tomorrow if she's got someone to look after her. I've told her she can come and stay with me.'

'Claudia, darling,' her father began, 'is that wise?'

'She hasn't got anyone else.'

'Will you be able to cope?' Mac asked, taking her hand. 'It doesn't sound like such a good idea to me.'

'Of course it's a good idea. There's nothing wrong with me and my life is back to normal. No more nonsense,' she said, not quite managing to meet his eye.

'I was thinking of her. After what she did it's going to be difficult for her to accept anything from you. The

358

letters, the dress – ' he dismissed them as minor problems – 'but when she sees the paint . . .'

'I'll get decorators organized this morning. She won't have to see it.' She regained possession of her hand and turned to her father. 'And there's no need to worry about tonight's performance, I can handle it.' She cut off her father's protest. 'Once I've had my hair sorted out. Will you drop me off at the hairdressers, Gabriel? It's not far out of your way home.'

There. She'd said it. Set him free with her casual dismissal. Let him know that she quite understood that last night was just one of those things that happened when two people were thrown together in emotional circumstances. She'd needed someone, he'd been kind. More than kind. But there was no need to make a big thing out of it, pretend it meant more than it did, hang on until it all got horribly messy. That way it could only end in tears and what they had shared had been too important, too special to end like that.

'Drop you off. You don't want me to wait for you?' he asked. The words were slow, careful, as if he wanted to be certain that he understood her.

'Good heavens, no.' She laughed at the very idea. 'I don't need a bodyguard any more and I've put you to far too much trouble already. I can easily get a taxi back to the flat.'

'The flat.' There was a moment of silence. Then, 'Well, yes, I suppose you're right. I've got a million things to catch up on. Tony's been doing two jobs, Adele is quite out of hand . . .'

Edward cleared his throat. 'I'm going your way, Claudia. Maybe, if Mac is so pressed you should let him get back to work.'

'Oh, yes – ' Claudia began quickly.

'There's no need – ' Gabriel said, at the same time.

Edward glanced from one to the other. 'I'll leave you to sort it out, while I make a call from the car.'

'Well, there,' Claudia said, as soon as her father had gone. 'What could be better? Now I won't have to feel guilty about dragging you out of your way.' She put out her hand in a formal and unmistakable gesture of farewell.

She wanted him to shake her hand? After last night? He couldn't believe it. But he took it, because it gave him a last chance to be near to her. But he didn't shake it, he held it and had to fight the urge to pull her into his arms, to pour out his feelings. But she looked so distant, so far from him. So, instead, he leaned forward and lightly kissed her cheek. 'You don't have to feel guilty, Claudia,' he told her. 'About anything.'

Despite the overheated temperature of the hospital Claudia's hand felt cold in his and she shivered a little. 'I'll never forget what you did for me. Truly. I hope . . . one day . . .' She hoped one day he would discover a new love, a new happiness, but he wouldn't want her sympathy any more than he wanted her love. When she stepped back she had a smile firmly fixed to her lips. 'Goodbye, Gabriel,' she said. 'Mind how you jump out of aeroplanes . . .'

360

He wanted to seize her, make her look at him while he told her how much he loved her, how much he would always love her. But he didn't because he knew she wouldn't want to know. And with a little flutter of her fingers she turned and walked away from him.

'Goodbye, my love,' he said, softly. She didn't hear him. She was already clipping smartly down the corridor, head held high, apparently oblivious to the ripple of head-turning recognition as she passed. She turned a corner and disappeared from sight. For a moment Mac remained where he was, then, unable to bear the emptiness he began to follow her, breaking into a run as she disappeared through the door to the car park. But then he stopped. The ever present newsmen were there, no doubt alerted by a porter with a contact on a newsdesk. They surrounded her as she waited at the curb for her father and she threw back her head and laughed at something one of them had said.

He could still see her, Mac thought, but she was gone. She was back in her own world. He'd known how it would be. But he hadn't realized just how hard it would be to let her go, how much it would hurt.

'Joanna is going to be fine. Just a few bumps and bruises.' Her clear voice carried to back to him. 'When *Private Lives* goes on tour later in the year she'll be playing Amanda, you can put money on it.'

'And what'll you be doing, Claudia,' one of the men asked.

'Having fun, darling, what else?' And she blew them a kiss before stepping into her father's Daimler.

Claudia Beaumont. Her name was like a brand between his eyes, her scent clung to his skin. She was a hot ache that wouldn't go away. Before he met her, he had believed Claudia was just another trivial, careless, almost certainly amoral woman. He had learned that he was wrong, in every respect. She was warm, funny, loving. Who else would have rushed to offer comfort to a girl who had done everything in her power to frighten and hurt her, who might even have blinded her.

He frowned. He had been so certain that it had been a man who had been behind the campaign of terror. He should have insisted on speaking to Joanna himself. While the slashed dress and the letters had fitted a certain kind of female cattiness, it had been a man in the delivery van, watching the apartment . . . And there was something else. What? He rubbed his hand hard over his face. Something. He needed sleep so badly. Maybe with a clear head . . .

The urgent burble of the telephone cut across his train of thought.

'Yes?' he snapped, bad-temperedly.

'Mac. I need help.' It was Adele and something in her voice loaded his blood with adrenalin and he was immediately alert. 'I've started having contractions and Tony flew to Cardiff first thing. I phoned him but there was a problem with the plane – '

362

'Where are you?'

'At the airfield.'

'Idiot!'

'Thanks, and I love you too. Someone's got to keep this place ticking over while you're off holding Miss Beaumont's pretty white – ' She broke off.

'Adele?'

'Ummm. Mac, this is a bit tricky. Everything is moving rather quicker than I was led to expect. I've called an ambulance but – '

'I'll meet you at the hospital.'

'I'm sorry to disappoint you, but it's not you I want. I need Tony. Now . . .' Her breath caught on a gasp. 'Oh . . . ooohhh. *Mac*! Do something!'

'Cross your legs, sweetheart. I'll get him to you somehow.'

'Are you sure you did the right thing, Claudia?' her father asked as they drove out of the hospital car park.

'Oh, yes. Joanna must come to me.'

'I wasn't talking about Joanna Gray. I was referring to Gabriel MacIntyre.' She glanced up, startled. 'He seems . . . fond of you.' She didn't respond and he continued. 'He's quite a hero, you know. He got a gong for something he did in the Gulf.'

She wasn't a bit surprised to hear it. 'Did he? How do you know that?'

'It was in the paper yesterday. Your little *contretemps* in some restaurant made quite a splash and someone must have been doing their homework.'

Claudia groaned. 'Oh, good grief. I'd forgotten all about that.'

'There was quite a bit about his wife, too. He was married to Jenny Callendar . . . the climber? But I expect you knew that.'

'Yes, he told me.' And after that he'd still had the patience to listen to her petty problems, the generosity to make love with her, when he had seen her need for him, as if she was the last woman in creation. It made her heartsick that he should have been so exposed because of his determination to protect her.

'He's a good man, Claudia. Luke checked him out.'

Claudia stared at her father. 'Luke did *what*?'

He shrugged. 'Mac promised to look after you, sweetheart, but Luke didn't know anything about him.'

'Gabriel wouldn't hurt me, Dad.' She sat back and closed her eyes. And she wouldn't hurt him. She'd done her best to see that he wasn't. More than her best. 'He's about as close to a "parfit gentil knyght" as a girl can hope for these days. He even knew how to bow out without making a fuss.'

'That's a pity.'

'Oh?'

'I was rather hoping he would know when to hang in there. He's the first man I've met who looked capable of keeping you in line.'

Claudia forced a laugh. 'That's reason enough, don't you think, to beat a hasty retreat.'

★ ★ ★

364

Claudia left the salon after a couple of hours during which she had been treated like a Dresden shepherdess by a stylist shattered by the ruins of her hair. She had been pampered, cooed over by his staff, offered every combination of coffee, tea and snack that it was possible to dream up. They all assumed that her distracted mood was the result of the disaster that had befallen her hair and she didn't disabuse them.

She'd sent Gabriel away. She couldn't believe she'd done that. Another few days, a week even, wouldn't have made such a difference, would it? Except of course, that it would have. Once she was out of danger there could be no pretence and she would have to admit her feelings. Then he would feel guilty for not loving her in return and he would try to pretend. She couldn't do that to him. Or to herself.

'Claudia?' She realized that her approval was awaited and she gave her attention to her reflection. 'What do you think?'

'It's . . . oh, heavens, it's so different.' She turned her head to the side. 'I've never had short hair, before. I feel positively lightheaded.' She touched the soft golden tendrils that curled around her ears and lay on her neck. It gave her a gamin look that was entirely new. 'I just love it.' There was an almost audible sigh of relief from around the room and she laughed. 'It's wonderful. Thank you.'

'Just stay away from paint and that will be thanks enough,' the stylist warned her. She'd spun them a story about knocking a tin of paint from a stepladder at the theatre and they hadn't questioned it.

Back on the pavement she didn't know what to do. For days her whole life had been dictated by Gabriel. Now, suddenly, she was on her own. She ought to go back to the flat, try and sleep for a while. The flat. The paint. She needed to organize an emergency clean-up so that Joanna wouldn't have to face the mess she'd made. She shuddered as she thought of it and wondered, briefly, if Gabriel had been right.

Tony didn't wait for his plane to be repaired. He borrowed a car and beat Mac to the hospital by seconds and they met in the entrance to the maternity unit.

'How is she?' Tony demanded.

'In a hurry to be a mother. You'd better get in there.'

Tony hesitated. 'I hope I don't faint.'

'I advise against it, she'd never let you live it down.'

'No.' He dragged his hand through his hair. 'You're right.' Then he looked at Mac more closely. 'If you don't mind my saying so, you look as if you could do with a bed yourself.'

'Mr Singleton?' A young nurse looked at the two men and waited for one of them to own up. Tony stepped forward. 'Your wife is getting impatient. I wouldn't keep her waiting if you want to see your baby make its entrance into the world.'

Mac watched him go, then sank onto a padded bench that lined the wall and tried very hard not to think how it could have been for him, if he hadn't made the mistake of marrying a woman who put herself before everything. He'd so admired Jenny's single-mindedness when he had first met her. Her lack of fear. Her determination to succeed. It hadn't taken him long to discover how much blind selfishness it took to fuel that kind of ambition. And to discover the only reason she'd married him was because she thought he had money. He'd just inherited Pinkneys Abbey and she had assumed, quite wrongly, that he would be able to finance any and all expeditions she cared to pick. Expeditions of which she would be the leader so that all the glory would be hers.

If she'd bothered to ask he would have explained what three lots of death duties in ten years did to an estate like Pinkneys, that inheriting it was a burden and not the bottomless piggy bank she had anticipated. It would have saved them both a lot of heartache.

'Hey, Mac.' A touch on his shoulder brought him awake and Tony was grinning down at him idiotically. 'It's a boy. He's . . . oh God, Mac, it was amazing. I mean I was *there*.'

'I take it you didn't faint. How's Adele?'

'Happy.' Tony's state of mind was not in question. 'Come and see them. I mean . . . it was incredible.'

'Just try and stop me,' Mac said, easing himself up off the bench. He felt like hell and probably looked it, he thought, as he rubbed his hand over his face and

367

realized he hadn't shaved. 'Tony,' he said, as his brother-in-law turned away, eager to get back to his wife. He looked back and Mac held out his hand. 'Congratulations.'

Adele was sitting up in bed, holding her baby and grinning from ear to ear. 'Good grief, Mac,' she exclaimed, on seeing him. 'Don't come any closer or you'll frighten my poor baby out of his wits.' She handed the infant over to his father. 'What on earth did that woman do to you last night?' she demanded.

'Last night?' Mac repeated, blankly.

'Last night. You're keeping a close watch on her, right? So I don't imagine you left her in London while you spent the night at the cottage?'

'You're too clever for me, Adele. I don't know what I'll do without you until you come back to work.'

'Come back to work? You must be joking. I'm a *mother*.' She beamed as if no one else in the entire world had managed the feat. 'That's a full-time job. Why don't you ask Miss Beaumont to give you hand? It might keep her out of trouble.'

Mac wasn't prepared to celebrate his unexpected victory just yet. He knew his sister too well. 'You just be careful. I might do that.' His forehead creased in concentration. He had been dreaming about Claudia when Tony woke him. She had been explaining something to him. Something important.

Adele touched his arm. 'Mac? Are you all right?'

He patted her hand. 'Sure. I just need a few hours' sleep.' He bent over her and kissed her. 'Well done, sweetheart. You've earned straight sixes for both technical merit and artistic achievement.' He turned to his nephew and touched his downy head. 'Right then, young Harry. Let's have a look at you.' He took the baby from Tony, cradled him for a moment.

Tony and Adele exchanged a glance. 'Actually, we thought of calling him James,' Adele said.

'He's the first boy of the new generation. He should be named for his grandfather.' He looked up, met Adele's eyes and smiled. 'He's beautiful.' He handed the baby back to his mother and then turned to Tony, laying a heavy hand on his shoulder. 'I hate to break up the party, but hadn't you better give some thought as to how you're going to get that plane back from Cardiff?'

'What plane?' Tony asked, still grinning idiotically.

Mac laughed. 'I'm kidding. No one in their right mind would let you loose with an aircraft right now. I'll send someone else to do the job.'

Someone else to do the job. A stand-in. Like Joanna Gray. That's what Claudia had been telling him in his dream. '*I telephoned her yesterday evening.*' Why was that so important? He dragged his hand over his face as he headed for the car park. Half an hour's nap on a hospital bench hadn't exactly set him up to think straight.

He climbed into the Landcruiser, slid the key into the ignition. *Telephoned.* Why was that so important? He hadn't stopped to listen to the telephone tapes last night. Now he wished he had. It would save him having to waste time going back to the airfield.

Once there he sifted through the tapes and found Claudia's at the third attempt. She'd called Fizz. It was just a friendly, how are you, how's the bump coming along, call. She'd called her father to tell him that she needed a few days off and suggested Joanna Gray as a stand-in. Then she'd called Joanna. '*I telephoned her yesterday evening.*'

He sat there and began to go through what had happened right from the beginning, from the moment he had noticed the envelope sticking out of Claudia's parachute pack until Joanna threw the can of paint over her. And then he knew what had been bothering him. He knew he had to speak to Joanna Gray and he didn't have time to catch up on his sleep.

By the time Claudia had organized a crew of decorators, she was asleep on her feet. But there was no point in returning to the flat – she'd get no peace there with workmen all over the place, making a noise, wanting to use her kitchen to make their tea.

Melanie didn't look surprised to see her, she didn't even ask any questions. She simply steered Claudia into her bedroom, found her a clean nightdress and tucked her up in bed. 'I'll give you a call in plenty of time for curtain up,' she promised. 'Don't worry about a thing.'

CHAPTER 6

Joanna Gray was sitting up, staring blankly at a magazine. For a moment Mac watched her through the glass. Then he tapped on the door. She jumped nervously and when she looked up he saw from her eyes that she recognized him but he introduced himself anyway.

'My name is Gabriel MacIntyre. I'm a friend of Claudia Beaumont's. Can I talk to you, Miss Gray?'

'Why? What do want?' She edged up the bed away from him.

'I believe that Claudia may still be in some danger but I don't want to frighten her unnecessarily. Can I ask you some questions?'

'I'm not going to do anything else,' she declared. 'I promise you. I promised her – '

'And she believed you,' he said, reassuringly. 'So do I. May I?' He didn't wait for her permission before lowering himself onto the edge of the bed.

'Then why are you here?' Joanna asked nervously.

'Because I want you to tell me exactly what you did to Claudia and how you did it.'

'But I told her – '

'Tell me.'

Joanna shivered. Mac had spoken softly, but there was no mistaking the determination in his voice. 'That's all?' she asked.

'That's all.'

'What about anyone who helped me? Will you want to know who – '

He hid his impatience. He needed to know the truth, but losing his temper wouldn't get him anywhere. 'I just want to know everything that you did. I'm not interested in names and it won't be taken any further. You have my word.' She still looked anxious. 'Claudia wouldn't allow it.'

'Only the photograph . . . someone else put that in the parachute. A friend, one of the film crew. He didn't know what it was. I told him it was a good luck message. I told Claudia that this morning.'

In Mac's opinion, Joanna Gray's friendship was not something to be eagerly pursued, but his smile remained friendly, his voice reassuring. 'I thought that was probably it. Tell me about the letters.'

'Oh, God.' She covered her face with her hands. 'I can't believe I did that. She put the idea into my head, you know. She said if she hurt herself I could take over as Amanda . . . I thought if she was really nervous she might be tense . . .'

And it had worked. She had been nervous and she had hurt her ankle. But she hadn't made a fuss, she'd just had it strapped and carried on. He put his hand on

372

her shoulder. 'We all do things we regret, Joanna. The important thing is learn from our mistakes. Come on now, tell me about it.'

'I just pushed the first one through her front door. Someone was going out and he held the door for me. After the first one the others just seemed to happen . . .'

'And the dress?'

She balked. 'Look, I've admitted all this. I don't want to talk about it.'

'But you slashed the dress.'

'Yes!'

A nurse looked in. 'Is everything all right here? Joanna?'

For a moment she looked as if she would complain, but Mac held her gaze. 'I'm fine,' she muttered. 'No problem.' She looked sullenly at Mac. 'I slashed the dress, I sent her nasty little notes, I cut up her photograph and had it put in the parachute. Now will you go away and leave me alone? Or do you want a confession in blood?'

'What about the car, Joanna?'

'The car?'

'Claudia's pretty new car. The brakes were tampered with. Did your friend in the film crew handle that? Or was that another friend?'

She stared at him. 'I don't know what you're talking about.'

'And the man watching her flat. The man in the delivery van. Was that another friend?'

She was staring at him as if he were mad. 'I don't know what you're talking about.'

'Don't you? Then tell me about the paint.'

'What paint?'

'Didn't you wonder why Claudia had her head covered up this morning? Why she was wearing so much make-up? She doesn't normally as I'm sure you know, since you're such a friend.' The woman in the bed visibly flinched but she didn't answer. 'Someone flung a litre of scarlet paint over her two nights ago. She reacted badly to it and her skin came out in great blotches. And they had to cut her hair off in the hospital. She could have been blinded, Joanna.'

For a moment Joanna Gray stared at him. 'Do you really think I'd do something like that? Try to *hurt* her?' she asked in a disbelieving whisper. He didn't answer. 'Oh, no,' she said, shaking her head. 'Oh no, you can't really believe that.'

'Why? Because you're her *friend*? Tell me, Joanna, would you have stopped at nasty letters if Claudia hadn't handed you her role on a plate when the strain got too much for her?'

'I wouldn't have done anything else. Please.' She clutched at his hand. 'You've got to believe that. I felt so ashamed of myself. I was going to call her, confess what a bitch I'd been, then out of the blue she phoned me, asked me if I'd take over from her for a week or so. As a favour to *her*. I thought . . . I *knew* if I'd told her what I'd done she wouldn't let me near the theatre.' She covered her face and began to sob quietly. 'Oh,

374

God. She was my friend, my very best friend and I've ruined everything.'

Mac stared down at the girl. He'd given her a hard time because he'd had too. She'd been a fool, but she hadn't hurt Claudia and he didn't believe she ever would. 'I'll tell you something about friendship,' he said, quietly. 'When Claudia came to see you this morning, rushing to comfort you, reassure you, offer you the sanctuary of her own home, she believed you had done every one of the things I've told you about. But she was more concerned about how you were feeling than with what you had done to her.'

'But I didn't!' She clutched at his arm, looking up at him with her tear-stained face. 'You've got to believe me. I didn't touch her car, or throw paint at her.' She gave a little groan. 'And if I didn't, someone else must have. You were right, she is still in danger. For pity's sake – '

But Mac hadn't waited to hear any more.

'I have to go home, Mel. I need some fresh underwear and much as I love you I have no wish to borrow yours. You're just too damned skinny.'

'Do you want me to come with you?'

'To hold my hand?' Claudia knew Melanie meant well, but she would have to face it sooner or later and she needed to begin to reclaim her life. Make some decisions about her future now that the horrors were behind her. The first hurdle would be facing her flat on her own. This morning hadn't counted. It had all

375

been too frantic. And Gabriel had been there. 'No, really. I just needed a couple of hours' sleep, that's all. I'm fine now.' Maybe that was an exaggeration, but she would make it the truth.

Gabriel was no longer a physical presence for her to lean on, but he would always be with her in spirit. He had cared for her, looked after her, put her first. Discovering that she loved him, was capable of falling in love with him, had taught her so much about herself. She felt as if she had taken a step forward out of the black hole of the past.

'If you're quite sure.' Melanie still sounded uncertain so Claudia kissed her cheek and gave her a hug.

'Don't worry, darling. I'll see you later.'

Twenty minutes later, stuck in a traffic jam, she paid off the taxi and began to walk.

Mac put his finger to Claudia's bell and held on. There was no answer, but that didn't mean she wasn't up there. She may be hurt, or worse. He rang Kay's bell, but before she had a chance to answer he caught sight of Claudia. She was strolling along the street, her long legs swinging in that easy, seductive gait that sent the blood rushing to his head. Just seeing her, so unexpectedly, took his breath away.

And then she saw him too and stopped. Just stopped, the look on her face unmistakable. It was joy. Pure unadulterated joy and his heart felt as big as a haystack.

'Gabriel?' She took a step towards him, then hesitated as if she wasn't sure she could believe her own

376

eyes. Then her face changed, the teasing smile was levered back into place and her thick lashes were doing their flirtatious tango as she hid her deepest feelings behind a mask of careless nonchalance. 'What on earth are you doing here?' she asked. But it was too late. She would never fool him again.

He'd thought she was like Jenny. Hard, selfish, uncaring. He'd been so wrong. And he was there because there was nowhere else in the entire world he would want to be. He covered the ground between them without any particular awareness of putting one foot in front of the other, taking her hands in his as she looked up at him with those extraordinary eyes, the little black flecks darkening the silver irises.

'I'm here because – ' because he couldn't live without her, because he had to tell her how much he loved her – 'because I wanted to ask you a question.'

'A question?' Claudia lifted one shoulder just a touch awkwardly. For a moment she had thought that he had come back because . . . well, just *because* . . . 'You're always asking questions,' she said, and he saw the disappointment in her face. Twenty-four hours ago he would have missed that. Now he knew what to look for.

'Two questions, actually.'

'Two questions,' she repeated disgustedly. Claudia didn't care for the way he was looking at her. As if he knew something that she didn't. 'What do you think I am? An encyclopaedia? Why don't you go for broke, darling? Three's a charm, or didn't you know?'

Oh, yes, he knew and there was a third question. A very important question, but that would have to wait. 'Tell me who threw the paint at you last night?'

He kept fooling her. When would she ever learn? Over and over she fell into the trap of thinking he might be able to care for her because even when she had gone to such heartbreaking pains to let him see that he was free to walk away without giving her another thought, he didn't seem to be able to do it. And every time he came back her heart would keep *hoping*.

'You know who,' she said, crossly. 'Joanna – '

'It wasn't Joanna. She sent the letters, she slashed your dress, but she didn't know anything about the paint.'

She pulled her hands away from his. She hadn't a clue what he was talking about, but she wasn't prepared to play any more. 'Gabriel, it's all over. I don't want to talk about it.'

'Claudia, darling, if you're protecting someone, it's time to stop.'

'I'm not protecting anyone. Let it go.' She waited for him to step aside, let her passed. He didn't. 'Gabriel, I need to pick up a few things before I go to the theatre.' She tried to get past him but he blocked her way, gripping her shoulders.

'Claudia, listen to me.'

'It's over,' she insisted, pulling free. 'You've been great, Mac,' she said, reverting to the name that everyone used, distancing herself from him. 'I'll write you a reference any time you want, but it's over. You have to know when to let it go.' She couldn't say it any more clearly, she thought, sweeping around him, desperate now to get away.

'There are two questions. You haven't heard the other one.' Claudia stopped, her back to him and waited. 'Who is David Hart?'

She spun round, absolutely furious. 'David is a friend. A sweet, kind man who never judges me, never criticizes me and never, ever plagues me with stupid questions – '

The squeal of tyres cut off her words and she stood, open-mouthed, as a small delivery van swung across the road heading straight for her. She remained transfixed, glued to the pavement as everything happened in slow motion around her; the van mounting the pavement, a glimpse of the driver's face contorted in pain, or rage, someone shouting from a long way off for her to move. Then Gabriel caught her, lifted her and flung her out of the way. She threw up her arms to protect herself as she hit the pavement and rolled, automatically using the method Tony had taught her so painstakingly before her parachute jump and which she had so notably failed to employ at the time. She lay there for a moment, winded, trying desperately to suck air into her lungs so that she could scream.

It was so quiet.

Then the sounds began to fill in the eery silence around her. The crash as the van piled into something. The pounding of feet running towards them.

Someone shouting instructions to call an ambulance and the fire brigade. A low moaning. Then she realized the moaning was coming from her and she opened her eyes.

Her eyes were a few inches above the grey pavement and for a moment she couldn't think why. Then she remembered Gabriel and she turned her head. He was lying a few feet from her. He was horribly still and blood was beginning to pool at the side of his head. And then she did scream.

'Gabriel?' She'd been sitting beside him for hours, waiting for him to come round fully from the anaesthetic. He'd drifted in and out several times. Once he'd spoken to her but she could see that he wasn't absolutely conscious.

Now when he turned his head his blue eyes were clear and bright against the pallid colour of his skin and he smiled as she stood up and took his hand. 'I like your hair. I didn't have a chance to tell you before.'

'No.' Damn. She hadn't cried so far. Now, when he was conscious, her eyes were filling with tears.

'And you're not hurt.'

She gave a little sniff. 'Thanks to you. You saved my life.'

'Not really. If I hadn't kept you talking on the pavement you'd have been inside your flat well out of harm's way.'

'Not quite.' She hesitated. 'It wasn't an accident, Gabriel. He was trying to kill me. That's what you were trying to tell me, wasn't it? That there was someone else?'

'Who was he? Who was the man in the van?' She told him the man's name, who he was and watched the slow realization cross his face. 'The man who crippled your mother?' She nodded. 'But *why*?'

Claudia shrugged. 'Who knows. Dad believes it was the photograph that set him off. I look sufficiently like her in all honesty, but the photograph was touched up and I had my hair done in exactly the same way. I was even wearing one of her dresses. He probably recognized it. He might even have bought it for her.' She closed her eyes, trying to blot out the horror of it all. 'I suppose he thought she'd come back to haunt him, to expose him. By attacking me he must have hoped to get rid of her, put the genie back into the bottle. The trouble was I kept bouncing back. I was on the television, three times in four days as well as in the *Stalker* promos. The guilt had probably been eating away at him all these years . . . it just needed something like that photograph to make him snap.'

'I suppose his death will be put down to a heart attack? Another cover-up?'

'I hope so. Let the dead keep their secrets.'

'Yes, well, I'm glad it's over.' He turned away, staring straight ahead at the clock. Then he said, 'Shouldn't you be at the theatre?'

'Should I?'

'Well, someone should be. Losing one leading lady

might be construed as bad luck; two looks a touch careless from where I'm lying.'

'There's always another actress waiting in the wings, Gabriel. Tonight it's the turn of the girl who has been playing the maid to get her chance as Amanda, and the ASM gets to play the maid's role. Dreams, you see, really can come true.' She paused to gather her breath. 'As for me, well I have to tell you, Gabriel MacIntyre, that there isn't a play, or a film, or a television series, or a part in any one of them that would have kept me away from you.' He didn't answer and she stared down at her hands, awkwardly twisting the corner of the sheet. 'You might so easily have been killed. All the time in the ambulance I kept thinking that you might die and I wouldn't ever have the chance to tell you how much I love you. You don't have to do anything about it. But I wanted you to know.' Still he said nothing. 'That's all.'

'Can I ask you a question?'

Claudia sighed. 'Weren't you listening? Or did that car knock what sense you had clean out out of your head? I told you, David is just friend. He's never – '

'Forget David. Three's a charm you said.'

'Did I? Oh. Well, yes, I suppose I did.'

'Then let's hope it works.' He turned to her then, regarding her gravely before motioning her closer. She leaned over him. 'Closer,' he murmured. Then as she put her ear down to his mouth, he caught her and pulled her down beside him, ignoring the cry of alarm as she toppled over, ignoring the pain that shot through his leg. That was a familiar pain and he knew that it would go in its own good time.

'Gabriel, for goodness' sake, your leg . . .'

'Stay exactly where you are and my leg won't be a problem.'

'I can't stay here!'

'You'll have to.' His mouth widened in a broad grin as she glanced nervously towards the door. 'I want to ask you a question and I want your undivided attention.'

She was inches above him, her body pressed along the length of his and suddenly she didn't care who might be outside in the corridor. She only cared about him. 'You've got it, my love. I'm all yours.'

'Then there's only one more thing to settle. Are you going to marry me without a fuss, Claudia Beaumont? Or will I have to take a leaf from Luke Devlin's book and lay siege until you surrender. I warn you that unlike him I have the training for it so you might as well give up without a fuss.'

'Is that right?' She looked into his eyes, saw that he meant every word he said and a warm glow began to spread through her entire body. 'Will we live in the cottage?'

'Would you like to?'

'I think I'd like to bathe by candlelight and swim as the sun rises.'

'But only in the summer,' he advised. 'We'll extend the place, I've got the plans drawn up already.' He paused. 'And we'll put in electricity.'

'Who needs electricity, when I've got you to keep me warm?'

'Can I take that as a yes?' he enquired, huskily.

'Mmmm.' She eased herself down onto him, avoiding the cage that protected his injured leg. 'How's your head?' She lightly touched the dressing pad that covered the small cut that had produced so much blood.

'A bit sore.'

'Would you like me to kiss it better?'

'I thought you'd never offer.'

And her kiss was everything he knew it would be. All the promises, all the answers to any question he had ever asked. And after a while, he eased her down beside him. 'Well?'

Claudia put her head on his shoulder and snuggled against him. 'Ask me again when you're not concussed and I'll take you seriously.'

'I've never been more serious in my entire life.' He yawned. 'Or had so little sleep.'

'Sssh,' Claudia murmured.

And when the nurse looked in half an hour later, they were curled up in each other's arms in the narrow bed, fast asleep.

'How's our hero doing?' the ward sister asked, as the nurse returned to the desk to write up her notes.

'Oh, he's doing pretty well,' she said. And she smiled to herself. 'In fact, you'd be surprised how well he's doing.'

We're sure you've enjoyed Mac and Claudia's story, the second book in Liz Fielding's Beaumont Brides Trilogy, which feature the delightful Beaumont sisters. On the following pages, you'll find an extract from WILD FIRE, the final book in the trilogy . . . and we know this will make you want to read on!

So, do look out for Melanie's story later this year . . .

WILD FIRE

'With this ring I thee wed, with my body I thee worship, and with all my worldly goods I thee endow. . .'

A sigh rippled through the congregation as Edward Beaumont placed a ring on the finger of Diana Archer and made her his wife. He had been alone for a long time, since the death of his first wife, the beautiful and talented actress Elaine French and everyone who knew him was delighted with this September love that had come to him so unexpectedly.

Only Melanie, his youngest daughter, balled her hands into tight little fists and blinked back a tear. Why couldn't she be happy for them? Diana was the kindest, loveliest of women, even if her daughter took some swallowing.

She looked around her. Her older sisters, her half-sisters, she adjusted the relationship mentally, although they had taken her so fully to their hearts that distancing herself from them in this way seemed another betrayal, were so obviously delighted by this turn of events. But then they had seen Edward suffering at the hands of their mother. Maybe that was the problem. On the other side of the world she had witnessed her own mother's loneliness, her suffering. That was the gulf that set them apart today.

Her mother had never had any of this, the old church decked out in spring flowers, the solemn vows, the expensive reception that would follow it. Not that Juliet would have bothered about the rich trappings of ceremony. A simple register office wedding would have been enough, but her mother had been denied any public acknowledgement of Edward's passionate love for her. She had lived out her life with only her daughter to remind her of a love so great that she had sacrificed everything for it. And she had died before Edward had discovered what she had done and been able to put things right. If she had lived this might have been her day . . .

She caught her lower lip between her teeth and made an effort to concentrate on the service. But as she looked up she caught Heather Archer's gaze fixed upon her from the other side of the church and saw the shocking reflection of her own thoughts in the younger girl's face. Maybe she was remembering the other ghost at the feast, her own beloved father.

Melanie, the smooth skin between her dark eyes momentarily creased in the slightest of frowns, continued to regard the other girl, this new member of a family that seemed to be growing almost daily, first with the birth of Fizz's daughter, then Claudia's marriage to Gabriel. Now Edward was taking a new wife. There seemed to have been nothing but celebrations in the last year. But Heather, his new stepdaughter, eighteen years old and dressed like a black scarecrow in her student uniform of Oxfam castoffs that would have looked more at home at a funeral than a wedding, wasn't celebrating.

The only difference between the two of them, Mel decided, was that Heather didn't care who knew it.

If she didn't make an effort to counteract the tears stinging at her eyelids, everyone would know how she was feeling too. Not that there was anything wrong with tears. Both Fizz and Claudia were dabbing at their eyes with delicate lace-edged handkerchiefs. Tears at a wedding were to be expected, almost mandatory, but they were supposed to be tears of happiness. Irritated with herself, reminding herself that she had been acting professionally since she was ten years old, she assumed a serene smile. But the need to lever a smile to her lips on what should have been the happiest of days forced her to come to a decision that she had been putting off.

It was more than a year since she had come to England. It had been a momentous year, a wonderful year. She had found a family she had never known existed, they had taken her to their hearts and she had wallowed in the kind of family life that she had never experienced before. But when she had added Beaumont to her name, Melanie Brett had somehow got just a little bit lost.

Luke should have understood. Her mother's younger brother, he was surely sharing just a little of her feelings today? Except that he was now a part of the extended Beaumont family. Married to Fizz and with a darling baby daughter to take up every moment, he was distracted by his own happiness and she couldn't deny him that. Maybe if she had had a love of her own she would have been less wrapped up in the past. But for weeks the past had been tugging at her sleeve, calling her back, and it was, Melanie decided, time to take a look back, remind herself who she was. Before she forgot.

After Edward and Diana had left the reception, she sought out Luke to tell him what she intended to do.

'You're taking a year off?' he repeated, in all too obvious disbelief. 'Are you mad?'

'I've been working practically non-stop since I was ten years old, Luke. I'm not complaining, I nagged Mum to let me do it, I was the envy of all my friends and I loved every moment of it, but I'm entitled to a holiday. So I'm adding up all the holidays I've missed out on over the last ten years and I figure a year off is about right.'

'Can you take a year off in your business? Aren't you afraid that when you come back everyone will have forgotten you?'

'I'm prepared to take that risk.'

He still looked doubtful. 'You'll be bored to death in ten minutes.' Melanie stifled her irritation. Luke didn't *mean* to be patronising, it was just that he'd been a surrogate father to her for so long that he couldn't quite come to terms with the fact that she was an adult.

'I won't be bored. And if I am I'll get a job. Something ordinary. I've never done anything ordinary.'

'I think you'll find that "ordinary" is over-rated.' Luke, still regarding her with concern, was distracted by his wife waving frantically from the other side of the room. 'Fizz wants to get back to the baby, Mel. Can we talk about this later?'

'There's nothing to talk about, Luke. I'm not asking your permission here, or asking you to hold my hand. I'm just letting you know my plans so that you won't worry. Will you say goodbye to everyone for me?'

Melanie watched Luke struggle to keep his silence knowing that he wanted to tell her that nothing would ever stop him from worrying about his sister's little girl. Instead he said, somewhat gruffly, 'We'll miss you, Mel.' Then he bent and kissed her cheek. 'Keep in touch. If you need anything – '

'I'll send you a postcard.'

THE EXCITING NEW NAME
IN WOMEN'S FICTION!

PLEASE HELP ME TO HELP YOU!

Dear *Scarlet* Reader,

As Editor of *Scarlet* Books I want to make sure that the books I offer you every month are up to the high standards *Scarlet* readers expect. And to do that I need to know a little more about you and your reading likes and dislikes. So please spare a few minutes to fill in the short questionnaire on the following pages and send it to me. I'll send *you* a surprise gift as a thank you!*

Looking forward to hearing from you,

Sally Cooper

Editor-in-Chief, *Scarlet*

*Offer applies only in the UK, only one offer per household.

Note: further offers which might be of interest may be sent to you by other, carefully selected, companies. If you do not want to receive them, please write to Robinson Publishing Ltd, 7 Kensington Church Court, London W8 4SP, UK.

QUESTIONNAIRE

Please tick the appropriate boxes to indicate your answers

1 Where did you get this Scarlet title?
Bought in supermarket ☐
Bought at my local bookstore ☐ Bought at chain bookstore ☐
Bought at book exchange or used bookstore ☐
Borrowed from a friend ☐
Other (please indicate) _____

2 Did you enjoy reading it?
A lot ☐   A little ☐   Not at all ☐

3 What did you particularly like about this book?
Believable characters ☐   Easy to read ☐
Good value for money ☐   Enjoyable locations ☐
Interesting story ☐   Modern setting ☐
Other _____

4 What did you particularly dislike about this book?
_____

5 Would you buy another Scarlet book?
Yes ☐   No ☐

6 What other kinds of book do you enjoy reading?
Horror ☐   Puzzle books ☐   Historical fiction ☐
General fiction ☐   Crime/Detective ☐   Cookery ☐
Other (please indicate) _____

7 Which magazines do you enjoy reading?
1. _____
2. _____
3. _____

And now a little about you –
8 How old are you?
Under 25 ☐   25–34 ☐   35–44 ☐
45–54 ☐   55–64 ☐   over 65 ☐

cont.